# Billy Bowling

## An American Novel

by
Steve Stitzel

"If a man does not keep pace with his companions, perhaps
it is because he hears a different drummer. Let him step to
the music he hears, however measured or far away."

(Henry David Thoreau)

Llumina
Press

This is a work of fiction. Names, characters, places and incidents are either the product of the author's imagination or are used fictitiously, and any resemblance to any actual persons, living or dead, events or locales is entirely coincidental.

ISBN: 978-1-60594-681-8 ( PB )

Printed in the United States of America by Llumina Press

Library of Congress Control Number: 2011900421

*To Jane, Especially*


*and to the memory of Dan Rumer,*
*a great guy to work for,*
*and someone who I wish could have read my book*

# *Acknowledgements*

I want to thank up front three people who made this book possible: Jane, for her encouragement and sanctuaries, both in Florida and Michigan. . . Maria, for her magnanimous, if at times provocative, editing. Forgive me, Maria, for defending and salvaging at least 'some' of my questionable literary idiosyncrasies. . . and my daughter, Annie, who graciously provided my graphics and sketches. Your commission will start, Annie, after I bank the first million.

Also

Especially to Scott, Brady, Brett, Brien (and Kathy) . . . and Holden (my dog who lived the entire process). Jeff, T.C., Chris, Dave, Bud and Kelly (Chamberlin's Ole Forest Inn, Curtis, MI), Jim and Sue, Ed and Tony, Dave and Barb, Toni and Lewie, Jim Rafko (God, he cracked me up), Gayla, Sam, Tammy, Sandy, Dale (the bartender), Joe (the bartender), Lucas (the bartender/teacher/ Harbor Springs city employee), Tim (who taught me the finer points of bartending), LB (the busboy who made me laugh), Adam (from Poland), Steve, Steve & Steve (and actually another Steve (me), but a long story for another novel), Craig B., Jake and Tommie, Cosmo Creamer, Dr. Bud from Texas, Marty, Dr. Rick, the Dotys, my sisters Tonda and Connie, and of course my children, Annie (Steve), and Ian (Jenna). Oh, and to Karen Lea, whom I hope is still in my life when my book is finally published.

Thanks are also due the Llumina Publishing Family, who have been wonderful to work with . . . Deborah Greenspan . . . and especially Shari Reimann.

And thanks to my mother, Amy King Stitzel, the (future) language arts teacher, who taught me to write a complete sentence when I was four or five years old, I think.  Hard to imagine she has been gone nearly thirty years. I've led a BIG life . . . so I may have missed someone with due credit . . . and if so, I apologize.

Sincerely, Steve

# Prologue

*U*ncle Marco was supposed to write this story! That had been our agreement five years earlier when Krissy and I moved to Northern Michigan to manage Marco's summer camp. I would tell him everything I knew—everything that had happened to me—and he would do the writing. That seemed to make perfect sense, Marco having already authored at the time two popular mystery novels, which he had written under the pen name, *Carson Bradshaw*, who was actually supposed to be a knockout MILF from Grosse Pointe. His publishers had even hired a hot fortyish Chicago model to pose for the glamour shots they ran on the dust jackets.

But our lives exploded, and though exciting, became incredibly demanding for all of us—Marco, Mirella, Krissy and myself, not to mention our young son, Eli—and well beyond our wildest dreams. So the chapters of pain that had defined most of my life (and the particular one of horror) faded, and eventually I decided perhaps it was best to just leave it all behind, even as deep inside I knew I was wrong . . .

. . ."Billy . . . Mirella and I can't thank you and Krissy enough for what you have done with Camp Romano. Because of you our dreams have been consummated and if I haven't said it enough, thank you . . . thank you both very much," Marco Romano said with a big smile, raising the rare Riedel of vintage *Machiavelli Chianti Classico* for a toast, magnetically drawing a triumvirate of arms to a thirty degree salute.

It was a beautiful early-October afternoon on *Escape Lake* in the heart of Michigan's Upper Peninsula. A bright sun showcased the emerging gold, orange and red upon distant hills across the lake to the north. We sat upon comfortable lodge chairs, positioned around a linen draped utility table that Marco had appointed upon the vast boathouse dock. The accompanying late day snack included an aged Wisconsin white cheddar that Marco had recently decided rivaled the finest European matures, sliced into crumbling wedges and placed around a blue crystal bowl of pickled onions and sliced avocados, but our favorite treat was the still scrumptious leftover student hard rolls, generously cloaked in Wensleydale butter and served in a wicker basket on loan from the *Trattoria.*

Quiet, beauty, and fellowship reigned—*for we were family*—though just the day before the last of the culinary students had left, most returning to the projects and inner-city schools of Cincinnati; a month delinquent, but by special arrangement. We had especially celebrated those students who had completed the second year program and qualified for scholarships to attend some of the finer institutes around the country, a rare few to even study abroad. So the day following was always a very special and proud time for the four of us, and a tradition that Marco had founded four years ago that month.

After a wondrous hour of wine, cheese and conversation, Krissy and Mirella adjourned to the lodge to prepare a simple evening meal, for simplicity was something that we actually looked forward to on that momentous evening. Eli was staying the night with a friend across the lake, and after the meal we would go our own way as couples, *finally* to have some truly alone time with our spouses and my groin had been stirring with a mind of its own, achingly teased by the sexy winks Krissy had been flashing throughout the afternoon. . . .

. . . "Billy, it's been ten years. It's time you told your story; time you finally wrote that book," Marco said softly, taking me by surprise.

I felt my body stiffen, reflexively, though he waited me out until I finally answered. "What do you mean, Marco? *You* are the writer, not me," I replied, turning my attention back to the exquisite Tuscan and consciously avoiding his eyes

"It's a story that needs told and it's time, but *you* need to write it."

"I'm not a writer, Marco," I answered without pause, casually scanning the placid blue lake, my eyes settling upon Doc Stambaugh's tiny aluminum fishing boat bobbing at anchor in the distance off Eagle's Nest Island.

"You can do it, Billy. You have all winter now. Start it up here and finish it in Jupiter before you and Krissy come north. I'll help edit as possible when Mirella and I return from Cortina in May. People *must* know the truth! You know that . . . and always have."

"But you were going . . ."

"You're the only one who can write it, Billy. I've thought about it a lot. I could never *feel* it, no matter how you might describe things. It's not like me writing those mystery capers I make up. The story's in your soul and that's what has to come across, for it's been butchered by the press and in those cheap movies and never truly understood. And Billy, you will never be at peace until you do, and you deserve that . . . even though you don't think you do. . . ."

. . . Krissy and Mirella had grilled burgers in the massive, now ghostly abandoned lodge, also deep frying a generous batch of ambrosial sweet potato fries which we dipped in our own Camp Romano maple syrup. After months of finely prepared European and American entrée's, the burgers and sweet fries ironically hit the spot . . . *though my beautiful wife was even yummier two hours later!*

Following lovemaking we donned warm clothing and Krissy made a couple of Irish coffees. From our deck on a bluff high above the lake we watched the Superman streaks of last light slowly disappear to the west. Across the lake a few dim lights flickered about Camp Row (as the kids all called it), but it was oddly quiet and dark now for the first time in nearly four months, and though we welcomed the seclusion and the privacy, there was still the twinge of once common life having passed now beyond us that was somehow sad.

I looked at Krissy as she lifted her eyes from the lake, turning toward me. Having just turned thirty-one, she was still the most beautiful and sexy woman a man could invent in a dream . . . *but God could only know what a road we had traveled!* That good fortune was finally ours was true, and something for which we both thanked our Lord, yet I would never have survived to enjoy it, I am now certain, except for the strength of *Krissy Kurtz Bowling.* And no one saw that coming a decade earlier—*no one*—least of all, myself.

"Marco says it's time, Kris. Time to tell the story and that I should write it myself," I said quietly, staring now into darkness.

"And how do *you* feel about that?" she asked, simply.

"I know he's right, but it scares me. I can only do it one way . . . as I saw things from the very beginning, and felt them over the years. But I worry about hurting good people when it's only the assholes I want to indict, Kris; the people who turned their backs and allowed it all to happen because of their distorted and sick values."

"If you write it, write it as you lived it, Billy. It's the only way. Otherwise what would be the point? People *need* to see themselves so that maybe they'll face the truth and it'll never happen again, whether in Fort Harrison or another town somewhere else. That's what you've always said, what haunts you so, and why you've got to get it out," she said, passing her hand behind my head where her fingers twisted curls in my neglected long hair.

The wisdom of Krissy Bowling was profound, though springing from an incredibly tough background. She was the kindest, funniest, strongest human being I had ever met, and yet had every reason in the world to feel sorry for herself, blaming a neglected childhood and horrendous family life or the cutting comments of school classmates. Yet early on she'd swept that all aside, choosing instead to fashion life on her own terms.

"But what if I hurt people I like, maybe even you? I just know I've got to write what I lived *then*, even though I am no longer that person. It's the only way, Kris. *The only way!*"

"*William James Bowling*," she scolded, "I've known what's been bottled up in you for a long time and I've always believed that once you get it out our lives will be even richer and more honest. There's no way you can hurt me, and I'm disappointed you'd even think that. I know what my life once was and *nothing* you or anyone else ever thought, or that you could write about my past, has anything to do with now. You know me, and when have I ever cared about what people think? I love you and nothing could change that. *Ever!* But more than that, Billy, nobody can touch us, not any more they can't, and you know that. So shoot from the hip!"

A gentle breeze blew in from the lake as darkness enveloped us, and now instead of seeing the falling leaves, you could feel them, hear them. The cry of a loon somewhere far out on the lake broke a long silence that we had become practiced at, appreciating the quiet and closeness . . . and understanding there were times when words were simply uninvited guests. Yet it was I who broke the silence. . . .

*"Kris, it wasn't Jimmy's fault. He wouldn't have done those terrible things . . . or killed those people. All he needed was one moral adult in his life after Mom and Libby died. Just one! How many kids had to be destroyed . . . how many, Krissy? And everybody thinks it was just Gwen."*

I felt the coolness of tears teased by the northern October breeze and as I looked at Krissy again could no longer mouth the words I knew she was hearing anyway. And somewhere deep inside of me a demon was preparing to pack his bags.

*BB*
*Escape Lake, Michigan*
*Seventh, October, MMVIII*

# Author's Note

The prologue preceding was written, as noted, the first week of October, 2008, having just passed my thirty-first birthday, while the bulk of this book was written throughout the year immediately before. To say I am an educated man would be stretching the point, yet my personal growth this past decade relative to the unusual events I lived through have changed me in a way that few people could ever experience. In the process, I have come to believe I have inherited a certain modest sophistication that transcends a formal education, though it is certainly not something I write of boastfully.

Further, as I have pointed out, I am not a professional writer and the dilemma that I faced when Uncle Marco convinced me to assume the responsibility of telling my own story was particularly one of establishing and portraying the progression of time and the changes that all humans experience as life moves forward. A well meaning person suggested that I read William Strunk and E.B. White's 'The Elements of Style,' which I did, but that confounded me all the more. Though I acknowledge its value in formal writing, it simply won't work for me. Somehow, however, I stumbled across Stephen King's amazing little book on writing, simply titled—On Writing. I found it exceedingly helpful and so different from what might come to mind when considering the Author, yet it managed to issue me license for writing the story as I believed it needed to be written.

It has been at times morally challenging to employ the graphic language and depict the explicit scenes that I felt necessary for *the story to reflect credibly upon life as it unfolded around me throughout the years I have written about. Krissy and Marco, however, were both adamant that I stay the course relative. This was the most difficult obstacle that I have had to overcome in order to render my story as genuine and honest as I possibly can. So please, both literary guests and family alike, consider that as you continue.*

*Sincerely,*
*Billy Bowling*

# Part One

## Fort Harrison, Ohio

## the 1990's

*"The nice thing about living in a small town is that when you don't know what you're doing, someone else does."*

*(Billy Bowling, 1993)*

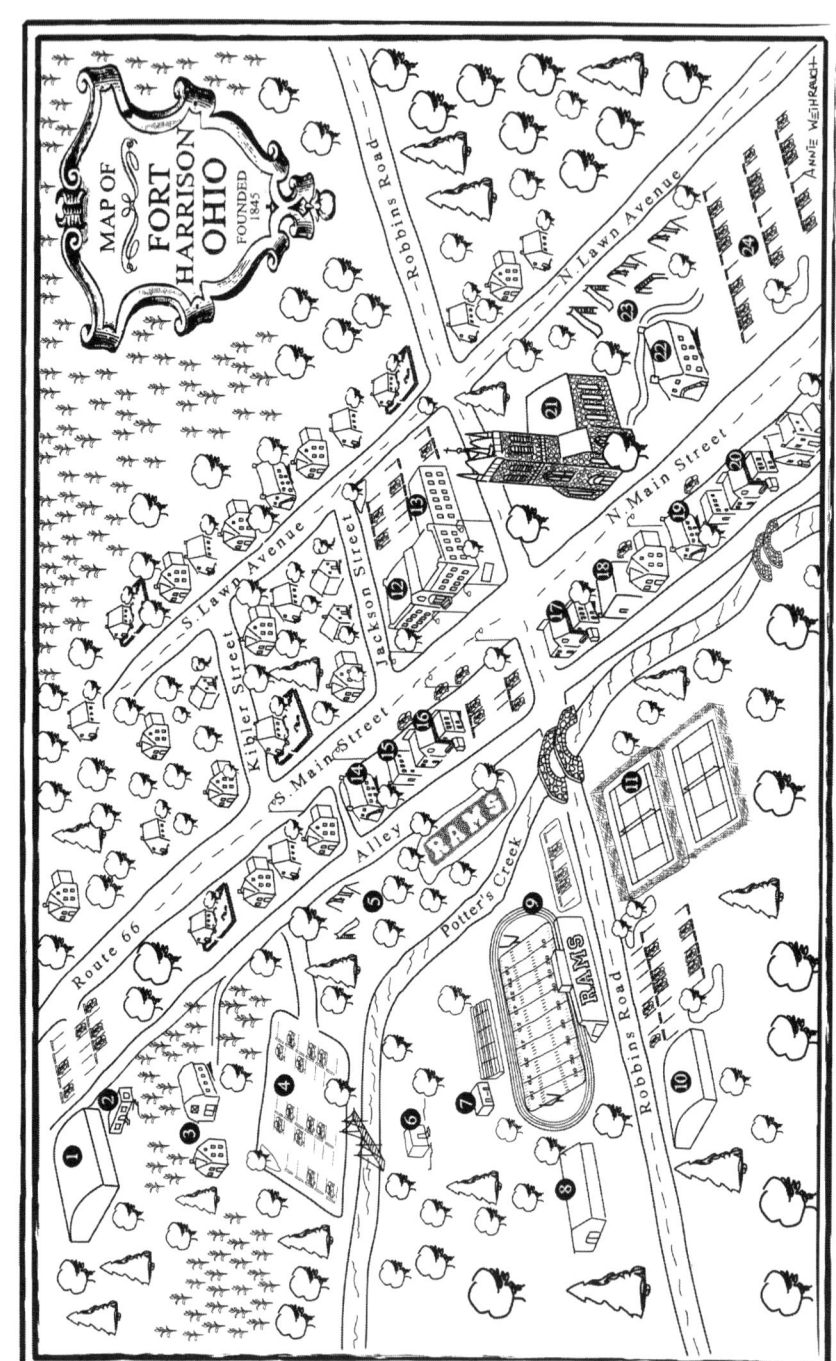

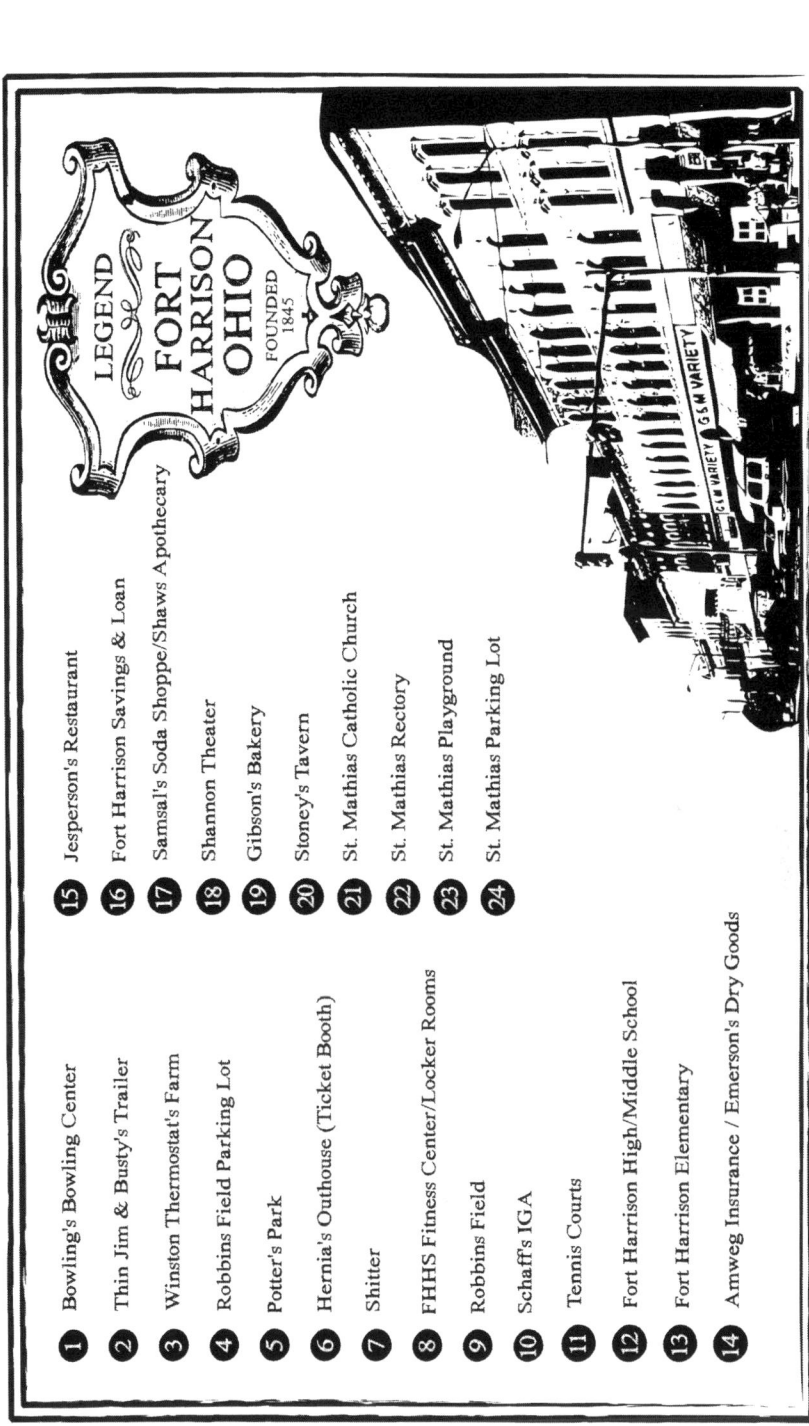

# LEGEND
## FORT HARRISON OHIO
### FOUNDED 1845

1. Bowling's Bowling Center
2. Thin Jim & Busty's Trailer
3. Winston Thermostat's Farm
4. Robbins Field Parking Lot
5. Potter's Park
6. Hernia's Outhouse (Ticket Booth)
7. Shitter
8. FHHS Fitness Center/Locker Rooms
9. Robbins Field
10. Schaff's IGA
11. Tennis Courts
12. Fort Harrison High/Middle School
13. Fort Harrison Elementary
14. Amweg Insurance / Emerson's Dry Goods
15. Jesperson's Restaurant
16. Fort Harrison Savings & Loan
17. Samsal's Soda Shoppe/Shaws Apothecary
18. Shannon Theater
19. Gibson's Bakery
20. Stoney's Tavern
21. St. Mathias Catholic Church
22. St. Mathias Rectory
23. St. Mathias Playground
24. St. Mathias Parking Lot

# Chapter One

I was in seventh grade at Fort Harrison Middle School when I became part of the cult that was drawn hypnotically to *Gwen Putnam* . . . along with farmers, bankers, Ford and Honda guys, teachers, plumbers, housewives, students—and on and on. In fact, almost everyone who lived in Fort Harrison, Ohio, whenever possible, would abandon professional responsibilities, household chores, studies—and sometimes even 'other' team practices—to watch the long legged blonde farm girl glide across the planet with the grace of a species before unknown. And that, *more than anything else*, characterized Fort Harrison, Ohio, in the late 1980's and early 90's . . . for everyone knew Gwen's days were numbered and she would soon move on to share herself with a much larger world.

By graduation in 1992, Gwen Putnam had won *twenty* individual, and her Fort Harrison High teams, *eight,* Ohio State Championships in Division III track and cross-country. But to really put this in perspective: *in four years of varsity competition, neither Gwen as an individual, nor FHHS as a team, had ever suffered a loss; a perfection that no other known high school athlete in United States history had ever achieved or likely ever will*. At one time Gwen held four national high school distance records and went on to the University of Notre Dame where she won three NCAA Division I cross-country titles and set national records in four track and field events . . . and all while pursing a pre-med degree in the pioneer field of Kinetic Medicine.

By Gwen's sophomore year at Fort Harrison, growing numbers of unattached strangers also began to show up for her track and cross country meets, and sometimes even practices, usually unannounced and more often than not at the most awkward of times, forcing Coach Chappell to close practices to the public. Police Chief Wade Borger even took it upon himself to monitor the team, assuming his most important assignment as a Fort Harrison lawman since the John Shorter 'investigation' twenty years earlier, when John had murdered his wife, Clarice, and Cal Otte, while they were having sex in his bed at 224 South Lawn Avenue, before turning the gun on himself.

Oh, and by the way, Gwen Putnam was also incredibly beautiful, though not in the heavy mascara, mini-skirt and pumps sort of way that was all the rage at the time. At 5'10" with long natural blonde hair and the bluest eyes you could ever look into, Gwen Putnam had no need for beauty enhancement products, but it was those long perfect legs on display to the world that were the true hypnotic draw; legs, which by the age of 22 as she prepared for the '96 *Atlanta Olympics,* had logged over 20,000 miles.

Yet somehow there was much more to the mesmerizing pull of Gwen Putnam than the multiple state championships, blond pigtails flying in the wind and perfectly sculpted legs. After all, Fort Harrison's athletic reputation was already well established among the small band of rural Catholic schools that dotted the central Ohio border with Indiana and comprised the Western Ohio Athletic Conference. For decades the conference had dominated Ohio small school athletics and garnered countless state titles, in the process commissioning a notable army of graduates to succeed upon the playing fields, hardwood courts and running venues of small colleges and large universities throughout the Midwest. Yet above them all, Gwen Putnam stood alone. The world lay before Gwen like the bright red doors of a *Chucky Cheese* welcoming a virginal eight year old and friends for a birthday party. Professional athlete, actress, physician, concert cellist, journalist, research scientist, even President—pretty much whatever she decided—that's where Gwen Putnam would someday go the people of Fort Harrison were certain, and confident that they would always being invited guests to the party. Gwen Putnam was destined for *big things*. That was a given; *and everyone knew that!*

......................................................................

Fort Harrison was also home to *Sam Giovanazzo*, who at age 45 when Gwen graduated in 1992, had already coached Fort Harrison High to *seven* State Championships in Division III football and *three* more in wrestling. Sam had arrived in Fort Harrison with his wife, Bobbie, in 1970 after serving one year as a high school assistant at Youngstown Boardman where he had also gone to high school, even though at the time he'd listed his hometown as Cleveland, a questionable representation of the true facts that would only decades later be understood.

The storied history of Sam Giovanazzo and the FHHS Rams had reached folklore status by the 1990's and had always stood *alone and above*—until, that is—Gwen Putnam captured everyone's hopes and dreams while toting a personality to boot. Not that Sam Giovanazzo didn't quarter a personality, because he did— loud, obscene, repulsive, controlling—and though growing more obnoxious with each state championship his success had seemed to insure him immunity to criticism no matter what else he may have done. For you see winning football games, and especially State Championship ones, was all that the majority in Fort Harrison *really* cared about . . . until Gwen secured a spot on the American Olympic team and an even brighter light flooded the small village as the '96 Atlanta Olympics drew near.

Just over a year into Sam's tenure at Fort Harrison, his wife jumped ship and was never seen again, though it had never seemed to much bother Sam, nor apparently did the rumors surrounding her flight. To hear the ole' boys talk, Bobbie was a beautiful girl, even though sporting an ugly scar that connected the right side of her mouth to her right eye as if disfigured by a drunken fisherman trying to extract a deeply swallowed hook. She had worked at the Fort Harrison Savings and Loan just prior to an embezzlement scandal that had driven vice-president Reldon Fox from both Fort Harrison and his family . . . to Sacramento, California. For whatever reason never communally understood, legal action was dropped, and of course, Reldon was never heard from again. It was shortly thereafter that Bobbie vanished. One story had her joining Reldon in California though another claimed the FBI had been in Fort Harrison asking *much* different questions related to her disappearance, as if perhaps something more sinister had been at work. But that was all in 1971, a very long time ago now, and since nothing illicit had ever been proven nor relatives shown up to cause a stink, it was assumed Bobbie had surfaced somewhere to the satisfaction of the authorities and the case itself had faded along with the memory of Bobbie Giovanazzo . . . in a day long before Greta Van Susteren could storm the small village on a white horse to solve the case and save the day.

When Sam was hired by the Fort Harrison school board the only round peg in his resume at the time that meshed with the small community was that he was Catholic, but when the state championships started rolling in a few years later, both the mysterious rumors of his past and his increasingly questionable behavior around the girls at Fort Harrison High were always conveniently swept under the carpet. If you wanted to survive as an administrator in Fort Harrison, you didn't fuck with Sam Giovanazzo—cause he was first, and for many years the *only*, person to really put Fort Harrison, Ohio, on the map—which was exactly where it intended to stay. Sam Giovanazzo *was solid* in Fort Harrison. That was a given; *and everyone knew that!*

················································

There *had* been other Fort Harrison notables, like Nick Santoria ('79), starting linebacker for the AFC in the Pro Bowl in '87 and '90 . . . and Darf Pannabecker ('93) who would become a regular on *Saturday Night Live* and go on to star in many movies along side Adam Sandler, Dana Carvey, Vince Vaughn and the Wilson brothers. Darf, just a few years ahead of me, hadn't been all that popular with Principal Dick Wickman (Wickerdick) and had spent considerable time in the small exile alcove of the high school office, assimilating million dollar material and guarded by Melvina Tannenbaum who'd been high school secretary at FHHS since the Indians moved west. A couple of other less notable NFL guys had also been spawned by Giovanazzo and (then) there *was* my best friend, Brent Sturdivant ('95), who would graduate 'Magna Cum Laude' from Kenyon College with a degree in 'French Philosophy' and go on to become a Vermont Teddy Bear Counselor in 2004, followed by a promotion to *Director of Bear Counseling (DBC)* just a few short years later. Oh, yeah, and Brent's younger brother, Baxter, would one day become the most exclusive sports agent in the history of professional sports.

.........................................................................................

*So the tiny village of Fort Harrison, Ohio, (population 1712 by the 1990 census) was indeed unique by any account—and believe me—wore its deserved pride without a hint of modesty.*

.........................................................................................

Then there was me, *Billy Bowling*, whom the people of Fort Harrison, Ohio, would forever hold responsible for demise of Camelot. I'm actually William James Bowling V, son of James William Bowling V, brother to James William Bowling VI, grandson to William James Bowling IV and great grandson to James William Bowling IV and so on back to the Norman Invasion (not the Invasion of Normandy, mind you). Well, you get the picture, and I guess it's good for a laugh because, believe me, the Bowlings were about as far removed from royalty as a family could get!

For nineteen years I was pretty much wallpaper as far as Fort Harrison was concerned, and the dysfunctional family (*fucked up* is the way people coin the term in Fort Harrison) from which I was begot was my only true notoriety . . . other than the occasional hot shot game I'd bowl at *Bowling's Bowling Center* (*the BBC)* that might make the small print in the weekly Fort Harrison *Reinforcer.* It wasn't that I was a weasel or couldn't have been a decent athlete and probably even dated cute girls, but you see I was chained to a fucking bowling alley and never around to lead the *normal* life that most high school kids do. Yep, that was 'my lot' in life, or at least the one I'd accepted, cause on the other hand my brother, *Jimmy*, who was four years older, was a huge football star at FHHS, playing for Sam Giovanazzo on two state championship teams and even named Ohio's *'Mr. Football'* in 1991. By graduation he actually held every rushing yardage and rushing touchdown record in the storied history of FHHS, along with being Homecoming King twice, a standout in track and State Runner-up in the 110 hurdles his junior year. *Oh . . . and he was also the guy for whom all the girls dropped their panties!*

Yet Jimmy could never quite land Gwen Putnam, his one true love. So after his last football season (and a year after our mother and little sister had been killed) he pretty much did a *360*, settling for a string of sluts, a party apartment in 'downtown' Fort Harrison and just managing to graduate from good ole' FHHS by maybe an ear hair. Nevertheless I looked up to Jimmy for having told Dad early on to get fucked, escaping the slavery that had snared me and allowing him to be the hot shot around school that he was.

My mother, Maria, and little sister, Libby (who never much got a chance to be anything awesome) were killed when I was in eighth grade and Jimmy was a junior, at which time our father, *Thin Jim* (don't ever call him Slim Jim) *Bowling* launched a disciplined campaign to drink himself to death. Now it's not like he was so happy or a wonderful husband and father even before they died, though, so don't get that idea, because he had always pretty much been an asshole. Though I will admit he became a much more committed asshole following the accident. Still, I made it *almost* to my sophomore year before ole' Thin Jim dropped the 'bowling ball in my lap,' forcing me to pretty much run the BBC in order to pay the family bills and put beer and vodka on the table. Some kids get handed lives where you'd better grow up fast because the adults in your life are the real children and survival itself demands a role reversal. I was dealt one of those hands, and though ultimately it has served me well—*trust me*—you wouldn't have wanted to trade me for the ride.

...............................................................................

*Most Fort Harrison people think they already know this story, but they don't! Nobody really does but me! Newspapers, books, entertainment shows, national newscasts, magazines, made for TV movies, and most of all that jerk, Geraldo Rivera . . . it was all bullshit, I'm telling you . . . bullshit! The sad part is that it is a story that should have never taken place at all, and the incalculable damage to the youth of Fort Harrison High School for twenty-six years is a fact that the abundant supply of assholes in Fort Harrison, Ohio, have never faced. The truth needs to be known and has for a very long time.*

*This is what REALLY happened!!*

# Chapter Two

I was in freshman math, Room 205, and though the second bell had rung like five minutes earlier, *Hernia* (Milton Hernemann, that is) was still in the hallway shootin' the shit with Lance Klaus who'd landed the other high school math job that past summer when Howard Bockratt retired after teaching at Fort Harrison for about a hundred and fifty years. It was only the second week of school, but I could already see that becoming a freshman was no earthshaking climb up the ladder of joy, at least not for a guy like me. The buzz was still muted, but it would get louder as the year moved on and Hernia stretched his hall time from five to maybe fifteen minutes, then once every month or so fire a dictionary against the wall after closing the door and glare at the class like James Cagney in *Public Enemy*. That was supposed to insure domestic tranquility and keep us shaking in our shoes, or so ole' Hernie figured.

Occasionally he'd scrawl some numbers on the board that would have stumped Will Hunting before passing out cheap handouts for us to work on and then burying himself in *The Wall Street Journal* or a John Grisham novel. Any moron, however, could tell his eyes were more often fixed upon the squirming crotches of the freshman class's finest young co-eds rather than seriously picking preferred stock or solving a vexing crime. Not that he was the Lone Ranger, understand, since that was pretty much the script for every male teacher at Fort Harrison.

I didn't know for sure (on that mid-September, 1991 day) exactly what to expect in Hernia's class, but Jimmy said it would get real ragged before the year was over and that I'd come to wish the guy actually did have some discipline. *And it did. And he didn't. And I did!* I mean in my class there was always an abundant supply of assholes around to see to that, so freshman math at Fort Harrison High School was more of a forum for budding 'Comedy Centralians' than potential stock brokers or accountants, that much was pretty clear by October. But I guess some things you'll just have to take my word for—unless you had Hernia for a class yourself. . . .

. . . "Ok, ladies and gentlemen, remember our theme: you're not in junior high school anymore, you are adults! Now repeat after me . . . 'We are all adults!' I don't HEAR you," Hernia shouted comically. "Ok, again, repeat . . . *We are all adults!"*

Dirk Salisbury burst out with a screaming laugh as a sprinkling of comical 'We are all adults' squeaked around the room. He followed that with his own deep operatic 'WE ARE ALL ADULTS,' at which time Hernia flashed him a wicked look, but otherwise pretended that the dramatic declarations were satisfactory and had now prepared us all for paying taxes, procuring mortgages, raising children, and choosing an appropriate divorce attorney.

"You're grown up now and should be ready to take on the challenges of a new world, which starts right here in the classrooms, hallways, and on the playing fields of Fort Harrison High School," Hernia proclaimed, comically crossing his arms and staring into space, proud of himself. I had a flash he was entertaining delusions that he was Socrates and we were his students gathered in a grove of olive trees and lusting for knowledge. Of course I would soon find that I was the delusional one since Hernia never taught ten minutes straight the entire school year. Anyhow, it was all just a bit too weird for me and pretty much everyone else it seemed as I glanced around the room and watched the chaos slowly unfold.

"Oh, and yes," he then said, breaking his meditative trance. "It was quite loud in here when I was conferring with Mr. Klaus a few minutes ago. You *do* understand that when the second bell rings, we expect you to be mature and respectful, even though I am not in the room, and that means quiet . . . as in DON'T TALK!*"* he said, raising his voice and again trying to act tough. Now I'm no thespian, but drama just wasn't Hernie's bag. I mean, he sure couldn't have been an actor, except maybe in like *Ferris Bueller's Day Off,* and especially because he was always a half step behind the points he was trying to make as far as his dramatic overtures went and it was really quite comical.

"Now I can understand on this wonderful September Friday, that we are all filled with excitement and looking forward with great anticipation to the game with St. Michaels tonight, but we still have the responsibility of education to attend to and I'm sure you understand that quite well . . . *don't we, Mr. Uhlenkamp?*" Hernia shouted, staring bullets at Brad Uhlenkamp in the back seat of the first row right, who not only had his arms and head on the desk, but was snoring noticeably.

Laughter broke out around the room like slowly popping corn and Hernia flashed another Cagney glare. Slowly he walked around his desk, starting toward Brad when Justin Westerheide smashed his desk backward against Uhlenkamp's, who first stirred, then jumped awake with wild eyes and a large pink oval on his forehead where it had pushed against his fist. Uhlenkamp was one of the *mice* and a perfect victim for Hernia to hang. Teachers loved to make examples of and hang mice. Athletes, board member's kids and most girls were immune, but mice were fair game and when they were fried everyone else was supposed to shape up too . . . another big laugh.

"Mr. Uhlenkamp, we must have had a *hot* date last night, is that it?" Hernie queried maliciously, inviting now, even soliciting laughter as he panned the class with a ridiculous smirk on his face. "Or perhaps it's that we're *smarter than Einstein* so there's certainly nothing to be learned from Mr. Hernemann," he said, proud again and pleased with his witty castigations, completely oblivious to the rapidly decomposing class.

Milton Hernemann, however, was a pretty typical teacher. The classroom was his stage to be King, Scholar, Cynic, Comedian, Magistrate and Executioner, but above it all, ole' Hernie truly believed he was *Superior*, which was the biggest joke of all, since every teacher at Fort Harrison pretty much had the same act (yeah, I know . . . said that before, didn't I? Sorry. Just give me some time to get into the 'swing' of things).

On the left side of the room just then Dirk Salisbury shot a BB that caught Ryan Ruckhaus just below the jaw, stinging . . . hard!. He'd had a miniature slingshot since like third grade that he was always able to come up with when the opportunity arose. Of course it wasn't the original, the weapons having been confiscated about a hundred times over the years, but he now manufactured them with mature perfection, was a dead shot from hours of practice and mean enough to want to really hurt people. Ryan rubbed at the skin hard, tears welling up, but he would never say anything—*ever*—cause Ryan was pretty much another mouse just like Uhlenkamp. No one else seemed to notice, but I'd learned the skill early on—just kind of watching things unfold while everyone else either rushed through life on a roller coaster of activities and false hopes or were imprisoned in a bubble of numbness like Brad and Ryan.

Then there was Ty Neumeier. He was turned completely backwards in his seat, oblivious to the berating comedian, Milton Hernemann. Ever since the commotion started he'd seen the opportunity to zero in with Superman eyes, far up and into the crotch of Mindy Dalinghaus, whose torso was turned at the waist looking toward Hernie, her legs open wide to the world, though discovered only by Ty sitting two seats forward and possessing a practiced knack for such things. Again it seemed only I noticed, and by the way, I would have enjoyed looking too—I mean it wasn't like beyond my moral sense of propriety or anything—but I was 'north' of the action at the time.

Ty's father was a chiropractor in Fort Harrison whose claim to fame was that he was the team physician for the varsity football team, which was pretty strange if you really thought about it, but ever since Doc Jones died in '88, the closest GP (other than Norma Perkins who had no interest in the position) was in Minster about ten miles away and in a different school district. So every game Dr. Richard Neumeier cruised the sidelines with a comical air of importance, wearing a ridiculous blue vest, huge gold bowtie, and carrying a medical bag which only God could know what dwelt within.

Hernia returned to his desk, dramatically addressing the class. "I hope we're ready to attend to some serious work now. We are, *aren't we, Mr. Uhlenkamp?*" Milton Hernemann sneered.

"Yes sir," Brad mumbled.

"I didn't HEAR you, Mr. Uhlenkamp," Hernie returned, cynically.

"Yes sir, we're ready," Brad returned, wanting to strike out in anger, but it just wasn't in him, for he knew it would have meant certain death for a mouse.

# Chapter Three

*H*ernie then smiled with noticeable perversity, which we would all shortly understand as he began. "Ok, for two weeks now I've let you settle in wherever you wanted, but we've developed some problem pockets that need to be corrected so I have devised a seating chart that will be in effect as long as is necessary," he said, doffing a pair of bizarre Woody Allen glasses and elevating a sheet of construction paper on which he had meticulously drawn five rows wide and six seats deep, large square boxes penned with each student's last name in black magic marker.

I knew the drill by heart and had understood it since seventh grade, though it would probably get even more interesting in high school as the girls passed further along the road to and beyond puberty. *The good ole' male teachers of FHHS and their seating charts!* In general I was convinced most teachers were stupid, if for no other reason than because they thought we all were.

"Ok now," Hernia began . . .

. . . By the time the dust had settled, Mindy Dalinghaus, Krissy Kurtz, Brooke Schweiterman, Abby Bertke, Haley Obringer and Sarah Pleiman had been placed like chess pieces re-arranged while a dumb opponent was away taking a shit. I think every girl, except for maybe Haley Obringer, knew exactly what was up. Krissy Kurtz had the prime seat, she always did—front row, second row in from the door—the seat where ole' Hernie's eyes couldn't help but settle as he feigned reading his lousy *Wall Street Journal.*

Krissy played the role too, already well practiced in an art I was yet a few years removed from even understanding. I mean, she'd been around the block a few times if you could believe what kids said, even at fourteen. She wasn't like a volleyball player or a cheerleader or any of that stuff and never had been, but goddamn, any way you sliced it, she did a *thing* on the male species, period . . . and I mean me not withstanding, I've got to admit that. She'd been in my class since third grade when she moved with her mother and sister from Lima, thirty miles north on I-75, to *Sunrise Mobile Home Court* just outside Fort Harrison, north on Route 66. She was the *first* girl I ever got hard over, I've gotta tell you that. It was sixth grade recess and I was perched atop the jungle gym while she swung high in the swing, her legs spread wide. And Jesus, even in sixth grade she was wearing red undies and fixing me with a look most girls would never master in a lifetime of moves. I took a deep breath, bid a quick 'uncle' to my brain, and began to feel the alien presence move, eventually pushing against the unyielding thread of my Lee's and scaring me shitless. Once my friend, Brent Sturdivant and me, for some stupid reason, were talking about getting our first hard-ons and pretty much agreed that it probably scared the hell out of everyone the first time. Of course try to get a guy, even like a young teenager, to tell you he was once scared by an erection, and well, good luck.

Math was right before lunch and I'd noticed ole' Hernia after nearly every class beatin' it down the hallway to get to his house across the street from the high school. I didn't much know his story except that he lived alone and had for years. Anyway, I was pretty sure it wasn't lunch he was in a hurry for cause from the position of my desk it wasn't too difficult to see his eyes peering over whatever he was feigning to read and fixed on Krissy's fourteen year old crotch each day just before the bell. Nope, Hernia was hot footin' it home to beat-off, or so I figured, and poor Krissy Kurtz was getting dicked daily by ole' Hernia's brain cells, though somehow I was pretty sure she knew it every bit as well as I did.

Abby and Sarah were really nice girls and uneasy with their seats I pretty much thought, which wasn't fair cause it would become something they had to always fight that guys and homely girls didn't have to deal with . . . worrying about *how* they were sitting, that is. I mean if you were a good-looking girl at FHHS, you either had to dress like a Quaker or a Ninja . . . or 'bust your ass to hide your ass,' at least from the sizable population of male lechers that taught at Fort Harrison.

I didn't know how Brooke felt about it all, but Mindy leaned more toward the 'Krissy Kurtz School of Finishing' I'd always thought. The main difference was that Mindy's father, James, was the pastor at the *Fort Harrison United Methodist Church*, while Krissy's mother, Lacy, was a pole dancer at *Three Blind Dice,* a shit hole in the wall bar over in Sidney, the county seat. Now I'm not saying everyone knew that, but Brent Sturdivant told me his twenty-two year old cousin told him once that one of the strippers at *TBD* had a daughter in our class at Fort Harrison. After that you didn't have to be Columbo to figure it out.

Except for George Thomas, all the male teachers had the same script and the girls pretty much the same roles. Krissy and Mindy took a lot of pressure off the other girls, however, since at least freshman year they stood far above the crowd as far as 'development' went and I guessed that was sort of good in a way (for the other girls). Yet they were about as different as two girls could be, even beyond their social chasm . . . .

. . . Mindy was cute as hell, that was for sure, and had huge boobs, though short yet nicely shaped legs, but she was painfully phony even though she had no idea she was. Still, her naive phoniness was preferable to the more common premeditated phoniness of some kids (and pretty much all adults), at least from my point of view. She meant well and all, but being a cheerleader and wanting stuff like to be on the homecoming court, date an upper class jock, and all that kind of crap drove every last molecule in her body. She was definitely one of those girls whose life could only go downhill after graduation and the sad thing was that probably half her school days she managed to fuck up anyway by getting all hot and bothered about something she had no control over and then going home to cry about it till the next morning. That was really too bad, I remember once thinking . . . cause Mindy could have been really cool if she'd just been able to loosen up and not worry about stupid shit.

Krissy Kurtz, on the other hand, was funny as hell I always thought, and didn't give the first shit about anything that Mindy Dalinghaus got all knotted up about. In a way Krissy was an outcast, I suppose, but it never much seemed to bother her. The hot shot girls talked about her non-stop and you almost had to figure she dressed sexy as hell and did her own thing more than anything just to piss them off. She was kind of a hard one to really figure though, cause she was never around anymore than she had to be. She had a sister in Jimmy's class that was on the rough side, but still damn good looking. I'd heard all the stuff about her Mom and the older dropout types Krissy supposedly ran with and how she was supposed to be so wild . . . but sometimes you had to wonder if it was really all true.

But she was sexy all right . . . short skirts and heely shoes with frilly little socks that could cause a freshman to ride a bike off a cliff or an upperclassman or adult perv to drive into a tree—well you know what I mean. Natural dark skin, maybe 5'4ish, with perfect legs and great perky tits, even though only a freshman, and not the sloppy-loose sort of boobs that 'ole Mindy trussed up. Her hands, nails, face and hair were always perfect and that pissed off the other girls more than anything . . . the way I figured, anyhow. Krissy Kurtz was just downright beautiful, and coming from Sunrise Mobile Home Park . . . well, I mean everybody knew the rules, didn't they— *and that just wasn't allowed!* She was also sweet and friendly to guys, which of course, again by the rules, meant she was a *ho.* But regardless, when the last bell rang it was 'Hocus Pocus Fishbones Chocus' and she was gone. So like every other guy I just gawked at her most of the time . . . trying to act cool about it, of course. She knew what she did to guys though, I was pretty certain of that, and I was convinced she'd sized me up that day nearly three years earlier when the highflying swing and tiny red panties had welded me atop the jungle gym like a perverted gargoyle.

Anyway, while we were playing musical chairs Dirk Salisbury nailed poor Brad Uhlenkamp in the back of the head with one of his fucking BB's. It definitely wasn't Brad's day. I sort of wanted to just stand up and kick Dirk in the balls, which I passed on, cause I was pretty much a lousy rebel when it was likely I'd get into trouble, but I did give him a shitty look which he returned with a big smirk. It pissed me off and yet at the same time I had to admire his skill cause the shot had to pass like right across Natalie Dunn's nose and just behind Eddie Otte's head to hit the mark. He knew what he was doing, I'll give him that, even if he was a royal asshole. Dirk was also a hot shot quarterback in junior high so everyone always told him that his shit didn't stink, and especially his old man, Clarke, who owned Salisbury Excavation. Oh, yeah . . . and I'd already seen Dirk hanging out talking to that asshole, Sam Giovanazzo.

He knew better than to shoot me though, but mostly because of my brother, Jimmy, more than because of who I was. Dirk understood the safe targets, that was for sure; the ones who wouldn't cry wolf or didn't have a snowball's chance of kicking his ass, and he tortured them pretty much daily, including poor Thelma Noblet who was over two hundred pounds and had to go through Fort Harrison High with a name reserved for grandmothers fifty years earlier. Oh yeah, Dirk Salisbury was a real prince all right . . . and the perfect type of asshole for Sam Giovanazzo to turn into an even bigger asshole!

# Chapter Four

Below me *Robbins Field* resembled one of those Christmas snow-globes that hadn't yet been shaken. The stadium lights bathed the blue and gold of the dominate rabid while across the field a smaller rectangular patch of St. Michaels green and muted white was poised like an Old Town canoe about to strike out upon a sun drenched lake. From my vantage the mid- September darkness enveloped most everything and my second impression was that the activity below looked more like the last piece of a brightly decorated birthday cake on a huge greenish-gray platter. I was always thinking about shit like that and you should probably know that up front, but don't go gettin' the idea that I'm like artistic or anything.

I sat on a small bench in the alley behind *Fort Harrison Savings and Loan.* The bench was something new that Carl Robbins III, the bank president, had anchored in the ground near the back entrance to the bank after smoking had been banned from the employee break room a year earlier. It was actually pretty comical how employees lurked around the ass end of businesses and restaurants to smoke, and particularly the characters out at *Twilight Village*, the old folks home on 66 where a small army of them were always lounging around on half busted tables and chairs they'd drug out of the cafeteria. You pretty much had to figure that if anyone was ever short a chair, one of the custodians would take a hammer to a good one so it could be pulled out back for a smoker. One thing about smokers though—I mean it could be ten below and they'd still be hanging out in their anterior sub-culture. Yep, I'll give them that—smokers are very dedicated people.

It was maybe a couple of 'football fields' to the football field, I guess, from where I was perched. Far enough so that everything below me seemed to be moving in slow motion, which I liked because except for the fact that my brother, Jimmy, was a big star, I was pretty cynical about the whole operation. So I looked for diversions, at least before the game started. For instance I thought the alley that ran the block behind the bank, Jesperson's Restaurant, Amweg Insurance and Emerson's Dry Goods had to be about the prettiest alley in the country. I mean Fort Harrison really is a pretty town, I must admit that, even if most days I wasn't too positive about it. A sweeping lawn just across the alley dropped away to Potter's Creek and at the top a long flower garden about eight feet in width ran the length of the hill and was where they planted blue and gold mums each fall that spelled out RAMS with a blue R, gold A, blue M and gold S. Four poles about fifteen feet high each had a spotlight that shined down on the letters and from the home bleachers you could read it real clear. It was kind of corny, but cool at the same time, although it'd been over a year now since I'd seen it from that side of Potter's Creek . . . back when Mom and my little sister were still alive and Dad was 60% human.

Main Street runs along a pretty high ridge where the businesses sit, probably 'five football fields' if you counted 'The Depot' ice cream parlor on the north end and our bowling alley to the south. It's not that I'm a huge football fan, please understand, but Fort Harrison's 'standard of measurement' is *football fields,* so after awhile it just rubs off on you I guess. Anyhow, the buildings were mostly built in the 1880's and 90's, I think, and they're really quite charming and maintained nicely too; I'll give the townies that. The high school's right in the middle of town, directly across Main Street from the bank and across Robbins Road from St. Matthias, so it's a straight shot down Robbins to the football field and a really big deal before each home game for the band, cheerleaders, and the football studs and to parade themselves to the field like the return of a fucking conquering Roman army. That's pretty much always around 6:30 so I've learned to be pretty scarce til that business is all over cause to see that asshole Sam Giovanazzo leading his charges is enough to make me wanna' chug an antifreeze slurpy.

Anyway, St. Matthias Catholic Church dwarfs everything— *and I mean everything*! I think they started building it like in 1870 and finished it about 1895, or so I'd once overheard at the BBC. Its single spire soars 215' and is the second tallest church in Ohio and the nineteenth tallest in the *entire country*, and on a clear day you can see it from over twenty miles away. Story says it sits on the exact spot the Fort Harrison stockade did 200 years earlier when William Henry Harrison and the boys fought off Indian attacks. Of course every little Catholic berg along Western Ohio had a big shot church, but St. Matthias took the cake, the pie and the scalloped potato casserole! One legend about ole'St. Matthias was that God favors the FHHS football teams because the Catholic forefathers had built the incredible church to humble every other spire in the Western Ohio Athletic Conference. As for me, I'd side with God any day rather than ever give that fucker Sam Giovanazzo any credit, I can tell you that for sure.

Ok, I'll try to lighten up. Well, like I said, across the alley behind the loan-company where I sat, the terrain drops away steeply to Potter's Creek and the football field is just beyond that. The main bridge over the creek is on Robbin's Road to my left which runs between FHHS and St. Matthias, across Main and along the Saving and Loan before dropping down the hill and crossing the creek to the field. A suspension footbridge crossed the creek to the south and came in on the backside of the field near the visitors' bleachers far off to my right. After a few state championships they built a big parking lot over that way and the footbridge across the creek to the field area. It was a big fucking deal at the time, just like everything is that happens in Fort Harrison I guess, the way most people act. They even had a big ceremony when they built the new shitters just off the visitors' twenty-yard line. The bank had slapped down most of the dough, I'd heard, so ole' Carl Robbins gave a big speech . . . which was actually quite appropriate the way I saw it.

One hoot I always got was Hernia manning his stupid outhouse just across the footbridge, selling tickets and collecting passes and stuff like that. I always thought of The Black Knight guarding the bridge in *Search for the Holy Grail*. One time I even saw Hernie freak out and chase a couple of junior high kids from Cliffton who tried to sneak in. He chased them into the darkness clear across the railroad tracks, like a 'football field and a half' east, hugging the cash box and all while he ran about like Icabod Crane. It was pretty funny, but at the same time you had to respect him a little for doing it. Anyhow, Hernia, Nancy Baldwin, one of the English teachers, Ted Turner (no shit), the guidance counselor, and Millicent Conner, the home-ec teacher (who was like ninety) all ran around doing silly shit at the games. They'd all wear this nutty blue and gold stuff on Fridays and act all *rah rah Rams*, but you knew it was phony and they were just trying to nab an extra forty bucks or so. But some phoniness I guess you have to respect when you really think about it cause somebody had to do that kind of crap.

By game time there wasn't much chance anyone would be around to bother me, that was for sure. I used to think that if I'd studied lock-picking and safe-cracking I could have probably been sitting on the beach in Aruba or somewhere by Sunday with babes draped all over me and a Pina Colada with an umbrella straw in my hand. I mean, all the big shots and cops were at the game and you'd have to drop a nuclear weapon uptown to get them to budge, so robbing the bank would be cake if you just had the basic skills. The bank had a pretty good history of that stuff already since John Dillinger and 'Baby Face' Nelson robbed it back in 1934, killing Chief Merle Denton and shooting up the place good. Five or six bullet holes are still in the bricks up front and now Carl Robbins III thinks they're *tits*. I guess it was Carl II who had like a 24 karat gold plaque or something bolted beside them with a bunch of historical shit on it, but I bet *King Carl I* wasn't all fuzzy warm when the guns started blasting away, his coffers were raped and ole' Merle Denton lay dead in the middle of Main street.

# Chapter Five

$\mathcal{N}$ow it's not that I didn't have any friends; I mean that wasn't my reason for sitting alone and feeding you a bunch of pre-game bs about the town cause I actually got along quite well with most people. I sorta had no choice but to be social, working at the bowling alley about a hundred hours a week along with going to school. It's really pretty much why I was there, cause I had to leave anyhow by half to get the alley bar ready to baby-sit a few drunks from the *DCA* (Downtown Coaches Association) after the game. So there'd really be no point getting all involved with friends and stuff at the game when I'd have to leave anyhow. I did like to watch Jimmy up close sometimes, I'll give you that, but overall the whole atmosphere makes me wanna puke, especially that asshole Sam Giovanazzo pacing the sidelines like he was fucking Vince Lombardi or Woody Hayes. Not that I'm a football historian or anything, understand.

I mean, I don't think I'm fooling myself that I got along ok with most people, but I could be wrong I suppose. Still, pretty much everybody in Fort Harrison, at one time or another, comes to Bowling's Bowling Center just South of town on 66—*where Billy Bowling is the resident indentured servant at your beck and fucking call*—so I learned to be fairly social a long time ago cause overall it makes things a lot easier.

Besides open bowling and the guys that just hung out at the bar, we get Catholic and Protestant church groups, both youth and adult out the wazoo; men's leagues, women's leagues, senior leagues, after school leagues, P.E. classes, every kind of school group and club you can imagine, post Prom, class reunions, family reunions—hell, even Monday night Fantasy Football league. One winter years back Dad even set up an afternoon league for 'Friends of the Library.' I was at school, but he swore they read books and held literary discussions while waiting their turn to bowl. They also refused to keep score, which I guess was some kind of pacifist declaration somebody once told me.

When the church groups, youth groups and prissy clubs have the lanes reserved, Dad did close the bar, I'll give him that much, cause we always had a few pretty skilled drunks glued to the seats and it was kinda hard to pretend they weren't there. He hated to though, I do know that, and believe me, it's not like he's a moral crusader or anything and in general he's pretty Jewish . . . but my mother laid the law down about not mixing the drunks with the kids and church people years ago, so even though she's dead now, I guess Dad does respect that much of her memory. On the other hand, I've begun to think lately that it's more likely he's just too drunk so much of the time that he hasn't figured out yet that he could change the rules.

DED league (Distributive Education or the 'Dedheds' as everyone called them) was on Mondays before the Fantasy Football guys and much as I get sick of the alley, it was one group you didn't want to miss. DED league was Tammy Kurtz and company (Krissy's older sister who could knock your socks off, too). There was also Candy 'Busty' Bailey, one of Jimmy's shags whose job was right there at the alley, which was a royal joke that no one understood better than I did. Sal Navarre, Dick Hudson, Turner Gibson, Missy Campbell, Toby Neuenschwander, Rosie Haufbauer, Bullnuts Kaiser, Eddie Creps, and House Gardner were also Dedheds who bowled at the BBC, as of course did their princely instructor, George Runser. I pretty much knew the whole class cause they were interesting, at least the way I saw things, I've got to tell you that. It's true that the Dedheds were actually pretty fucked up, but for the most part they weren't phony, and I've concluded that I'd rather be *fucked up* than *phony*. My best friend, Brent Sturdivant, says I'm crazy to have that philosophy, but if you knew his parents it wouldn't be all that hard to understand his point of view.

The real fun was watching the Dedheds actually bowl, then trying to guess what drug they were on that night. Brent usually hung with me for DED league and we made this game up we called 'Guess the Drug or Drink.' There were times it seemed Brent actually had some balls, but you can easily mistake that with someone who pretty much is just in 'la la land,' which Brent was about half the time. Anyhow, by the third game he'd infiltrate and collect some pretty good intelligence, which I know is an oxymoron if you're talking about a Dedhed. Then he'd come back and we'd mark our scorecard. It was stupid and all, but somehow when the two of us were together there didn't much seem to be an intelligent second option.

Another attraction was ole' Runser telling them about a hundred times that they weren't allowed to smoke since they were a school club. Of course while he was talking, Bullnuts Kaiser would be standing right in front of him blowing smoke rings around his nose. It wasn't like Runser gave a shit or took his job serious, but one night Karen Fish, the school board President, had stopped at the alley to retrieve her purse that she'd forgotten earlier that afternoon while bowling in the 'Catholic Wives League.' Anyway, as she was leaving she noticed ole' Runser and spied the nuclear cloud settled in over the Dedheds. What turned out to be bad luck for George though, was that she was on her way *to* a school board meeting at the time and reasonably sober cause on a normal night she would have just gone home and hit the sauce and forgotten all about it. So after calling the meeting to order she went ballistic on 'Soup' Beckman and Principal 'Wickerdick' . . . before they knew what even hit them. Runser got called on the carpet and the last thing he could afford was to loose his cake job as General Dedhed, so he'd gotten pretty rattled I guess and determined then and there to establish discipline. That, of course, had turned out to be about as effective as Barney Fife trying to arrest Al Capone.

Those nights were a good time though and I knew Brent went home and jerked off thinking about Tammy Kurtz and maybe even ole' Busty. I ragged him about it for a long time and he'd get all mad and embarrassed, but eventually I quit cause I guess it really wasn't fair since I did the same thing every once in a while too. I probably shouldn't admit this, but even at fifteen I could already tell you that there's something about the 'hooker look' that could make you stupid. . . . and Tammy Kurtz had it *all* going—*and more*! I mean there was just no end to the number of 'stupid tickets' those Kurtz girls had to pass out to guys. Still, there was something different about Krissy from Tammy—something I couldn't quite figure, but just sort of respected—given the unlikely chance that you could get sex off your brain long enough to actually *think* that is.

Dedheds go to school for a couple of hours in the morning in this dungeon of a room in the basement of FHHS where they're sort of exiled like lepers and then they'd go off to jobs at Dean's Sunoco, Steinman Ford, Jespersons Restaurant, Hoffman Lumber, Westerheide Meat Market etc. etc. . . . along with *always* providing an 'ass jockey' to work the village garbage truck while Orville Hocker drove and smoked cheap cigars in the cab. Orville had come by his job honestly, however, as a former Dedhead and ass jockey and was now, not only worshipped by the Dedheds for his move inside the cab, but for having even landed a paying job at all upon graduation.

Runser hits the road by noon each day to make the rounds 'checking his charges,' but everybody in Fort Harrison knows he just goes back to his apartment above Doc Neumeier's office where he moved after splitting from his wife. Brent says he probably sleeps all day or beats off watching porno, but since it's a state funded program nobody much gives a shit and Dedhed parents aren't the type to bitch about something like that.

I got along pretty well with the Dedheds and knew where most of them worked except Tammy Kurtz, which seemed to be a pretty big mystery. Brent figured she stripped at *Three Blind Dice* with her mother, but I never believed it, cause I'd say that'd be a pretty hard gig for even Runser to forge the paperwork on, but I knew he got off just thinking about it so it was no big deal to me. Personally I figured she didn't work anywhere and just copped ole' Runser's nob every once in awhile so he'd find a way to fix it so she could graduate with everyone else . . . and if you think shit like that doesn't happen you should probably be sloppin' down a few beers at TBD.

Brent told me the Dedheds graduated with everyone else in the spring and that Con Stephens sat next to his sister, Kylie, during graduation last year and made her sick. I guess she'd held her breath for most of the speeches and crap, but following the recessional (or whatever) puked in some bushes right outside the school doors while standing like two feet away from their grandparents. Con was an 'ass jockey' at the time and Brent said he'd come straight from a special Sunday morning run to Krantz Slaughterhouse over in Maria Stein, got off the truck and just threw his gown on over his Carharts, so he'd probably smelled pretty tough. It's one of those situations that's funny as hell, but still you had to kind of feel sorry for ole' Kylie at the same time. I wish I'd have been there though, I've got to admit, cause Brent said his Mom started crying and then she started to upchuck herself and had to run to the can through all the well wishers loitering about, loosing one of her heels in the process which Brent had to retrieve. Then Brent said she wouldn't come back out of the toilet until everyone cleared out to go home or to dinner or whatever it was they were gonna do, but you know how long people just hang around slow-like for stuff like graduations, and especially if it's a really nice spring day, which Brent said it was. It was the kind of thing that in some families could actually be a hoot years later, especially if someone had got a shot of ole' Kylie tossing her cookies in the bushes or Lorinda Sturdivant hot footin it to the john with one heel on, but after I thought about it for awhile, I could see that it wasn't the type of hoot that would have ever worked for the Sturdivants. So on second thought it's probably good that I wasn't there cause I would have laughed . . . and it's one of the things about myself I wasn't too proud of. . . .

. . . The game was 21-7, Fort Harrison, at half, when I had to start my trek to the stupid bowling alley. Jimmy had a touchdown, but I would miss one that he scored on a 68-yard return from the second half kickoff. Still, it was better to miss some of Jimmy's big shot moments or watch from a distance in the dark, I reasoned, than to hear the gossip about our fucked up family up close, which my presence always seemed to spawn when I ventured into the *real* world, that is, which in reality is the *phony* world. I heard enough of it at the alley when people actually thought they were *being kind.* I mean Jimmy wore a helmet and was all involved, but if I lurked around the bleachers people kind of like whispered shit and glanced at me, acting all private, though you really knew they wanted to make sure you heard them. People can crack you up when you stop to think about it, if you can learn to keep a sense of humor, at least. *And what's really hysterical is that they think everybody else is fucked up.*

Dad and Jimmy fought constantly and pretty much always had, but especially since my Mom and little sister were killed, a year upcoming that February. Thin Jim advertised in the *Reinforcer* that the alley would be open every Friday that fall to try and snag some of the post-game derelicts away from Stoney's Pub uptown and turn a few extra bucks. At least that's what he'd tried to claim, but I knew it was just a convenient excuse for him to hide out in his office, get schnockered, and avoid Jimmy's heroics.

A small group would come, but even the townies were pissed with Dad's attitude about Jimmy and the Rams cause most of them would have exorcised a testicle to have a son like Jimmy to brag about, and especially in Fort Harrison. I pretty much just let it all go like I'd learned to do with most of life in order to survive, but since I was still an indentured servant, my 'season ticket' was on Carl Robbin's pretty bench at the ass end of the bank so that I could hot foot it back to the alley by half to help do pretty much nothing . . . pretty much fucking nothing at all.

# Chapter Six

*L* egally I couldn't bartend at fifteen though the law allowed me to stock the coolers and monkey around behind the bar 'cleaning or cooking,' but it was all a big joke. Let's put it this way: I pulled more beer out of the coolers than I put in, I mean it seemed that way anyhow. I was also quite skilled at tossing together G&T's, T&T's, V&C's, J&C's, VT's, LIIT's, Cosmopolitans, Martinis, Manhattans, Rusty Nails, Harvey Wallbangers, Mudslides, B-52's, Kamikazes, Fat Frogs, Salty Dogs and probably the best Margaritas in Shelby County. Bartending could pay my bills anytime I might need it in the future, that was for certain. Not that I'm saying the drunks of Fort Harrison, Ohio, were the most discriminating lushes on the planet, so ninety percent of the time it was simply Miller Lite, Bud/Bud Lite, PBR's, or Jack or Jim and Coke.

The real joke was that the state liquor inspector, Tom Borges, was one of Dad's friends and they'd gone to Fort Harrison High together like a millennium earlier. He even bowled leagues twice a week while I was snagging beers and mixing drinks and Jimmy's part time shag, Busty Bailey (who was supposedly the bartender), 'Detroit leaned' her tits all over the place. She was quite a draw, though; I'll give her that, even if she never did five minutes of work in a five-hour shift. But she was eighteen and behind the bar so of course it made all *my* moves legal, which certainly made sense to me cause I'd long since learned how the real world works and I had been educated *honestly*—at the good ole' Fort Harrison Exempted Village Schools *and* Bowling's Bowling Center.

What really cracked me up though was how about once a month ole' Borges tipped Dad that he'd be stopping by for an *official* State inspection. Dad would position me over with the goddamn rotten rental shoes and Busty would march up and down the bar asking, "Can I get something for anybody? Just let me know." Borges would come in with a clipboard and his state employee game face on and ask Dad questions as if they'd never fucking met. I mean talk about phony; fucking Monty Python couldn't have come up with that silly shit. Anyway, he'd check off these boxes and stuff, stick his nose under the sink, go down to the stock room in the basement and once in a blue moon check something ridiculous that Dad needed to change to *meet code*, like move a case of beer at the bottom of the steps three inches to insure employee safety. Then he'd hit the door, mount his free ride white Sable station wagon with the magnetic 'State of Ohio, Department of Liquor Control' sign and ride off into the sunset to slay another morally threatening dragon, and all for the bargain tax salary of about forty-five grand a year, a pretty fucking penny for anybody in the early 90's.

Then there was *Winston Thermostat!*

Winston Thermostat, who was pushing 80, was perched at the bar like he always was when I pushed through the door a little after nine that night. Everyone in Fort Harrison had a Thermostat joke and after awhile I had come to believe it was his only real connection to people, so even though he feigned offense I pretty much thought he actually bathed in the attention, sad as that may have been. He was a strange ole' boy, that was for sure, and lived on a tumbledown farm a quarter mile back a long sandy lane off 66 just north of the alley.

The counties knew Thermie was drunk 25 hours a day and he'd been carted off to Sidney lockup too many times to count before he finally gave up and parked his rusted-out '52 Ford pickup in ten foot weeds out behind a rotting corn crib. The last time I can remember him fucking up on a public street was like when I was a seventh grader I think. He was driving his Oliver tractor down Main on the way to Schaff's IGA and had rear-ended 'Sterile' Cheryl Fox's VW Van. Cheryl was like a clerk for the village sanitary department and a recycled hippie who lived with fifteen or twenty cats and a white cockatoo that could make a bald eagle say 'uncle.' The cozy Fox menagerie was housed in a big ole' run down Victorian on Beal Street where rumor had it she raised the finest pot in Shelby county in her attic on the fourth floor (for her exclusive use, of course). Anyway, since there'd never been an ATF raid or anything, a low profile was exactly what Cheryl hoped to preserve. Twenty years earlier she'd been married to Reldon Fox who'd blown town leaving Cheryl behind (go figure) because of the bank scandal . . . and more than likely also because of his lust for Bobbie Giovanazzo. Two common children had left the area years earlier and never come back that anyone knew of, so Sterile Cheryl had tumbled into her own unique world and most people now forgot she had ever been anything much different.

Dog Noblet, a part time special deputy for the Fort Harrison PD and the full time dog warden for Shelby County, was on cop duty at the time because Wade Borger was away fishing in Canada. The story was that Winston promised him a gallon of moonshine to let the accident slide if Cheryl would. Sterile, being a peacenik type, felt sorry for Winston anyhow, although it was more likely she was high and just wanted get the hell out of there for pretty much the same reason Winston did . . . before a *real* cop happened by. Anyhow, it was rumored that she just flashed a peace sign and with tears in her eyes, for either Winston or the trashed peace-mobile (nobody knew for sure), beat a beeline home to her cats and mega-bird. For years thereafter she drove the peace-mobile about town with the bumper pushed up and into the ass end and wired to the frame with coat hangers, which somehow was fitting anyway, the way I saw it.

Doggie must have taken Winston up on his end of the offer cause about a week later he was arrested by a statie for DUI after losing control of the dog-mobile and mowing down Clarke Berke's Springer Spaniel on Howard Road in Miami County. Of course he lost both his job as county dog cop and part time gig as defender of peace and morals in the village of Fort Harrison. At his hearing at the courthouse in Piqua it was said he went completely bananas and (as quoted by Ned Shriner in the *Reinforcer*) stood and yelled at Judge Goldsnake: "I'd like to see you round up those (bleeping) mutts sober, your honor," he cried, sobbing out loud. "You couldn't do it, judge, you couldn't (bleeping) do it!" He was then led away for a thirty-day jail gig and psychiatric tests crying like a baby.

. . . "Hey Bi l l l y y y, how are y a a a?" Winston slurred as I stepped behind the bar to check the coolers. I could see Dad had already lined up five Beam shots and four sat dead upon the bar as he raised the final one in my honor, I guess. I did feel sorry for the poor guy though. I mean the only reason he came to the alley was to be around warm bodies, I figured, cause he could have stayed on the farm and drank his Beam for pennies on the alley's dollar.

Thermie'd never married and owned a big chunk of land a lot of people had tried to pry away from him over the years, but Winston wouldn't much do anything anybody would have liked and that was the main joy he took in life I always felt. Dad was nice to him though, so Winston was there day after day after day, dropping thirty or forty bucks, drinking Beam shots and getting a sandwich or something to eat every night. Word was he probably had money buried in his yard and with the wad of cash he always carried around you pretty much had to believe it. With the game on, Winston was the only one there, and by then Dad was off buried in his office with his head up his ass and feeling sorry for himself like he had every day for as long as I could remember

# Chapter Seven

There'd be few, if any bowlers, so I'd run the entire show as usual while Dad drank, slept, and hid from hearing about Jimmy's exploits. Everyone in the county knew I was fifteen, but Dad figured that since th3e explosion the chances of being busted had been reduced out of respect (or pity), so he didn't much worry any more about even having an adult around to be seen on 'Football' Fridays and I must admit he was probably right. Busty always had Fridays off so Jimmy could take his turn screwing her after the game unless he'd turned up something better, which he usually did. I could have cared less about Busty being a whore cause Jimmy knew it anyway, but I was beginning to wonder if Dad was somewhere in the cue line too? And if so, I wasn't too choked up about that, I can tell you.

It was maybe five to ten when the door burst open and Tic Forgett (which he pronounced *for-jay* of course), Joe Smith and Garth Schmutz stumbled in singing the goddamn Fort Harrison fight song.

"Billy Boy Beanie Baby Bowling, how duh fuck are ya?" Tic bellowed, already trashed. "Didn't you see big brotha' kick St.Michael's gonads? What duh fuck's wrong with you, boy, and where's duh fuckin' proud papa anyway? Just what duh fuck's wrong with him these days? I don't mean no disrespect for your mom, but it's been awhile, Billy, and you'd think the ole' man would wanna watch Jimmy play."

"Yeh, whatever," I'd said out of habit. "I saw first half, Tic. So what happened second?" I asked, wanting to know and not needing to listen any longer to a drunk's theories about my fucked up family. I set two Miller Lites and a Bud up bar like I'd done a thousand times before.

"Your fucking brother ran back the second half kick seventy yards for a fucking touchdown, dat's what fucking happened . . . just like Tic here did in the state semi game against Twinsburg in '83," Garth slurred, slapping Tic on the back and raising his Miller to toast position.

Tic basked in his glory on cue. They had the script down pat and I'd heard it five hundred times if I'd heard it once. It was always 'state championship this, state championship that;' 'Sam Giovanazzo this, Sam Giovanazzo that.' The bowling alley was thick with state champion heroes—'72, '75, '82, '83, '87 and last year. I'd heard the play by play of every state championship and most of the other three hundred or so games played the last quarter century a hundred times and it seemed like each week another hero was born, and these days sometimes from someone who'd never even been on a fucking football team.

Tic added, "Scored another one late in duh third too, Billy. Dat's what fucking happened, what your fucking bro did! Three fucking touchdowns! Only needs eight more to break Doff Shannon's fucking record. You do fucking *know* that I hope, lil' bro."

Now I'll admit I sometimes struggled with the King's English, but should the words *fuck, fucking, fucked, fucker, fuckhead and fuckable* somehow be banned, communication in the Western World would be threatened and at the BBC rendered obsolete.

Tic chugged the Miller and slammed it on the bar. "Reinforcements, cowboy, and be quick about it. We got injuns to shoot."

"So what was the final score?" I asked.

"41-10, fucking 41-10," Tic burped. Tic was the king and Joe and Garth his court jesters and a stranger could have figured that in nine seconds. Joe Smith never said squat. I wasn't even certain he knew how to talk. They'd all played at Fort Harrison in the early 80's, but I only much had heard about Tic having been a big shot running back and didn't know what Garth and Joe had played, or if they even had . . . as if I much gave a bobcat's butt.

"Hey Thermie, what's the fucking temperature?" Tic shouted at Winston (who'd polished off his fifth Beam) then roared in laughter, joined by Garth and Joe. Joe did laugh at Tic's jokes a lot, but usually not before looking at Garth to see if he laughed. So at least I knew Joe could make sounds.

Winston was 79 and had for years sworn at the cops, challenged the drunks to fistfights in the parking lot, and generally prided himself in being cantankerous and difficult. He was sitting right there on his seat the night the explosion shook the alley, but had shown up sober the next morning to ask if there was anyway he could help. Dad had been kind, but dismissive, and Winston disappeared never to be seen by us again for nearly six months. Mom had always been kind to Winston and stewed about how to get him to wash his clothes (and himself) since complaints about his BO were common. She would bring clothes from Emerson's Dry Goods, where she worked, and stick them behind the bar in a brown paper sack trying to find just the right time to give them to him, hoping to tiptoe around offense. But somehow it just never seemed to take. . . .

. . . "Winston, we had a mix up with an order at Emersons this week and Ray gave out some really good work clothes to myself and Carol Fisher. They weren't Jim's size, but I bet these would work for you, otherwise they'll just get tossed," she'd said one day, lifting a brown bag on the counter and showing Winston a couple of pair of Lee Jeans and three shirts, not unlike what he always wore, but new. "I'd bet they're about your size. Oh, and there was a bunch of under-clothing and socks overstocked too so I threw some of them in the bag if you could use them by any chance," Mom had said trying to be flippantly casual.

"Oh thank you, Mrs. Bowling, but I wouldn't wanna take no charity. There's still a bunch uh Pa's stuff I ain't even touched yet that'd fit me fine. But you sure are nice fer thinking bout me," he'd said with a big smile as Mom tucked the bag back behind the counter, maybe to try another way in another month. She was always worried about offending him so she just gave the soft sell, admitted defeat, and the day moved on—Winston as certain to return rank next time as would the complaints.

It was probably about the first of August that Winston reappeared after the February explosion, sliding back onto his old seat and tossing down Beams one after the other, just like old times. Somehow that made me happy though it's pretty hard to explain, but most of all Winston had *changed.* He was wearing clean clothes, maybe even new ones, it had seemed, and he was smiling, or at least tried to, which he had seldom done for years. No matter where I stood or how close, there wasn't even a hint of BO and his hands and face looked literally scrubbed. Tic and the boys would still spout jokes, but strangely he started laughing *with* them instead of getting pissed, though I'm not sure for a long time that those assholes even much noticed the difference. I didn't completely understand the change though I suspected it was somehow connected to respect for Mom and one of life's good little twists, and it had made me happy.

Tark Cowan and Bert Andrews were the next through the door, followed closely by Nick Fisher and Dennis Shindeldecker. Two more Miller Lites, a Bud Light and a Jack and Coke. They were sprinkled throughout the various years of Ram Football and the irony was that it always seemed everyone had played on a state championship team, which honestly was a laugh if you really thought about it. I mean I'll give that there were a lot of championship years, but there were a lot that weren't. So what happened to those guys? But any way you sliced it, the 'Good Ole' Boy's Club' in Fort Harrison, Ohio, was a big one, and as long as the football team kicked ass it would only grow, cause leaving the home turf was unnecessary in those days—north to Ford in Lima or south to Honda in Anna—good jobs were everywhere, money was abundant, and the *GOBC* thrived . . . *and never more than Friday nights after a Fort Harrison Ram football victory!*

# Chapter Eight

F riday, November 3, 1991, was unusually mild and by mid afternoon the temperature topped 50. The last football game of the season would be played at Robbins Field and the hallways were littered with all fashion of blue and gold paper which had fallen or more likely been torn from over doorways and across lockers. At least half of the 'Good Luck Chet,' 'Go Rams, Tackle Raiders' or '10-0, No Other Way, Hey!' signs that cheerleader advisor Shannon Edwards and her joined-at-the-hip gynoids had slaved away creating to tape on the lockers of the football studs were now 'dead soldiers,' torn and kicked across the floor, collecting an artistic array of boot, plimsoll and cross trainer tread imprints. Blind loyalty and both sanctioned and unsanctioned festivities ruled the day—and anarchy reigned—with rebels from the usually apathetic subterranean emerging to assume the role of antichrist. So when Lane Phillips grabbed the restroom pass during sixth period study hall I knew exactly what he was up to: the rape and pillage of hall decorations like a Goth attacking Adrianople. Now it's not that I'm like a major historian or anything, but I'd actually picked that up in World History earlier in the week (while looking at the pictures, that is, when I was bored out of my gourd) and it seemed to fit.

Now big shot athletes, board member's kids, scary Dedheds or hot girls who knew how to flash their ass and boobs hadn't always held FHHS hostage, but that's sure what I deducted during all the free time I had on my hands as I surfed the hallways and classrooms of good ole' Fort Harrison High. I guess though, like fifteen years earlier, Catholic Law had still pretty much ruled and Priests from St. Matthias roamed the halls so that kids fucking up didn't worry about getting a wack or being suspended, but rather going to hell.

The administrators were also Priests back then, despite the fact FHHS was a public school. It's just the way it had been for about two centuries and nobody bitched, not even the Protestants.

I knew this because 80% of Fort Harrison was Catholic and the bowling alley was a karaoke forum for whiners and the biggest assholes to formally walk the hallowed halls of FHHS. Half of their sentences started with 'Now when Father John was . . .' or 'Father John didn't put up with no shit . . .' etc. etc. I mean they probably had a point cause I'd understood for a few years by then that we were a good country on the road to fuckdom and that we were gonna get there a lot quicker with the liberals driving the bus. Anyhow, school discipline at FHHS was pretty messed up by the time I was in school. In my opinion, at least.

Fort Harrison stood 9-0 and the game that night with the Rexton Prairie Raiders, who were 8-1, was the game all West Central Ohio's attention was hopped up about. Jimmy had over 1300 rushing yards and 26 touchdowns for the season and was likely headed for first-team all state after being second-team the season before. Yet the conflict with Dad had never been worse. Two weeks earlier he'd moved out and got an apartment downtown over Gibson's Bakery, which he shared with Clint Obringer who flew the coop also. I was pretty numb about the whole thing, but kind of glad the screaming had stopped and I was able to get a bit of sleep. I'd gone to Jimmy's apartment once and it was actually pretty depressing, but I made Jimmy feel like it was big shit. I guess that was good practice though, cause I had already figured out that lying about stuff like that was really what people expected and especially if you were like someone's brother.

Somehow I bet the most depressing times were after Jimmy boinked Busty then had to give her like fifteen minutes or so of small-talk before he told her to hit the road. I was pretty sure she'd already lobbied to move in, but I hoped Jimmy didn't give in to that cause that could get really depressing, though I pretty much gave him credit for being smarter than that.

Brent said Tommy Pleiman saw Clint going up the back steps with Tammy Kurtz one night, so it made you wonder what all really goes on up there, I guess. I wasn't really sure how I felt about it all, not that it made a shit bit of difference anyhow of course. I mean, like on one hand ole' Busty and Tammy had some shit going for them and any guy could get pretty hot and bothered, but they could be depressing too. I could picture the excitement, the lust and all that—naked bodies bouncing off the walls and all kind of weird positions that Brent was always panting about—but it was the flip side that really brought me down. I mean you wouldn't much want to hang out with them for conversation or even like play Monopoly or that kind of stuff. At least I wouldn't.

Dad didn't give a shit when Jimmy moved out. In fact I think he seemed relieved (which I would *later* come to understand was because it gave him more shots at 'ole Busty), but their (Jimmy and Dad) relationship wasn't too popular around town. We were losing people at the alley because of our fucked up family, though probably not all that many when I really thought about it. I mean a lot of people are always gonna bowl cause life's about finding shit to do so you don't have to think about other shit and in Fort Harrison the choices were pretty thin. So all in all the bowling alley was pretty solid, even if it *was* being run by fucked up people.

Word was, however, that the Obringers were hounding everyone from Soup Beckman to Chief Borger to do something about the 'Pleasure Dome,' and even went crying to the school board. Jimmy and Clint were both 18 though and could pretty much do what they wanted. The Obringers knew that too, but they were desperate to find someone to blame. I mean, those kind of people never wanna much look at themselves cause that's no fun. If they'd really wanted to find someone to blame they should have gone after that asshole, Sam Giovanazzo, cause Jimmy told me that Sam had given him and Clint the money for the security deposit and even first months rent. But blame Sam Giovanazzo? Everyone knew better than to do that, including the Obringers. That'd be like short-sheeting Hannibal Lecter.

. . . "Sturdivant, what's in your mouth? Approach the desk," George Thomas yelled above the circus. Sixth period study hall was in the freshman science room, which was in the basement of FHHS. I turned to Brent who flashed me his 'what the hell did I do look' as he walked up the far side of the room. Brent was probably my best friend, but he was far too dramatic and had a persecution complex about the size of Texas, which could really get on your nerves at times.

George Thomas was not really a bad guy and a pretty good teacher I thought, which was rare at Fort Harrison High. I'd learned some interesting stuff from him during first period science and it was about the only class I looked forward to, which meant my entire day was a downhill slide of course. My class had 16 kids in it and we were always busy, so things went quite well, but GT was short on control for the afternoon study hall I have to admit and that day it was like being at the Battle of Gettysburg. GT was about ready to slam his (own) head into the wall you could tell and for once Brent was probably right about getting fucked, I'll give him that. But GT was in desperate need of a sacrifice and Brent was the first 'quasi-mouse' that had caught his eye just as he was about to crack. I must admit though, I was biting my tongue not to laugh. Some friend I am, I know, and I should be ashamed, but it was funny as hell—you just had to be there.

"Spit that gum out! You know the rules," GT screamed at Brent, scanning the room severely. I guess they taught *all* teachers to do the Cagney thing, even ole' GT, though I'd only seen it work once in a blue moon . . . and *never* for George Thomas. GT held the wastebasket for Brent to spit the gum into and looked like he was about ready to cry, seeing nobody was even watching the drama unfold. Brent then flashed me a peace sign and a big grin, having regained reality and remembering it was only GT and that ultimately nothing would happen to him. Then without consequence he returned to his desk, now wondrously proud of himself.

Dirk Salisbury nailed Brad Slavik in the back of the head with a BB, maybe a minute later. Slavik's ole' man, Russell was a vice president at the Savings and Loan and a pretty big cheese in Fort Harrison. Of course there's like fifteen vice presidents at the bank, which I've never much understood, but ole' man Slavik could be a real asshole I'd always heard. Brad was a little like me though, cause he had an older brother, Sal, who was a big shot football star like five years earlier who'd gone on to play for Purdue so Brad was in the 'trick bag' with the ole' man for not measuring up. I suspected Dirk had it all figured—that Brad wouldn't run crying to the old man and that if he did it was Brad who'd probably get his ass booted. Dirk wasn't stupid, I'll give you that, even if he was the biggest asshole in our class which I know I've said ten times now.

When George Thomas's attempt to gain control by making an example of Brent for chewing gum failed, he just gave up and walked to the back of the room, burying his head in the metal cabinet where the jars of pig fetuses and snakes in formaldehyde were housed. Then someone fired a tennis ball that rebounded off the blackboard before hitting Stan Fisher in the front row and knocking his glasses off. The entire room went beserk, but GT never even turned, his mutt still stuck in the cabinet where I was pretty sure he was crying. I hadn't seen who'd thrown it though I suspected Eddie Candle who was an excellent tennis player and always seemed to have tennis balls with him even though Fort Harrison didn't have a team. I've got to admit it was all pretty funny; I mean I gotta tell you that. Stan was one of those kids who could study in the eye of a hurricane and I admired his discipline. A small red circle began to form on his forehead, but ole' Stan just picked his glasses up, put them back on and stuck his nose back in his book without any noticeable emotion at all. The only thing I thought I detected was that he'd seemed to duck a bit lower in his seat so that it was probably gonna take like Robin Hood next time around to bring his glasses down.

I felt sorry for GT, but I always sort of tried to look for the good in stuff and was just glad the freshman science room was in the basement instead of second or third floor, cause I was pretty sure George Thomas would have jumped out the window before the bell rang that day. But then maybe they'd figured that out years back when they stuck ole' GT down there in the basement in the first place.

*R I N G* ..................

# Chapter Nine

By seventh period you had to wonder how the football players would ever get their heads out of the cheerleader's asses and actually be ready to play a game by 8 pm. It wasn't like I knew much about concentration or coaching football, but things were pretty chaotic. But if you never went to a small Ohio high school with a good football team, or like if it's been years since you were in high school at all, then I doubt I can quite explain just how stupid football Fridays can really get.

Take for example seventh period World History, Room 211, at the southeast corner of the building overlooking Main Street. Dick Hamilton was the teacher, which was a joke, but at least you'd think he'd put in an appearance sometime during the period that day, but it never happened. He was one of the assistant football coaches, duh! I mean this *was* a history class and they always stuck the coaches in either Phys. Ed. or History; they weren't rocket scientists, were they? He did have discipline when he was in the classroom, I'll give him that much, but mostly I figured so he wasn't bothered reading his *USA Today* or drawing up his stupid football plays. It's not like he ever taught or anything and needed order to make some kind of profound point.

At least two, often three days a week, he'd walk in and say, 'Study hall today, get busy and don't let me hear any shit from you.' And that would be it for 55 minutes. I mean, between the football coaches and your actual study halls, a Fort Harrison High kid should be pretty smart with all that time to study . . . unless of course actually being *taught* something was supposed to be part of the deal too. Other days ole' Hambone would show cheap movies about WWII, the Romans, or whatever he could get the library to send upstairs. But it was never in any order and he'd never turn the lights off or even pull down the window shades so we couldn't really see them anyhow. The guy wouldn't even put the reel on the projector. (Yeah, I know it was the 90's, but Dick Hamilton still used reel projectors, which I'd always assumed was like a 'football' superstition, or something that dated back to his days at Ohio State). Anyway he had Eddie Candle thread the tapes and even had Brent lined up as a backup in case Eddie ever got sick; you know, the kind of thing an assistant football coach is supposed to do, I guess.

We'd never had a class discussion so far in two months, or even a test, and I hadn't yet figured out how we were gonna be graded. Jimmy'd said, 'Just don't piss him off and you'll be fine. Don't worry about grades. You'll probably get a B. Besides, you're my brother so I don't think he's likely to fuck with you. You can only fuck yourself, cowboy, so be smart.' Now a lot of kids would take comfort in stuff like that, but all in all I thought it was pretty cheap. I mean Giovanazzo and Hamilton ruled the school and anybody could see that. Wickerdick and Larry Beckman were just ventriloquist dummies, but somehow everybody in Fort Harrison was ok with the arrangement and it looked like it was working just fine that year again, with another state football championship likely just weeks away!

I noticed that Dirk Salisbury and Tyler Boeke, two big shot freshman football players, had flown the coop and Mindy Dalinghaus was in a twit scooting around her seat so much I began to think she might set it on fire or something; you know, Boy Scout friction and all that. She had her freshman cheerleading getup on and was actually crying because so far she hadn't had the balls to bolt and join the anarchists. Haley Obringer had her outfit on too, just like all the cheerleaders, but she was actually doing science homework two minutes inside the door, which even to me was extreme that day I must admit, but you had to respect her in a way cause I thought the world should be more like that than the way the other assholes were pushing it.

Part of my shining reputation that year was from having a window seat that period, for which I was envied. I was pretty sure if it wasn't for Jimmy I would have gotten booted and replaced by even a second rate freshman football asshole, but ole' Dick and Jimmy were tight and Hamilton could have given a shit about the freshman players, except for Dirk and Tyler, and they had seats in the same row. So I figured as long as I had to be there with nothing to do all year that a window seat was definitely a bonus and exactly why everyone was jealous.

On the street below, big shots were as thick as August flies in Jim Byrnes's dairy parlor. Marcia Schweiterman was sitting on Turk Otte's lap on a bench beside the flagpole right below Wickerdick's office. I might have had a better vantage point than Wickman, being one story higher, but it was pretty easy to see Turk's hand embedded in Marcia's cheerleader tights and from the expression on her face I'm pretty sure I wasn't wrong. Talk about ballsy! Even at my age I had to wonder whatever happened to sneaking into the band instrument room at the end of the stage in order to engage in a sex act while at school?

Except for open lunch for seniors, students were not to leave school property at any time during the day, but that was a big laugh. Sometimes they'd nail a few AWOL's if they could catch a mouse here and there, but I doubt Wickerdick would have kept his job til Monday if he'd nabbed any of the big shots cruising Main, which included my brother Jimmy who I saw emerge just then from Samsal's Soda Shop playing grab ass with Kendra Pleiman, captain of the cheerleaders that year. At least she had a little class compared to Busty who was out of the picture working at the alley for Friday afternoon senior leagues. Not that Jimmy would have given a shit, that is, or that it would have changed anything he was doing.

I was tiring of the whole scene, but noticed when I turned that 'ole Mindy had finally made her prison break which in an odd way I was happy about cause, like I said, she was the type whose life was certain to be downhill forever once she graduated. Her 'time' would actually come much sooner, however, when she got riffed from the yell squad the following summer. It was pretty much the fate of most of the big shots when their time ran out and they were kicked in the ass into the real world, though I'd hoped that wasn't true with Jimmy.

From my seat I had a straight shot through the door and across the hall into Constance Badderly's English room. There I could see Gwen Putnam and Mrs. Badderly sitting together, probably working on lesson plans. It's what I figured, anyhow, since Gwen was a student assistant for Mrs. Badderly. Gwen Putnam was beautiful and perfect, she just was, and there was no other way to say it. She was friendly to everyone and involved in everything, but that didn't include a need to skip class and party on school time. Gwen was also about the only big shot who could take the high road and never be made fun of. I mean Gwen was by far the *biggest big shot* at Fort Harrison in one way, and on the other hand not a big shot at all. It's kind of hard to explain, but no one was *ever* gonna rag on Gwen. It would just never happen. Period!

Gwen would be at the game that night early, cheering from the stands and playing flute in the band's half time show before leaving to get her rest for the regional cross-country championship the next morning in Troy, which of course she would win. Jimmy had been in love with Gwen since grade school, but then everyone was in a way, including me. A year or so earlier they'd been on a few dates, but Jimmy'd come too see it would never be anything serious cause Gwen had goals no one understood but herself and she possessed a laser focus and discipline to achieve them. Much as Jimmy might have wished for more, he had still remained a good friend and would defend her to the end, which was something it seemed Gwen Putnam instilled in people, but would likely never need. From the mice to the subterranean cynics, right through the big shots and on into the adult world, I'd never known anyone to say a negative thing about Gwen Putnam . . . *well, except for Sam Giovanazzo, that is.*

## Chapter Ten

*A* comically large clock on the wall above Dick Hamilton's desk said it was 1:45, so there were still 23 minutes in the period although it seemed to me like it should have been summer vacation by then. I found myself reflecting and slipping into cynicism, which I often did to kill time, though it could be quite depressing. I mean if you figure you sleep 30% of your life, it's pretty much a given that you'll be forced to spend 60% of your life doing crap like sitting in a seventh period study hall that was supposed to be a history class, so if you're lucky that gives you a sliver of a chance to do something fun or productive the other ten. And to be honest, even that theory seems optimistic when I really stop to think about it. Anyway, everyone stares at the stupid clock pretty much all period as if that will make time go faster, which of course youth craves and age fears. So no one hardly studies in any of the classrooms cause they all have the same damn clock. I mean if they wanted kids to study, don't put a fucking clock on the wall. It's really a quite simple concept.

I could see Jimmy and Kendra Plieman crossing the street on their way back to the high school for the big pep assembly in the gym last period. In less than six months Jimmy would graduate and I knew he would leave Fort Harrison and probably never come back.

Suddenly that thought made me really sad. . . .

. . . "Billy, quit it. Mom, make Billy quit. He's laughing and making noise and I can't concentrate."

Jimmy was trying to solve a Rubik's Cube. He was in junior high and I was probably a third or fourth grader. We were headed to Cincinnati to see Grampy and Grammy Romano. I lived for those trips and had every farm, town and landmark memorized on 66 all the way to the edge of Cincinnati. I knew the dairy farms, smelly hog farms and turkey farms, which, from a distance, loomed like fields of summer snow that had refused to melt. For miles the old Miami-Erie Canal chased the highway and my mom told me why it had been built and what it must have been like a hundred years ago. Then there was North Star where Annie Oakley was both born and buried. Mom told me about her and about all the Indian battles which had been fought around towns just like Fort Harrison. She told me about the Treaty of Greenville and one time Dad stopped at the fort there, which they'd rebuilt and I didn't want to leave. I always begged him to stop again, but he never did, probably because he knew I'd liked it so much.

"Billy, look. You can see the old canal over there running along the tree line. See it? We cross it pretty soon again, so let's watch for it," she said, turning and smiling with a wink as I sat forward, straining to see the canal and forgetting all else.

Mom never yelled at you. She was quiet most of the time and had a way of turning a fight between Jimmy and me into a game, but it's hard to explain cause I never really understood it myself or even knew it was happening. I thought Mom had to be about the most beautiful woman in Fort Harrison, and even when I was pretty young I used to wonder how Mom and Dad had gotten together cause they never seemed all that happy. That's when I first started understanding sadness because I thought it was stupid that if you had a chance to be happy and adults were the big shots who could make all the decisions, then why did they always seem to be so sad? So I learned early on to be cynical I guess, even though I didn't much understand it at the time. At least if you're cynical you sort of prepare yourself for being an adult, but if you skip around all happy as a kid and then *boom*—one day you're an adult—well that could be pretty rough I reasoned. So it's probably just as well to understand the bullshit early on, then just try not to fight it all that much when you get older.

Still, Cincinnati at my grandparents was just about the best thing in the world, I always thought. Grampy Mario and Grammy Louisa Romano ran an Italian Restaurant called *Romanos* right in the middle of the city and had a great big wonderful apartment on the 19th floor high above it. From there you could look out over *Fountain*

*Square* and watch all the people below who looked like brightly colored bugs darting in an out of the buildings. Christmas was best of all though, when the city lights were up and the tiny storefronts sparkled like distant stars. One week each summer Jimmy and I got to stay a whole week with Grampy and Grammy and we always did it when the Reds played at home all week. Our Uncle Marco, who helped run the restaurant and had an apartment in a building across the street, would take us to the games at *Riverfront Stadium* about every day and when it was time to go back to Fort Harrison it was like the bottom dropped out of my world.

All I ever really knew about my Mom and Dad meeting was that it had been at Romanos when Dad was on leave from the service, just before being shipped out to Vietnam. Mom had told Jimmy and me this once in our room late at night (while she was hugging us tight and crying). She'd sort of seemed happy talking about it, but at the same time she was crying and I didn't understand. She just said: 'I was a waitress at the restaurant when your father walked in wearing his uniform. He was just so handsome . . . he . . .' she'd be saying, then broke out sobbing before wiping away her tears and kissing us both on the forehead, then leaving. Dad had been yelling downstairs before Mom came up, so I sort of knew what was going on, but when you're six years old you don't want to think about it cause there's nothing you can really do to change things.

"Mommy, we're almost there aren't we?" I squealed, seeing the skyscrapers looming in the distance.

"Billy, just relax, goddamn it, and quit yelling in my ear," Dad said crossly, so I sat back in the seat and fought to box my excitement. Mom turned and gave me a quick wink, softly touching my hand, but turned back quickly so I wouldn't see her looking sad even though I knew in some ways she was excited too. Dad was always pissed about going to Grampy and Grammys and I never knew why, but I could tell it, even as a little kid. I knew Mom loved it, but somehow I always understood Dad made sure she couldn't love it too much.

Jimmy was still on a mission to solve the Rubik's Cube and never even looked up as we drove down the city streets where you had to crane your neck to see the top of the buildings, surely the most exciting thing in the world I thought. Dad took the ticket for the parking garage where Grampy Romano had four spots on the 12$^{th}$ tier, but bitched at every turn. Even as a kid I used to think that if I ever had my own family this would be the most fun thing in the world we could do together, but it sure wasn't like that with us. There is so much innocence in children that even well meaning adults usually find a way to fuck up, let alone an asshole like my father.

Jimmy could get excited too, but usually only when he knew we were going to go to a Reds or Bengals game and it wasn't in the plans that trip. Otherwise he said he'd rather be back in Fort Harrison with his friends, so he was a close second to my Dad as far as attitude issues went that trip. Eventually I just learned to forget about everyone else and whatever their stupid problems were. I figured this out early on and I don't think most kids do, but we were in Cincinnati and I wasn't going to let anybody spoil that . . . not even my Dad.

. . . Just before the bell, reality sliced like a paper cut. Below, the blue and gold hot shots had evaporated while I'd been lost in my daydream. In five minutes the entire student body, including the middle school, would be crammed into the gymnasium on the south side home bleachers for the biggest pep assembly in the history of Fort Harrison High School—at least that's what I heard Mindy Dalinghaus harping about at the beginning of the period. 'This is going to be the biggest day of my life and I've *got* to go get ready,' I'd heard her sob to Tara Neumeier, who could have given two shits, but smiled at her with practiced empathy. Tara was one of those kids who would smile at anything and you never quite understood whether she had a functioning brain or had just decided long ago that everyone else was a dumb ass. Either way I sort of respected her, and given that she'd grown up with that nutjob, Doc Neumeier, for a father . . . well, I had to give her a lot of credit for possessing even marginal sanity. Anyhow the good ole' freshman space cadets had a cheer on the program and were also going to be a part of some stupid skit where they'd probably be made to look like asses, getting plastered in the face with Gillette pies and stuff like that. But with cheerleaders that silly shit goes right past them anyway, so I guess it doesn't much matter, does it?

RING………….

# Chapter Eleven

I wasn't too choked up about Dick Hamilton, like I already said, but I must admit he was about the only guy that could keep something like a pep assembly from becoming a full blown insurrection. As a teacher he was a joke, but he *had* been a lineman at Ohio State, so if he gave you a 'Cagney look,' you sort of started to get nervous. He and fuck-head Giovanazzo stood like bookends on each side of the main door into the gym as we stumbled and filed in like cattle slipping on a shit covered slaughterhouse ramp. Ole' Dick had already planted a half-Cagney look on his mug that made you think a bit about really doing something stupid in the bleachers, like throwing a bolt you'd ripped off from Industrial Arts at the cheerleaders, and if you think stuff like that didn't happen, you'd be wrong, whether you'd like to believe it or not. Not that I would do it, mind you, because I wouldn't, but in a way would have been just as guilty if it *had* happened, I suppose, cause I was the type of guy who woulda laughed, which is exactly why the real derelicts did that kind of stuff in the first place. It's a bit of a chicken/egg thing I guess you could say.

I mean one of the biggest stories in the history of FHHS pep assemblies was how Karen Obringer, Haley and Clint's Mom and former cheerleader, lost two front teeth back in '69 from a bolt tossed at a pep assembly. I figured that was why Haley was so low keyed, I mean not flamboyant or anything, so as not to call much attention to herself and multiply her chances for being a target since she was a cheerleader too. Nevertheless, after ten minutes or so the really skilled and dedicated seditionists would surface and I must admit it was pretty exciting waiting to see what would come down.

*Hambone* zeroed in on the ex-cons, cause believe me, a lot of guys had been nailed in the past and booted out of school for awhile, which most of them didn't much mind, wearing their expulsion papers from a pep assembly prank like *" The Red Badge of Courage.*"

A couple of years earlier they'd quit hammering kids assess with Swiss cheese boards and since then the ranks of the anarchists had exploded. I knew some of this stuff cause Jimmy told me, but at Fort Harrison they dragged in the junior high kids to vaccinate with *school spirit* before you could ever much began to think for yourself so I'd already seen some pretty great monkeyshines in two seasons of pep assemblies already. What really cracked me up again was the stupidity of the adults. I guess they thought that if they imprisoned the junior high kids in the auditorium during the pep meetings, they'd get all fuzzy-warm and want to be on the football team or yell squad. That was another big joke. I mean I knew kids like Lane Phillips who *didn't* go out for football just so he could follow in the footsteps of Darf Pannabecker and disrupt pep assemblies, and that's no shit. And the crazy thing was that ole' Lane was a hell of a running back in junior high football. In fact, sometimes I even wondered if Lane loved pranks so much that it was the reason he repeated freshman year and fell a class behind us—just to give him an extra year so he could perfect his pranks even more. I loved it though when someone like Lane slipped through Sam Giovanazzo's fingers, and ultimately those people had no idea how truly lucky they had been.

Everyone knew that Hambone could only concentrate so long on potential terrorism before his attention became diverted and glued to a cheerleader's crotch, hoping I guess to see a few stray pubic hairs peeking out from beneath their tights, or perhaps cast lecherous glances upon yell squad coach Shannon 'Hooters' Edward's gigantic boobs. Of course that was almost honorable (in a distorted sort of way), I remember once thinking to myself, since everyone in school and around town knew he was shagging her anyhow. Well, everyone, that is, *except* Dave Edwards, her witless husband.

Jimmy and all the jocks sat in the front row wearing jeans and their home gold jerseys. If they had like a steady girlfriend or even some chick they wanted to lay that weekend, they'd let them wear the away blues, which was I guess an age old tradition that sometimes produced little *weekend mistakes* that would one day down the line help keep the Giovanazzo football machine chugging along. Jimmy let Busty Bailey wear his once I'd heard, but he took so much shit that even his big shot status took a major hit. Anyhow today Kendra Pleiman had Jimmy's # 30 on over her cheerleader get up, but somehow even I wasn't sure Jimmy could score that weekend cause Kendra was known as a pretty tough sell. I mean there *were* still a few girls left who weren't flaming hoes, just not many. Jimmy was always two steps ahead, though, and if Kendra wouldn't give up her cherry, he probably had somebody else already lined up . . . or as a last resort Busty would always be waiting in the wings. It was a matter of strategy and timing, and believe me, Jimmy Bowling had those down to a science.

Mindy Dallinghaus had somehow landed Ron Falk's # 87, so there wasn't a real big secret about what Mindy would be doing after the game or at least by Saturday night. I mean when a JV or freshmen cheerleader like Mindy snags a varsity jersey it should have made her parents pretty nervous cause it almost certainly meant she'd get poked about as soon as they lost track of her global position. I figured most parents knew this, especially if they were FHHS graduates, but after awhile I guess they began to believe that stuff never really happened anymore, and especially if they hadn't been laid in a decade or so.

A small plywood podium made by the shop boys (which was easy enough to tell) sat in the middle of the floor. Ted *"no shit"* Turner (which had for years by then actually been his nickname), the guidance counselor, was in a tizzy trying to adjust the mike so it wouldn't screech like space aliens were invading the town. When he finally got it anesthetized, Wickerdick got up and walked to the podium. As he was clearing his throat an alarm clock went off somewhere high up in the rafters, eventually winding down while the bleachers roared and a flustered Wickerdick tried to regain composure. Near the north wall, two short rows of folding chairs were set up for the football coaches, Wickerdick, Soup Beckman, Karen Fish and a couple of other clowns from the school board, Hooters Edwards, Father Casey from St. Matthias, Ned Shriner from the *Reinforcer* and of course Doc Neumeier, who was decked out in his blue blazer and clown size gold bow tie. Everyone knew he'd stand up and do his Soupy Sales bullshit and lead the last cheer. I mean you couldn't invent anything that dumb if you'd been born in a different galaxy, but somehow the school board, Beckman, Wickerdick & Co. thought it was *tits*. All we really needed were the Simpsons arriving late to make everything perfect.

Wickerdick started again. "I know we're all proud of Coach Giovanazzo and the Rams. Let's stand and let them know how we feel," he said, starting to clap furiously. Most of the indentured students stood clapping and cheering, but small pockets here and there stayed put. I loved this part because of guys like Darf Pannabecker who now cupped his hands and ducked behind Ron Martin (who weighed over 300 pounds) and began yelling obscene catcalls at the top of his voice, but just muddled enough so that it was pretty hard to make out the words from the floor where the prison guards were, but *Cheerleaders are Sluts* and *Beckman Sucks* were pretty clear from where I sat. Dick Hamilton glared into the stands toward Darf, but without enough evidence at that point to cause a scene. The jocks stood and faced the bleachers on cue from Giovanazzo and then started to laugh their asses off cause they all thought the school clowns were tits. I always thought the insurgents did a lot more to loosen up the jocks than the stupid cheerleaders ever did (*at least before the game*), which is sort of supposed to be the point of the pep confabs, isn't it?

When the cheers, jeers, and catcalls subsided, Wickerdick stepped back to the podium just as a second alarm clock weakly wound down from the rafters and the bleachers roared again. He waited patiently, if noticeably rattled, before continuing: "Let's also give a hand to Ms. Edwards, our fearless cheerleading coach, who would now like to say a word."

Wickerdick returned to his seat and Hooters started to the podium. "*Show us your tits, show us your tits*," Darf barked through muffled hands, expecting to remain concealed by both Martin's bulk and the hoots, howls and noise that echoed throughout the gym as she walked toward the mike, but a freak lull gave Darf center stage and the third '*Show us your tits'* echoed clearly around the gymnasium, and even as he tried to hide, his cover was pretty much blown. That was when the chant of '*Darf, Darf, Darf'* spread through the bleachers like soft margarine and half the football players joined in, clapping in unison with each 'Darf.'

Dick Hamilton jumped up and practically ran to the mike. "Darf Pannabecker, you are excused to go to Mr. Wickman's office immediately. We will meet with you following the assembly." Hamilton cast a laser stare upon Darf as he levitated briefly above his foxhole before tripping toward the aisle. Hooters stood behind *'Sterodick,'* which Hamilton was sometimes called along with Hambone, if from well behind his back, and most kids I knew wouldn't use the nickname until they were past the Indiana state line. The hot shots on the chairs sat like disciples at The Last Supper looking toward Christ in charge at the podium.

I glanced at Giovanazzo who was in a world that none of us would truly understand for years yet to come. Since Hamilton had signed on, he'd assumed the enforcer duties shouldered for a decade or so by Giovanazzo I'd heard the boys at the alley say. Most of the time Giovanazzo, I thought, seemed to be suspended in some kind of drug induced catatonia. Anyway, Darf, who was nearly as big as Ron Martin, stumbled off the last step nearly pitching himself to the floor as several football players reached out to give him *low fives*. Hamilton glared at them, but I knew how it worked—the players *and* coaches would all have a good laugh later in the locker room and share hoots and jokes about Hooter's tits and laugh about Darf's monkeyshines. I mean it wasn't like Sterodick and company didn't think it was funnier than hell, but with ole' Fishface, Father Casey and a few parents here and there, there was a script to follow and it required a human sacrifice, which of course was 9 times out of 10, Darf Pannabecker . . . *who would one day get the last laugh.*

Darf cut his throat a bit that day, however, when he turned to the bleachers just before passing through the doors and flashed a double victory/peace sign. That started the 'Darf' chant again and more disgusted looks from the board members who stared at Wickerdick for his obvious lack of control. I mean as stupid as the assemblies were, the comedy was priceless. Darf would get a three day suspension, his second that year already, but still be the *biggest story* from the *biggest pep meeting* in FHHS history . . . at least according to Mindy Dalinghaus.

The remainder of the Pep Assembly was predictable and anticlimactic after Darf's departure. Hooters introduced all the cheers and skits, making sure to take the mike in her hand so she could stand out in *front* of the podium, showcasing her tits that were packaged in a tight gold sweater and stealing the show from her charges in their heavy sweaters and varsity jock jerseys. Of course there were some nice legs on display and the occasional crotch shot you hoped you didn't miss, which you wouldn't if you kept your radar up. The freshmen pretty much fucked up their big chance and I later saw Mindy Dalinghaus standing by the door of the girls' locker room, crying. A couple of the second string football studs took Gillette pies in the face, which was getting pretty old I thought, and then fucking Sam Giovanazzo gave his 'last words and testament' which about made me puke, before turning it over to Doc Neumeier to perform his silly shit just before the bell rang and turned loose a stampede for the doors that would have made Buffalo Bill proud.

Since he was my brother, I didn't want to think Jimmy was a phony and I honestly thought he was pretty good at playing both sides, which all in all was a good way to go through life I'd figured awhile back, though I was pretty certain it wasn't something I could ever become very skilled at. I mean I know I'm far too cynical and will probably always have a pretty miserable life . . . *if I really decide not to become a phony, that is.*

In some ways though, I guess you had to appreciate ole' Fort Harrison High School and even the town. I mean the whole world is pretty fucked up, and all in all things were calm in our neck of the woods, at least since John Dillinger and 'Baby Face' robbed the bank and nailed Merle Denton like a turtle's age ago. Sure, there'd been a few suicides, car wrecks or accidents at the stone quarry that snuffed somebody out here and there, but the only real capital crime the past half-century had been when Shorter had blown Clarice and Cal away in the heat of their *embrace* back in '75. So I guess we should be pretty happy with the place overall and learn to put up with the phoniness cause I figured if I lived somewhere else, things would still be just as phony and probably even more dangerous to boot.

# Chapter Twelve

Fort Harrison won the game over Rexton Prairie Raiders that night, 52-20. Jimmy had four touchdowns and 164 yards and so now pretty much owned every major record for a running back to ever play Fort Harrison football. Dad had been buried in his office at the BBC as always and it had been over a month since Jimmy had been home or at the alley, and even longer since the two of them had talked.

Winston was settled on his bar stool alone with a litter of Beams when I returned that night a bit later than usual, having stayed on my bench until end of third quarter. I got to see all of Jimmy's touchdowns and was lucky because I remembered to take this tiny pair of binoculars I'd found, still in perfect condition, and hanging from a high tree branch a couple of days after the explosion.

Fort Harrison went on that year to win their *seventh* Ohio State Division III football championship and close out an undefeated season without a close game. Jimmy was *Ohio's Mr. Football,* the state's greatest individual sports honor, and asshole Sam Giovanazzo got State *Coach of the Year* for the fifth time. I saw the playoff game with Dayton Carver, but missed the Fairview game and state championship with Youngstown Mogadore because, of course, Dad needed me to run a bowling alley in a town where everyone was fucking gone but him and me.

But the real highlight of my freshman year, if you'd really care to know, was that I was able to watch Gwen Putnam run quite a few times before she graduated. Cross-country and track meets were Saturday morning events and I could usually get away for a few hours here and there, and as Dad got weirder and his hangovers longer, I just started leaving without saying anything and a lot of times wasn't even missed.

Gwen was individual state champion for the *fourth* straight year in cross-country and the Rams won their *fourth* straight team title.

Though I was unable to see the championship in Columbus, Brent Sturdivant and I had gone with his Dad to Troy to watch the regional meet that was run along the banks of the Little Miami River. Gordon Sturdivant, who was a CPA in Piqua, had no connection with the team or anything, but once we crossed the bridge from the parking lot and caught sight of Gwen doing her warm-up stretches, ole' Gordie was hooked and never took his eyes off her for like the next two hours. At least I'm pretty sure he didn't, but I wasn't spending a lot of time watching Gordie because, like everyone, I understood that Gwen Putnam's Fort Harrison days were numbered and soon she and her long graceful legs would pack up and journey down the highway of the world.

I understood cross-country fairly well (not that it was exactly profound) and had always wanted to go out for the team, except for the fucking alley of course, duh! I mean they like plotted a course through woods or around a lake and you ran around it to see who came in first. Fairly simple stuff. The Troy course was great because you could pretty much see Gwen run the whole race. On some courses I'd gone to, the runners disappeared before you knew the race had even started and when you saw them again, like 15 minutes or so later, they'd be emerging from a woods or from behind a hill and crossing the finish line, which I thought all in all was pretty much a low blow for the spectators. But at Troy the runners started on this wide open stretch on the 'flood plain' down by the river, ran straight for a half mile or so and around a few cones or something and back along the river for like a mile, up the bank and around the football stadium and tennis courts and back down for another tour of the river bank before finishing in the open where they started. You could actually see the whole race, which I somehow thought was supposed to be the point of a sporting event. Cross-country was pastoral and all, but overall it sucked for the spectators cause if you were like a fan for a good team and they disappeared into a woods you could get sort of worried about sabotage or something like that taking place behind your back.

Anyhow at the mile mark of the race (which was around 3 miles) Gwen looked like a gazelle being chased by a tribe of one legged and particularly stupid Indians. Eventually when she crossed the finish line with a time of 17-twenty something, she was nearly a *mile* ahead of second place and you'd swear she wasn't even tired. I've kind of always thought the word *phenomenon* is used too often so that it screws stuff up when something or someone really is! Well Gwen Putnam needed to have a new word invented to describe her and that's about the only way I can put it.

"Oh my God, Billy, I'm in love. What I'd give to bury my nose inside those little shorts. I'd lick the ole' sweat right off . . ." Brent was saying as Gwen once passed right in front of us . . .

"Fuck you, Brent, and *don't* talk like that about Gwen. You can think that stuff about Busty or Tammy Kurtz, but shut the fuck up about Gwen or I swear I'll kick you in the balls right here in front of your Dad," I shot back angrily and meant it. You couldn't think like that about Gwen Putnam—you just *couldn't*! Not if you were gonna stand around me. I glanced over at Gordie who looked even more disgusting than Brent and almost unconsciously I found myself walking away, wanting to distance myself from the 'Stupidents.'

After Gwen crossed the finish line, about four minutes or so passed before Jenna Clarke and Kris Fisher, both from Fort Harrison, showed up and another five minutes or so later, the last runner brought up the rear. The Harrison girls disappeared for their warm-down and slowly *The Children of the Corn* began to disperse, returning home to their mostly miserable lives.

It would still be nearly four years before I *really* came to know Gwen Putnam, which I could have never predicted would happen anyhow; I mean, why would I? But there would come a time, when in a sense, we would become close . . . the phenomenal and beautiful Gwen Putnam and *wallpaper boy*, Billy Bowling. It wasn't anything serious of course and don't think I ever had that illusion, but it was wonderful for a few short days . . . *just before the Nightmare that snuffed out the moon, the sun . . . and my freedom upon Planet Earth.*

# Chapter Thirteen

*A*s the spring of '92 rolled around everybody hit the golf course and I could get away from the alley easier than any other time of the year and was really looking forward to going to as many track meets as I could to watch both Jimmy and Gwen run. With Gwen running on her last FHHS team, attendance at track meets rivaled a home football game and half the village businesses cut their Saturday hours as nearly all of Fort Harrison turned out for the meets, blending with a regiment of disconnected spectators who often drove hundreds of miles to watch the blonde phenomenon run.

But as for Jimmy, I soon found my spectator days were history since he didn't even go out for the team that last year, a year after being State runner-up in the 110 hurdles. He was partying big time and his attitude sucked. It was probably only because of the state championship and Player of the Year crap that the cops didn't bust Jimmy and Clint Obringer for underage drinking and who knows what else they probably could have been nailed for. It was well known by then that the parties and noise from their apartment were a pretty big thorn in Chief Borger's ribs . . . or so I'd heard from PI Brent Sturdivant.

One day Brent was going ape-shit to show me something behind Jimmy's apartment, so I agreed to take a walk down the alley with him after school to see what he was all feathered up about. Right above the back stairwell to their apartment was a crude sign that read 'Shack Up Shack.' Brent thought it was hysterical while I thought it was about 60% stupid and 40% sad. I never much talked to Jimmy anymore and wasn't too choked up about him, not that I was a moral crusader or anything. You gotta remember, though, if a guys ever gonna get sad and all about another guy fucking up, seeing that your big brother's the 'fuck-up' will usually turn the trick easier than seeing it was someone else . . . because when it happens to someone else, for the most part, it always seems funnier than hell.

Wade Borger was pretty much the whole police force in Fort Harrison, especially since Dog Noblet got the heave, and one thing he didn't need was any kind of problem at all because the Wader liked his sleep . . . and that meant pretty much all night *and* all day. Chief Borger would have probably had reasonable backing to bust up Jimmy's apartment, especially that spring when people were pissed with Jimmy about track and also because he was old news as all attention was focused on Gwen's last days in Fort Harrison. But Sam Giovanazzo lurked in the background and Jimmy and Clint were *his* boys. Jimmy might have faded from radar, and Gwen's days were coming to an end, but then Sam would reassume center stage, promising another state championship. So the people of Fort Harrison didn't want to step on his toes and that included Wade Borger who had learned many years earlier that there were *other* very good reasons not to fuck with Sam Giovanazzo. And for the most part that meant you didn't fuck with his boys either.

Gwen won four events that spring at State and Fort Harrison their fourth team track crown and eighth (total) state championship in Gwen's four years. She set three state records and the one she didn't break was hers from the year before. Gwen tried to decline a *Gwen Putnam Day* with a big parade that the town council and school board were planning, saying 'every mountain climbed was a team achievement,' or something like that. Most people would just say that kind of stuff and not mean it, but Gwen did, and people knew it. Still everyone agreed with the plan and teammates, coaches, teachers and even her parents, Don and Clare, finally convinced her the recognition was deserved and that her teammates would be honored with an equal emphasis (even as *everyone* really knew is was mostly about Gwen).

The day turned out to be the biggest single event in the history of Fort Harrison, dwarfing even the football parades and countless championship celebrations over the years, which had (of course) been impressive. It's just the way Fort Harrison was. The parade even included the *Budweiser Clydesdales* and Gwen was perched high upon the wagon with her uncle Max Frantz, the driver, and *Buddy*, the Dalmatian. Max was Clare Putnam's brother and had for years been a renowned horseman around the state and at national draft horse driving championships. He'd been hired by the St. Louis hitch in 1985 upon the death of their long time driver, Clive Churchill, and good ole' AB turned the hitch over to him for Gwen's parade—free of charge—the usual fee for a weekend appearance being around twenty grand.

The other big attraction was the *Notre Dame Marching Band*, which had assembled that June for summer parades around the Midwest. Gwen had signed to attend Notre Dame and an open date allowed the band to make the hundred-mile trip. Word was that Phil Burton, the FHHS *band man*, had pulled off the coup and that he was bouncing around Fort Harrison the day of the parade, readying the Ram Marching Band and grinning as if he'd just won a contest where the grand prize was a date with Elton John.

Saturday, June 20, 1992, dawned a glorious early summer day in West Central Ohio. The ten AM parade assembled on the north end of town in the parking lot of Tibbet Electronics and the route took it up Main to St. Matthias, right on Robbins, left on Elm three blocks to Kibler, back to Main at the south end of town, back to Robbins, then right and over the bridge to Robbins Field. In a town of 1712 people, it was estimated that over 5000 showed up that day to honor Gwen . . . or more likely just to get a look at her.

I caught the parade when it turned off Kibler onto Main cause the intersection was only about two 'football fields' from the alley so I'd ridden my bike up while Dad was doing whatever it is he does, or rather usually doesn't do. I had to be back for open bowling at eleven, even though not one person would show until after one, except of course for Winston Thermostat. The Clydesdale hitch was incredible, even though I had seen it a couple of other times at the Minster Octoberfest, but graced with Gwen it was ten times better and I was really pissed that I hadn't thought to bring a camera. There weren't many people hanging where I was cause they wanted to hit the stadium for the big shit stuff and when Gwen looked me right in the eye and winked, calling out 'Hi Billy, thanks for coming,' I about shit my pants (sorry, but that's the truth of it). God, that excited me, cause I didn't know she hardly even knew my name. After the hitch was out of sight I grabbed my bike and turned to go cause I didn't much care to see all the phonies riding in convertibles as if they were somehow a part of it all. But I can tell you this: my legs were rubber, my heart was in my throat, and I damn near fell off my bike like three times before I made it back to the alley. Gwen Putnam could do that to you . . . even though it's one thing I can't even try to honestly explain.

Turk Smith, the state senator from Minister, gave a speech I'd heard, along with the girls' coach from Notre Dame, Coach Sadie Chappell, Beckman and Wickerdick (of course), Roger Edmunds, the mayor, and good ole' Karen Fish, the school board President. Brent told me later that Gordie thought Fishface was *jolly juiced*, which I assumed was Sturdivant family lingo for drunk. I sure didn't mind missing all that stuff though, cause it probably would have made me puke, but I would have loved to have seen Gwen up there giving her speech; I mean that would have been so cool cause I had the same feeling pretty much everybody did . . . *that we wouldn't be seeing much of Gwen Putnam around these parts anymore.*

# Chapter Fourteen

*Authors Note . . . Though I didn't know the following at the time, eventually when all the facts were known . . . well . . . read this chapter and you'll understand, cause the facts as they would later come to light need to start here.*

*W*hile Gwen Putnam was standing to a deafening ovation at Robbins Field on that beautiful mid June morning, Sam Giovanazzo was in Youngstown, two hundred miles across the state, and fuming. Sam's background, which was much shadier than anyone really knew, had been kept secret from even his few friends and assistant coaches in Fort Harrison for decades. Sam was a Youngstown boy and the grandson of Vitrialli Cardone, the most notorious mob boss in the history of the city. His father, Vitorio Giovanazzo, had died of a heart attack when Sam was nine; his mother Lila passing from leukemia just a few short years later . . . so he and his brother, Vincent, were raised by Papa Vitrialli and Nana Ariella in the spectacular Cardone estate in Youngstown Heights. Sam excelled in football and wrestling at Youngstown Boardman and had been a standout halfback at Slippery Rock University in Pennsylvania, a few short miles across the state line. From the time he was a kid, Sam wanted to be a football coach and Vitrialli encouraged it, oddly hoping to distance both Sam and Vincent from the organization rather than assume roles that would have been inherent.

Sam had taken an assistant job coaching at Boardman in 1969 right out of college, but was determined to run the show for himself—and to him, that meant *yesterday.* He had married Roberta 'Bobbie' Smith, whom he met at Slippery Rock, one weekend after flying to Las Vegas in the spring of their senior year. Papa Vitrialli was unhappy with the decision, but no more so than Sam himself who quickly saw Bobbie as a millstone that would not only interfere with his coaching style, but also impede his lust for young girls, which had perhaps been as much a motivation for coaching at the high school level as was his drive to win football games and championships.

In the spring of 1970, Sam and Bobbie left Youngstown in their new blue '69 Plymouth Road-Runner, heading first south on I-77 before striking out west on the old Lincoln Highway, U.S. 30 North. He had three interviews lined up for a head football position at small Catholic area high schools in far Western Ohio. Sam knew that if he stayed in the Youngstown area he could never be his own boss, for no matter how well meaning Papa Vitrialli might be, his larger than life aura would not only dwarf Sam, but also dispense an intimidating presence that would prevent him from truly being his own man. Sam needed a fresh start where hopefully no one knew of his background and a backward Catholic farm community 200 miles away might just work. For you see, Sam Giovanazzo wanted to be not only his own man . . . *Sam Giovanazzo wanted to be King*!

In 1970 employment standards and procedures at public schools were pretty loose, especially small rural schools. There was no fingerprinting, blood tests or background checks which would have turned up not only a few scrapes with the law and Sam's obvious connection to the Youngstown mob, but very possibly a rape charge pressed by a 14 year old high school freshman during Sam's senior year in college. He'd been student teaching at Seneca Valley H.S. in Harmony, Pennsylvania, when Gretchen Nixon and her parents filed the charges in Butler Country municipal court. They were filed on a Tuesday and Sam was suspended from the substitute program immediately, returning to Youngstown after a phone conversation with Vitrialli. By Friday, however, the charges had been *mysteriously* dropped and on Monday he was back in his Seneca Valley classroom where he completed the teaching program, graduating SR University five weeks later with his degree in education.

Sam interviewed at Minster High School, Delphos St. Johns High School and Fort Harrison. He provided each school with his teaching certificate, a letter of recommendation from his college football coach, Pike Wilson, and letters of recommendation from head coach John Pissarelli and Principal Dolf Hatcher of Boardman, both whom were smart enough to have written *anything* that Sam Giovanazzo asked for.

When Sam was offered a contract at Fort Harrison, he reasoned it was the most backward town of the bunch, yet loaded with both big Catholic farm boys he was sure he could mold into mean football players . . . and attractive blue eyed blondes who just might come in handy also. Setting himself up as the King would be easiest at Fort Harrison he reasoned, and the raw materials he both needed and desired were in place to bow to the King. He would start with the Podunk conference that he was certain he could soon dominate and within a few seasons move well beyond that, and when he did, the whole town would be eating out of his hand. *And he was right. And soon they were.* From the very beginning Sam Giovanazzo was about not only dominating football games, but dominating an entire community with the explicit goal of creating total immunity for himself.

Vincent Giovanazzo, Sam's older brother, had made what could probably be called a reasonable attempt to go straight. He'd spent two years at Youngstown State pursuing a business degree with the idea of taking a branch of the family business and making it legit. The targeted division was the development of high-rise parking garages in mid-size cities throughout the country. Numbers, strip clubs, prostitution, drugs and trucking were divvied up between his cousins Al, Mario and Giermo Cardone while extortion of everything from the cops to city hall to the corner baker was controlled by his uncle, Mastriano Giovanazzo, who probably raked in more income than all the other branches combined.

Then in 1974, Vitrialli Cardone disappeared from the face of the planet, which brought on a four-year mob war, vicious by even New York and Chicago standards, yet oblivious to most of the greater world. After the smoke cleared in 1978, Mario Cardone and Mastriano Giovanazzo were history and Vincent Giovanazzo was the new boss, having fashioned a rather uneasy peace with Al and Giermo, his cousins. Fourteen years later not much had changed, although the role of the mob in Youngstown was somewhat diminished with the deterioration of the city, the steel industry, and the flight of a sizable chunk of the moneyed populace to sunnier shores.

During the years of the mob war and after his grandfather disappeared, Sam never once returned to Youngstown. Vincent understood and was ok with it, but Nana Ariello grew old and confused wondering why she never again saw Sam. As for Sam, it's hard to imagine he had a gentle thought in his brain for anyone and had even skipped Nana's funeral in the winter of 1977, though partially on the recommendation of Vincent who had expected a graveside assassination attempt although it never came to pass.

Through it all Sam Giovanazzo was supposedly never connected to the mob by the people of Fort Harrison, at least that was the story, as if anyone in their right mind would have paraded the revelation. No matter who you were, what you thought you knew, or what you really knew, it would be smart not to fuck with Sam Giovanazzo— not in the little town of Fort Harrison, Ohio—and certainly not as long as the State Championships continued to roll in.

# Chapter Fifteen

*A* s Sam Giovanazzo sat across from his brother, Vincent, in his office at the loading docks of *Giovanazzo Trucking*, and as Gwen Putnam was being awarded the first *Fort Harrison Key to the Village* two hundred miles to the west, the seeds were being sown in Sam's distorted brain that would one day wreak no less havoc upon the small Catholic village of Fort Harrison, Ohio, than if it had played host to the Ten Plagues of Egypt. . . .

. . . "Sammy, just what the fuck is your problem? I haven't seen you all these years and when you show up I have to put up with this pissing and moaning? I don't need that. You and I should party, Sammy, not whine and cry," Vincent Giovanazzo said, slapping Sam on the back and pouring them each a double shot of Bowmore single malt before silencing Sam for a toast.

"Vinnie, I win this Podunk town *seven* football state championships and *three* more in wrestling; more than any coach in the state. I even live my life in this cow pasture and what thanks do I get? They give the *first* fucking key to the town to a fucking high school girl. Christ, I've coached three guys into the NFL and even *they* never got a fucking key to the town."

Norm Otte, the local State Farm agent, had come up with the idea a month earlier: *A Key to the Village*, and the simple truth was that no one had ever thought of it before, or more than likely Sam would have been the first recipient. A Fort Harrison *Hall of Fame* was now in the works which would include Gwen, Nick Santoria, who'd just retired after nine years with the Miami Dolphins and Minnesota Vikings, Marty Barhorst who had played with several NFL teams in a short career and Tim Denton, the grandson of gunned down Police chief Merle Denton, who currently was playing with the San Diego Chargers. They were still debating on whether to posthumously vote Merle in along with Tim at the ceremony they were planning for the end of the year. *And of course Sam Giovanazzo would be in the charter group* because honestly he deserved it more than anybody else based on his incredible record of State Championships and no one denied that. (Well, I would have voted against it, but I didn't carry much weight with the village brain trust).

"Sammy, you sound like a baby. I respected that you chose a new path and stayed away from the business; was glad about it even, but if something like the key to a two bit cow town makes you piss and whine like a hooker with the clap, then you and I ain't got much to talk about and I guess I got better things to do. SO GROW UP!" Vincent snapped loudly.

There was a lot Sam didn't know about his brother and why should he? They had only seen each other a few times the past quarter century and each of their lives had changed drastically. Vincent Giovanazzo could be ruthless, for it was the nature of the job—a job, which to that very day he loathed, but above all Vincent Giovanazzo was a family man. In the fourteen years he had maintained the often uneasy, though relatively restrained peace in Youngstown, it was his abhorrence to family convulsion that ruled many decisions and had stamped his moderate reign.

"Ok, ok. I know what it sounds like and you're right, but this bitch is like the fucking second coming of Christ to these assholes and it makes me want to puke; and all because she can run? Give me a break! Give me a *fucking* break. What she needs is slammed on my office desk like the rest of them. Tear that soft lily white pussy open, wrap those long frog legs around my back and drive my dick in her so hard my desk would splinter in thousand pieces, just like my desk in '83 did when I nailed ole' Wendy Borgstrum. You shoulda seen that, Vinnie! I had to pick splinters out of my nut sack for a week, but she was a hell of a fuck that girl, a hell of a fuck . . . and she loved it too!" Sam said with a reflective grin.

"So you're still fucking the young ones, are you Sammy? Is that what you're telling me? Just how many little girls have you fucked?" Vincent asked coldly, though it went right past Sam who had slipped inside his own demented world.

"I don't know, what do you mean?" he replied lightly.

"Underage girls—you know *exactly* what I mean," Vincent said with a restrained, yet building rage . . . and standing now.

"I don't know the number . . . a few or so I guess, but they want it, Vinnie . . . they *all* wanted it. Sometimes it takes a little talking, a little schmoozing, you know, but . . ." Sam was boasting when Vincent leaned across the desk and smashed Sam hard across the face with a backhand, his large pinkie diamond slicing deeply into the corner of Sam's mouth, drawing first a trickle then a steady dripping of blood which Sam finally dammed with a white silk handkerchief that Vincent had thrown across the desk. Sam looked up, shocked, but stayed put, stayed quiet, cause he knew it was what he had to do just then.

"You know what, Sammy? I was proud of you. I followed the papers and bragged about you to the old boys . . . hell, to everyone I knew. Bragged about the games you won, especially the championship last year against Mogadore. I bragged about you going straight and now I find that you're bigger scum than the two bit hoods I use to do my dirty work. You do that shit back here in Youngstown and you wouldn't need to worry about splinters in your nut sack cause it *and* your dick would be hanging from the flag pole at the courthouse for the turkey buzzards to fight over. In our business sometimes bad things happen to people, but only for a good reason, and only to those who choose to play the game outside the lines. Innocent young girls are a gift of God to be respected. I have two daughters myself, Sammy, and now I give thanks that you were *never* around to know them. I'm sorry I ever said the first thing good about you because you are dog shit and I want you out of here right now before I cut your dick off myself and stick it in your mouth, cause that's what we do around here when we find someone messing with little girls or boys. Get out RIGHT NOW, or at the count of five I will do it—*I swear to God I will.* That's one thing we don't wait to see if the law will handle; we take care of those bastards ourselves. Bastards just like my brother I guess . . . ONE . . ."

Sam understood, at least enough to hit the road *quick,* and was soon back on highway 30 traveling west, seething, and forever distancing himself from Vinnie and his bullshit, cause neither he nor anyone else was going to tell Sam Giovanazzo what to do . . . EVER! If Sam wanted young pussy, he'd have it. If he wanted revenge, he'd have that too. But the sweetest thing of all would be to dip into young arrogant snatch *and* get revenge at the same time . . . and especially the virginal exalted pussy of Gwen Putnam, despite the fact that she was older than Sam's usual girls. Thinking about it just then even gave him an erection, though he well understood the encounter could necessarily involve another very *different* virginal dimension that Sam had never yet experienced. No matter how long it took for the time to be right, Sam Giovanazzo would show Gwen Putnam *exactly* what her purpose on the planet was . . . fucking Key to Fort Harrison or not!

Though Sam Giovanazzo may not have dwelt upon it, nor given it much reflective thought at all, his trip to Youngstown had gone terribly wrong. Why he'd even gone in the first place was probably as much a mystery to him as it was to his brother? Maybe it was just for sympathy or perhaps in some odd way he'd meant to solicit mob assistance to right an imagined wrong. Honestly even Sam wasn't sure, but he'd dismissed it all with a yawn. Yet one day his grave miscalculation relative to his brother's values would prove as deadly to Sam Giovanazzo as an assassin's bullet had been for his favorite cousin, Mario Cardone, nearly two decades earlier.

# Chapter Sixteen

Jimmy had accepted a football scholarship to *Bowling Green State University* soon after the first of the year. He joked with me once saying, 'Bowling Green, duh, where else would I go?' At 5'9," 160, he was never much considered by the big boys as a running back although with Player of the Year under his belt the football brains at the alley said it was more because of his color than his size. Of course in the early 90's, Fort Harrison was 99% Redneck Caucasian and 1% Hispanics who'd missed the bus back to Texas after the tomatoes were picked so political correctness around Fort Harrison was about as rare as 'queer bait,' which was how the good ole' boys at BBC bar would likely put it.

Jimmy graduated with a C+ average, despite nearly flunking every class his last semester, but that had been cushioned by nearly all A's he'd collected before Mom was killed. There were rumors that the scholarship was nearly pulled when Jimmy's grades hit rock bottom and he'd AWOL'd high school track that spring, but I suspected that since Sam Giovanazzo had sent a legion of players to BG, he'd probably schmoozed things over easy enough and by the first week of August, 1992, Jimmy Bowling packed up, closed down the 'Shack up Shack' and headed off for pre-season football camp. Clint Obringer likewise headed off to Ball State on a football ride although I couldn't imagine who'd pulled those strings, but he flunked out by Christmas anyway and was once again living at home and spreading cow shit across the extensive Obringer spread.

As brothers Jimmy and I were never close and I was sad about that. When I was too young to understand and while Jimmy was still young enough for Dad to control they had spent a zillion hours together in the bowling alley while Dad groomed Jimmy to be this big shot bowler to go out on the pro circuit some day and win a shit load of bucks, I guess. It's really pretty funny when you think about it cause bowling isn't exactly loaded with hotshot millionaires and guys doing megabuck commercials for deodorants and automobiles. Besides, things can't get much more boring than bowling. It's not like you get to inhale nature looking for a lost ball or even have fun driving a cart like an idiot . . . or get a good laugh when a guy hits a ball in a pond six times in a row or maybe even off somebody's skull, which is usually good for a roll on the ground laugh. I mean a bad bowler can only fuck up so many things and after awhile the laughs get thin.

By the age of twelve though, Jimmy jumped ship, and I've always had to respect the balls he had for doing it, especially at that age. I mean I'm fifteen and I'm still a candy ass who pretty much puts up with Dad's shit twenty-five hours a day; when he's conscious that is. When Jimmy did quit bowling—*and I mean quit*—he had bowled three 300 games and seven 800 series and hadn't yet turned thirteen! He'd won a truck load of kid's tournaments all over the place and had about a hundred trophies or so which is the only thing I ever much remembered because I was there the day he decided to throw them all away.

*I was about eight, I think, the day Jimmy quit bowling.* He had me help him carry all the trophies out of the house and throw them in the dumpster behind the alley one day while Dad was away at a tournament and Mom was at work with Libby, who was only like two at the time and Ray Emerson, I guess, allowed Mom to bring her along to work at Emerson's Dry Goods. Anyway, along with Dad's huge trophies at the alley, the whole house was nothing but bowling trophies. Everywhere you looked you saw them; everywhere you walked you tripped over them. They were in the living room, the bedrooms, the kitchen and even the bathroom. They were on cupboards, on top of the fridge, sitting on the floor, on the steps going upstairs and the steps going to the basement. Oh, and there were so many in the garage you could only get one car in. Some even went clear back to Grampa Bowling I found out later on. One thing you didn't do if you were a Bowling was throw a bowling trophy away and there I was getting ready to help Jimmy throw out, by his count after the fact, 79 bowling trophies. Believe me, even at eight, and even as I didn't understand it all, the one thing I *did know* was that Dad was gonna be pissed—*real pissed*—but that somehow that was making Jimmy all the more gleeful.

. . . "Billy get your wagon out of the garage and pull it over by the front door. I want you to help me," Jimmy had said.

I ran to the garage and pulled the old Radio Flyer Mom got me once at a garage sale around to the front door. I was real excited about helping Jimmy cause he never paid much attention to me at all and was always away with his friends or in the bowling alley with Dad.

"Here shrimp, throw these in the wagon," Jimmy said, coming to the front door with an armful of trophies.

"What you gonna do with em, Jimmy?" I asked eagerly.

"I'm gonna throw em in the fucking dumpster—that's what I'm gonna do shrimp," he answered, handing a couple to me and tossing a big one toward the wagon that I remembered hit the metal side and bounced onto the sidewalk, breaking in half—a big plastic gold cup with a bowler on its top skidding down the front sidewalk and off onto the lawn.

"No, Jimmy," I pleaded. "Let me have em."

"Billy, shut the fuck up and do what I say or get out of here and I'll do it myself. Nobody's gonna get these but the garbage man. You're always whining about wanting to help me, so just shut up and help."

I knew that *fuck* was a bad word and had heard Mom get really mad a couple of times she caught Jimmy saying it, especially if I was around, but I'd also heard Dad say it and the guys at the bar said it all the time though Mom told me I wasn't supposed to be there or talk to them. So I was pretty confused about it all. There were other bad words too, I knew, but that was the one I heard the most. I didn't like Jimmy calling me shrimp, but at least it usually meant I was getting to do something with him, so I didn't want to complain about it. I didn't understand Jimmy throwing his trophies away and I just wished he let me have some of them, but I knew I had to shut up then or it would be curtains for me. Still, I was pretty sure he shouldn't be saying all the bad words.

"Jimmy, *fuck's* a bad word. Mom said. . . ."

"Shut up, Billy. You gonna help me or not?" he said, again from the doorway with another arm full of trophies. "Go play on your stupid swing set then if you don't want to help; I can do this myself," he said crossly and I almost started to cry, thinking he wasn't gonna let me help him anymore.

"I'm sorry, Jimmy, can I still help you, *please*," I pleaded.

"Ok, look: I'll pile them here on the top step and you load the wagon. When it's all loaded we'll haul them to the dumpster," he said, disappearing again inside.

I had to quit asking questions cause the next time I knew I'd be done for. So I just shut up for awhile. We must have hauled five or six loads of trophies out of the house when he came out with the keys to the alley in his hand and told me to bring the wagon along as he started across the parking lot.

Inside, Jimmy went to Dad's office and came back with the keys for the big glass case which he opened and took out three trophies that were almost as tall as I was. "Here, take these out to the wagon," he barked.

"But Jimmy, Dad . . ."

"They're mine, butthead. The others are Dad's, but these are mine. You gonna help me or not? If you wanna help, keep your trap shut," he snapped and again I almost started to cry. I could only carry one at a time and when I was done I saw Jimmy with a screwdriver taking two big plaques off the wall and a framed article from the *Dayton Daily News* with Jimmy's picture on it for winning the State Junior Bowling Congress two years in a row. At least I figured that out a few years later.

After we pitched them all in the dumpster Jimmy looked happy and turned to me. "Thanks shrimp for your help. I'm gonna catch a lot of shit for this, but I don't care. Now let me tell you something. Dad's gonna get his claws in you one of these days and make your life miserable. He'll make you bowl and bowl and bowl. Maybe you'll like it and if you do, fine, but if you don't, just don't do it, that's all I can tell you—*just don't fucking do it!"*

"But Jimmy, I *wanna* bowl. I never get to and it's not fair . . ."

"Look shrimp, you'll get your chance, believe me, and you might not like it so much then. That's all I'm gonna say."

"But Jimmy . . ."

"That's *all* I'm gonna say, didn't I tell you? Now *can* it," he said crossly and walked over to the garage to shoot baskets at the hoop I remembered him and Dad arguing about when Jimmy wanted to put it up two days earlier.

The garbage truck came about an hour after we trashed the trophies and I later understood that Jimmy knew exactly when it would get there, and that if he hadn't planned it that way, Dad would probably have dug them all back out when he got home and made Jimmy carry them back in the house. When Mom came home it was pretty hard not to see all the trophies that were missing and she sent me out of the kitchen, telling me to go watch TV because she and Jimmy had to have a talk. But I hid behind the stairs and listened.

"Jimmy, your father's going to be furious with you. Where are your bowling trophies? You threw them away, didn't you?" she had said almost telepathically (which of course I didn't remotely understand then).

"Mom, I *hate* bowling and you know it. Why can't I do things I like? I can't be on a baseball team cause I always have to go to tournaments and now Dad says I can't go out for Midget Football because of the same reason. He probably won't even let me go out for junior high basketball next year and I'm sick of it. I don't care it he beats my ass for a week."

"Jimmy, there will be no swearing in this house . . ."

"*No swearing, Mom*? That's all I hear from Dad and . . ."

"Jim Bowling, we've had this discussion before and you know *exactly* what I mean and how I feel."

"Ok, I'm sorry, but I'm done bowling and I'm going out for Midgets," Jimmy cried. I peeked around the corner and saw Mom holding Jimmy tight up against her chest and then she began sobbing herself. It seemed like all of Mom's life was sad, at least ever since I knew her . . . and then she was killed, and it wasn't fair! It just wasn't fair.

Sunday afternoon when Dad was due home Mom sent me over to the Rohrbachs, our neighbors, to play with Casey who was in my second grade class. Sometimes I stayed there while Mom and Dad went somewhere and sometimes Casey stayed at our house, but not near as much. The whole deal was to get me away from the shit that was about to hit the fan, though I didn't completely understand it at the time. I thought I was just there to spend a few hours, but later Mrs. Rohrbach came in and said Mom had dropped some clothes off and that I would be staying the night.

*Things were never the same after that night. Not even close.* Mom and Dad hardly talked at all and Jimmy and Dad never did anything together even though Jimmy was still just a kid. Jimmy did play Midget Football that season and Mom took me to most of the games, but Dad never went. And almost immediately, even that first year, Jimmy Bowling was the star.

Dad went to bowling tournaments almost every weekend after that and Mom had me start helping her at the alley when Dad was gone, which I liked cause it was a lot more fun being with her than with Dad. Jimmy'd help when Dad was away, but when he was home he wouldn't. Sometimes when Mom had to work at Emerson's, Ted Howard, who was a college kid going to OSU in Celina, would help out. I'd hear people at the alley asking Mom about why Jimmy wasn't bowling in tournaments and stuff, but I never paid too much attention to her answers. After a few years I kind of forgot Jimmy ever even bowled at all, along with pretty much everybody else since he had become a major football hero . . . *everyone except for Dad that is.*

## Chapter Seventeen

By ten I was working and bowling with Dad at the alley every day, and I liked it pretty much, at least at first. He taught me a lot, but honestly I never felt that he forced me, in fact I was pretty sure he didn't even much care. Later on I figured out that someday he wanted me to run the alley and thought I should at least be a better bowler than most of the idiots who thought they were hot shots . . . for the reputation of the alley and all that.

I bowled tournaments here and there and actually won most of the time. Dad put a few of my trophies in the case at the alley and I thought it was big shit when I was younger, but you could tell he had lost his 'heart' when Jimmy rebelled and I soon understood I was just being groomed for the role of bondsman. I entered the Junior Bowling Congress a couple of years, but never made it to the finals. I was good for a kid, but I was no Jimmy I would find out later on. On the other hand, Dad and me never fought like Jimmy and he did. All Thin Jim Bowling much cared about as far as I was concerned was that I was at the alley in time to *pick cotton* every day.

After Jimmy's rebellion Dad was never the same, but in a way you really couldn't blame it on Jimmy, cause I mean Dad was supposed to be the adult. I later figured Dad's whole life had been about control and when he lost it over Jimmy, his every waking moment was about blame and feeling sorry for himself. Eventually I came to understand he was just one of those people who actually loved being miserable and expected everyone else to be the same, even if it was something that hadn't taken on a life of its own until after Jimmy's declaration of independence. The best kind of rebellion against Dad was being happy I came to understand—not that any of us were of course. Yep, the Bowling Family was fucked up all right—anyway you sliced it—we just plain were! But it was Mom I always felt saddest for and that's something I'll never get over my whole life long. Why do people do what they do to each other? *And especially those who had once said 'I Love You.'*

During junior high I was working at the alley pretty much every night, all day Saturdays, and Sunday afternoons. Even when I was knocking the pins around pretty good, people would still talk about Jimmy's bowling sometimes and almost never mine, but I never much thought about it and honestly didn't care. After he became a major football star at FHHS, Jimmy's bowling never came up that often and like I said, I almost forgot he'd bowled at all. Fact is, I never really understood Jimmy's younger magic until one day in the spring of 1991, and a couple of months after Mom and Libby were killed. Dad was away at a tournament and Jimmy and Curt Martin came to the alley after getting back mid-afternoon from a Saturday track meet. I was getting things ready for open bowling at 4 and still really struggling with the accident. I knew Jimmy was too, but he put up this cocky front, almost pretending it had never happened, at least that's what it seemed to me. One thing we *didn't* do was talk about it . . . Jimmy, Dad, or me. I guess that's how a professionally fucked up family handles things though.

. . ."Hey, Billy-boy, hotshot brother bowler. I'll bowl you for fucking beer. You win and I'll leave without taking any. I win and I take a six pack and you keep your mouth shut; how's that sound cowboy?" I remember him yelling as he burst through the door that day as if all the world was cotton candy, easy girls, beer and roller coasters.

I was in eighth grade and yet for years had been Dad's slave, or whatever you want to call it, but totally ignorant about Jimmy's hard core incarceration in the early days. My only frame of reference with Jimmy and bowling was the day we'd trashed the trophies. In the meantime, I'd bowled a 300 game just the week before and an 800 series earlier in the winter, though like I said, I could see Dad had no great illusions that I was going to deliver a treasure chest of cash to insure security for the Bowling family by becoming another Dick Weber. Dad expected I'd take over BBC someday and that was pretty much it. He still picked up a few hundred or even a thousand or so bucks at tournaments here and there, and he said it was good

PR for the alley, which I suppose in a way it was, but to be sure the extra bucks came in pretty handy—especially with a budget of about five hundred a month for Dad's booze.

"Yeah, ok, Jimmy, but I don't wanna get in no trouble with the beer and all," I replied.

"Fuck that, Billy. Dad's in fucking Dayton and he don't give a shit about anything anymore except getting drunk and maybe even getting some young pussy . . . and before the grass even covers Mom's grave. He's a fucking asshole and someday you're gonna understand that—mark my fucking words. Besides cowboy, nobody can beat you, right? So get that pretty ball of yours Dad paid all the dough for; I'm ready!" he said, leaning over to pick up the first ball he touched, never even checking for grip, trying to be flippant about everything, but boiling with anger I could easily see. The lanes were turned on cause I had been checking the spotters and Jimmy just walks up to Lane Six and lets it fly and bingo—pins danced off the sidewalls with a vengeance—*strike.*

"Ok lil' bro,' you're up," he said, sprinting to the bar and pulling out two Millers for himself and Curt, then pausing, pulled out another. "Hey cowboy, have a beer on me," Jimmy yelled as I started my approach, but turned just in time to catch the Miller flying through the air straight for my head. He then burst into a roaring laugh that only stopped when a beer can sealed off his lips. Jimmy strode forward, passing a beer to Curt before turning to me with a huge grin on his mug. "Sorry cowboy, hope I didn't mess you up," he'd spouted, again followed by the roaring pain-masking laugh.

I sat the beer in the holder at the scorer's table, sent nine pins flying, then finished off the spare. "Jimmy, I don't drink much, besides Dad's gonna count . . ."

"Goddamn it, Billy, open the fucking can and drink it and don't be such a goddamn pussy. You gotta start getting real about life; we don't get much time on the goddamn planet. *You sure the fuck ought to see that by now!* You gotta learn to drink beer and eat pussy; that's what you gotta do, now hear me now," he yelled back at me while collecting his second strike without even taking the can out of his left hand. Then turning around continued, "and fuck Dad, Billy, you hear me. FUCK HIM! There's so much you just don't know and I ain't gonna waste my fucking breath trying to tell you. Just keep your fucking eyes open and don't let him run your whole fucking life cause that's what I'm seein,' cowboy. Jesus, don't you get it? Dad didn't want sons, Billy—HE WANTED FUCKING SLAVES," he screamed at the top of his lungs causing even Curt to look about nervously.

Jimmy and I would never have any golden moments as brothers, it just wasn't going to happen—*not ever*—and I could see it so clearly just then. Drinking my first beer with him under normal circumstances could have been one of those moments and probably was for a lot of younger brothers, but we were the *Bowling Family*—what was left of us—and normal for us was about as fucked up as it gets. I could see a bitterness in Jimmy that was frightening, and suddenly I was nearly suffocated by a vast emptiness, and not just the realization that there was no longer a Bowling family, but an even more devastating understanding that there really never had been.

After five frames, Jimmy had five strikes while I had two, a spare and two opens. The old black alley ball sent pins flying like I'd never before seen and I was embarrassed using my $150 Brunswick Inferno. He was not only kicking my ass big time, but in the process my arms had turned to steel and I was choking in a way I never thought possible, while Jimmy and Curt Martin roared and toasted their beer cans every time I fucked up.

"Billy, I really ain't got all that much time—there are maidens awaiting rescue. Are you ready to say *uncle* yet, cowboy?" he said with that deafening laugh.

"Jimmy, Jesus, I've never even seen you bowl. I mean I know you used to, but you never even practice," I said, shaking my head. Believe me there were some pretty hot shot bowlers around and Dad was like a robot, but I'd *never* seen anyone bust pins like Jimmy.

"I used to, lil' bro.' You fucking know that. It was just before you remember, that's all, and before I realized Dad meant to make me a fucking slave. So I said *fuck it.* And that was the day we threw out all the fucking trophies. Surely you remember that, cowboy," he said, continuing his boisterous laughter and it was evident he was feeling the three beers he had already sucked down.

. . . "And let me tell you something else, cowboy. I've heard him whine to people about being all depressed over Mom and Libby, but don't you believe that for a second. He made Mom's life miserable; didn't want her spending time with her folks or brothers; didn't want her going anywhere *ever* with anyone, like shopping with friends and stuff. He didn't want her working at Emersons either, cause he expected her at the alley all day, every day. When she took the job anyway they fought like hell and then just quit talking at all for the most part. Mom was a wonderful person, but if she'd have left that asshole ten years ago she'd still be alive, Billy . . . *SHE'D STILL BE FUCKING ALIVE,"* he'd screamed at the top of his lungs, and though quieting down, continued, bitterly, "Fuck it all, I'm shuttin up now."

I could tell he was holding back tears, but he chugged another Miller and after tossing the can careening off into the seats, turned, and with but a couple of forward steps, fired *another* strike . . . *and this one from nearly five feet behind the foul line!*

"Ok, ok, can you let it go for awhile, Jesus! I just don't see how you can bowl like that. I mean you don't practice or anything. It just don't make sense."

"Billy, bowling is so *goddamn simple*! It really is. I mean its not fucking golf. Once you got the basics, its all just *concentration and anger,* so it's easier for me than you cause I'm a pretty fucking angry person. I learned the mechanics and to concentrate when I was a kid and I also learned to *hate* those fucking pins. I taught myself to see ten fucking Dads standing down there giving me the finger. After that the rest was easy. *So fucking easy,"* he said, turning to me again with a big grin. "Now how about that six pack, cowboy? Naw, let's make it a twelve. Beat you fair and square, right?" he said, slapping me hard on the back, grabbing the still rolling ball from the return and turning to fire one last ball down alley six, exploding ten more pins for *seven* strikes in a row—*a truth I swear that was frightening.*

"Jimmy, you'd better not take that much. You know as well as I do he'll count . . ."

"Don't give me that bullshit. You're in charge of everything in this fucking dump; I'm not stupid, so you'll figure it out," he roared, pulling open the cooler and grabbing a twelve of High Life. Then with a numb Curt Martin, he rounded the bar, pushing through the door and disappearing into the muted late-afternoon spring sun.

# Chapter Eighteen

It was just after 7pm on Thursday, February 8, 1991, that Mom (Maria Romano Bowling) and my little sister Libby (Elizabeth Chloe Bowling), who was seven, were killed in a gas explosion that completely leveled our house across the parking lot from the bowling alley. Dad was away, as always, for a three day bowling tournament in Cleveland and Jimmy was working men's league with Busty Bailey. They were tending bar, making burgers, pizza and French fries, and playing grab ass. Jimmy'd been dorking Busty pretty much forever I'd learned by then, along with half the guys in Fort Harrison, but Jimmy didn't much seem to mind cause he was first in line whenever he wanted. In a weird kind of way it was a healthy attitude I figured, cause Busty wasn't like wife material or anything and nobody to waste your energy getting jealous over, that was for sure.

She really never much did *anything* except hang her huge tits out on the counter to keep guys around and sell more beer, which I was pretty sure was why Dad hired her, at least at first. Usually I got stuck working with her, which meant I did 98% of everything, but that night I had Dad's job troubleshooting the pin spotters or once in a blue moon darting in shoe rental to fit someone, which was pretty rare league nights.

Leagues were actually kind of comical, especially the guys with the fancy shit that was supposed to guarantee 200+ games, like Moe Picklesimer who worked at Simmon's Feed and Grain. Ole' Moe was a fat-ass bachelor who made maybe two hundred bucks a week, but had $150 Lind shoes and a $200 Elite 'Alien' ball which he'd ordered through Dad, although I'd never seen him bowl a game over 140 in all the years I was around. These were the kind of guys who tried to carve out an identity at the bowling alley and when they were having a bad game (which was always) they just started drinking heavily so they could laugh off the scores as having 'partied a little too much!' But Bowling's Bowling Center won any way you sliced it with those guys, as did the fat-cats in the bowling equipment industry who made their millions with God's blessing, since on the fourth day of creation he created *idiots* so they could populate Thursday night men's bowling leagues.

Mom stayed late at Emerson's on Thursdays to pick Libby up from a gymnastics class in the basement of St. Matthias. Libby was in first grade and would go to Emerson's after school and about 4:30 they'd go to Samsals or Jespersons for a sandwich or something before Libby went to her class at 5:30. Mom called it *girls night out* and you could tell it was a big deal for both of them, and one of the only times it seemed that anyone in the Bowling family actually had some fun.

Getting home at seven, Mom had pulled into the garage where they would enter the house through the laundry room. I guess there was a gas leak and it had been building up all day; or so they (the good ole' 'they' people) later said. In the February cold, the house was shut up tight as a drum so the gas had no way to get out. We can't know this, I guess, but the fire people and insurance investigators figured mom opened the door, flipped the switch, and the house exploded in a million pieces from a spark that was a form of *kinetic energy* generated from the light switch. It's supposedly more common than people realize, at least that's what Tuck Adams, the fire marshal said; which in some weird way it seemed he thought was supposed to make us feel better or something.

The alley was shaken with an impact that knocked down standing pins, sent the TV over the bar crashing to the floor, along with half the liquor bottles, and created a spider web of cracks throughout the concrete block walls of the entire building. As everyone raced into the cold winter evening to fathom what had happened, I lapsed into a shock that I'd only heard about, but never really understood. Everything just kind of went dark amidst a blur of surreal thick gray smoke, sirens and patchwork screams.

I partly remember being taken away by the EMS and across Rt. 29 to Wilson Memorial hospital in Sidney and lying in a room with nurses checking on me all the time until they let me go the next morning. Carl Talbot, a friend and neighbor rode beside me in the ambulance, but Jimmy stayed behind even though I didn't know it at the time. My only conscious memory before being taken away was of cars covered with debris, partially shrouded by the heavy smoke . . . and one of Libby's blonde Barbie Dolls laying on the sparse snow beside a Shelby County Sheriff cruiser which had just pulled to a stop. It was like everything was in slow motion, at least that's the way I remember it now . . . the way I probably always will.

I'm fairly certain, even now, that I've never really come to terms with the explosion that night and the deaths of my mother and sister. Ted Turner, the school counselor for both the middle school and high school had me stop in his office before returning to classes when I went back to school a week later. . . .

. . . "Have a seat Billy. I know all this has been very difficult for you. How do you think you are doing?" he asked kindly enough, I guess.

He seemed like a nice guy and genuine in a way he should have been and not all that phony. Still, I think, given everything that happened, I probably gave answers I figured he wanted to hear instead of stuff I really felt, but it's just kind of what you learn to do when you get trapped inside four walls with a guy like that. We shot the shit for a half hour or so and he said he was going to talk to Jimmy, which he may or may not have done because Jimmy never said anything to me about it and I never asked him. He also said he was going to call Dad and suggest I see this psychologist in Piqua. Again, if he did, I never knew it and never heard anything about it again, but I guess he was just doing his job and I sort of respected that and didn't start thinking he was a complete phony. He probably did call Dad, but Dad wasn't the kind of guy to send me off to a psychologist, no matter what had happened—and especially if he thought the tab was going to find its way back to him.

Some kids at school, especially the girls, were googly nice and all, but I figured about one in maybe five wasn't phony. Boys just acted funny around me and even Brent seemed to wish it hadn't happened more so that he didn't have to be uncomfortable than that I would still have a mother and sister, which could have really depressed me if I'd allowed myself to think much about it.

Even teachers didn't want to face nervous shit like that and have their day ruined you could tell, except for Mrs. Blanchard and Mrs. Smith who sort of seemed to be caring and sincere without being all that phony. Of course they were both getting pretty old and you had to figure they were just brushing up on skills they'd probably need to use sooner than later anyhow when their friends started biting the dust on a fairly regular basis. As for the other teachers, most of them are so practiced at being phony anyhow that flashing a fake smile and acting concerned is pretty easy stuff to pull off. I mean that's what they *think* anyhow.

If you gotta be around a lot of people at a funeral home cause your mother and little sister were killed, the biggest challenge is usually to buy into all the grief that you know most people are faking. It's not that I don't understand it cause I do, it's just that it sucks to have to be a babysitter for the phony emotions of phony adults and it involves some seriously skilled theatrics in order to let them believe you think they are being sincere—which is a dimension you just don't really need at a time like that.

Watching kids at school deal with a tragedy can actually be fairly comical at times, blasphemous as that may sound. I mean let's face it, school is not much more than this machine sort of thing spitting out another batch of phonies each June—*a la Pink Floyd and Another Brick in the Wall stuff.* And honestly I think that the little schools obsessed with football and town spirit and that kind of junk actually spit out a higher percentage of dedicated phonies than the larger city schools. I mean that's my opinion, not that it's worth all that much I suppose.

In general school grieving is sort of like: 'which dead animal did you just pass on the road . . . a dog or a possum?' Ok, here's what I mean. Two years ago a silage auger ate Craig Nestor, and then last year Dawn Campbell died from leukemia. Craig had been a big shot football player and wrestler a year ahead of Jimmy, while Dawn Campbell was a Dedhed. I mean I know this sounds like a social commentary, I'm sorry; I'll try to make it brief. Anyhow, Craig Nestor was plastered across the front page of the *Reinforcer*, the football game that week with New Bremen was moved to the end of the season and school was called off for two days. Girls were going ape shit everywhere and balling their eyes out for like two weeks straight and the football guys were all long faced and wore these black arm bands for like a month plus they put big black CN initials on their helmets. Teachers donned their somber suits for quite a long time as did Beckman and Wickerdick of course, and if you dared look at a football coach sideways and weren't a football player, you could bet on detention for a month of Sundays.

On the other hand when Dawn Campbell died . . . *nothing, absolutely nothing* . . . other than the Dedheds and George Runser going to the funeral four days later, and George even then, I'm bettin,' only because it would have looked pretty bad if he didn't. No Beckman or Wickerdick . . . or school board president, Karen Fish. Dawn's obit was right beside Glen Fysinger, who had died at 84, and his column was five times as long, although I sort of understood that since he'd lived so long. At school it would be safe to say well over half the kids hadn't known she'd died or who she even was, and the teachers didn't have to dirty their *extra phony* suits. And life went on.

Now don't get me wrong, Craig Nestor's death was tragic and unexpected and of course he was popular and Dawn Campbell wasn't. So sure there would be some differences and even I understood that. But Craig Nestor was bestowed privilege in death just as he was in life at Fort Harrison High School while Dawn Campbell's life was noticeably much less important and pretty much sucked all the way around. The End.

It took probably ten days tops before everyone at school and most of the people at the alley considered it fair game to return to their happy selves and normal lives (around me, I mean), which included the phonies not having to concentrate on an alternative phoniness and just getting back to being a regular every day phony. Jimmy, Dad and me did funeral duty and I cried a lot when I was alone, but I never much saw either of them cry and the worst thing was I never knew how they really felt since not once ever did any of us talk about the explosion. I had understood we were already a pretty fucked up family before the accident and afterwards not a family at all. Dad and Jimmy had a few knock down drag outs within days and then they each went their own way more than ever, so I was on my own. But it was a role I was already well practiced at, so life just pretty much went on.

When I was little, and until Jimmy quit bowling, I used to think we were sort of happy. At least I wanted to think that. We'd eat together at the table sometimes and even once in a while Dad would smile and give Mom a quick peck on the cheek which made me feel really happy. Trips to Cincinnati without Dad were maybe the happiest times of all, which was sad in a way, but I still want to remember them. But as I really try to think . . . *no* . . . there was never much happiness at all, but maybe that's the way it is for everybody and I just don't understand it. Or maybe it's God's way of preparing us for what's to come, and just making sure we don't get our hopes up that it could ever be anything much different.

# *Chapter Nineteen*

I was in the third row of bleachers waiting for the bell to ax another second period Sam Giovanazzo freshman P.E. class; a moment in time Brent Sturdivant called *Escape from Auschwitz.* Rebecca Kaufman sat in the front row, sobbing and holding a baggie of ice on her eye. Fuck-head Giovanazzo had at least given it to her, which, in-and-of itself should have qualified him for the Medal of Honor—though he just wanted her (and Molly Schmuckel) to shut up and could have cared less about the swelling and rapidly closing left eye. Willie Freytag sat ten feet further down, ice-nursing a nose now the size of a blue ribbon county fair pear. He was a boy so he had gone and pinched the ice himself, cause nobody was gonna *sissy wait* on any guy in Sam Giovanazzo's class. Ironically, it was a mild session so far for a football Friday—and the casualties acceptable— since some Fridays the gym resembled a Red Cross mobile infirmary following the attack on Pearl Harbor.

Clint Obringer, Thad Otte and Jason Berke, all senior football players, were on one of Giovanazzo's cheap study hall passes to hang out talking football and scoping out freshman pussy, but in particular so that they could fire tiny red rubber balls a hundred miles an hour at the freshman boys, and especially the mice like Ryan Ruckhaus, Brad Uhlenkamp, Tyler Crepts and Willie Freytag— guys who had abuse heaped upon them day after day after day, yet refused to turn 'state's evidence' that they knew would fall upon deaf administrative ears.

Fall Friday's also always meant 'study hall,' and Giovanazzo never made you dress out. Most girls sat in the bleachers gabbing with the exception of the girl jocks who shot baskets with the boys or organized pick up games. The freshman cheerleaders like Mindy Dalinghaus flaunted themselves for Giovanazzo and his animals— and I'd just seen Clint goose Mindy while Giovanazzo laughed. I also quite clearly heard him joke right along with the seniors about the size of her boobs, but Mindy would just smile and giggle, bathing in their lechery; desperate for the attention, but particularly because she figured it was the surest political platform from which to strengthen a continued spot on the cheer squad.

Most of the time I shot baskets cause there wasn't much else to do and if you were a boy and just sat in the bleachers reading, the hot shots would make fun of you and you'd be pretty sure to take a few hard rubber rockets in the chops. Probably because I was Jimmy's brother I'd never really been picked on much and yet my position wasn't worth all that much if you really stopped to consider it. Still, I was a little bigger than most of the mice, and that probably gave me some additional leverage.

*'If you aren't Football, you aren't shit!'* That was *Sam Giovanazzo's Motto from Day One in Fort Harrison, Ohio . . .* except I guess in the winter when it changed to, *'If you aren't Wrestling, you aren't shit.'* There *was* one exception though—*girls*—and particularly cheerleaders, but I had the distinct feeling that any hot girl could win ole' Sam Giovanazzo's favor, whatever that meant or whatever it was they had to do which didn't seem to be any great secret.

Rebecca Kaufman had just been sitting in the far bleachers talking to Allie Crosier when the little red ball pretty much took out half her face. Sure, it was an 'overthrow' and not intended, but it only qualified as a 'mini-tragedy,' since Rebecca was a far cry from being a candidate for *Sam's Club.* Any girl who was either fat and homely, skinny and homely, just plain fat, or just plain homely, had no shot at making the ballot for Sam's Club, even if they'd wanted to. I mean, truthfully, even most of the hot girls (if they possessed at least a partial brain) tried to steer clear of Giovanazzo and his thugs, though usually without much luck. Anyhow, Molly Schmuckel was first to the rescue and glared across the gym toward Giovanazzo and his court jesters. Molly, who would have never qualified for the club, was a naïve crusader for justice in Giovanazzo's dictatorship and I suspected he would one day take out a serious hit on her if she didn't cease and desist.

Leading Rebecca by the arm across the gym—and on a bee line for Sam—I could tell Rebecca wasn't really into it at all, no matter the pain, cause she well understood the script by then.

"Rebecca is hurt, Mr. Giovanazzo. I'm going to take her to the office," Molly had *said* boldly—not asking . . . pretty much *telling*—which is something just not done with Sam Giovanazzo. *Nobody tells Sam Giovanazzo what to do. Period.*

"It's Molly, right?" Sam had asked with controlled cynicism. You had to at least give him credit for coming up with her name the first time—and to this day I have no idea how that happened.

"Yes," Molly answered, starting for the exit, pulling Rebecca along, arm in arm.

I was watching from beneath the near basket at the time and saw Giovanazzo give an almost unnoticeable nod to Clint who slid sideways and blocked the exit. Even as I try to tell this story I know people will never really grasp the immunity and power of Sam Giovanazzo in Fort Harrison. It *was* mob rule.

"You're not going anywhere, Miss Molly," Sam said cynically, turning to Clint. "Hey Clint, ain't there a song or something about Molly here?" Clint looked stupidly toward Sam, the joke lost amidst the denseness of his cranium.

Jason Berke's face lit up though and he turned toward Giovanazzo: *"Good Golly Miss Molly!'* Is that what you mean, coach?"

"Yeh, that's it, Jason. Sure is," he said to the cat that ate the canary.

"Mr. Giovanazzo, Rebecca's eye is swelling shut. She needs ice and attention and should be going to the doctor. My parents are . . ."

*"W- e - l - l . . . Good Golly, Miss Molly . . . can it a bit*! Jason get a pack of ice out of the training room." Jason disappeared and Sam continued. "This really doesn't much have a thing to do with you . . . Molly? . . . uh, Molly?" Sam glared at her with raised questioning eyebrows, waiting for her to provide a last name. "Your last name, Molly?" Sam finally said impatiently.

"Molly Schmuckel," she replied, pointedly.

"Well boys, that's quite a mouthful isn't it . . . *Molly Schmuckel*," he said, chuckling and turning his smirk toward Clint and Thad who imitated their God like mirrored glass. "And Molly, what was it you were saying about your parents? I take it the Schmuckel family has moved here recently, right? Cause I never heard of no Schmuckels around these parts before. You boys heard of any Schmuckels around here?" Sam asked, as Clint and Thad stumbled over themselves to come up with the perfect and expected responsive 'no's' and the dumbly shaking of their heads.

"I was saying my parents are nurses and . . ."

"Whatever, Molly. So what does your Dad do?" Sam asked, getting noticeably tired of her presence.

"I just said . . . *my parents are nurses!*"

A huge slow grin crept across Sam's face. "Now let me get this straight . . . your *father* is a nurse? Is that what you're telling me? *That your father is a nurse?* Do you believe that boys? Molly here's ole' man is a nurse! Boy, that's a new one on me. Was he also a cheerleader for the high school football team?" he mocked, turning toward Clint and Thad with roaring laughter.

Clint had a big smile on his face, but I could tell Thad knew Sam was going too far, making fun of a girl's dad right in front of her. Thad Otte, who was Turk's twin brother, was a friend of Jimmy's and a pretty good guy I always thought. Of course Jimmy hung with Clint all the time too, but I kind of think it was because Clint was pretty much a gofer and sometimes—much as I hated to think about it—Jimmy had a lot of Sam Giovanazzo in him, and having Clint at his beck and call gave Jimmy a rise.

Poor Molly Schmuckel stood before Sam fuming, but luckily bit her tongue and soon Jason returned with a small pack of ice, which at Sam's nod he handed to Rebecca. Molly continued to glare which only brought out a shaking head laugh from Sam while the flunkies refined and adjusted their smirks appropriately, even Thad. "I think you can return to your seat across the gym, *Mssss Schmuckel*. Things are quite under control now, but thanks *for all your help*,' he'd said with cynical venom. "If someone needs an enema or something we'll be sure to give your dad a buzz," he'd dismissively spat, followed by the laughter of himself and his jokers, even though it seemed that Thad had made a conscious attempt to disconnect, hopefully without Giovanazzo's notice.

Molly took a deep breath, obviously not finished, but Sam headed her off. "I said we are *quite* finished here, Ms. Schmuckel. Return to your seat . . . NOW." He screamed the NOW at the top of his voice and with a frightening anger. All heads turned and all bodies froze. Even his pet jocks held their breath. Sam stood over Molly Schmuckel with clenched fists as it he were going to just up and kick her ass. I had seen him like this before, but *never* with a girl and it was almost beyond belief that such a confrontation could take place in a public school—well, except of course—in Sam Giovanazzo's dictatorship at Fort Harrison High School in Fort Harrison, Ohio.

He backed off a bit then, almost willing himself to break his own angry trance, and then turning toward Rebecca in a normal tone said, "Rebecca I think you'll be fine if you keep the ice on your eye. I think you should go back to your seat with Ms. Schmuckel."

By the end of the period, Willie Freytag's nose looked like a firecracker had been tossed inside the right nostril and Rebecca's eye was completely swollen shut. She *was* excused last period to meet with her mother who worked at Twilight Village, since Doc Holliday (no shit) from Sidney was on duty. He dressed it up with a patch and gave Joan Kaufman a few pain relievers. Rebecca said she got hit by a ball playing tennis and claimed it was her own fault. Joan Kaufman was a harried single parent and not the type to much bitch, particularly given Rebecca's story. Sam Giovanazzo definitely had a way of making liars out of a lot of usually honest people, but nobody was willing to face that stuff—not as long as there were football games to be won and more state championship trophies to squeeze into the trophy case.

Molly Schmuckel's liberal parents (in staunchly conservative Republican Fort Harrison) were indeed both nurses at Twilight Village and had recently moved to Fort Harrison from God knows where; I certainly never knew. They had been to the lanes one Saturday afternoon during open bowling as a family I remembered; I mean how could I forget? Molly, her father Kevin, mother Wisteria and sister Tangy (Tangerine). The family thing didn't fly too strong anymore in Fort Harrison and much as I hated Giovanazzo, I could tell the Schmuckels weren't gonna get too far or carry much clout around Fort Harrison, even if Molly prodded them into progressive measures. Kevin, who was nearly bald, wore a pair of dress black shorts, dingy yellow socks to the knee, a long sleeve lavender turtleneck and a crudely fashioned peace pendant affixed to a discarded leather shoe string and framed against a concave chest. Wisteria, with hair resembling a busted bale of straw strewn across a highway, donned a South Pacific sarong that she was always tripping on, a tie-dye madras blouse and resembled a half completed jigsaw puzzle of the beach at Ipanema. The whole family was shod in Birkenstocks and socks and if the dates would have meshed, I'd have believed that they were refugees who'd survived the Jonestown massacre—and decided to go bowling first thing—once they'd caught their breath.

Within the first month of school, the Schmuckels had twice ascended the hallowed granite steps of FHHS to question Wickerdick's educational philosophy, expertise and leadership. Ole' Wickerdick, however, was quite skilled at nodding, smiling, raising his eyebrows on cue and shaking his head in obvious consternation, then slowly arising with the promise of an internal investigation before deftly moving his constituents toward the exit as if they were carnival patrons whose time on a ride was up. Then as the door hit them in the ass, he'd re-engage neutral, stuff a pinch of Kodiak deep within his gums, and for the eight thousandth time pick up and fondle the picture of himself standing beside Arnold Palmer at the 1975 PGA Championship at Firestone Country Club in Akron. Then he'd take a deep and satisfying breath, knowing his ducks were nearly all in a row and that he would soon be able to play golf all day—every day—the rest of his life; moving to Palm Coast, Florida, and his condo at Pine Lakes Country Club *in exactly three years, eight months and six days.*

# Chapter Twenty

The second week of summer practice at Bowling Green, Jimmy broke his collar bone, but rather than wait to heal and rehab, rejoining the team at mid season, he just up and quit school and joined the Marines. The recruiter's deal, I found out later, was that he'd report in four months after he was patched up, but rather than come home to Fort Harrison, he moved to Columbus with Curt Martin and Ron Falk who had rented an apartment just off High Street while going to Ohio State. Jimmy'd decided that, before reporting for duty, he would party major-league throughout the Buckeye's '93 football season on his $7500 recruitment bonus—and he was especially excited because Bobby Hoying, from nearby archrival St. Henry, was poised to quarterback the Bucks as a sophomore that year. He and Jimmy had been serious rivals over the years, and although never friends, Jimmy would have been the sort to root for Bobby's success. In fact Jimmy had succeeded Bobby as Ohio's *Mr. Football* in 1991—Hoying having been awarded the honor just the year before—an incredible coup de'etat for the good ole' WOAC. Yet less than a year later, Bobby was set to direct one of the top Division I teams in the country . . . while Jimmy Bowling was headed only God knew where. For the Buckeyes, the season would prove to be a typical John Cooper joyride. Toting an undefeated season into Michigan, they would be trounced 28-0. For Jimmy, though, the year had been a non-stop party—*'High on High.'*

It was several weeks before either Dad or I ever heard about it though, not that Dad cared all that much, of course. It was like one of those deals where the milkman is fucking somebody's wife and everybody in town knows about it before the old lady's husband does. Come to think of it, a Dave Edwards sort of thing I guess you could say. I heard it first from Brent one Saturday night in early September when he came to help me at the alley. It seemed like two thirds of the crap I had in my brain got lodged there by stupid stuff Brent Sturdivant said, so I tried not to believe him at first, but by the time nine words were hatched I knew this time that he was telling the truth.

"So just where'd you hear that, Brent?" I had snapped angrily.

"Jeez Bowling, don't get pissed at me, I didn't do anything," he said, hurt. I knew it was wrong to take out my frustration on Brent, but I couldn't help it. Somehow when something's going wrong or you're getting bad news, Brent Sturdivant is the last person you want around, much less be the mailman. But I couldn't much help it in this case, I guess.

"Sorry Brent, please and thank you, where'd you hear it?" I asked cynically this time around instead of maliciously, for I knew Brent was fairly comfortable with cynicism, especially since most of it went right across the top of his head anyhow, so he continued.

"My Dad heard it up at the bank from Russell Slavik, I guess. I'm not sure where he heard it. Pretty much just that Jimmy broke his collar bone a couple of weeks ago so he quit school and signed up for the Marines and now he's down in Columbus staying with Curt Martin. You never said anything to me about it so I figured you didn't know. Does your Dad know about it yet?"

"I don't know, Brent. He doesn't give a fuck about Jimmy anyway. Are you positive about this Brent?" I questioned, knowing without a doubt he was right and that it was a script that fit Jimmy like a tailored suit, given his last six months in high school.

Just then Tic Forgett rounded the corner alone and slid onto a stool. At that point I was indebted to Brent, for I'd rather he'd ambushed me than an asshole like Forgett, which is exactly what would have happened five minutes later.

"So what the fuck's wrong with that brother of yours?" Tic asked, snapping the High Life out of my hand before I could even sit it down.

"He broke his collar bone and can't play," I said, trying to act like I'd known it all along.

"Jesus Christ, Billy, I heard that. I mean why the fuck did he quit school, join the Marines and that shit. Best goddamn half back

Sam ever puts out and he goes and fucks us all! That's bullshit, Billy, fucking bullshit," Tic said, chugging the beer and slamming the bottle on the bar.

"Who told you all that anyhow, Tic?"

"You're not telling me you didn't know, are you Billy. Jesus Christ . . ."

"No, no Tic. Of course I knew. I just wondered where *you* got it. Maybe you really don't have it all that straight," I said, as much as anything trying to find out more for myself.

"Tark got it from Dick Hamilton up at Stoney's. Ok then, what's the official Bowling family line? And what's your ole' man say about it, Billy? Naw, fuck that, I *know* that answer . . . its like everything else, he doesn't give a fuck does he?" he said shaking his head and grabbing the next beer I sat on the bar.

I didn't want to even respond to the asshole. One thing I never did, much as I'd long believed Dad truly *was* an asshole, was join ranks with someone else to call him one. It really wasn't their business, but when you run a bowling alley it's pretty damn hard to be private . . . and fucking impossible to defend my Dad about anything; especially anything connected to him and Jimmy.

"What else do you *think* you know, Tic?" I finally asked, feigning enlightenment and yet wanting more information on Jimmy which I thought maybe I could get by lobbing the ball back to his court.

"Like what, Billy?" Tic said, slurring, as I concluded this was his second stop after probably a few hours at the Downtown Coach's Clubhouse, Stoney's Bar.

"Like where he's gonna go after he reports?" I'd made up my mind to spit that one out no matter how much shit he wanted to give me. It was a good move, too, cause Tic *was* getting drunk and so now would pretty much shit out info without trying to flog me with his stupid shirttail superiority.

"Parris Island's what Dick Hamilton says. It's where all the recruits go so they can find the pussies and kick their ass to the curb. "

"Where's that?" I asked, ignorantly, which gave Tic a big shit laugh, but I honestly had no idea where Parris Island was at the time.

"It's fucking boot camp in the fucking ocean, cowboy. Where the fuck you been all your life?" he spat, again shaking his head in that *you stupid dumb ass* manner. Later on when I looked it up and saw it was off the coast of South Carolina, I realized Tic didn't know where Parris Island was either, except *'in the fucking ocean, cowboy!'*

I did get a post card from Jimmy about a week later, addressed to me, not Dad, and since I got the mail like everything else, I never even showed it to him cause I guess if Jimmy'd wanted that, he'd have sent it to him.

*(It would prove to be the last time I ever heard from . . .or communicated with . . . my brother, Jimmy . . . to this very day).*

*Billy.*
*You probably heard I quit school. It just wasn't for me. In January I'm going into the Marines. I'm not coming home before that though, but it's not because of you and I just wanted to make sure you knew that. Got $7500 to sign up so gonna have a good time for awhile. I'm not going to say nothing more cause you heard it all from me before. I just want to tell you good luck, cowboy. I'll try to let you know what's going on in a few months.*

*Jimmy*

A couple of nights after I got the post card, Dad and I were having one of our typically *profound* conversations while repairing the spotter on Lane 3. It was a process that took two people and we had the mechanics down like a Dale Earnhardt pit crew.

"Your brother's goin' off to shoot Indians, I heard," he said in grunts as always, and of course, never making eye contact with me. His vodka breath about choked me and I had to tuck my nose in the armpit of my sweatshirt at times just to collect some free air. I played dumb, like I was hearing this for the first time . . .

"What are you talking about, Dad?"

"Ya hard of fuckin' hearing, Billy? *Shooting fucking Indians*! He's in the goddamn Army. Jesus Christ, sometimes if I didn't know the difference I'd think you were born in a barn."

Dad had such a wonderful way about him. His entire life had pretty much been dedicated to making sure everyone on the planet knew that they were idiots . . . and taking particular care that they knew that *he knew* that they were idiots . . . which I think had even sadly included Mom at times. The only good thing these days was that he was passed out so much of the time that the egg shells I used to have to walk on—along with the vicious verbal enemas my sanity was always cleaning up—could now be swept aside for hours on end. I guess any way you sliced it, I was just fortunate to have such an inspirational role model. I mean the relatives of serious alcoholics have no idea how fortunate they are to have the freedom that they do since the assholes are passed out and the horizontal so much of the time. So whoever came up with this 'intervention' crap to 'solve' that problem just ain't quite right . . . at least the way I see it. . . .

. . . "You've got to try to understand your father, Billy, and you've got to find a way to be nice to him, even though he gets so angry," Mother had said to me (and Jimmy) on more than a couple of occasions. "He's just not happy cause he never really wanted to run the bowling alley. There were other things he wanted to do. And there are other reasons too, Billy. I just can't talk about them, not just yet. *You've just got to try to understand him.*"

. . . *Bowling's Bowling Center* was built in 1950 by Grampa William James Bowling IV and had been his life long dream. I'd heard the story more times than I wanted to remember, but I honestly think I probably need to tell it to you. It was spoon fed to me almost daily by my Grandmother (Emma) Bowling, a mean and angry woman who cheated her grandkids at cards and kicked her little dog, Blackie, if she ever lost . . . *just to make certain that we always did!* Having a mean grandmother isn't all that much fun I can tell you, especially if you're a little kid and get dumped off there like five times a week. Most kids I knew had wonderful grandmothers. I mean that should really be a law or something, I'd often find myself joking quietly, as my youthful cynicism was slowly constructed.

Grampa Bowling, who died before I was born, worked at the feed mill in Fort Harrison part time and farmed the small Bowling farm outside town before his father died. I guess at FHHS clear back in the 1930's everyone joked that he should build a Bowling alley because of his name, though in the 1930's bowling alleys could only be found in the big cities. When his father finally croaked in 1949 and he inherited the farm, he sold it within a few months and boom—nine months later the BBC was completed just south of town on Route 66—one of the first anywhere around in small towns the size of Fort Harrison or even in much larger ones.

It was his pride and joy and I guess Dad pretty much played the role I do now while he was growing up, becoming a damn good bowler in the process, but was drafted during the Vietnam War and gone four years. Returning home in 1972, Thin Jim Bowling assumed management of the alley when Grandpa died a year later, although Grandma Bowling technically still owned the alley and lived another decade. Picking his game back up, he soon became a renowned bowler, always on the edge of the big time, but never quite making it, though in the process collecting an occasional nice paycheck in addition to developing an appetite for his singular weekend absences. He and Mom *eloped* and got married that same year and she moved to Fort Harrison. Jimmy and me both were tired of hearing that the alley was a job that he never really wanted, but rather than break from ole' Mamma Bowling and strike a new life course, he chose instead to cultivate a personal cancer from which could only be gleaned a maturing crop of bitterness.

Mom said Dad had wanted to be an insurance agent because he said Ed Sorgenfrei, the State Farm agent, raked in dough like fallen October leaves . . . and did it just sitting on his ass in his office or even while up on Lake Erie sailing his forty foot yacht. If he wanted that so bad, why didn't he just do it, Jimmy and me had always wondered? Why not just sell the fucking alley—at least after Grandma died in 1982—and be a fucking insurance agent? I mean how hard could that have been? Even though I thought Jimmy fucked up a lot, I could definitely see early on that he had more balls than Dad—given how he vaulted the prison walls at twelve when he quit bowling. So I suppose in a sense he became a *reverse hero* and I always respected him for that . . . even as I could never find *anything* to respect Dad for, pretty much no matter how hard I tried. . . .

. . . "Your father *had* to run the alley boys! It's been in the family for years and your grandmother would have never let him sell it when she was alive cause she was still the owner. Please try to understand that boys," Mother told us time and again, always defending Dad, no matter how wrong, angry or obnoxious. *Always defending Dad.* She would often add: "there are other things too; things we'll talk about when you're both older," but she never told me whatever that *mystery* was, and if she ever told Jimmy, he never told me. Jimmy and me loved Mom, but it was hard to respect her cause her whole married life was doing what Dad expected and defending him like a stoolie juror in fear of the mob. I mean to us, Mom never had a life of her own . . . and then one day still young, she died.

*Then there was Libby.* Of course she deserved more, but she was a happy kid and I was pretty certain that when she died she had still remained immune to most of the Bowling family bullshit, and that made me feel good in a way when I really stopped to think about it. Nobody should die young like Libby, though most kids her age around the world die having known only pain and fear and hunger, which is terrible. But Libby was all smiles and happiness. Her life was kindergarten, first grade, gymnastics, learning to ride a bike and getting to stay with a friend all night or spending girl time with Mom or Grammy Louisa in Cincinnati. I think Libby's world was pretty much all happy, I really do. So sad as it is, you still have to try to find some good and I have, cause there's not many people that get even a handful of years on Planet Earth without having to don boots and roll their pants to the knee just to wade through the bullshit and pain of life, but Libby didn't have to . . . and somehow I have to try to believe that was mostly good.

# *Chapter Twenty-one*

*"J*esus, Billy, you're not gonna believe this,"* Brent Sturdivant squealed, catching up to me at my locker. I had seen him running toward me like an idiot as soon as he'd rounded the east doors at the top of the steps, third floor, fifty feet away. Brent seldom swore and I hardly ever remembered him taking the Lord's name in vain so I've got to admit he threw a curve at me that day. I'd learned to discount most of Brent's theatrics over the years, but there was definitely something big about to come down although I was probably the only person who understood Brent well enough to see that.

It was October, 1994, *and we were finally Seniors*. Football was in high gear so I was dodging blue and gold streamers, signs, and balloons, just trying to get to my locker. Because Brent was always so dramatic, the girls he was nearly knocking down to get to me gave him little notice except to shake their heads, laugh, and poke jokes his way.

"*Now* what's up, Brent? A teacher fucked you and you got an A-, right?" I joked, having second thoughts about my first impulse and deciding it had to be something more like that. Goofy as Brent was, he was a nearly perfect student and according to him, he and Molly Schmuckel were neck and neck for the top senior grade point average which would eventually determine the '95 Valedictorian, so anything below an A would be equivalent to being impaled up the butt by a heat seeking missile, at least the way he would see it. Still, he was acting stranger than I could ever remember, and with eyes as large as golf balls, but what really caught my attention was that he seemed almost tongue tied which just *never* happened to Brent Sturdivant! It was lunch and seniors were free to go uptown although with only thirty minutes it didn't give you much time to score food at Samsal's if you didn't beat the rush, which we'd already pretty much blown.

"Brent, we going to Samsal's or what? There's not much time."

"Billy, you *gotta* hear this and you *can't* tell *anyone*—and I mean that—hear me?" he'd exclaimed, gasping.

I'd heard that a thousand times over the years—the 'don't tell anyone' bullshit—only to see Brent motor-mouthing the same story three minutes later to someone else, then seven minutes again after that. And of course *everything* Brent had to say was like God passing the Commandments to Moses on Mount Sinai. So it was food on my mind that day more than what Brent had to say.

"Ok, then, can we grab something ala carte'? I'm hungry," I conceded.

"We can't be where anybody can hear us, Billy! Oh, God, you're not going to believe this! *It's huge!*"

I grabbed a half sub and a Sprite in the cafeteria ala-carte line. Brent said he couldn't even eat, which was *really* hardcore cause he wasn't one to miss a meal, tipping the scales by our senior year at over 200 pounds, and without a muscle in his body. He said we couldn't sit at a table or someone might hear him so when ole' GT, the lunchroom monitor, had his back turned, we slid through the side door into the alley which ran behind the school and sat on a pile of lumber outside the wood shop.

"Ok, Brent, what's the big fucking secret? You're really acting stupid this time, you know."

"*Billy . . . Billy! I just watched Sam Giovanazzo screw Mindy Dalinghaus in his office.* He had her bent right over his desk with her cheerleading skirt flipped over her butt and he was doing her doggie," Brent gasped—nearly hyperventilating as he tried to talk—but eventually taking a deep breath before he collapsed backward until he came into contact with the brick wall.

"*What?* What do you mean you *watched* them? Where were you?" I was shocked, but somehow there was still a flash of comedy thinking of Brent Sturdivant hiding to watch people fuck . . . but pulling it off around Sam Giovanazzo's office was suicidal.

Sam Giovanazzo had a big office off the stage in the old FHHS gym that served now as both a sacred shrine to honor all Sam's football and wrestling teams and also the site for all Ram home-wrestling meets. When he came to Fort Harrison twenty five years earlier—and before the new gymnasium was built in the mid 80's—the old gym was a buzzing center of activity and the P.E. office Sam was assigned was exactly where he still held court. When the new gym was built with two P.E. offices, Sam turned his office into a training room for football and stayed put in the old office. A nearby door that could be opened from the inside only (without a key, which only Sam and the custodians had), led into a short alley and then to the back door of the new gym maybe fifty feet away. Sam was a smoker anyway and so the short commute back and forth between classes provided him with convenient smoke breaks.

Story is, over the years there'd been more than a few complaints and pressure on the school board to utilize the old gym more efficiently, and especially since the middle school basketball teams were forced to use the tiny St. Matthias gymnasium that had only three bleacher rows on one side. Sam stood firm, however, proclaiming that *The Pit*—as his wrestlers had christened the gym—was the *exclusive* domain of the wrestling team and not available for any other use! With each new football or wrestling state championship, democratic opposition was always forced underground . . . and the Sam Giovanazzo dictatorship thrived unchallenged.

The two main basketball bank boards and side practice boards were removed via Giovanazzo edict years earlier and wrestling mats were fitted across the entire gymnasium like custom carpeting. The old wooden chair seats that rose on the north side and seated about 400 were refinished and varnished to a sparkling sheen, and a stunning blue and gold paint job around the entire gym jumped out at you like a kaleidoscope. But it was the trophy cases and hanging banners that—even I had to admit—were pretty impressive, regardless of how you felt about Giovanazzo. On both the east and west walls were mounted twin trophy cases that measured 35' wide by 10' high (I'd heard the dimensions and all that from bar talk at the BBC, understand please). The east was for football and the west for wrestling, each with their large state championship trophies centrally placed. There were actually more total wrestling trophies because of Invitationals, but on the football side, along with the District, Regional and State trophies, sat 21 WOAC league championship trophies out of the 25 years Sam had coached. Dropped from the rafters were maybe a hundred blue and gold banners, noting the myriad of championships and it could take an hour just to read them all. If the whole deal wasn't so pukingly disgusting, you'd have to almost think it was actually kind of cool. Jimmy always thought it was tits, but why wouldn't he, I guess—after all, he was one of *Sam's boys!*

Personally I'd only been in The Pit a few times—to a couple of wrestling meets with Abby Bertke (who I sorta dated for a brief period one winter) cause her brother, Chuck, was a pretty noted wrestler . . . and once or twice with Jimmy when I was in junior high school. Sam always wanted Jimmy to wrestle, but he never did, and I respected Jimmy a lot because he didn't do *everything* Sam Giovanazzo had wanted him to do. I mean—when you really thought about it—Jimmy Bowling was pretty much his own Captain any way you sliced it, and that was pretty cool . . . *even though it sure didn't mean he wasn't capable of fucking up.*

# Chapter Twenty-two

"Brent, Jesus, tell me the story! What were you doing around Giovanazzo's office . . . or are you just shitting me?"

Brent turned to me slowly, his eyes bigger than before. "Ok, Billy, you know I'm the stage manager for *'Drop Dead, Juliet,'* the school play Badderly's directing at St. Matthias," he said, pausing.

"And?"

"Well, years ago—before Giovanazzo got here—the plays were in the old gym and they'd toss backdrops, props, and that kind of crap up above his office where it's like a loft, you know where I mean?"

"Whatever, Brent, go on."

"Well some of that stuff is still up there and it's about the only place Giovanazzo and his goons haven't messed with over the years."

"And ?."

"So I'm in 'Gallbladder's lit class fourth period, pretty much doing nothing after I handed in a test, and she signals me to come up to the desk. She tells me to go check out the loft to see if there was anything we could use for the play and writes me a pass."

"Jesus, Sturdivant, you *know* that's shaky ground. That's like James Bond shit and you're no James Bond. Had she cleared it with Giovanazzo?" I'd queried, but as soon as I'd asked I knew that was a joke since Giovanazzo had pretty much nothing to do with anyone except his stooge assistant coaches.

"No . . . I mean I didn't ask her, but you know ole' Gallbladder! She thinks all teachers are honorable and perfect and all that stuff. She's not part of the *real* world, Bowling, you *know* that. There's a boatload of stuff she doesn't get."

"That's fine, Brent, but *you* do. Anyhow, hurry up—the bell's gonna ring."

"Well, there's these black metal rungs bolted to the wall that go up to the loft, right around the corner from Giovanazzo's door. So I climb up them and don't even know anyone's around cause I thought Giovanazzo had a class . . ."

"He's got a student teacher, dumb ass. He *always* does during football, so he's never in class except to watch his thugs kill freshmen or scope pussy. You ought to know that Brent. Sorry, let's hear the rest."

"Well, I get up there and I think I hear something below so I'm real quiet. It's pretty dark and I can't much see the crap Gallbladder wanted me to look for, but there's this old metal grate, like a two-foot square on the loft floor right in the middle of Giovanazzo's office and right over his desk. So I lean over it a little and the first thing I see is Mindy's chin pressed on a white gym towel on the desk and sort of sliding back and forth like a metronome—you know what I mean, Bowling. I was scared, but I crawled a little more so I could see the whole thing. Giovanazzo had her cheerleading dress flipped up over her butt and her tights down around her ankles and was pounding away with his eyes closed. Geez, Billy, he even still had his whistle around his neck and it was jumping around like a kid on a trampoline. Mindy was grunting and breathing hard and all, but not real loud, so I figured Giovanazzo'd told her to keep it down."

"So what if you got caught? Didn't you think about that?"

"Sure I did, but what could I do then?"

"You could have left, Brent. Giovanazzo would have never known, never even heard you, not right then. His brain was in Mindy's pussy. You could have run straight across the fucking mats and burst in Wickerdick's office and forced him to catch Giovanazzo. You could have screamed it out in the office around everyone. *Then they would have had to do something.* But you wanted to watch them finish, didn't you? Christ, you're as big a pervert as Giovanazzo is," I said angrily, though I must admit I probably wouldn't have done anything much differently. It's just the truth, even if I'm ashamed to say it. I mean, I'm bettin' a lot of kids thought about reporting Giovanazzo's disgusting behavior over the years, but it never happened—and more than likely never would.

"Screw you, Bowling . . . like you would have. I didn't know *what* to do. I was scared and I wasn't going to rat on Giovanazzo. No one would and you wouldn't either, so don't act so superior."

"Ok, ok, so what else happened?" I asked, knowing there was more, yet almost not wanting to hear it.

"Well, pretty soon he pulls out and turns Mindy around. Then he whips her cheerleading sweater and bra up to her chin, telling her to bend over and then he starts screwing her tits. I couldn't really see much cause Mindy had her head and back to me and it covered up most of the action . . . along with Giovanazzo's gut, that is. Anyway, Giovanazzo pulls out and comes all over her tits and face which I could see real clear when Mindy straightened back up. Then he grabbed the towel off his desk, cleaned his prick with it, and then just sorta threw it at Mindy, almost mean like. After he did that he walked over to this big mirror on the wall and starts combing his hair. Can you imagine that, Billy? He just starts combing his hair as if nothing had even happened?"

"Didn't they talk or anything?"

"Not really. Mindy wipes herself off and pulls this lacy black bra back down over her melons. Jesus, Billy, she's got awesome hooters and . . ."

"I know, Brent, remember . . . Schweiterman's party, sophomore year."

"Shit, that's right, Billy, I forgot. Jesus, you dorked her too, didn't you?"

"Let it go. Sorry I brought it up. I'm not a fucking teacher though, am I Brent? A little different don't you think?"

"I know, Billy. They should hang Giovanazzo by the balls, but they won't. Everybody knows he fucks the girls. They always have."

"That's why you gotta spill the beans, Sturdivant. *You've got to!*"

"Bullshit, Bowling, you think I'm *crazy*? I'm the one who would be nailed to a cross. I've heard you say it a hundred times, Bowling . . . '*nobody fucks with Sam Giovanazzo!*' And you know it. I know it makes you mad; it makes a lot of kids mad, but that's just the way it is and the way it's always been. Wish I'd never told you now. I'm trying to get a scholarship to Kenyon and I'm not gonna wreck that. Nobody's ever gone to Kenyon from Fort Harrison and my folks would kill me if I messed that up, so you can go to hell," Brent said, standing to walk away.

"Brent, calm down, I'm sorry. I hate Giovanazzo and a lot of people do, but nobody ever does anything. I mean, Jesus, he should go to prison! Mindy's not even eighteen yet, not until next June, yet he'll probably get another fucking award of some kind this year, then give a speech while he scans the crowd looking for new girls to ruin."

It was time for the bell and I felt sick. This wasn't anything I didn't already suspect, just as half the people in Fort Harrison did— *at least the kids*—and I was furious and depressed, but more than anything else, felt helpless. Somehow it seemed Brent should be able to expose that asshole and have the next parade thrown by the town for him, but it wouldn't work that way. Brent knew it and I did too. So the world would continue to be a fucked up planet and Fort Harrison, Ohio, a small open sore near it's asshole, oozing a stream of infinite pus that would never dry up . . . *not as long as Sam Giovanazzo was around.*

The bell rang and we started for the door when Brent stopped and turned to me. "There *was* one more thing, Billy."

"What?" I asked, numbly.

"I think they do it every Friday, fourth period."

"Why do you say that?" I asked, listening closely.

"After tossing the towel to Mindy, Giovanazzo said, 'You know the drill, Mindy. You were on a pass for cheerleading supplies at Emerson's, just like always. Oh, and Mindy, I'm thinking you're gonna need more supplies next Friday, right?' he'd said, laughing out loud as Mindy pulled on her sweater and tried to smile at him, but then he just turned his back on her and she left."

"So what'd you do then?"

"I had to wait till Giovanazzo came out of his office and went out into the alley. Then when the door banged shut and it was quiet, I got down, sprinted across the floor and up to the hallway above the seats. Nobody saw me, I'm sure of that," Brent said . . . as I found myself wondering if that were good or bad.

"Ok, Brent, fine; whatever. I've really got to do some thinking about this, but I wanna burn that fucker. I want to burn him in the worst way."

"You're not gonna say anything, are you? Billy, I can't . . ."

"No, Brent, I'm not gonna tell anyone what you saw. I just wish *you* would. Now let's just get to class," I'd said as we numbly filed in through the alley door and back into the cafeteria unnoticed.

# Chapter Twenty-three

*W*ith more than a little curiosity, people wondered how Mindy Dalinghaus had recaptured a spot on the varsity cheer squad after being voted off her sophomore year. It was something that seldom happened—but especially because few girls would have even tried out again the next year. Normally once you receive the *kiss of death* . . . you *are* dead! I could have cared less about cheerleading, but when Sturdivant once told me who was on the voting panel, I had practically rolled on the ground laughing, but now I was beginning to understand something completely different.

The voting panel was appointed and presided over by Hooters Edwards, the cheer coach, who at 33 still had the best tits in Shelby County. A graduate of FHHS in 1980, she was reputed to have been one of Giovanazzo's squeezes years back, but had lately been adopted by Dick Hamilton. Then there was LuAnn Shriner, another airhead cheerleader from the early 80's and even bigger airhead adult, who supposedly was *also* having an affair with Dick Hamilton although married to Ned Shriner, editor of the *Fort Harrison Reinforcer*. Third was Ted "*no shit*" Turner, the guidance counselor, who was supposed to provide political correctness I figured, but in reality was terrified of Sam Giovanazzo, making him a perfect 'yes man.' Dick Hamilton, *and of course, Sam Giovanazzo*, completed the voting panel. What more needs said?

However she did it, Mindy had lost a few pounds over the summer heading into our junior year and looked pretty damn good, but the biggest surprise of all, at least for those who hadn't a clue how things at Fort Harrison High School *really* worked, was that she had re-gained her spot on the varsity cheer squad after failing to make it the year before. I hadn't given it much notice at the time, but now understood that there was no mystery nor fate nor any great surprise to it at all—for obviously Mindy was one of *Sam's girls* and if she had wanted to be a cheerleader again, well, she knew what she had to do and after that who was going to vote against her?

The school was a zoo game days our senior year, just as it had been when I was a freshman. The only difference was that I could have cared less and was more cynical than ever since Jimmy now was long gone. The team stood 5-1 on that particular Friday, having lost to Cliffton, which, even though it was a non-league game, was a tragedy none the less in Fort Harrison, and served to make Sam Giovanazzo more disagreeable and mean than ever. The game that night with St. Michaels, who was 4-2, was a big one and Giovanazzo could now pace the sidelines with a singularly focused anger—his lustful seeds having been bisected from his disgusting nature and planted across the chest and face of Mindy Dalinghaus but a few hours earlier. . . .

. . . It was late summer before my eighth grade year that I really learned what Sam Giovanazzo was about and learned from that day forward to hate him. I was riding my bike to the town pool, passing the practice football field, when I saw Jimmy and Turk Otte sitting on the bleachers, their morning workout just over. I decided to ride over and say hi, but just as I started across the foot bridge, Sam Giovanazzo and Dick Hamilton came out of the stadium weight room and stopped to talk to Jimmy and Turk . . . never even noticing my approach cause I'd stopped my bike about twenty feet behind them.

"Hey Bowling, gettin' any of that Putnam pussy? Come on; tell Dick and me what it's like. We're bettin' she can wrap those legs around you twice. Tell us about it, big guy," Giovanazzo barked as Hamilton and Turk laughed and Jimmy smiled uneasily, looking toward the ground and not saying anything. He made darting eye contact with me as if to say *get lost*, but I didn't budge cause no one else was giving me any notice.

"She's getting pretty big for her britches around this town, Jimmy, but at least it's one of Sammy's boys that's getting inside them so I guess that ain't all bad. And Jimmy, if she don't put out easy, *just take it*! You know what I mean, boy. That's really what they all want anyway and that Putnam girl needs it more than most whether she thinks she'd like it or not. But Jimmy, just remember—your mind's for football and your dick's for women, so don't go mixen' the two up and fallin' in love. W*omen are to use; women are to fuck*, but don't let 'em make you stupid—and *never* let em run the show, son. You *do* know what I mean, don't you Jimmy?" Jimmy dumbly nodded, continuing to look at the ground before looking up with a weak smile on cue as Turk Otte slapped him on the back and Giovanazzo and Hamilton walked off laughing.

I'd turned and rode off, knowing it was the thing to do right then. I had known who Gwen Putnam was before Jimmy ever brought her to the alley a few times and since seventh grade had been watching her run at cross-country meets which were held in the community park not far from the alley. I knew they'd sort of dated off and on, but never serious, no matter what Jimmy might have wanted. One thing was certain though, their deal wasn't sexual and even if it had been, Sam Giovanazzo was a despicable human being to talk like that about Gwen to Jimmy that day and it made me want to throw up I remember thinking, even then as an eighth grader. But mostly I remember being really pissed at Jimmy and wondering how he could just sit there and let that man talk like that about Gwen? Everything about that day was wrong . . . *everything* . . . and I never forgot it. *Ever!*

. . . During the week following what Brent Sturdivant told me, I tried to think of every possible way to nail Sam Giovanazzo while he was fucking Mindy Dalinghaus the following Friday—hidden video, hidden tape recorder, trying to shoot video through the grate—or just plain telling Wickerdick or Beckman or Karen Fish about the impending act. I even had the idea of busting the door open with a loaded camera ready to shoot myself and taking it to Wade Borger, the chief of police. But in the end I did nothing but sit and observe and let life unfold around me, just like always. And I was disgusted . . . *disgusted with myself.*

October 14, 1994 . . . *Fort Harrison Rams, 42 . . . Saint Michaels Saints, 7*

October 21, 1994 . . . *Fort Harrison Rams, 24 . . .Minster Wildcats, 10*

# Chapter Twenty-four

The 1994 Fort Harrison High Rams *failed* that fall in football, falling to Norwalk St. Paul in the state championship game, 24-16. Runner-up was simply not acceptable to Sam Giovanazzo, although it was the third Runner-up spot for FHHS to go along with their seven Championships throughout his twenty-four year reign. Sam was *bitter,* but particularly because of the headlines in the *Reinforcer* the very next Wednesday, November 23, which was the day the weekly rag hit the newsstands . . .

## Gwen Putnam Looks toward '96 Olympics

*Fort Harrison's Gwen Putnam, who last weekend won her second NCAA Division I Cross Country title as a junior at Notre Dame, will attend a special Olympic development camp this summer at . . .*

The article was plastered across the front page of the *Reinforcer* with inch-and-a-half headlines, while the State Runner-up story for the football team shared the bottom half of the front page with a smaller article about a commercial expansion in New Bremen and even a tiny piece on the opening of the English Channel tunnel to France.

Though pissed about the runner-up finish, it was the *Reinforcer* headlines that infuriated Sam more than anything had in all his years in Fort Harrison, and he was particularly angered at himself for having abandoned his impulse to deal with Gwen Putnam two years earlier when he'd had the motivation and had actually come up with a plan. But Gwen had left for college before Sam could act and his anger and humiliation had faded eventually as he turned his attention toward the conquest of Mindy Dalinghaus and the upcoming '92 football season.

As far as I was concerned, the fact that Dirk Salisbury and the other football assholes in our class failed to win the state championship our senior year sure didn't cost me any sleep. I mean school spirit and having unassisted orgasms when your football team kicks somebody's ass—and the rest of that silly shit—just doesn't matter that much to most of the kids in school, and honestly, crying over a state Runner-up spot is actually quite funny, at least the way I saw it. Now as for me, Billy Bowling—my cynicism and negativism were gleaned because of the despicable Sam Giovanazzo, the morally bereft adults of Fort Harrison, and the drunks at the BBC—and didn't have all that much to do with the players in my class, although to be sure there were a few assholes besides Dirk. Personally, however, not one player has ever much messed with me over the years so I've got nothing against them.

The summer before my Junior year I had gotten totally disgusted living with Dad in the trailer that he'd placed on the old house foundation, so I moved into the back of the alley, behind the pin setters where I had an old couch, dresser and TV. The men's room up front had a shower, so all in all it wasn't a bad deal. When Mom was alive, Dad smoked some, though never in the house or around her, but now probably choked down two or three packs a day . . . and trying to sleep in the trailer was like sleeping in an ash tray and using a cigarette butt for a pillow. Besides, I was sick of doing his dishes; sick of ditching wasted, rotting food; sick of stumbling through a hundred empty beer cans and vodka bottles, and sick of the depression and hopelessness which seethed throughout the trailer like a starving dog chained in an abandoned alley.

People still came to the alley—pretty much looking past our *fucked-up-ed-ness*—because there was only so much to do in Fort Harrison. I know, I've said that like ten times before, haven't I? Sorry, but there's a point there. Anyway, I worked more hours at the alley than hours spent at school just to keep the place from falling into complete disrepair. I ordered the food, beer, liquor and pop, called the Brunswick repairman when necessary and by my senior year had pretty much assumed responsibility for the alley payroll and seeing that the bills were paid on time. I educated myself more at the alley than FHHS ever educated me, though it doesn't mean I'm down on the school completely, even though I'm sure it sounds like that most of the time. I do know it worked for some kids—those who weren't in one way or another destroyed by Sam Giovanazzo. I had even learned to temper my cynicism over the years . . . *just joking!*

Being forced into doing payroll meant actually paying Dad (which was a joke), myself, Busty and Brent Sturdivant, whom I had hired myself because there were days Dad never even came out of the trailer. Brent was perfect though cause like myself he wasn't into a bunch of sports and I could call him at the drop of a hat and he'd show; besides, Brent was one of the *last cowboys* who still thought that working at a bowling alley was big shit.

My four years at Fort Harrison, even as boring and depressing as my life usually seemed, oddly passed quickly—as I would later come to find that all life did. By my sophomore year I went to games, dances, and parties here and there on the occasional night the alley was closed . . . and sometimes when I just decided to close it myself with Dad drunk in the trailer or away for a bowling tournament. I guess I didn't have a lot of friends, but I got along pretty well overall I think. I certainly wasn't a big shot like Jimmy had been by any means and I couldn't go out for sports and stuff because I had to run the alley, but it seemed most people sort of respected me in a way for doing it and I got my share of party invitations. Since just about everyone came to the alley from time to time, they had pretty much written Dad off and connected with me—kids and adults alike. If it weren't for Billy Bowling there would be no *bowling* in Fort Harrison—and so I guess in some kind of perverted way—it made me important.

I had grown quite a bit after my freshman year and was taller than Jimmy had been by several inches. I had a weight bench behind the pin spotters and since the end of sophomore year had lifted religiously, though no one really knew that except Brent. I was far from a vain person, but I knew I was decent looking and the lifting had made a big difference too. I mean Jimmy and me *had* inherited Mom's Italian Romano genes, although Jimmy more so than me, and even though Dad was pretty much a total fuck up now, in his day he wasn't a bad looking guy . . . back when he used to take care of himself and in a way what must have trapped Mom.

I had a few dates and sort of went with Abby Bertke for a while, but it pretty much ended cause I always had to work at the alley though we were still good friends. I'd lost my virginity to Mindy Dalinghaus (*before* Brent had witnessed her get fucked by Sam Giovanazzo) during a party at Jon Schweiterman's house while his parents were away on a cruise, but I was sure I'd been pretty lame and it bothered me a lot for months cause I never got a second shot with her. That was at the end of our sophomore year. Mindy never came to the alley that summer and acted all weird around me when we got back to school in the fall, but after a while I reasoned it was probably just as well. I mean, Mindy *was* a girl you really could have fallen in love with, *at least in those days*; even though she had a checkered reputation. Still, besides her boobs of course, she was cute as hell and even though she was an airhead, she could be funny and fun and people liked her. The biggest problem with Mindy was that her priorities were really messed up and even if I'd had the chance to seriously date her, I could have never comfortably digested the stupid stuff. I mean when she'd lost her spot on the cheer squad, she'd cried all day—*every day*—for like two months straight. An enemy could have wiped LA or New York off the map and Mindy would have still been balling her eyes out over losing her goddamn cheer spot. A guy can't live with that silly shit—at least I can't see it—although I know her tits could, at times, scramble even the good sense of an educated prince.

*Then Mindy changed.* Sometime late during our junior year, I now remembered, but I honestly didn't give it much thought at the time. *Not until after what Brent witnessed the beginning of senior year.* I'd sometimes watch Mindy after that and it was sad cause she wasn't even close to the same person she'd once been. There was dullness in her eyes and a quiet about her that had never been there before. At least before—stupid as cheerleading might have seemed to me—she was excited and spontaneous about it, but after Giovanazzo got his claws (and dick) in her she just went through the motions. She used to bounce between laughing and crying, but after that, she did neither. So much had been stolen from her, and that fun-loving, emotional, sparkly girl was gone and it made me sad. It made me want to just talk to her and ask her to cry on my shoulder and tell me all about what troubled her . . . even if she had just wanted to lie.

*But most of all, it made me want to see Sam Giovanazzo in prison . . . or dead!*

# Chapter Twenty-five

Then there was *Krissy Kurtz*! When I was writing about doing payroll, I left her name out because I was still trying to decide whether or not to write *this* chapter. But since most of the rest of this book is about Krissy, I guess I should give you the *full* tale. Krissy *did* say to write the whole story as it unfolded, didn't she? But more than that, I wouldn't be here today to write it at all *if it weren't for her*! We've had quite the ride, and here is how it all started . . .

. . . Krissy *had* been working at the alley since early in our junior year, partly cause we needed the help, but *especially* because of the way she rendered her application! Now if you're a kid, or even an adult with a strict moral posture, you might be advised to bow out until next chapter, cause this chapter is pretty XXX. But I don't really know how else to write it so that you understand the *real* truth about (us) at the same time. Well, I warned you.

Like her sister, Tammy, Krissy became a Dedhed and was in the Monday night league. She went into the Dedhed program at the beginning of our junior year and if they didn't already have a job they had to land one within a month in order to stay in the program. So Krissy stopped by one Friday soon after school started to see about working at the alley. I was alone cleaning up behind the bar, but her scent hit me the second the door swung open—a scent every guy and male teacher at FHHS could have pinned on Krissy Kurtz, even if they'd been blindfolded. I'd told Dad a hundred times we needed more help, but didn't lay the truth on the line by blaming his drunken laziness as the reason, at least not that early on. Anyway, it took maybe nine seconds and Krissy started turning on the charm, which is putting it modestly—*very* modestly. At first I told her she'd have to talk to Dad . . . but . . .

. . . "Billy, come on, I've been out here two times bowling and I never even seen your Dad. Everybody says you run the place. I gotta get a job or they're gonna kick me out of the program and I like it out here, Billy . . . and I like you too . . . *a lot!*" She ducked under the walkthrough and leaned up against me, grabbing my left cheek (*ass cheek*) in her hand hard, and I mean *real* hard. Then she buried her nose in my ear and nibbled on my earlobe. "Don't you like me, Billy? I've always thought you were *real* cute, and I've seen the way you look at me since clear back in grade school. Haven't I?" she teased, blowing soft warm air into my right ear before sticking her tongue in it and licking all around, as my knees got weak and my dick got hard—very hard!

I'd never been so close to Krissy Kurtz . . . well, duh! That she could turn heads everybody knew, but the perfection of her dark skin and the soft intoxicating smell of her hair was unlike anything I'd ever before experienced, and the intensity of my erection was frightening. Whether eight or eighty, Krissy Kurtz could stir the gonads of every male with a pulse and probably raise the dead if she stood near enough an open casket I remember thinking at the time. I was seventeen and Krissy Kurtz was kneading my ass and chewing my earlobe in the dark vacant alley, and I was about to succumb to temptation . . . just as surely as Krissy Kurtz was about to land a job.

"Think your Dad might come in, Billy? Or anyone else?" she breathed in my ear, suddenly sliding her hand deftly inside my pants, cradling my balls, planting her lips on mine and sticking her tongue halfway down my throat.

I disconnected, breathing hard and mumbled, "Dad's gone, Krissy. He's at a tournament in Akron so you should probably come back on Monday," I said weakly, knowing exactly what was about to happen, my resistance now as soft as my penis was hard. But why should I have even resisted in the first place, the thought flashed? I mean it wasn't like I was married or anything—or even dating anyone. And everyone I knew would have killed to have a shot to get in Krissy Kurtz's pants. But there *was* Butch Clayton, I suddenly remembered—a Minster High School dropout who, with his brothers, beat the shit out of people for fun as often as other guys teed up a golf ball—and everybody knew Butch and Krissy were *a thing*, . . . at least that was what I'd always heard.

"I know you like me, Billy. I've seen the way you look at me. Remember sixth grade? You haven't forgotten that, have you naughty boy? You've dreamed about this and you beat off thinking about me, don't you? It's ok, lots of guys do, and especially those perverted teachers at Harrison High. Now wouldn't you like to get what they all dream about? I don't put out no matter what people say, but I like you, I really do . . . and I want you as bad as you want me. You won't be sorry," she said, squeezing my balls hard, which though painful, was incredibly exciting at the same time. Getting hit in the nuts with a baseball wasn't fun, but Krissy's hand squeezing hard was somehow a pain that I didn't want to stop.

"Krissy . . . I know you and Butch . . ." I started to say with chopped breathing.

"Fuck Butch, Billy! He's not my keeper and he ain't gonna know, so quit worrying. Besides, most of that's just talk, Billy, it really is. Butch Clayton's never fucked me, no matter what he says, or what a hundred prissy Fort Harrison bitches yak about. I do what I want and that doesn't mean I fuck, cause I don't, but right now I *really* want you, Billy Bowling . . . *just you and nobody else.* I could care less if you give me a job cause I'd want you anyhow, but I hope you do so we can spend a lot more time together," she cooed.

Then it was Krissy who was panting and getting hot. Her grip on my testicles moved to my penis and she started pumping it slowly, chafing it against the roughness of my jeans and I had flashbacks to that first hard on I had gotten in sixth grade. Then as I was an inch from ejaculating . . . she stopped.

"Billy, don't come yet. I can tell."

"Jesus, Krissy, how could you know that?" I stuttered.

"Billy, Billy, Billy, you've got a lot to learn and it'll be fun to learn together, so let's have a lesson right now. Where do you want to fuck me? Here on the bar so you can think about it every day you're here working . . . or maybe in the middle of one of the alleys? You pick the spot, but I don't wanna wait much longer--*I'm so hot!*" she said, growling.

"Krissy, I gotta lock the door, ok?"

"Hurry, Billy . . . *hurry.*"

I ran to the door and slid the dead bolt then started back, but remembered the key we hid in the shrubbery just outside the door so I pushed the door back open and leaning around the corner, grabbed it. Brent Sturdivant was actually due, but screw him. Hopefully he'd just go away if the door was locked and he couldn't find the key, but *Jesus*, Krissy's beat up old Escort was parked right in front of the door. So if the key was gone and her car here, he'd pretty much figure . . . oh screw it all, I decided, and suddenly I wanted Krissy Kurtz in the worst way and was about to join an infinite string of men that stretched into both the past and would into the future— men whose brains were more easily lobotomized by the wiles and ways of a Krissy Kurtz than by the precision of a neurosurgeon with a court order.

When I rounded the corner of the bar I nearly passed out. Krissy was half sitting/half leaning backward onto a bar stool, wearing only a pink thong and matching bra. Her short skirt and tube top were tossed upon the bar to her left and she was playfully scuffing the heel of one of her ankle boots erotically out in front of her, as if mimicking a vicious bull with murderous designs upon an arrogant matador. I froze before her as she seductively pulled up her bra, releasing a perfect, incredibly firm breast, and began tweaking its almost sable nipple with the fingertips of her right hand. Hypnotized by a sexual intensity I couldn't have dreamed up in a century, I swear I nearly fainted as Krissy thrust forward magenta pouting lips that she had formed into a teasing kiss.

"Here on the bar, Billy—is this where you want it—here on the bar?" she teased.

There were long narrow windows without curtains behind the liquor shelves that ran the length of the bar, allowing a certain amount of light in so things weren't so dingy. They were probably seven feet off the ground from outside, but I knew Brent would find a way to elevate his mug to get a look, especially when he saw Krissy's car, so the bar wasn't a good idea I reasoned, though my brain cells were organizing a new colony on Mars about then.

"Krissy," I said, panting, "I have a couch in the back where I sleep. Sturdivant will be here anytime and he'll try to look through the windows behind the bar, I'm sure of that."

"Whatever you want, Billy. We could give Brent a show, if you'd like. He swallows his tongue every time I cross my legs. Wouldn't you like your ole' buddy to see you get something he can only dream about?" she joked, playfully.

"You said *nobody'd* know . . . Butch . . ."

"Ok fine, Billy, *let's go*," she cried, pushing quickly away from the stool, her right breast bouncing about with a life of its own. She grabbed my hand and started to pull me toward the cat walk that led to the back of the alley when I noticed she'd left her micro clothes on the floor. I disengaged and ran back, scooping them up.

"Clothing's one thing we *don't* need Billy, that's for sure! You're *way* too up tight. I'm gonna untie those knots, Billy. I'm gonna turn you into jelly *and* hard steel. Come on, hurry, and you'll see what I mean."

Halfway down the catwalk Krissy moved her hand back inside my jeans and used my dick now to pull me forward. We stumbled through the door and fell upon the old couch as she pulled at my jeans and ripped at my sweatshirt. I kicked my shoes off and allowed Krissy to do the rest. She whipped her bra off, releasing both perfect breasts with their blackberry tiaras. They were so different from Mindy Dalinghaus's, whose were larger, but mushy-like and with blue veins running across them like state routes on a road atlas. Krissy's were *exotic* . . . like the breasts you might have found on Cleopatra, I remember thinking. She grabbed a pillow and threw it between my feet as I sat upon the edge of the couch. Then kneeling she took my penis deep into her mouth. Mindy hadn't done that and it was exciting. Then suddenly she stopped!

"You can't come, Billy, not yet!" she said, pushing me back until I was fully reclined. She still had her boots on, which I found incredibly exciting and I suspected Krissy well knew. "Make me wet, Billy," she said, swiveling to plant herself on my face while taking me back into her mouth, her incredible boobs brushing across my stomach. And then the *real* lessons began . . . and with chapters on positions that I'd bet even Brent Sturdivant had never before fantasized about. . . .

. . . The pounding which started first as a distant soft rumble somewhere in the front, moved around the building, pausing at each door like a solo for African drums and actually served to intensify my orgasmic crescendo on Krissy Kurtz's belly and across her pubic hair. We collapsed together in an alien satisfaction as Brent Sturdivant's percussive talents on the service door behind our head continued. Krissy roared in laughter and then screamed, even though already spent . . . *"O H H BILLY BILLY B-I- L- L- L-L- Y . . . you're S-0-0-0H BIG."*

Krissy sat up and grinned, leaning over to kiss me, before giggling and rubbing some of my own goop from her belly across my cheek and then pinching my nipples with her black acrylic nails—*hard*—and until she drew a trace of blood. I'd never seen her mother, who danced at *Three Blind Dice*, but I found myself trying to imagine her . . . and trying to understand where the gene came from that turned these Kurtz women into the forbidden fruit that men so craved.

I knew that Brent was going crazy outside and was certain that he'd heard Krissy's mischievously brazen screams while he was at the back service entrance. But once again you could hear a dull thud emanating from up front.

"Guess we gotta go, eh boss?" Krissy joked, poking me in the ribs, then leaning over to give me a long passionate kiss before retrieving her panties and bra, both of which had somehow become deeply planted between the cushions and the backrest.

"Yeah, Krissy," I replied, numbly.

I sat up on the edge of the old couch, spellbound as Krissy slipped her thong over the sexy black boots which she'd worn throughout our intense sexual encounter. After the thong disappeared into the crevice of her perfect ass, she then doffed the remainder of her micro clothing before grabbing my hand and pulling me toward the door with almost childlike frolic. Near the front of the catwalk I disengaged to go liberate Brent and Krissy went to retrieve her purse from the bar. When Brent entered, his eyes were nearly the size of the bowling balls in the sales counters to his left. Krissy approached us almost skipping.

"Well, I gotta go, guys. Let me know about that job, Billy. You'll like me working here. I'll do whatever you want, babe, and that means working too," she teased with a bubbling laugh. "Oh, and Billy, honey, you were *great* . . . and I mean . . . as in like an *animal*!"

Then she was out the door, the beat up old Escort backing away and disappearing right on 66.

I was pretty certain Brent Sturdivant had completely forgotten how to talk, which was about as unlikely as it had been that I had just gotten laid by Krissy Kurtz, so the world as I'd known it an hour earlier had suddenly taken a sharp turn. Brent stood there dumbly, his mouth open, until I popped him lightly in the gut.

"Brent, not a word of this to anyone, you hear me . . . *to no one* . . . and I mean it. Butch Clayton would kick my ass so hard you'd feel it, and since you're here he'd do the same to you, so I'd feel it twice. And neither one of us needs that!"

"I'm not gonna tell anyone, Billy, but what was that about? I could hear Krissy screaming just like my Dad's pornos. Did you really screw her?" he mumbled, looking at me in awe.

"Well, what do you think?"

"How did *that* happen? I didn't know you guys had a thing going."

"We didn't. I mean we don't. She needs a job so she can stay in Dedheds and she wants to work at the alley."

"So she screws you for a job? Is that what you're saying . . . she screws you for a job?"

"I don't really know cause I'm just now starting to think about it. My brain hopped a train to Timbuktu the second I smelled her perfume and I realized we were alone. The rest is all a blur, Brent . . . all just a fucking blur."

# Chapter Twenty-six

I did hire Krissy Kurtz that fall of our junior year and she would end up working at Bowling's Bowling Center nearly three years. From the very beginning Busty Bailey was pissed, but she had to get used to it because Krissy was a worker and Busty wasn't and *somebody* had to actually work to keep the place open. However, between Krissy and Busty, we nearly *doubled* the bar crowd, though I can't say it did much for the family reputation of the alley. The women's adult league was the only serious mutiny though, pulling out to go to Starburst Alleys in Minster, ten miles away. It hurt, but even Dad admitted we made more money selling beer to the lechers than we lost when the women hiked. We lost a church group or two, also, but not enough to make much difference.

Brent Sturdivant worked church and school outings and the girls divided men's leagues and open bowling, with one behind the bar pretty much always. I, of course, was there every single fucking minute that anybody was. For the most part, Krissy was too, though when off clock she'd go in the back and watch TV, which was a real trick with twelve lanes of exploding pins a few feet away. Then one night we realized that some good old WWII fly-boy headsets and thirty foot of lead did the trick just fine. I will give Dad that he pretty much respected it as *my space,* except when absolutely necessary and I was at school. From the very beginning I realized he was glad to have me out of the trailer, especially since, within a few weeks, Busty was staying there more than half the time.

Brent worked hard and was a good employee, but as graduation approached he would move on to college, just like I should be doing . . . well that's good for a laugh anyway. The rest of junior year and as seniors, Krissy and I worked side by side at least five days a week and though we still got it on quite often, for whatever reason, it never went beyond that. Early on Butch Clayton and his brothers once threatened me at the car wash in Minster, but when I mentioned it to Krissy, I never saw them again. *Ever*. Which was exactly what she told me would happen although I never much understood how she had pulled that off and to this day have never asked.

The way Krissy dressed was just Krissy, but without even talking about it, I somehow knew she wasn't dating anyone and I would have oddly staked my life by graduation that no one else had even touched her since that first afternoon we'd made love. The sex was still incredibly intense and toward the end of our senior year she'd started staying overnight at the alley quite a bit—though we oddly went our own ways otherwise almost up until graduation. It's one of those impossible things to explain because I'd never understood it myself and I was pretty sure that Krissy didn't either.

Krissy said later that after that first afternoon of wild sex she was ashamed and believed she'd done everything wrong. If there were ever a chance for real love I would have to make the first move she had decided, although sadly afraid that I never would. Maybe our pasts were fucking us over finally, despite that we were both extremely independent people and had been long before any of our peers . . . but it was an independence founded out of sheer survival and we understood it didn't mean we were honestly adults.

I don't mean to say that our promiscuity was right or that we would condone it for our own children; it's just where we were in our lives at that time and what happened. Krissy and I answered to no one and my Dad and her Mother could have cared less. The actual sex was easy, felt good, and the passion incredibly exciting. It was the love—a love that we had each strongly felt for nearly two years—that we didn't much know how to do . . . maybe because neither of us had actually ever seen it practiced. Kind of a strange deal when you think about it I guess—that we had passionate sex for over two years before we ever *consummated* our love. Perhaps it's supposed to be the other way around, but then our entire lives had pretty much been lived backwards so in that respect it made perfect sense.

Krissy once said she thought I would have been embarrassed to be with her around school or in front of our classmates as a couple because of her reputation. Oh, but to have those two stumbling years back so I could have shown her how proud to be with Krissy Kurtz I would have been! It wasn't that we weren't connected by a lot of people, because we were, and the honest truth was that we weren't exactly high profile students and, except for Krissy's knockout looks, nobody much gave a shit about us or what we did. I mean the Dedheds left school at 11:20 each day . . . and . . . well, and . . . I was still just Billy Bowling.

After that first night of teasing Brent Sturdivant, Krissy buried that act immediately, leaving Brent in a confounded state and yet it was a subject he never again touched on around either of us. Sorta one of those deals where he understood what to do (or not do), even as he understood absolutely nothing at all. We had never talked about it and I never asked Krissy to change anything, she just did! To say I was never jealous wouldn't be accurate, but I knew early on that Krissy Kurtz could take care of herself around men and that had once even included Sam Giovanazzo . . . a story that I wouldn't, however, learn until much later on. She also told me one day that the reason she could handle about anything was from having to fight off two stepfathers and a string of low life boyfriends that her mother was always bringing home. . . .

. . . "Billy," Krissy softly said one night when we were cleaning up, having just locked the alley doors—and a few weeks before we finally fell in love like Romeo and Juliet. "I'm not a virgin, Billy, but there was only one other before you and . . ."

"You don't have to tell me this, Krissy," I said, cutting her off and really not wanting to know.

"I know, and I don't want to, but still it's not what people say about me—not even close. I've always just somehow *known* about stuff, you know—the sexy clothes and the stuff I do to get you all hot and bothered. I guess in a way I used to like it when I knew the boys and even the perverted teachers were always watching me. I know that was wrong, but it didn't mean I was out screwing guys like everyone thought and I know that part was mostly my own fault. One night, Billy, just one night, and it was really goofy— not anything like you and me. You do believe me, don't you? It's important to me that you do."

"Yeah, Krissy, I do, but I'd never try to tell you what to do. I don't ever want to do that to a person—*ever*! Cause that's what my Dad did to my Mom every single day of her life and I *hate* that. *I hate that so much!*"

"Billy, because of the way I was that first afternoon, you thought I'd been like that before didn't you, so you probably don't believe me now because I was so wild with you, right? Please tell me the truth; I really need you to. We're still pretty crazy at times, I know, but it's that first night that has always bothered me and the way I was around Brent. I would give anything to take it back, and especially how I acted around him, cause everything just came out all wrong. We've never talked about it, but it's always bothered me so much," she said, breaking into tears.

"Krissy, it's ok, it really is; whatever you tell me I believe. Since junior high I've always kind of seen you as apart. You did your thing and didn't worry about what others thought and I'd never doubt your honesty. I watch people, Krissy; I always have—and you're the best; you just are—and though I can't explain why I feel that, I have for a long time. And Jesus, Krissy, I *love* sex with you. I would never want that to change!"

There *was* a part of me that in the very beginning thought there had to be some experience behind her flirting and erotic nature, though I can honestly say it wasn't something I thought much about, even as I began to fall in love with her. Yet there was no need to say that now, and no reason for hurting Krissy with thoughts long since deceased.

"One more thing then, Billy. Should I dress different? If you want me to, I will," she said, sniffling.

"No, Krissy, I don't!" I said without pause and meant it. First of all, I loved the way Krissy dressed and had become comfortably practiced at living half my life with a hard on. But mostly it was just plain Krissy, and you don't ask people to be something else for the wrong reasons. I abhorred jealously and control and had I even hidden in my gut the desire for Krissy Kurtz to be anything other than what she was, it would have been hypocritical to air it, and I wasn't about to live my life like that.

That the guys in school and the men of Fort Harrison (and especially the lechers at the bowling alley) needed goggles to keep their eye balls off the floor was one thing that had never once bothered me about Krissy as we gravitated magnetically toward each other. I had made my mind up years earlier that I wanted to surround myself with people of confidence and sincere individuality and Krissy Kurtz sure as hell possessed both by the truck load and is why to this day we are a perfect match. I had decided that a person couldn't be honest with me if they were incapable of being honest with themselves, so her sexy outfits were a moot point, having absolutely *nothing* to do with the *person*. That was just Krissy Kurtz and how could I not love it . . . *especially since I was the one who got to take them off!*

"One more thing, Billy. I broke a guys arm one night with a hammer. I never heard no one say it around here cause I don't think anybody knows, but I want *you* to know," she'd said, now clearly holding back tears that I, of course, couldn't understand. I didn't really know how much of this I wanted to hear, but Krissy had brought it up and I could tell she wanted to tell me, so I asked, "When did you do that, Krissy, and why?"

"It was my second step-dad. He raped Tammy and I knew about it. I think Mom did too, but she always said later that she didn't, since Tammy hadn't ratted. Then one night he came into my room and after that Tammy made sure she knew what he had done to her. I was eleven and this asshole comes creeping into my room one night and sat on the edge of my bed, starting to feel my tits. I'd always wanted a gun, but I couldn't pull that off so I bought a hammer at a garage sale one day for $2. It was sort of one of those extra big ones and I always kept it beside my pillow. My Mom never knew cause she never cleaned or anything, so I reached across for it in the dark and he never saw it coming. I could see his arm framed by the streetlight shining through the window and I swung as hard as I could and was lucky because it caught the bones right between his elbow and his hand that had been wedged against the bed frame and snapped both of the bones in half. I know it was a lucky hit, but I gotta tell you that one swing changed me and sort of even Tammy's lives, crazy as that sounds," Krissy said, neither laughing nor crying, just serious and with even temperament.

"Jesus, Krissy, what happened then?" I asked.

"This fucking Cal jerk . . . Cal Johnson was his name, which is still my mom's name and kinda makes me wanna puke. Anyhow, he's screaming and wailing and running around the room in circles. It was really weird. It was about 3 in the morning and Mom and Tammy came running to the door and flipped the lights on and Cal's arm is like just hanging by the skin. It almost made me sick, too, but I was goddamn proud, Billy. I know that sounds bad, but I was proud. From that point on I was determined that *no one* would ever again touch me that I didn't let touch me. *Ever!* It would *never* happen, even if I had to kill someone the next time—or even if I had to die. And it never has. That's what's so funny about you thinking Butch Clayton ever touched me. Butch is a candy ass, Billy, and he knew better than to even try. He got off just thinking that people *thought* he fucked me. That was his game and after a while even that began to bother me, but only after you came into my life, because I don't give one shit about what anyone *else* thinks."

"It's ok, Krissy, I understand . . . and I always have. You don't need to explain one thing to me, girl, because you're a jewel and I've always felt that way," I said, reaching over with my right arm to pull her close to me. "So what *did* happen to Cal? I *would* love to know that," I finished with a light chuckle that I could feel served to loosen things up all the way around.

"Well, he was screaming at Mom to take him to the hospital, but Mom had picked up one of my boots beside the bed after she'd come over to me and, turning, threw it as hard as she could at him with an almost better luck shot than I'd had, cause the heel hit him just under the eye and cut a big gash that started bleeding like crazy and took five stitches to close. The guy was messed up, Billy. *Big time.* It was pretty much, Kurtz women 2, Assholes 0 that night. Mom screamed at him to get the fuck out and I never saw him again. Later she told me he went back to Kentucky cause she said if she ever saw him again or he filed papers to get even one thing out of the house, she'd file rape charges for Tammy. She wanted to do it anyhow, but Tammy talked her out of it although I wished she wouldn't have, and a few years later Tammy wished she hadn't too."

*Krissy Kurtz was special then and she is special now and if I wrote a hundred books I'd probably never quite be able to explain her to you. She's just one of those rare people who make you happy to be alive and to know her . . . and to be her husband (you did get that from the Prologue, I think?) . . . well, to be her husband . . . oh, forget it . . . cause there sure as hell is no way I could possibly explain what that's like and I guarantee that you're never gonna know! But should you ever decide to take the wonderful summer trek north across the great Mackinac Bridge to Romano's North, just outside Curtis, Michigan, she may very likely greet you at the Trattoria door. Or if you should find yourself south, stop during the winter months in Jupiter, Florida, at Romano Rinata, where she might just happen to be doing the same . . . and then with confidence I am most certain you will then understand.*

# *Chapter Twenty-seven*

*A*fter Jimmy and Gwen graduated in 1992, my freshman year, nothing too earth shaking came down at FHHS with the exception of Brent spying Sam Giovanazzo screwing Mindy Dalinghaus early during our senior year. . . . oh, and of course, the priceless monkeyshines of Darf Pannebecker. As for football state championships, Giovanazzo's charges never pulled off another (after Jimmy's senior year in '91), until '95, the first year Krissy and I were out of school and pretty much running the alley full time together. The asshole did manage another state wrestling title in the winter of '94 though. Dirk Salisbury was state champion at 166 that year and 172 the next, although the team didn't place top five our senior year. I only know about the weights and all that crap because, after awhile—working the BBC bar—that kind of shit starts to echo off the walls. Otherwise, everything was fairly boring and uneventful . . . unless you counted as excitement watching everybody head off to college in the fall while Krissy and I got the bonus opportunity of spending the *entire* day now at the alley so Dad could get drunk early in the morning instead of mid morning.

I must say, however, that graduation itself did turn out to be pretty special—in fact a fantastic day for Krissy and myself that remains one of the most magical days of our lives—though understand, it had absolutely *nothing* to do with receiving a diploma or going through the painfully stupid ceremonies! . . .

. . . Senior Commencement was Sunday, June 4, 1995, at Robbins Field. Dad actually said he was going to come, which in and of itself (just saying it, I mean) sorta blew me away, but ultimately he was a *no-show,* which was no great surprise nor something that much upset my day. Besides, I knew he was drunk anyhow when he'd said it to me one Monday in a rare good mood after winning $1500 at a tournament that weekend. My Grammy Romano was too sick to come, but Uncle Marco came and *it caused quite the stir* . . .

Uncle Marco was 46 and a widower at the time, having been married when he was quite young. Mom once said that his wife, Holly, was very beautiful and that Marco had worshipped her, but when he was 25 and Holly 24, she died of a rare form of ocular cancer. According to Mom, for over ten years after her death, Marco never once dated despite his movie star good looks, as Mom always put it. Even later when he did she said she was certain he'd probably stay a bachelor for life, though the single women on the planet would be the biggest losers she used to joke with bright eyes, of course always in the absence of Dad.

So anyway, Marco tools up I-75 in his black BMW 750IL, which I would come to find out years later he had just snagged the week before for $72,000 cash. But more than that, and what kicked Krissy's ass, is that he is the *absolute* spitting image of Michael Douglas, the actor . . . so much so that everyone in Fort Harrison thought he *was* Michael Douglas and honestly a lot of people still believe Michael Douglas attended the 1995 FHHS Commencement to this day.

Now Marco is cool and as genuine as they come and not a phony, but he has fun on occasion with the Michael Douglas gig and thought that I would get a hoot from it, knowing I've really got no family to embarrass—and he wasn't wrong on that account, that's for sure. Marco's always been a car nut and had pretty big money, partly because he'd managed *Romano's* for a decade by then, the most successful restaurant in Cincinnati, but especially because he was one of the top *sommeliers* (wine steward) in the world, which I didn't know at the time nor could have told you what it meant. He would go to France, Italy and California (appraisal trips he called them), and then just by giving wine recommendations and lending his signature to fine restaurants all over the place, he raked in thousands.

Well, Fort Harrison's pretty easy to find—just West off I-75 about twelve miles—and Marco found himself getting there earlier that day than he'd expected. He didn't stop at the alley because he hadn't much use for my Dad and never had—surprise. So he tools down Main, finds Robbins Field, and as he's crossing the bridge takes the first vacant parking spot right outside the iron gates where everyone has to walk right by the ole' 750IL, which looks like a mobster's car and definitely the first of its type to pass within the village limits of Fort Harrison. An hour early, he decides to walk up town, stopping by Jesperson's Restaurant for coffee, which is always open Sundays for the church crowd. He had on a dark navy pin-stripe suit, Italian shoes—the whole works, you know—pink silk tie on soft blue dress shirt plus the slicked back, jet black Romono hair. I mean it is incredibly eerie . . . *he is Michael Douglas*! So people are like falling all over themselves, 'Mr. Douglas this, Mr. Douglas that,' though I guess he drew the line at autographs, which in Fort Harrison didn't much piss anybody off; after all, they were graced by his mere presence and the gossip that it would generate, which was always a welcome commodity in Fort Harrison.

Neither Krissy nor I got a chance to see Marco before the penguin walk cause they had us stashed in the football weight room so we could come in from the east side of the stadium. I guess Judy Tredway, the choir chick who was in charge of the graduation logistics, thought that tucking us away in Bum Fuck Egypt was a *choreographic coup* that would guarantee her a ticket on the fast train to Broadway. By the time the actual Commencement started, the buzz that Michael Douglas was in the stadium had reached us anyway. The entire town was beside itself, especially given that everyone had to file by the Bimmer (which, by the way, *is* the correct 'nickname' spelling for a BMW automobile—as 'Beemer' is a BMW motorcycle) mega-car that cost more than half the houses in the school district. When I first heard the buzz about Michael Douglas I got a rush because I remembered Mom once saying Uncle Marco always did Halloween parties as ole' MD, so I was pretty sure that the gig was on. Of course the truth is—he really didn't have to do anything but clean up a bit.

Krissy was in a row across the aisle from me and I never got to talk to her until the drag was over. Some Fort Harrison alumni—a Dr. Leonard Shope—who'd graduated from FHHS like a hundred years earlier and was now a big shot dentist in California and part owner of the San Diego Chargers, had been exhumed to give the Commencement speech. I caught both Soup Beckman and Karen Fish yawning all over the place, which in some ways I sort of respected because it was an almost human act instead of their usual phony horseshit. But seriously, I mean the guy sucked big time and if he was supposed to be a role model for the Class of '95, we should have just marched then and there straight up the stadium steps and trashed ourselves over the railing and onto Robbins Road like a legion of Alaskan Lemmings single-filing off a fucking cliff. I mean in 2004, several years after Beckman and Wickerdick had retired, they got Darf Pannabecker for Commencement! Can you believe that? *Darf Pannabecker*! Now I'll admit I heard later from Brent Sturdivant, whom I talked to occasionally on the phone over the years, that the big shots were kind of sorry they did cause Darf wasn't too politically correct and all, but give me a break, what did they expect? Still, it was a big deal for Fort Harrison at that time cause the town had been in a shambles since '96 and in desperate need of a hero of *any* kind. But seriously, I would have handed my diploma back to hear Darf Pannabecker speak at a FHHS Commencement.

. . . Anyway, when all the horseshit was finally over and everybody was plugging up Robbins Road all over the place, I met Krissy by the exit under the football bleachers. "Way to go girl," I said and kissed her, although at that time we *still* weren't yet Romeo and Juliet. Krissy was leaning back to kiss me when Marco walked up behind me and put his hand on my shoulder, but before turning I had noticed Krissy eyes double in size, I swear as truth.

"Billy, congratulations, kid," Marco said, pumping my hand. "And who might this lovely young lady be?" The resemblance to Michael Douglas *was* eerie I then really understood for the first time and later Krissy told me there was absolutely no doubt in her mind that's who he was at the time.

"This is my friend, Krissy Kurtz. We work together at the alley. Krissy, this is my Uncle Marco from Cincinnati. He's my mother's brother." Afterwards I could have kicked myself for not playing the game too and introducing him as my Uncle Michael, but I fucked up, what can I say? It was honestly the *only* time that I ever saw Krissy Kurtz frozen in place, speechless, and awed by *anybody*.

"You thought he was Michael Douglas, right, Krissy?" I said, laughing lightly, but making sure she knew it wasn't at her. Marco hooked his arm inside hers and started to steer us toward the big black Bimmer. Krissy was in heaven, and still admits that today, particularly after an hour or so of sitting around Escape Lake— *sampling* Marco's incredible wines. It's a fun story that never gets old.

We were standing beside the car when Lacy Johnson walked up by herself. She was between idiots, I found out later, and Tammy hadn't come for a reason I can't remember now. But honestly, Mrs. Johnson was kick-ass hot that night, yet dressed really very smartly. A shorter skirt and higher heels than most, but still quite tasteful— and now the *men* were scoping *her* out more than ole' MD. It was all incredibly comical in some ways, but for Krissy and me, it was really very cool . . . a*nd very much fun*. Marco did a double take on Lacy, and then looking from Krissy to her mother and back said (before I had been able to fashion an introduction), "You are obviously this lovely young lady's mother. I'm Marco Romano, Billy's uncle . . . and you might be?"

I'd met Lacy several times by then and she was a bit on the rough side, yet you certainly couldn't tell it that day. I mean not too many strippers at *Three Blind Dice* learned their trade at finishing school, but she was far from stupid and, of course, the cloth from which Krissy was cut. She'd obviously done the MD take like everyone else, but was very charming through the whole introduction and never really missed a beat star struck or tongue tied or spitting out a stupid phrase or anything. I was extremely impressed and so was Marco, I could tell, but like Krissy, Lacy was a survivor and surviving involves adapting and ultimately an unusual comfort in dealing with anything thrown your way.

Marco reached for her hand as she extended it and replied, "Very nice to meet you, Mr. Romano, I'm Lacy Johnson . . . and yes, I *am* Krissy's mother."

"Are there other family members coming?" Marco asked, looking from Krissy to her mother.

"No, Krissy's sister wasn't able to come today," Lacy answered.

"A Mr. Johnson?" Marco posed, waiting.

At that, Lacy let out an almost mischievous chuckle. "No, Mr. Romano, there is no Mr! I am on a *sabbatical,* I guess you could say."

I wasn't certain I had heard right, but Marco laughed out loud and somewhere an echo bounced back off Robbins Stadium and I knew I *had* heard right and was impressed. The cool thing that hit me about her almost immediately was that she wasn't *trying* to be, say, or act any way, which is exactly what had impressed me about Krissy since before junior high school, but took me so many years to really understand. The 'sabbatical joke' had rolled off her tongue spontaneously and nothing seemed forced with Lacy. I knew she'd had a tough life and that she and Krissy knocked heads from time to time, but she was a pretty cool lady and for the first time Krissy Kurtz made *total* sense to me.

"Well then, ladies and gentleman," Marco said, clasping his hands. "Are there plans for dinner or may we make them now? You ladies *will* join us for dinner, won't you?"

Krissy and I had talked of dinner after graduation, but since I wasn't sure what the deal with Marco would be we had never made plans. Now he was including Krissy's mother, which seemed quite appropriate and we all looked to Lacy for a reply when Marco spoke again.

"I have a delightful idea and if you accept my suggestion, I, of course, will stand as host for the evening. How does that sound? Are you game, Mrs. Johnson?" Marco asked, looking toward Lacy.

"It's not necessary, Mr. Romano. Take the kids; that would be fine," she replied.

"If you would call me Marco, please. Are you saying you are committed elsewhere? And may I call you Lacy?"

"Certainly, Marco . . . and no, I'm not busy, I just . . ."

"Wonderful, we shall all go together then," Marco said cheerfully.

"That would be very nice, Mr. Romano . . . Marco, I mean, but we shall split . . ."

"Nonsense—my restaurant, my tab. And besides, I told you the rules, and unless you have a local preference, my suggestion is *l'Auberge.* We're maybe 50 minutes away, but it's only 4:30. Would that be agreeable or are there other suggestions? Bear in mind, Chef Niahros is a close friend and that might be worth a few perks . . . and I suggest it highly."

I'd never heard of (*l'Auberge?*) or knew where it was, but suspected Dayton since Marco said 50 minutes away. Lima was much closer, but had no restaurant that would likely meet Marco's standards. Krissy was awash with excitement and words were lost upon her just then while something told me Lacy Johnson was very impressed by Marco's choice.

Lacy and Krissy looked toward me. "Marco, that's great I'm sure. Krissy and I aren't particular, just not sure where that is," I'd said, which had sounded a bit lame I then realized.

"*l'Auberge* is in North Dayton. Some say, after Romano's of course, that it's the finest in the Midwest. If agreed, I need to place a call to Chef Niahros. I'm sure we'll be ok; it's part of the pull I have," he'd said, winking with a grin. "Of course we might have to eat in the kitchen with the cook staff," he laughed, turning to open the Bimmer door for Lacy.

"Marco, are you sure I am dressed for *l'Auberge*?" Lacy asked, obviously acquainted with the restaurant and I was starting to get the idea it was quite special.

"You will be the most beautiful woman there, I assure you," he said, holding the door for her to slide in, then closing it behind her and asking, "Are you kids ready?"

"Sure, Uncle Marco," I said as I held the door for Krissy who slid inside, still in a dream state. The interior of the Bimmer was luxury like I hadn't known even existed. Krissy turned to me with dancing fun eyes and leaned over to give me a light kiss as my groin stirred. Yet it would still be most of a year before we understood love and that was probably a good thing. Most people jump way too quickly, though somehow at the time we were both afraid to even hop. But that night was golden!

As we drove away, the *Children of the Corn* followed us with eyes you could almost feel. I could have written a whole book about that afternoon and evening, and the Fort Harrisoners who truly thought then—and would for years to come—that Billy Bowling and the trailer park mother-daughter tandem from 'across the tracks' had just been whisked away in a limo by Michael Douglas.

Dining at *l'Auberge* that evening was special, and the owner and waitresses fell all over themselves as if Marco were the second coming. It was truly a surreal experience for us and to this day, except for the birth of Eli, I kid Krissy that I've never yet managed to top that night in her life. She scoffs at me, but I know it's true, for you couldn't have invented a night like that if it was your full time job for a decade. As far as what Marco and Lacy did that evening after dropping us off—well—I guess we'll never know cause neither has ever had any inclination to satisfy our curiosity. I'm fine with that, but as for Krissy . . . *it drives her crazy!*

# Chapter Twenty-eight

*A*fter Jimmy graduated I could have cared less about football, but trying to avoid the topic at the bowling alley was like trying to avoid idiots at a school board meeting, and in the fall of 1995, the DCA was having a banner year, tossing down beer and shots at a near record pace . . . which both 'lined our pockets' and provided Thin Jim Bowling with a much higher quality of vodka I'd noticed, having recently switched from Popov to Absolut, double the price. I saw the upgrade as I dumped the garbage from behind the trailer each week, which was bullshit, but something that would have never come to pass had I not done it myself.

There were three 'firewater' distributors who plied their wares at Bowling's Bowling Center. Nate Bertke, who had been a big shot football player at Fort Harrison in the 80's and had been on both the '82 and '83 state championship teams, was the sales rep for Griffin Beverages out of Wapakoneta. Apparently he had long ago inked a private treaty with Dad, stashing his vodka in a mystical spot I never did disrobe over the years. Tom Swift was the rep for C&G Distributors in Lima and the source for about three quarters of our hooch, and Sal Nichols from Ciminellos wine distributors in Dayton stopped by once in a blue moon to see if we needed any wine, which was pretty much a joke at the alley. A couple of gallons of white and red Gallo pretty much set up the year and I usually just bought it at *Wal-Mart* in Lima when I went to stock up on stuff the drive-by boys didn't tote in their saddle bags.

One day while making his rounds, Tom ordered a burger and we got to talking a little past mid-morning. . . .

"You're like an armadillo, aren't you, Tom?" I joked, sitting the burger down and throwing in a batch of our fairly famous onion rings that I told him were on the house.

'How's that, Billy?" he'd answered, curiously.

"Come on, Tom, think about it; you have the safest job on the planet. When times are good and people are happy and teams are winning and parties are planned, people drink like fish. When people are pissed, sad and lonely, when they've just been fired or found out somebody's fucking their wife or when their favorite team just got trashed, they drink like bigger fish. You can't lose . . . *ever!* Not until the planet flies off its orbit and burns up like a San Diego County wildfire. What a job you got, man," I said, reaching across to give him a good-natured slap on the shoulder.

"I know, Billy . . . and to think two thirds of my high school class went to college. Crazy world, huh?"

. . . Oh yeah . . . then there was *the thing* with Candy 'Busty' Bailey and Dad. I don't get too excited even thinking about it, much less trying to fashion it into words, but I guess it needs to get penned in the story somewhere. I mean if it weren't for who I am, it would be funny as hell I suppose, but I am, so it's not. But life's like that isn't it? It pretty much depends on which side of the fence you're on as to whether something's hilarious, painful or maybe even tragic. To everyone else in Fort Harrison it was a royal hoot, but what the hell, it *is* the Bowling 'family' after all, so where's the big surprise?

Candy Bailey started working as a Dedhed at Bowling's Bowling Center in the fall of 1990, her (and Jimmy's) junior year in high school. Jimmy not only held a peck of FHHS football records, but may have also been the youngest kid in the Fort Harrison School district to ever get laid, having kidded with me once that he'd screwed Candy the summer before they were in seventh grade in the dugout over at Sower's Field. That made Jimmy and Candy twelve at the time . . . *if that.*

Busty's huge tits helped considerably to steer all eyes south of her ole' banana, which was proportionately even larger and had anyone first seen a profile of Candy peering out the window of a car, their verdict would have necessarily rendered her a large Toucan. But the reality was that her tits were a gold mine and her entire life was defined by their majesty . . .so nobody much noticed her nose. Had she possessed even a marginal personality (which she didn't), it wouldn't have stood a snowball's chance in hell to get a word in edgeways. Huge, hard and haughty—that described ole' Busty to an 'H!'

Jimmy probably had the aggregate record for screwing Busty the six years preceding his Fort Harrison departure, but it was definitely a competitive event, cause another ten to twenty of Fort Harrison's finest derelicts also took their shot on a regular basis—the low number for straight fucks, the higher if you threw in blowjobs. Jimmy knew it all though, from the get-go, and didn't much care. One night when I went to throw trash in the dumpster I heard moans and squeals coming from Garth Schmutz's F250 Ford pickup where Garth and Busty were going at it like a pair of mink, even though the truck was parked right under the security light. I wasn't sure what to do, but decided to say something to Jimmy cause Busty was supposed to be on the clock at the time, which was a joke anyhow. He was a senior, and by then was rarely at the alley so he could have cared less about her clock time, and just laughed it off anyhow saying, 'Relax, cowboy, I always use a rubber; besides the more practice she gets the better she is when I take my shots.'

Early on I had my suspicions that Dad also held a ticket for the inside of her underwear, and even before Jimmy left Fort Harrison, though I honestly can't swear to that timeline and have no facts to support my theory. No matter though, because late my sophomore year, and a few months after Jimmy left for the Marines, I walked in on Busty giving Dad a blowjob in his office. They saw me and didn't even stop—and of course, Dad never mentioned it later. Norman Rockwell would have been proud.

I don't want to do this much longer cause it's fairly painful—and particularly stupid—so let me speed the timeline up. First of all when Busty graduated in '92 along with Jimmy, Dad hired her full time, which meant instead of working 7 minutes a day she now actually worked 11, but in retrospect, considering the blowjobs, I guess I understood. Even I've always admitted the 3 H's pulled in the bar bums and that the chances of pulling off a Garth Schmutzeroo in the alley parking lot were a hell of a lot better than winning an Ohio lottery scratch off card for ten bucks. And as far as I could tell it was all acceptable to Thin Jim Bowling so the years danced merrily along for the team—*the team at Bowling's Bowling Center . . . in Fort Harrison, Ohio.*

By the way, the happy couple, *Thin Jim* and *Busty (Bowling),* was married in Las Vegas on New Years Day, 1996. Dad was 49, Busty 23. But wait, it gets better. They were married at the Garden of Love Chapel with the *Deluxe Elvis Package Wedding.* So how'd I know that? Well (again) I was throwing out the trailer garbage when the invoice from Dad's credit card wafted away in the wind toward Winston Thermostat's soybean field with a life of its own— sort of dancing in the wind like that bag in *American Beauty.* For some inexplicable reason I decided to retrieve it and when my eyes focused on what it was, I wasn't sure whether to cry or laugh, but somehow the laugh button got pushed.

. . . The Garden of Love Wedding Chapel in Las Vegas, Nevada, offered Elvis Standard and Deluxe packages, a Tim McGraw package and a Rodney Dangerfield package. There was also an option of a drive-through wedding. The Elvis Deluxe had cost Dad $599. It included the marriage license, an Elvis look-alike pastor who also sang either *Love Me Tender* or *I Can't Help Falling In Love With You* per decision. The pastor's wife was the witness. Had Dad and the lovely bride chosen the standard package for $399, the musical score would have been deleted, so they'd obviously made a wise choice for a measly $200 extra bucks and certainly a much more romantic one. It could have been worse though, I suppose, for they could have chosen the Rodney Dangerfield package and then the wedding would have most certainly been a real joke. But then, by now you know just how cynical *I* can be . . . sorry.

So as the birds began to sing and the alley bequeathed its treasure chest of wondrous athletes to the Fort Harrison Golf Club in the spring of 1996, I had come to understand there was no way in hell I would stay in Fort Harrison long enough to entertain the arrival of another football/bowling season, even if it meant jumping off the village water tower into Mast Quarry. I had been in contact with Uncle Marco and we had talked about both Krissy and me moving there to get an apartment and work at *Romanos*. It was the first week of April that we talked one night on the phone . . .

"How's it going up there, Billy?"

"That's a dumb question, Marco. It sucks."

"And your Dad . . . and his new bride?" he'd queried with a snicker.

"That's not even funny, Marco. I'm a fucking idiot to be here. What else can I say?"

"How's that cutie of yours doing?"

"She's great. We stay together a lot and work together every day, but I've never really told her how I feel. I just don't know how, even though I know that sounds stupid. I love her and have for two years, but I've never even told her that. I've never told anyone I've loved them my whole life."

"I understand, Billy; I really do. She have another guy or something?"

"It's not that, Marco, cause I'm pretty sure she feels the same way I do."

"I think you and Krissy are afraid because you've never seen love work. It doesn't mean it can't work for you guys; in fact it probably guarantees that it can. I know you're still young and nobody's talking marriage here, but that bowling alley is going to destroy you both. I just know it, Billy. I know more than you think. Your mother and I were very close and talked more than anyone knows . . . and especially about your Dad. If you really love her, tell her, and then both of you get out of there. I can give you good jobs and teach you anything you want to know. We haven't talked a lot, but you've always told me you wanted to be a Chef. Even your Mom told me you said that when you were a little kid every time you went home from Romanos. You still feel that way?"

"Oh yes, Marco, but I never let myself think about it cause I knew I'd always have to stay here and run the alley . . . probably my whole life."

"That's all bullshit up there, Billy. Get out now and make a life for yourself . . . and bring that sweet little thing with you if she wants. She's a beauty. When I met her and her mother at your graduation, and we went to l'Auberge, I was really quite impressed with them both. There's real substance to that girl and that's not very common these days for a girl her age. She's got something extra and I might be careful not to lose her . . . besides being a knock-out which you well know."

"I know, Marco. I know it all."

"I gotta go. Your Grammy is very ill. I wish you'd come see her, but understand she may not even know you. I told you that before, but it's been getting much worse and you can almost see it now by the day. The offer's on the table," he said, as the dial tone trumped the last of his waning words.

# Chapter Twenty-nine

Then there was *Baxter Sturdivant*! Baxter Sturdivant was an enigma, a perfectly coined word that defined him *To a T!* Which of course meant we have absolutely no rational way to define him at all.

The summer following our graduation I realized someone would have to replace Brent at the alley. As Dad drank more, Brent had become very important and his presence was pretty much the only thing that had ever allowed me to once in a blue moon escape with the marginal goal of trying to maintain my sanity. Just watching TV in the back as the pins pounded about was still a break, knowing Brent could take care of most things without running to me. *(It's been nearly eleven years since I was last in the alley, and still the percussive sound of exploding bowling pins ring in my head. I once wondered how many million times in my life I'd heard that sound? And if it would ever go away?)*

Anyway, before he left for college, Brent had lobbied for his little brother Baxter to take his spot. Baxter would be a sophomore that coming year, which was the same age Brent had been when he started working for us so in a way it seemed to make sense. Yet for all the years that Brent and I had been best friends, I hardly knew Baxter at all, and like everyone else (I'm now sorry to say), the fact that he was named Baxter unwittingly had created the same image in my mind that it unfortunately had in pretty much everyone else's— *Baxter Sturdivant was surely a geek!*

Brent had landed his precious scholarship to Kenyon, though Molly Schmuckel had edged him for Valedictorian, which had driven Brent nearly to the edge of suicide, but by mid summer he'd gotten over it and was looking forward to whatever guys who are going to major in *French Philosophy* and minor in *Statistics* look forward to, let alone what they're going to do for a job afterwards.

The whole Molly Schmucker/Brent Sturdivant thing was sort of a hoot I thought, and there was a part of me that was pretty certain he had a thing for her, but Brent would have been slower to the draw than I was . . . and look at me. If two families should have gone off to rent a lake cabin together some summer, it should have been the Sturdivants and the Schmuckels. One of my favorite movies, *The Great Outdoors* with John Candy and Dan Ackroyd couldn't have held a candle to the silly shit that would have come down with those two families together. . . .

*. . . (Ok, I'm going to throw this in now cause it won't much fit later.) Brent Sturdivant and Molly Schmuckel did, not only get together, but were married in China, eight years after graduation, where Molly had taken a job as field representative for UNICEF (United Nation's Children Fund). Molly had graduated from Oberlin College with a major in Ethnic Studies and gone on to Stanford where she earned both an M.A. and PhD. in Advanced East Asian Studies (all of which I'd learned years later). I'd pretty much lost track of Brent when Krissy and I blew Fort Harrison for Florida in the Fall of '96, so I don't know the romantic course of their courtship. I just know the status now. Brent never did get a job, but then in 2005 Molly left UNICEF and took a faculty position as Director of International Studies at Middlebury College in Vermont, just twenty miles south of Shelburne, the corporate headquarters of Vermont Teddy Bear, Inc. where Brent eventually landed the job he now has as 'Director of Bear Counseling (DBC)' as I, somewhat cynically earlier noted. At last count I was told they were the proud parents of two Children of the Corn.*

. . . Anyhow, Baxter turned out to be a real unexpected gift and cool as hell. For whatever reason, Gordie and Lorinda, after choosing two quite normal names, Kylie and Brent, had saddled their third and last child with Baxter (and it wasn't like a family name or something as if Lorinda had been a Baxter), yet I soon found out that Baxter himself was quite proud of his name—specifically requesting no nicknames, middle name (Cameron) usage, nor abbreviated 'Bax.' *'Baxter was Baxter'* and he let that be known the first time I spoke with him about working for us.

Whereas Brent was incredibly excitable, Baxter was as low key as a person could get and still be breathing, but he was funnier than a pile of dog shit guilefully placed on Wickerdick's desk (which it was rumored had happened in the spring of '93, Darf Pannabecker's senior year . . .surprise). In fact, Baxter had the best sense of humor of anyone I've ever been around in my life—when you were lucky enough to hear him, that is—cause half the time he talked like Leslie, the *low-talker* who tricked Seinfeld into wearing the puffy shirt on the *Today Show*. So Krissy and I had to fine-tune our auditory ossicles, along with *asking* Baxter to *'FUCKING TALK LOUDER!'* We knew that Baxter loved profanity (although he never used it) and he reacted accordingly, never having been around it much. His take on life and people, however, was golden. I thought I had a pretty good grasp of cynical reality, but Baxter Sturdivant could put me to shame—and he was a Sturdivant to boot—go figure.

I always understood why Brent was pretty much a geek and I suspect almost everyone assumed the same of Baxter, which he honestly never much fought. My theory was that Gordie and Lorinda were much more comfortable with geeky kids than they would have been with normal ones so I had it figured that at home Baxter was a geek cause he was the type that would put up with ridiculous shit to make his parents comfortable—and especially, I came to believe later on, because he could look decades ahead and understood that since he would soon be flying the coop, what was the harm in keeping peace on the home front?

Baxter did things at work a light-year ahead of Brent, and Brent was the best worker we'd ever had before. Baxter would do things before I even thought they needed done and he was *always* right. It was at times almost eerie. He was a great help to us, that was certain . . . *and someone Krissy would eventually need to lean on more than we could have ever known.*

*Baxter Cameron Sturdivant graduated from FHHS in 1998, a year and a half after Krissy and I had settled in Florida and at a time the entire village of Fort Harrison was in ruins. He then attended Drexel University in Philadelphia where he would earn his Jurist Doctorate with an M.S. in Sports Management thrown in for good measure and would, just a few short years later, become one of the top personal agents in professional sports, carving out a niche for NFL quarterback representation with clients like Ben Rothlisberger and Drew Brees, for whom he has made kazillions while raking in already, at the age of 28, millions for himself in the process. Clever as he is, Krissy and I still joke that maybe he's low-talked the high-end contracts and that they really didn't understand what was coming down. (jk)*

# Part Two

## Paradise Lost

## 1996

*"Long is the way and Hard,*
*that out of Hell leads up to Light"*
*(John Milton, 'Paradise Lost' Book ii, Line 432)*

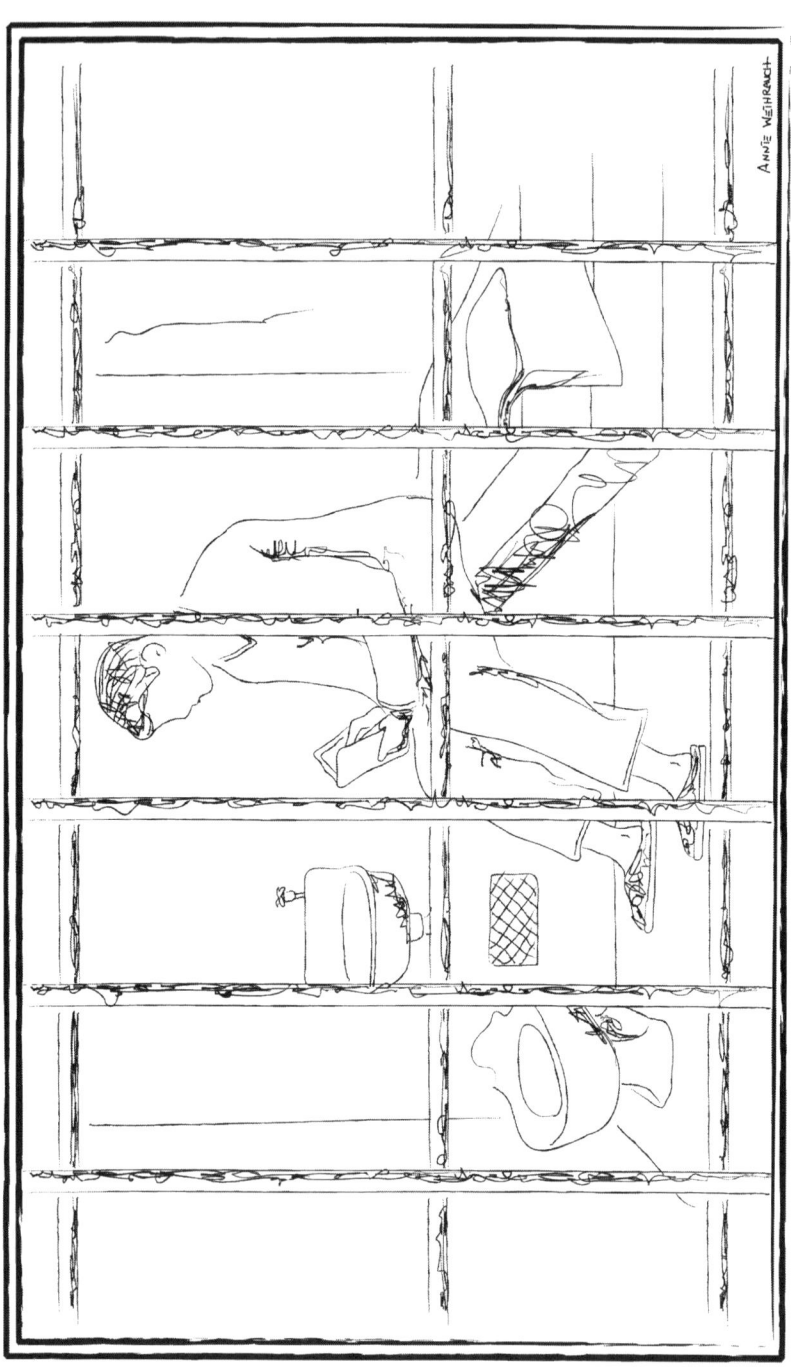

# Chapter Thirty

*A*s the spring of 1996 drew near, I knew I had to get away from the BBC and the town of Fort Harrison, Ohio. Krissy and I were both nearly twenty and it was time to tell her my heart and see if she felt the same. And if she did, I felt that the first step on that road would be to accept Marco's offer and move to Cincinnati where I believed the beginning of our dreams awaited.

That my father hadn't attended my graduation was no big deal, nor honestly was the fact that he'd never said he loved me, for I knew it was an 'old school' thing and that, as a son, I wasn't the Lone Ranger. But that he never said five words to me any day of the year except to give orders *was* a big deal—and that *he alone* was the reason there had never even been a Bowling family was unforgivable. I was *The Last Slave Left*, which should have been the title for this book . . . 'Open your eyes, Cowboy, just open your fucking eyes,' bombarded my senses these days more than the tympani of exploding pins and it was time to hold a funeral for both. *I had come to understand that what I wanted most was a purpose in life, not just a job or an income or an existence . . . and a family . . . which I hoped would one day be with Krissy Kurtz.*

Dad had Busty. She could have the fucking bowling alley; I didn't want it, although he comically still thought it was a carrot to hold in front of my nose that I would tremble to think of losing. I hated that bowling alley, hated the sound of busting pins and the putrid smell of rental shoes, and most of all I loathed the turnstile existence of the drunks who swung from the DCA to the BBC like the serpentine belt of an Edsel, living in a past that for most of them was a lie anyhow . . . and worshipping that perverted criminal, Sam Giovanazzo.

Above all, I was convinced that, with or without college educations—*twogether*—Krissy Kurtz and Billy Bowling could achieve success and discover a happiness that most kids our age couldn't hope to even understand. I also believed that, when we got there, we would be smart and we would be humble—for I had *finally* come to understand what I loved *most* about Krissy Kurtz! She saw a fucked up world and rose above it. I saw it too, but was pretty sure I needed her to help me climb up to where she had risen on her own.

*But as I was dreaming about the future with building confidence on that Wednesday, April 17, 1996, the phone call came that would change my life forever!*

. . . Incredibly, Dad was vertical that afternoon at 5 when the phone rang. He was also actually working, putting some new bolts in the old wooden chair seats, which though much stronger than the new plastic ones the reps were always trying to get us to buy, nevertheless took a beating and had needed attention for quite some time. I knew it too, but had decided to launch my *Fuck You Rebellion* (which Dad hadn't yet seemed to notice), having literally been taken hostage by the disturbing visions of that day Jimmy angrily blasted seven straight strikes on Lane 6—most of them from five feet or more behind the toe-line and while holding a Miller High Life can in his left hand to boot.

Dad had dropped what he was doing to go answer, probably figuring it was his lovely wife, Busty, whom I guess he still figured he was in love with—the Elvis wedding only a few months removed at that point.

"Billy, it's for you," he yelled with charm. I was behind the bar dumping a bucket of cocktail ice that I'd just snagged from the ice machine in the basement. Who would be calling me? Krissy had the night off and was going to visit her mother and go to dinner in Lima. Ever since graduation and l'Auberge, ten months earlier, their relationship had improved considerably. She told me Lacy had a new boyfriend that Krissy hadn't yet met, and though she really didn't want to meet him, figured it was the reason for the night out and that she was expecting to be ambushed. But, as always, I was confident Krissy could handle whatever came her way so I doubted it was her on the phone. Passing the double door on the way to the office I saw Baxter walking up the sidewalk, so the call was from God only knew.

"Do you know who it is, Dad?" I asked as I passed him.

"It's Gwen Putnam, that runner Jimmy used to date. Be quick about it, we got work to do," he barked, which was comical since I was the one who'd prepped and run nearly every league night for three years while he was passed out in his office or in the trailer.

Ambushed by a slow echo, I stopped in front of Dad. Had he just said Gwen Putnam? Surely not. He had to be mistaken. "Gwen Putnam, Dad? Is that who you said? Jesus, why would Gwen Putnam call me? Did she think Jimmy was home or something?" I asked, my heart all of a sudden pounding and jumping into my throat even though I hadn't thought much about Gwen for years.

"Billy, fuck it then; don't talk to her; I don't care. We got work to do anyhow. Goddamn league starts in an hour."

. . . "H'lo?" I said stupidly (no 'Billy here, may I help you' or 'Gwen, Dad said it was you, what a nice surprise.') Nope, not me . . . just a stupid lame, butchered 'hello.'

"Billy, is that you? It's great to hear you," she said as I felt my face and ears flush with a rush of blood even though I was just on the phone.

"Jimmy's not home, Gwen. Did you think he was?"

"No, Billy, I didn't expect Jimmy to be there. I know he's overseas. I'd really like to talk to you about a research paper I'm working on. I have a four-day break from school so could we meet sometime so I can explain how you could help me with it?" she asked.

"I guess, Gwen, sure. I mean how could I help you with a research paper?"

" I'll explain it to you when we meet. Is there any way you could meet me at Samsal's tomorrow around eleven for lunch, or do you have to work at the alley? Or Billy, is there a girlfriend that should maybe come along?" she'd asked, graciously.

*Me, Billy Bowling, being invited to have lunch with Gwen Putnam?* Somehow that just didn't fit. And how could I possibly help her with a research paper?

"Hello . . . Billy . . . you there?" Gwen finally asked, snapping me back to reality.

"Yeah, I'm here Gwen, sorry. That'd be fine, sure, I'm free I guess. I don't really have to be at the alley in the morning," I stuttered. It was spring and everybody was playing golf. Men's league wrapped up last week and women's did tonight. This was one time of the year that, yes, even Billy Bowling had some free time . . . so he'd just get his little ole' appointment book out and chalk Gwen Putnam in. Yes, that should work just fine.

"Great, Billy, I'll look forward to it. See you tomorrow—eleven o'clock at Samsal's," she said and hung up as I sat dumbly in Dad's chair, staring at the wall.

"Billy, goddammit, are you off the phone yet? Get your ass back to the bar and finish up, then . . . then . . ."

*It wasn't a dream.* Dad's bitching delivered me back to reality, but whatever, it was a reality that included lunch tomorrow with Gwen Putnam which was about as good as reality gets . . . *or so I thought at the time.*

"What the hell was that all about? What did *she* want?" Dad spat, not looking up as he lay on his back, a vodka tonic teetering upon the chair seat from under which the musical clicks of a tightening ratchet sung.

"Nothing Dad. Just wondered how Jimmy was doing." He would be the last person I would ever tell that I was going to meet Gwen Putnam. Dad blamed everybody alive in Fort Harrison for Jimmy's rebellious nature—and particularly old girlfriends—except for Busty, I guess. Jesus, I had to wonder what it was like having a wife that had been screwed by your own son more times than you would likely get it up the rest of your life? Oh, what a wonderful family I sprang from!

"She knows goddamn well Jimmy hasn't been around here for years, so I don't get that bullshit at all," he said absently and I decided to ignore him as usual, wishing he'd have a few more quick drinks, crawl off into one of his holes and just pass out. He usually stopped short of arguing with me like he used to with Jimmy though, but I figured that was mostly because (like I've said) I was the last slave in the boat and he couldn't afford to push me into the boiling vat of rebellion that had enveloped Jimmy. I knew he figured I was a candy-ass with small balls, but he nevertheless pushed only so far before leveling out . . . just in case there *was* a little fight in me. It didn't matter anyhow because I had already decided that within the month I would be outta there . . . one way or another.

*But I'd get back to that issue in a day or so . . . cause tomorrow I was having lunch with Gwen Putnam and I wouldn't miss that for anything . . . anything in the world!*

# Chapter Thirty-one

*I* sat at a small booth in *Samsal's Drugs and Sodas* the next morning, nervously nursing a chocolate malt, having arrived twenty minutes early. At exactly eleven, Gwen Putnam swung through the door like the day God created the sun, waving at Al Samsal and making a beeline for me where I sat almost trembling with muted excitement. I noticed Al glance our way with an open mouth and perplexed look. Here I was, Billy Bowling, pretty much an anonymous graduate of Fort Harrison High who lived in the back of a bowling alley about to have lunch with Gwen Putnam, FHHS's most famous and unquestionably most beautiful graduate. The same Gwen Putnam, no less, who was but a few months removed from running for the *United States Team* (and favored to win the Gold Medal) in the *Atlanta Summer Olympics*.

"Gee, Billy, it's great to see you, but wow you've grown up since I remember you tossing footballs in your yard or coming to the meets to watch Jimmy run hurdles. Oops, I'm sorry, Billy, I hope I didn't embarrass you," she said, sliding into the booth across from me.

A thousand emotions strangled my vocal cords, for I simply wasn't prepared for the reality of Gwen Putnam . . . I mean, not even close. I do remember almost comically thinking how I wanted to say: 'Gwen, I didn't come to see Jimmy run, I came to see *you*! And it didn't matter to me whether you even ran or not. Don't you understand that everyone in Fort Harrison felt like that?' Of course I didn't, which would have been inappropriate I know, but my thoughts froze me, forcing Gwen to carry the ball further, as I sat glued to the bench like an idiot.

"Billy . . . I did, didn't I? I'm sorry," she'd returned, breaking the awkward moment.

"No, no Gwen, you didn't," I managed to stutter, but with eyes fixed on the salt and pepper shakers pushed up against the ketchup stained wall.

I'd never been this close to Gwen Putnam before, even when she'd stopped by the alley with Jimmy years earlier or when I'd watched her bowling with school clubs and Catholic Church groups, and she was even more beautiful than I remembered. Somehow it was strange to see her long slim body encased in a pair of jeans and a blue Notre Dame sweatshirt when I had been so used to seeing her in nylon track briefs, her long perfect legs the object of everyone's admiration, male and female alike.

I was still half frozen and pissed at myself that I had greeted her with a dumb look and a mumbling sentence, followed by an open mouth, which I could now not change. I took a deep breath and looked up at Gwen who seemed to be comfortable with everything, however, her soft smile and blue eyes fixed lightly upon me in a way that seemed to slowly disarm my nervousness. I'd heard someone say once: 'Gwen Putnam just has a way of putting you at ease' or something like that, and though I couldn't then remember who it was, knew at that very moment that they were right.

"How is Jimmy? Hear much from him?" Gwen then asked.

"He's stationed in the Gulf and he's like a Captain or something now, but I'm not really sure," I replied, even though I'd made part of that up to cover my complete ignorance (but which years later I would actually come to find had been eerily right on).

"Sounds like Jimmy and I'm not surprised at all. I'm sure we need people like Jimmy Bowling defending our country and I'll bet we haven't heard the last from him. Please give him my best when you talk to him," Gwen said.

"Yeah, Gwen, I will," I answered, knowing Gwen herself would be about as likely to talk to him as I would.

"You going to get something to eat or just have your malt? We talked about lunch, right? Do you have any suggestions? I haven't been here for a few years I'm afraid, and Billy, it's my treat since I made the date," she said laughing and reaching for a coffee stained menu stuffed behind the napkin holder.

I should have cavalierly protested and reversed the lunch tab, but I was a dolt and again just managed to mumble, "I usually get the chicken salad sandwich. It's pretty good and always seems fresh." Jesus, I was amazing myself with profundity . . . 'always seems fresh.' Now all of a sudden I was a restaurant critic.

"That's perfect and it fits my training diet. Thanks *so* much; that was a *great* suggestion," she said as if complimenting me for inventing the wheel, yet surprisingly I felt myself begin to relax.

Samsal's was half apothecary, half luncheonette. Howard Shaw, who owned the building, in addition to being the pharmacist, slid in the back door every morning and filled prescriptions from what appeared to be a tiny elevated cage. Most of the people who came for prescriptions entered and left unnoticed at the rear of the building while the lunch patrons mostly filed in off Main Street. In all the years I'd been around, I'd never once seen Howard and Al hold a conversation, which seemed a bit weird. Howard not only owned the building, but half the block. My mind, which had drifted off to this Fort Harrison trivia out of nervousness, snapped to upon the appearance of Josh Samsal.

Josh, one of Al's sons, was a freshman at Fort Harrison and a strange bird to say the least. He came to take our order, his eyes fixed upon Gwen as if he'd just been released from a cage after having had no human contact for a decade. It had now been nearly four years since Gwen had run for Fort Harrison and he couldn't have been much more ten at the time, yet everyone knew who Gwen Putnam was, eight or eighty, it made no difference, and even if he didn't, her sheer beauty was enough to freeze a fox in a henhouse.

"Hey Josh, how you doing over there buddy? Got that order yet?" Al shouted from behind the counter, seeing that he needed to unglue the prodigal from the floor before us. When Josh turned to stumble away I was pretty certain he didn't remember . . . two chicken salad sandwiches, one Coke, one water . . . and I was right, since a minute later Al called across to us so we placed our orders again with raised voices.

Gwen replaced the menu and looked at me with a soft smile . . . as my heart sparred with my Adam's apple in a rush for the emergency exit. The story was that Gwen Putnam, even now as a senior at

Notre Dame, had never had a serious boyfriend. It had always been understood that Gwen had big goals which simply couldn't be stretched to include anything serious, not for a few years yet anyhow. Though Jimmy had been head over heals in love with her for years, he'd finally given up. You pretty much had to and then be glad to just count Gwen as a close friend. But one day—wow—some guy was gonna be lucky!

"Billy, tell me about your mother and little sister. I remember your mother a bit from the bowling alley, but didn't know your sister . . . Libby, right? Don't tell me anything you're not comfortable with and I mean that, but I just want to know what they were like because I didn't really know them. Is that ok with you? Just be honest with me and especially if I ever ask you anything that upsets you. Ok?" Gwen had said, actually reaching across the table and softly tapping the top of my hand.

I wasn't completely sure what that was all about at first, but she was soon to explain. It had been over five years since Mom and Libby had been killed. I don't even know if I ever thought about it much any more, terrible as that probably sounds, but I just plain don't *know* if I thought about it, just as I don't *know* if I didn't think about it. That's just pretty much the way it is when you haven't really made peace with a tragedy, I guess.

Gwen Putnam explained to me that day that she was doing her Pre-Med thesis at Notre Dame on *Kinetic Phenomenon and their Medical Consequences.* She told me that it had been the explosion that killed Mom and Libby that had motivated her to pursue the subject, which apparently had never been researched in depth although similar explosions were not uncommon. She said the idea that 'the light switch alone had been the reason for the accident was flawed in her opinion, although it may have interacted with kinetic phenomena to create the fatal result.' I didn't much get it all, but if Gwen did, that was all that really mattered.

I talked about Mom and Libby and what they were like that first day. It's what Gwen said she wanted cause she hadn't known them very well and wanted the motivation of hearing what their lives had been like with her goal being to develop a theory and steps to help prevent similar tragedies in the future. I agreed to meet her again at

Samsal's the next morning to share with her the 'fire marshal and insurance investigative reports.' I knew where Dad kept them and I knew he would not only *not* miss them, but had likely never even read them in the first place. If Gwen Putnam could use them to somehow make a difference, I would see that they were put into her hands. . . .

. . . "Billy, think you could put up with me one more morning or do you have to work? Or like I asked you the first time, would it be a problem with that girlfriend you mentioned yesterday?" Gwen asked as we were preparing to leave Samsal's the next morning after tea and breakfast rolls. I had delivered the documents I'd promised, telling her to keep them as long as she needed, knowing Dad wouldn't miss them the rest of his life.

I'd never said anything to Krissy about meeting with Gwen and really didn't plan to, though I had mentioned her briefly to Gwen when she'd asked me again as to whether or not I had a girlfriend that first day. Krissy and I still went our own way without questions, anyway, though I rarely went anywhere, period. That Saturday morning Krissy was going shopping with her mother in Dayton and so she had decided to drive to Sidney, where her Mom had recently bought a small home, and stay the night Friday so they could get an early start. Her dinner on Wednesday had gone well and, yes, the new boyfriend had shown up as she figured, but she'd told me he actually hadn't seemed like a jerk, whatever that meant. Anyway, they'd arranged another mother/daughter thing and I thought that was good. So tomorrow for me would work out fine, but what more could Gwen Putnam want to know?

"Tomorrow?" I asked.

"Yeah, how about going to the track meet with me at Minster. I can't stay all day, but I'd love to catch the prelims and the two-mile relay. I haven't seen a Ram track meet for three years."

"Gee, I guess so, Gwen. Do you want to talk more about the explosion?"

Gwen looked at me with sparkling eyes. "No, Billy, I just want a date. I haven't had one for a long time, with my training and all . . . oops I'm sorry . . . you've got that girlfriend don't you? Just kidding, really. I'd just like a friend along and we're friends, right?"

"Yeh, Gwen, we're friends, and I'd really like that," I answered, having regained most of my lost confidence after two days, though I have to admit I was still awed by Gwen.

"Do I know your girlfriend, Billy?"

"I don't know, Gwen, probably not. She works at the alley," I stammered.

"She's from Fort Harrison though?"

"It's Krissy Kurtz. She had a sister, Tammy, that was in your class."

As soon as I said it, I wished I hadn't . . . I mean, Tammy Kurtz and Gwen Putnam were sort of like two different species, and yet that was exactly the kind of judgmental bullshit that I always so abhorred and fought not to become part of. So I was ashamed of myself for thinking like that, but had I *really* known Gwen Putnam, I would have understood that nothing ever really needed 'sugar coated' for her.

"Oh, Tammy? That's right, she did have a younger sister though I don't remember her, but she's really lucky to have you for a boyfriend. Would she be ok with you and I going to the meet, Billy? If not . . ."

"We're just friends at this point and I'd like to go to the meet, ok?" The 'date' with Gwen Putnam was appropriate and sounded like fun. Besides, I wasn't stupid enough to harbor any fantasies that it was a *real* date.

"Ok then, if you're sure it's not a problem, how about I pick you up at 9. Or do you want to pick me up?"

"I can drive, Gwen . . . if you want me to."

"Great, you know my folks farm out on Boeke Road, don't you Billy?"

"Yep, Gwen, I know it."

"Do you have to work at the alley at all tomorrow?" she asked, sliding out of the booth.

"I should be there for open bowling at two," I replied, "but I could probably change that. I have a guy that's working anyhow and it really won't be busy." Dad and Busty had left for a tournament, God knows where, but Baxter could run the whole show on a spring

Saturday with no sweat at all if necessary, especially since the drunks didn't emerge from their burrows on Saturdays until well after 5.

"Billy, that works perfect cause I have to do my twenty miler tomorrow afternoon and so I need to leave the meet by one or so. That would give you plenty of time to be back at the alley by two. So I'll see you in the morning at nine," she said with a big smile that melted my heart.

"*Twenty miler!* You're going to run twenty miles tomorrow?" I asked in awe, but punctuated as quickly in my mind with a *duh!* This *was* Gwen Putnam after all—a member of the United States Olympic team—*so for Christ's sakes, get a brain Billy Bowling!*

## Chapter Thirty-two

*G*wen Putnam and Billy Bowling—*together*—were going to the high school track meet in Minster, and I was excited . . . *very excited*. Baxter was supposed to show at one to work and I called to tell him I might be late. The golf course was open and there were baseball and softball games along with the big meet in Minister so Baxter could easily handle the few families that might show up.

That Saturday morning, April 20, dawned pleasant, though cool. I wore a pair of nice khaki Tommy shorts I'd found at the St. Matthias thrift store, a decent Fort Harrison Rams gold hooded sweatshirt Jimmy had left behind that had been too large for him and a nice pair of Reeboks I'd had for a year or so, but seldom wore. I knew this wasn't a real date, but I scrubbed in the shower, spent an extra minute brushing my teeth, buzzed my face fuzz and lightly dabbed some Chaps behind my ear and on my chest. I had the kind of hair that looked different every day and though I'd never spent any time on it, girls I hardly even knew would sometimes get all excited about how they loved it. At first I thought they were making fun of me, but after awhile I realized they were actually pretty genuine and never seemed to care if it was even combed cause they'd mess it up anyway, so my grooming regimen got pretty simple, pretty quick . . . just keep it clean. The hair thing was kind of funny because I always envied Jimmy. He had the jet black Romano hair and I got the bushy curly brown Bowling gig, but I'd come to figure it was ok cause we always want somebody else's hair anyway, don't we? I mean, since these girls screamed about wanting mine it made sense to me to be ok with it, though it wasn't like it got me laid extra because of it or anything . . . back in the days before Krissy, anyhow.

I was pretty proud of my 91' Explorer Sport that I'd bought for cash a year earlier with the alley slave pay I'd saved for most of a decade. I'd washed and waxed, then scrubbed the interior into the wee hours of the morning, ending up sleeping five hours, if that. I double checked that the key to the alley was hanging from a twig in the shrubbery just outside the door where Baxter would expect it, started my shiny forest green machine and pulled out of the BBC at exactly 8:50 am, turning South on 66 toward the Putnam dairy farm about four miles distant on Boeke Road, just off the main highway.

From the time Gwen's foot touched the concrete parking lot, the staring, the smiling, the leering, the laughing, the waving, the reticent and the bold . . . all attention was focused upon Gwen Putnam, the pride of Fort Harrison village and High School, the WOAC, Shelby County, the State of Ohio—and soon the United States of America—having made the cover of *Sports Illustrated* just two weeks earlier. I was immediately self-conscious and surprised when Gwen reached for my hand and pulled me toward the entrance gate.

An old fellow with a bright orange Minster sweatshirt smiled dumbly at Gwen and waved her through, intending no charge, but Gwen held out an insisting five dollar bill, paying for us both and a dollar program. There was a buzz as we circled the track outside the short mesh wire fence and headed toward the smaller Fort Harrison bleachers, passing beside the long jump pit where everyone seemed to freeze, including a Minster kid a second into his takeoff. Gwen smiled and waved to old coaches; to a mix of young and old alike, then hooking an inclusive arm in mine we negotiated the gauntlet and found a purposeful seat in the top row. The whole thing was surreal, but I guess you had to be me to understand.

"Are you ok, Billy?" Gwen asked as we settled in. "It's kind of a circus, I know that; the Olympics you know." She was looking directly at me as if I was the most important person in the world. I had no illusions about why we were together and still figured that Gwen probably had a few more questions for her research project, but I also was pretty sure in a way she was just thanking me for my time, which was pretty silly if you thought about it.

"I'm fine, Gwen. Thanks a lot for letting me come with you. It's really special," I said, feeling mostly comfortable even as the legions of rubbernecks never took a break.

"Billy, don't you *dare* think I am any better or different than you are. You're a delightful fellow and I am so sorry that you lost your mother and sister in the horrible explosion. I want to take their memory and work to prevent it from happening to other families, and if I do, a lot will be because of you. And don't you forget that!"

Throughout the morning people leered, smiled and waved . . . and pretty much everyone stared at me with confusion, but particularly because Gwen was so bubbly, so inclusive. With every event I gained a little more confidence and shed a bit more self-consciousness, and by the time we left after the 3200 relays, the prelims, field events and the 3200-meter runs, I was actually pretty relaxed.

As we were leaving, Gwen would pause to talk with fans, coaches and younger athletes who worshipped her, and I started feeling weird again because people would stare at me like: 'What's your deal, Billy Bowling?' (Those who even knew who I was, that is). But mostly we kept moving and during one pause I bumped into Mrs. Badderly standing by the fence and we had a quite nice short conversation. Her daughter, Allie, had run on the 3200 relay team that had kicked Minster's butt and she was quite proud you could tell, especially when Gwen turned to her and raved about the race. When Gwen raved about your daughter you had to be proud, but when pretty much everyone else raved, you had to figure it was mostly phony . . . unless they were like the kid's grandparents or someone like that.

We walked around the track and across the parking lot toward my Explorer—just as the main running events were set to begin— and you could almost feel the eyes of all Shelby County following us and I had a feeling that most were wondering why we were leaving so early, which was no big deal of course, for Gwen had reasons that transcended time as others understood. I felt a pride that I knew was totally undeserved, but Gwen had put me at ease all day long and it *was* her show . . . *but the stark reality of that moment in time was that none of them would ever see Gwen Putnam again.*

# Chapter Thirty-three

*I*t was only about nine miles from the track meet at Minster to the Putnam farm, and yet we drove through three school districts, all of which would have probably sacrificed the testicle of a Saint to have had Gwen run for their school. The small villages of Western Ohio were often separated by less than five miles and there were spots where you could pan the countryside across the flat rich soil and see four or five looming spires, both near and distant. The whole scene was quite pastoral, even medieval I used to think, at least after taking world history (not that I'd learned anything from Dick Hamilton, but I'd had plenty of time to look at the pictures). I mean I had to admit that the small Catholic communities took great pride in their identity, and the villages and farms were nearly pristine, which I'd always felt was very cool.

These unique communities and their schools had also managed to maintain their autonomy throughout the years rather than consolidate traditional rivals, throw some gaudy new colors together and invent a stupid politically correct mascot like the Protestant districts around the state had done years back, taking names like *East Coshocton Schools, Big Valley Schools, Upper Scioto Valley Schools or Allen (county) East* . . . that kind of stuff. I wasn't a practicing Catholic, though Mom had been, but I mostly liked the Catholic stuff about the town and school and had never really felt shunned or anything. The crazy thing was, the little Catholic schools usually kicked the consolidated school's asses in sporting events— so far backwards that at times you'd wonder if the Reformation was a figment of the imagination.

In the three days we'd spent together, Gwen had explained her project thesis, which included negligent emergency gas shutoff valves, proposed insular electrical switches that would prevent the possibility of a spark and several other physically researched theories that I was glad she understood because I never would. Even as she prepared to run in the rapidly approaching Olympics, it was obvious that Gwen Putnam was driven to, not only complete a required thesis, but to *make a difference* by writing it.

I turned off Boeke Road and started back the quarter mile lane that led to the picture perfect Putnam farm. The lane centrally bisected a sweeping lawn about thirty yards wide and the wonderful old 19th century brick farmhouse was framed distantly by a grove of massive burr oaks. Beyond sat the Santa red gambrel dairy barn, upstaged only by side to side towering silos which made one think of circular, rural versions of Manhattan's twin towers (in those days when they were still standing). Along the lane to the left upon gently rising ground an already sprouting field of perfect corn stood in rows and poised like miniature soldiers along Seminary Ridge awaiting George Pickett's signal to charge the saucer eyed Holsteins passively chewing their cud in the pasture just across the lane. A few shrieking guineas (I found out later) scattered as we neared the house, darting in every direction like children on a church Easter egg hunt and I had to laugh.

"Those are Mom's watch dogs," Gwen said, laughing.

"The chickens you mean?" I asked in ignorance.

"Well they're actually called guineas and they really aren't much good for anything except as watchdogs. They're not very bright, but for whatever reason they hang around the lane and work like a charm. You don't get down this lane without notice and old Shep just lays over there on the porch watching the guineas do his work and thankful for the fact, I guess."

Gwen was unique among her gender, yet modest to a fault. The inverted blue hood of her Notre Dame pullover, randomly punctuated by cascading blonde locks, framed her beautiful perfect face. I had surprisingly become comfortable and seldom let my mind drift to thought of the perfect legs that lived in a world of their own just beneath the faded blue fabric of Levi denims. I pulled around a circular drive and stopped beside a walkway leading to a small patio area and rear door that appeared to be the path of family choice.

With her hand on the door handle, Gwen turned to me. "Billy, I've enjoyed your company these last few days and I mean it. I had fun today and I've learned a lot about your Mom and Libby and thank you so much for your help because I know it has been painful. I hope you understand I needed the personal motivation for sticking with a difficult project. What I will be pushing for is going to involve political change and hit the big guys in their wallets and it won't be popular, but I'm certain that many kinetic explosions could be avoided and someday your help will have been a big part if we can achieve that."

Wonderful as everything had been all morning, as I began to digest what she was saying I was nearly suffocated by sadness, although I would never let on that I was to Gwen. I was sad thinking about Mom and Libby, and that they had died in an explosion that could have maybe been avoided; sad because I never had, nor likely ever would be a part of a wonderful family like the Putnams—and particularly sad because in a few minutes Gwen Putnam would disappear from my life just as surely as Mom, Libby, and in a sense Jimmy had. And finally, I was sad because Dad had never been there for me or anyone else in our family . . . and because I knew that would never change.

"Gotta go, Billy. Got that twenty miler to run and then brother Mike's coming over to help me do the milking tonight. Dad, Mom, Carrie and Ryan all went to the livestock auction in Springfield and were going to stop in Dayton for shopping and dinner. I'll give you a call before I leave for the Olympics and maybe we can go do something again. That'd be fun. Then maybe you could bring your friend, Krissy, for me to meet. Goodbye, Billy," she said, reaching across to touch my forearm lightly before exiting, closing the door behind her and jogging to the back door where she let herself in without a key.

*It haunts me now to the point of almost vomiting. I can remember so clearly the faint sound of the slamming screen door behind Gwen that afternoon, followed by an evanesent, but noticeable silence, that had seemed almost surgically separated from the meter of a springtime barnyard . . . and it was the last time anyone would ever see Gwen Putnam alive again . . . well almost anyone!*

# Chapter Thirty-four

*I*t was a stunning spring day and the Putnam farm was a spot I didn't want to leave. It wasn't about Gwen at that point, it was just the moment in time—the kind we usually pass on because we have better things to do—things that cost good money. If it doesn't cost money, it can't be shit, people think. I mean a lot of people really do look at stuff this way, and especially because they don't think about what's truly free and that's sad, but then I've always seen the world differently, I guess, with no loving family to get in the way and no big stash of cash to buy *time toys*. I get a kick out of my Explorer, sure, but it's not like a huge deal. A long time ago I realized I had more reasons than a lot of kids to go around with my head up my ass, but I just decided not to cause I figured it was a choice. Now, I'll admit that I'm not as relaxed and buoyant about life as Krissy is, but I think I have been fairly grounded. I've got a bit of a shell around me, and to be sure, I'm terribly cynical, although I'm working on that. I understand that I have never really grieved for Mom and Libby in the healthiest sort of way, but I'm starting to think I'll get there sometime, especially after the things Gwen had just said those past three days.

If I'd have really let go back then (after the explosion and before I really connected with Krissy) and looked at my life, I'm pretty certain I'd have jumped off the water tower into Mast's Stone Quarry, cause back when Brent Sturdivant and me used to talk about how we'd do a suicide . . . well, that was our choice. But I didn't *want* to look too close at my life, so I traded that for watching the rest of the world, at least my stupid little chunk of the world there in Fort Harrison. Just watch and think, watch and think . . . and ultimately it's been a good thing for me in a couple of ways, I guess. I mean I see things around me very few people do, and I've found that's a good thing, and the second thing is . . . I haven't jumped off the water tower yet.

I had taught myself to stop for good moments, maybe not often, but sometimes. Moments like this—moments I was somehow sure the Putnam family didn't miss either. For some reason I was pretty sure that they were probably the type of people to walk out the back door each morning and appreciate that they were living a good life, that they had a wonderful large family, a beautiful farm—and especially an incredible daughter like Gwen.

I knew I needed to be going cause Gwen would be coming out soon for her run or might even be watching through a window and wondering if I was really weird since I was still sitting there and not this nice guy she'd just told me I was. Yet it was hard to drive away, to drive off this page of the storybook and back onto Boeke Road, thus to prove what the early navigators all feared so much—that the world was indeed flat, not round, and that somehow this part of it was not really connected to my world at all.

The waft of barnyard smells and sounds blended perfectly with that of the growing spring green. Darting swallows and wrens auditioned for mid summer Grammy's and the deliberate peaceful movements of a hundred farm lives you could almost feel without even seeing. Sheep with wobbly spring lambs, a first down away from cousins not yet met, grazed in a small fenced paddock beside the cornfield. A bearded goat, comically astride an old doghouse, held court beside a corncrib of muted yellows and gray while honking, brainless Chinese geese, chicken shit pretenders to barnyard bullies, loitered about in a large dirty barnyard puddle. And nearly everywhere, it seemed, spring-loaded leghorns, like popcorn balls, darted here and there devouring the heat-seeking worms of young spring. A handsome quarter horse, probably Gwen's, and book-ended by a team of placid blonde Belgians had their mugs stretched across a white gate in a small paddock beside the barn, watching me with longing anticipation. Even the aged *Shep,* who never budged from the back step, seemed to take comfort in my distant presence, as I reflected on the wonderful life he must have lived there on the farm. Most of all, however, were the omnipresent prize Putnam Holsteins with piercing ashtray eyes . . . and the still lazy tails of late April.

I simply could not face going back to the alley, not just yet, although it was time to vacate the Putnam farm, which had spawned placid thoughts I hadn't experienced for a very long time, if ever. Then I had a flash of the perfect place to stop—and where I could finish this surreal experience in peace and bleed my melancholy thoughts until they were exhausted. It was quite near, so I finally turned the key and the Explorer purred to life.

Turning right onto Boeke Road instead of left which would have taken me back to 66, I passed through a long flat stretch with youthful cornfields on my right and rapidly aging wheat to the left before the terrain changed and became the rolling green host to a hundred more grazing Holsteins. It was a beautiful drive, terminating at the old steel Boeke Bridge over Indian Creek, which was one of the last surviving dinosaurs of the early post covered bridge era. I'd had a grade school friend, Darrell Byers, who lived out this way ten years earlier or so. His family rented a small house down the road from the Putnam farm that I was approaching, the bridge was just beyond maybe a quarter mile. The house had burnt down, though I don't remember when, but it was sometime after the Byers' had moved to Missouri. A mammoth tumble down barn sat well back from the house ruins, but was now almost obscured from the road by a thick grove of virile young maples. Darrell and I spent countless hours there, swinging on ropes and shooting baskets at an old hoop in the mow, hopping between the busted floor planks, shooting rats with pellet guns, and building a maze of catacombs through a mountain of ancient dusty loose hay.

We would also often play in and around Indian Creek where it passed under the bridge just on down the road, sometimes in the heat and dryness of August, walking great distances across the flat exposed shale, the creek littered with hundreds of decomposing minnows and small fish that had been trapped in rock pools, first to boil, then bake, and I suppose finally to fry. One time we walked clear to New Bremen, miles away, then seeing the setting sun got scared of the time and called Darrell's Mom from a bar called *The Doghouse* to come pick us up, which she had done with a smile and without yelling at all, which at the time I'd thought incredibly cool.

Boeke Road was a mile long, dead-ending onto 66 to the East and Fletcher Road, just across the bridge on the west. From Fletcher stretching west were patchwork quilt square blocks all the way to the Indiana line about ten miles away. They had been perfectly laid out as provided by the Land Ordinance of 1787, I'd learned in seventh grade Ohio History from Mr. Crumb (Carter Crumb, that is, and a name for a million junior high jokes). Gwen told me that for her twenty-mile run, she ran a mile up Fletcher, then ran two 8-mile figure 8's around other sparsely traveled roads till she hit Fletcher again to Boeke and back home. The entire countryside was large dairy farms with a sprinkling of less attractive turkey farms. Except for the Amish in Eastern Ohio, the area was one of the last bastions of the family farm left in the state. Obscenely huge Dutch conglomerate dairy and poultry farms were now the rage in Ohio; farms with 10,000 cows or a million chickens, ten zillion flies, and shit you could smell two counties away. But for now, the area around Fort Harrison and the small Catholic villages of West Central Ohio was immune to that and still picture postcard pastoral, relatively obscure . . . and *seemingly* distanced from a distressingly changing world.

I decided to drive around a bit before returning to the alley and found myself cruising up and down roads I hadn't been on for years, if ever. I wasn't really sure where one school district stopped and the next started, but in the distance loomed the twin spires of St. Augustine in Minster, and just beyond, Holy Redeemer in New Bremen. St. Michael's in Fort Loramie was to my left and in the distance beyond, and a bit to the left, was St. Johns in Maria Stein. Then upon one turn, directly in front of me loomed St. Matthias, perhaps three miles distant and easily dominating the landscape beyond for miles.

One thing that I'd had plenty of time for over the years was reading, cause I would get stuck for hours on end babysitting a bar that was host to no one but Winston Thermostat. So after the chores were completed (and while dad was either trashed or away at a bowling tournament) I'd perch on a small chair in the corner of the kitchen and read whatever I could get my hands on. Winston was out of sight around the corner and after a couple of 'dead soldiers,' I think he even forgot I was around so he'd seldom ever bug me. I knew that it took him thirty-eight minutes *exactly* to execute five shots of *Beam* so I'd do a quick time check, begin reading, and appear magically (it probably seemed to him) to send in the substitutes, then return to my nest to read until the varsity was rested up. Well, you get the drift.

Anyway, a few weeks prior to Gwen's call I had just finished an epic Ken Follett book entitled *Pillars of the Earth.* Most of the novel (which was set in Middle Age England) revolved around the building of a massive cathedral and it almost gave me chills to consider that the European cathedrals would even dwarf St. Matthias. As a child, from Kindergarten through third grade, we used the playground behind St. Matthias for recess and there were times that I literally froze before the massive structure. In middle school English we had an incredible view of the entire façade and I used to try to imagine just *how* they had managed to build it . . . and in the mid-eighteen hundreds, to boot. Then after Brent returned from a trip to Europe with his family after our sophomore year and tried to explain the sheer stature of European cathedrals . . . well, I couldn't even imagine them and eventually just gave up trying to grasp their enormity. So I had very early on cultivated considerable respect for *all* of the noted churches that dotted the local landscape, and on that particularly pristine spring afternoon I was oddly warmed by their company.

Reflexively grasping for reality, I glanced at the dash and saw that it was nearly 2. I had told Baxter I might be a bit late and I knew he would have things under control, unlike Brent, who, though he had been a good worker, was very poor at adapting to change and with any schedule variation would have started to freak out. But it *was* Baxter, and that was considerably different. I thought briefly about heading straight back and getting real about life again, but somehow I wasn't ready . . . not just yet.

Driving beside Indian Creek on Fletcher Road for the second time, I found myself passing over a culvert where Darrel Byers and I used to play as kids. It was exactly the spot I had been thinking about while sitting at the Putnam farm, despite having been sidetracked for a while. I figured there wasn't a half a percent of twelve years olds, and maybe even adults, that knew what a culvert even was, but when you grow up as a kid in rural Ohio, they were kind of mystical places, a break in the beauty of nature, perhaps, but a place that as a kid you were magnetically drawn to.

I pulled over, parking on a spot obviously visited by other 'tranquilists,' or perhaps just kids trying to snatch a quick piece of ass. From recent April rains, the creek ran bubbly and below I could see clumps of already tall spring grasses that a few days earlier were likely bathing in the sun, but today performed an underwater ballet like a miniature octopus with a hundred green tentacles conducting multiple symphonies. Everywhere infant green peeked from behind the stage curtains, emerging from beneath the damp soil, if half an act yet removed from stardom and often still suffocated by the thick brown dead of last year life. Overhead, and sprinkled about like thousands of tiny green Christmas bulbs gracing the branches of anaconda-like tree branches, the art nouveau buds of spring blossomed everywhere, though sadly lost upon the tadpoles, cicadas, garter snakes, raccoons and the occasional opossum which inhabited the world below, bereft art appreciation courses.

There was today no shale sidewalk to New Bremen or half dead tadpoles and tiny fish trapped in boiling sun baked pools. It was spring, a time of renewal that we're usually far too busy to appreciate. It was all so placid and perfect and I found myself wishing Krissy were there to share it with me. It had to be why the culvert was wide and God had created moments like this . . . *to be shared* . . . and right there at that moment I started, *for the first time in my life,* to look forward to the future—a future I hoped and believed would be with Krissy Kurtz. *And I felt happy.*

I must have sat upon the culvert half an hour, maybe longer, and even then didn't want to leave. The bubbling, rushing water was almost hypnotizing, and had Krissy been there I may *never* have left. But there was the bowling alley—*there always was*—and even as I knew those days were numbered, still, I forced myself up and turned toward the Explorer.

# Chapter Thirty-five

*H*eading south on Fletcher Road, the shortest route to 66, I saw that the Obringer Farm was coming up on my right. I had been there once, maybe twice, with Jimmy years earlier. It was one of the largest in the area and I'd heard the boys at BBC once joking about how Clint had gone back home to farm after flunking out of Ball State. So I guessed he was back in his old bedroom, and now at 23 or so, I had to laugh figuring that his one great adventure in life would probably turn out to be those couple of months he and Jimmy had shared the 'Shack Up Shack.' I heard Clint hung out at Stoney's every night now, but so far hadn't graced us with his presence at the alley, though I figured it was just a matter of time and I hoped to be the hell out of there before that wonderful moment came to pass.

As I drew nearer, I noticed Clint with his back to me just off the right side of the road driving a megabuck John Deere and spreading manure. The smell was sort of grim in a way and in a way, not. I mean a town junior high or high school girl would probably pop a cork, but there was something about it on a bright April day that just kind of fit and didn't really bother me all that much. If you're a town or city person I doubt I can explain it to you, but if you're country, even a little . . . you'd understand.

I slowed down as I passed, though later wished I hadn't (*then much later than that would come to realize the incredible gravity of my decision to slow down and stop*), cause when Clint noticed who I was a huge grin spread across his face and with an animated wave of his arm motioned me to stop. I figured why not, although it wasn't like me and Clint Obringer had all that much in common, and especially because he was the biggest asshole in Jimmy's class I'd always thought . . . and the dumbest one for certain. But I pulled off the edge of the road anyhow and got out of the Explorer, approaching the big green machine, which I must admit, intrigued me cause I'd heard that they could cost over a hundred grand which was more than Uncle Marco's Bimmer.

Clint pushed open the door of a glass cab the size of a one car garage and I was ambushed by *Rage Against the Machine* by *'Bulls on Parade,'* blasting so loud it shook the ground *above* the roaring engine. He rotated sideways on a plush leather seat, wedging a shit caked Wellington sideways to keep the door open while swigging a Budweiser. Then he just looked at me awhile, shaking his head with a shit-eating grin on his mutt, like some alien farmer robot with a gear stripped. I've never figured out why dumb assess all had this thing about just looking at you for two minutes—while shaking their head and grinning—before being able to talk. I understand that it's a *reverse dumb-ass* sort of thing, and yet I've never understood how come they *all* did it. Clint's was particularly effective because he sat about eight feet above me in this massive machine and if there had been political offices for dumb ass farmers it would have made a perfect campaign poster.

*"Jesus Fucking Christ, Billy Fucking Bowling,"* Clint finally yelled over the still vibrating tractor, though he'd turned down the music with a remote control. Nope, the Obringers weren't exactly Amish. Clint certainly had a way with words, you had to give him that. Surprised the shit out of me that he flunked out of Ball State.

"What's up, Clint?" I found myself yelling. Have you ever noticed that when you start a conversation with "What's up?" it's pretty certain you've stopped to talk to someone you wish you hadn't stopped to talk to?

He reached behind him and opened a small refrigerator door as I tried to believe my eyes. It was actually built right into the corner of the cab, and upon closer look, there was even a microwave oven firmly attached above it. He snagged a *Budweiser* and I could see a regiment of them lined up as the door swung shut.

"Here, Billy boy, have a beer," Clint said, tossing one down to me . . . *hard,* as if hoping I would fumble it so he could laugh his ass off when it sprayed all over me. Clint hadn't much changed, that's for sure, and I was certain never would. I fielded the beer pretty slick, I must admit, even if it was an accident, which disappointed him, but since he had the memory span of a flea that passed quickly enough. I decided I'd better drink it even though I still didn't drink all that much cause with guys like Clint it'd be better to pour it out taking a fake piss behind the Explorer than refuse it cause that was a serious offense and they never let it go, not then, not five years from then . . . *despite* the memory span of a flea.

"What the fuck's Jimmy up too, Billy? Still shootin Injuns?" he snorted. ('Shootin Injuns' had meant being in the army for as long as I could remember around Fort Harrison, and I'd once figured ole' William Henry himself must have cast a spell on the town so that we never forgot about him.)

"Yep, he is, Clint," I answered, still needing to yell over the loudly idling tractor which I guessed Clint needed to keep running so his beer didn't get warm.

"So where's he at, cowboy? Still over with the fuckin ragheads?"

"Saudi Arabia, I guess."

"That's what I mean, dumb ass . . . *ragheads. Duh!"* Clint spat back with charm then said, "Ever talk to him?" Then swiveling around he grabbed *another* beer.

"Not for awhile, Clint."

"The ole' man ever talk to him?"

"No," I answered, practiced to say no more—*to anyone*—who might ask that question.

"What's Jimmy think about your ole'man and Busty?" Clint asked with a grin the size of a tricycle wheel before busting out in roaring laughter.

I didn't want to think of that shit again myself, but there was always an asshole somewhere stepping out from behind the fucking bushes and throwing it in my face.

"Probably don't know, Clint," I said, intending to say no more and starting to walk around the Explorer to get the hell out of there.

"Don't fucking know? How the fuck can he *not* know?" he yelled, chugging the entire beer and crushing the can in his giant mitt of a hand, then wheeling around *again* to retrieve another . . . his third already!

"I don't know, Clint, who'd tell him—*you*?" I yelled with a disgust that was lost on ears unfortunately attached to his skull.

"Fuck you, Billy, you're no fun," Clint yelled back at me.

('Fuck you, Billy, you're no fun?') Wasn't that clever I was thinking when it suddenly flashed that he'd expanded his vocabulary since the last time I'd held an intellectual discussion with him. It used to always be 'fuck you and the horse you rode in on.' He must have learned that one at Ball State. Clint was a real prize all right.

"I gotta go, Clint. Gotta work at the alley," I yelled, starting to duck inside the Explorer.

"Fuck you, Billy, you're a pussy, you know that?" he yelled, finishing off his third full beer in about four minutes.

"What the fuck'd I do?" I snapped, standing back up, pissed, then remembering Clint's whole life was about trying to back someone in a corner just for fun, so I forced myself to shut up.

"You kiss Daddy's ass, that's why . . . *kiss, kiss, kiss, kiss*," he said mockingly to me as I turned toward him one last time. "You'll never say 'Fuck You' to the ole' man like Jimmy did, so you're a pussy, Billy—the biggest fucking pussy in the whole fucking county. Nothing but a *great big fucking pussy!*" he screamed, now slurring his words comically.

I try not to let people get my goat, but Clint did that day, and that was about as low as I could have stooped. *And then I really stooped!* I looked over the hood of the Explorer and raising my right arm high, flipped him off, still cradling the nearly full Budweiser in my left hand which I then launched toward the tractor where it bounced off the windshield, followed by raising my left arm for a double bird before dodging behind the wheel. As I pulled away I heard and saw a full Bud bounce off my right front fender and in the rear view mirror could see Clint standing high upon the massive tire and flipping a double bird back at me—*but he was only able to do it just then because it was the first time all day he didn't have a beer in one of his hands.*

By the time I arrived at the alley, it was after three o'clock. I was still fuming about Clint Obringer, so I actually poured myself a vodka-cranberry (which was quite rare for me) and ducked into Dad's office, deciding to just sit tight for a few minutes and try to calm down. I couldn't believe that I had killed most of two hours just messing around out in the country after dropping Gwen off. Still, it was a golden day I wouldn't have missed . . . until I ran into that asshole Obringer, that is. Most of my still short life I had worked hard; harder than anyone else I knew in my high school class, and while most kids still needed to learn how to buckle down and work, Billy Bowling needed to learn how to just let work sit for an hour or so and fuck around. Which is *exactly* what I had just done. And it had been wonderful, just wonderful.

*Yet it was a chunk of solitary time that would forever color my life.*

# Chapter Thirty-six

*T*here were three cars in the lot when I'd gotten back, so I knew that Baxter had been fine, and also that we weren't making any money. Winston wasn't there, but I'd no more than sat down in the office with my drink when he showed, sliding onto his 'reserved' corner stool. Baxter was just returning from a reset I assumed or some other malfunction so I got up and started for the bar since I knew Baxter's parents were adamant about him not serving alcohol. My nerves were still a jangle from my encounter with that asshole Obringer and it must have shown as Baxter stopped before me.

"I'll catch Winston; are we set for the Young Saints?" I'd asked him absently.

"Yeah, I think so, Billy. Hey, are you Ok? Did something happen?" he returned.

"It's nothing; I'll be fine," I answered and turned toward Winston.

"How yah doing, Winston?" I asked, lightly sliding my hand across his Carhart as I passed.

"Hey, Billy, I'm doin ok, ah guess," he answered, coherently at that point and with a smile that was now nearly five years old.

After setting Winston up with a basketball team of Beam shots, I turned back to Baxter who informed me that things had been fine. Nobody'd been to the bar before Winston and his trip for a re-set was the first. He'd re-stocked coolers, swept the lanes twice, and thrown out all the garbage. Baxter was a gem.

The Young Saints Club from St. Johns in Maria Stein was due any minute. They had five alleys reserved from 3:30 – 5:00 and all needed shoes, balls and all that jazz, so I figured I had gotten back just right. Father Alex, one of the newer priests in the area was a cool guy, it seemed, but you had to wonder these days? I mean what with all the gay-priest/alter-boy scandals it could make you a bit nervous if you were one of the Young Saints I was thinking, since they were boys and girls about twelve, give or take. I sure hoped Father Alex was straight though cause he seemed like a great guy. I just don't know how a kid could really relax in that kind of club and that could sort of be a big subtraction if you were out for fun. Oh well, we had our side of the game to play and we still got their money.

I often found myself thinking about things like that—about kids who learned to smile when behind the smile was so much misery. Mindy was like that when we graduated, I could tell. Because I knew what I did, I could read her differently from the others and had wondered if her parents had even noticed the change? There was a dullness in eyes that used to sparkle and you could tell her smile was forced. It was a smile that she had to use face muscles to hold up instead of a real smile that washes like friendly waves upon a sunny beach. Jimmy was like that too, and always had been, I'd decided. But then there was Krissy, who'd fought off God knows how many degenerates yet had a joy about her that transcended anyone I ever knew that had seemingly had a perfect family life, so go figure. My theory sort of gets shot in the ass with her, I know. Still, how could the world ever get better when so many adults ruined so many children, turning them into a race of plastic androids for their own selfish and often perverted purposes?

I'd never mentioned anything to Baxter about being with Gwen Putnam and had decided there really wouldn't be much point to mention it to Krissy either, cause she was one of the few people I knew who just wouldn't quite get the draw. Krissy knew who Gwen was, but stuff like Gwen's career and football championships just never fazed Krissy Kurtz, which was just fine with me. In fact I thought that was very cool—I just did!

The door opened as I stood behind the bar. I figured it was the Young Saints, but it was Krissy rounding the corner with a huge smile and preceded by a hint of the bouquet that had driven me crazy for years—along, of course, with every male with descended testes in Fort Harrison and twenty miles beyond. She had once given me a brief education about her intoxicating scent: *Angel* (by Thierry Mugler), an expensive French fragrance she received from an Aunt who worked at ElBees (Elder Beerman) in downtown Dayton. Anyway, her aunt got a big discount etc., and, short of story, Aunt Lonny, who was married to an investment banker or some kind of big shot in Dayton, gave her a small bottle each Christmas *and* each birthday just as Krissy always requested.

"Didn't think you'd be back yet, girl," I said with a smile as she ducked under the counter and gave me a deft goose, oblivious to Winston, and followed up by a soupy nip on the ear.

"Mom has to work at 5:30, Billy. You know that; it *is* a Saturday."

Krissy and I still had never really talked about Lacy being a stripper at *Three Blind Dice*, but it was understood. She'd just turned forty, a week earlier, but was still incredibly striking in her hard life sort of way. Krissy'd once told me Tammy had been born when her mother was fifteen. She mostly just worked the bar I guess, but they had a tiny stage with dark lights and a pole and so a few minutes every hour or so she'd *do her thing*, which meant swinging around the pole for a minute or so and usually ending up being topless for like thirty seconds tops. That was pretty much it, I guess. Then she'd go back to waiting tables or behind the bar, hoping the nipple shot would land her an extra forty or so in tips each time.

I don't honestly remember where I'd heard that, but more than likely from some assholes awhile back at the BBC who go there every once in awhile. Nobody says boo these days about Lacy Johnson and the Three Blind Dice . . . *not at BBC anyhow* . . . since Krissy tore into Nick Fisher one night nearly a year earlier after she heard him say something about her Mom. Krissy never told me what he'd said, I just knew she'd grabbed him by the throat and it wasn't pretty. For a long time Nick didn't come back, but his buddies all did cause it had been a great hoot for them, though they sure as hell never laughed about it at the time, not in front of Krissy Kurtz they didn't!

You could look at, or even stare at Krissy all you wanted, but *never* touch . . . and never waste your time trying to pick her up cause it wasn't gonna happen. I never knew if there'd ever been an incident at the bar that put that drift straight early on cause Krissy never said anything, but I suspected some things had come down during the early years in my absence. The good ole' boys ogled Krissy to death, even as their talk to her was clean and straight, but they knew better than to expect any cheap action like they could get all night long from Busty if they started tipping her out good. After the Nick Fisher thing, the ground rules for the BBC bar were pretty much understood a county away, but I never felt we lost any business because of it. Krissy was just too damn spectacular to pass up for long and she never discouraged looking. The truth of the matter was she still probably raked in better tips than Busty anyway. Krissy Kurtz understood *BBC business* . . . and you, (I mean Krissy), could take that to the bank!

When Busty worked the bar alone things could get pretty wild, although I hadn't personally seen much of it. Candy Bailey's complete identity *was* her tits and that's why guys came. If you wanted to ogle huge perfect tits, even likely get them stuck in your face with cute little sly moves like Busty reaching across the bar for an empty, but stretching four inches further than necessary so she could smack your nose around a bit, well come to the BBC. Cause it was likely the best tit action south of Toledo and north of Dayton, and it didn't seem likely that it was gonna change all that much just because ole'Busty and Thin Jim Bowling had gotten hitched. After all, the likelihood that Thin Jim would be anything other than horizontal by evening was pretty 'slim' anyhow.

As for *Three Blind Dice*, I'd never been there, although I'd driven past it. It was a tiny triangular cement block building that I swear couldn't have been five feet from the railroad tracks on Compton Avenue in Sidney. The building had been painted pink years back, then decorated with three large goofy mice with oversize dice heads, shades and beggars cups on a big mural facing the street. The paint was chipping now and the last time I'd passed I noticed that the mouse in the middle no longer had a head, having been replaced by a big gray blob where the pink paint and dice head had pealed off. I had to wonder what kind of additional thrills the ole' CSX trains delivered when they blew through Sidney at about forty or so. I suppose it was quite a hoot to see a pole dance at the same time the train blew through town, though somehow I suspected I'd never now personally find out.

"You want me to work, Billy? Oh yeah, I forgot—Mom and I stopped at Arby's on the way back cause they had the 5 for 5 deal on and there's still 3 left for you and Baxter. Get's kind of old eating bar food everyday," she said, reaching across to pick up the bag she'd set unnoticed a few minutes earlier on the bar.

"Gee, thanks Krissy, I appreciate that. I love Arby's," Baxter spoke up much louder than usual just as the door swung open and a boatload of humanity flooded in laughing, everyone trying to out shout one another. The Young Saints had arrived.

"Yeh, Kris, we might need some help. Baxter, can you take shoes? Krissy, maybe you can help the kids find balls that fit. They've got lanes eight to twelve."

"No problem, Billy," she said, smiling, and as she turned I felt my dick stiffen . . . which *eleven years later* hasn't changed at all!

Krissy wore a denim mini skirt, a push up pink half bra beneath a deeply scooped white blouse, pink laced up ankle boots with frilly socks and matching pink panties, which I hadn't yet seen, but knowing her was certain completed the outfit. This week her hair was radiant platinum, though less than two weeks ago it had been jet black. I'd never understood how she could pull off the change, but she could, believe me! Her perfect nails were turquoise that day and her dark brown skin was lightly oiled and when close enough you could pick up on a secondary scent of some sort of soft body lotion. Kris was *something* all right—petite (about 5'4"-115), perfect face, teeth and pouting lips, beautiful natural breasts and with an ass like a Tour de France bike seat—and I'd never seen a man yet that didn't stare at her like the village idiot watching aliens land on Main Street. So the Young Saints were about to have their vows of future abstinence tested, which could prove to be pretty interesting.

Krissy darted from kid to kid checking out their grips and fitting them with the right balls. It was cool to watch because the boys were bouncing around like ping pong balls, asking her questions to get a closer look, yet at the same time torn sideways to get right to the lanes and get started bowling, but it was the girls who were glued to Krissy the most, though, and you couldn't quite tell what was going through their minds. Krissy was oblivious to it all though—

she really was. She understood lechers and drunks, but she was just another kid out there trying to help them with something she had learned and it was innocent wonderful fun just to watch her.

"Billy, thanks so much for having us," Father Alex said, approaching the bar and handing me the $90 check which was the hour and a half, five-lane deal that we had agreed upon several months earlier. Some of the Young Saints had filed through the door to the parking lot, but the bold ones lurked nearby; twelve year old boys who, now that the fun of bowling was over, turned their full attention on Krissy—stumbling into friends, the wall, or the door— mouths open, eyes popped, young dicks getting hard for maybe the first time and perhaps promising eternal damnation. And still the girls stole hypnotic looks upon leaving, they too stumbling about before spilling outside where they collided with the boldest boys sneaking back for another peek.

"You're more than welcome, Father Alex," I replied. "Should I book you again in two weeks?"

"Certainly, Billy, the kids love it here . . . and this young lady is?" Father Alex asked benevolently as Krissy approached, looking upon her with a kind, not leering face like she was used to.

"I'm Krissy . . . Krissy Kurtz," she said with a beaming smile before I could fashion an introduction.

"Well it's very nice to meet you, Krissy. I'm Father Alex from St. Johns Parish. You were very good with the kids and we really appreciate that—thanks. Well, you both have a nice afternoon now," he said and turned toward the door where three or four of the Young Saints now scrambled out of sight.

Even as I watched him closely, I still couldn't get a handle on Father Alex—I mean, like whether he would have been into the little boys who were bowling, into Krissy, perhaps, or exclusively betrothed to God, which was pretty much the way it was supposed to be I imagined. Whatever, he was either an exceptional actor or else I pretty much figured God had him in his pocket.

Some junior high kids from Fort Harrison were bowling Lane 1 and two families that I knew from Fort Recovery were on 3 and 4. The lowlifes hadn't yet arrived for late afternoon cocktails nor had the large group from Fort Loramie that had six lanes reserved at 7 for a good ole' Catholic family reunion. We'd hosted the Barhorsts since I was a kid and they would arrive after dinner, most already shit faced, and I knew Krissy would be busy at the bar where the leering men would stumble for another hundred beers or so as their wives slowly lost humor and assimilated domestic bombs I only hoped they'd wait to detonate in their own space.

Baxter finished re-racking all the stinky shoes, and after hitting the john to wash his hands, popped back to the bar for the last Arby's that I told him earlier he could have. He asked me what else needed done and I told him that everything was kosher and to take his sandwich and some pop and take a break in my 'apartment' and watch TV until a little before the Barhorsts were scheduled to arrive. Baxter thought my digs was tits and I had to laugh as his eyes lit up when I'd told him to go catch some TV in the back. A Reds/Astros game was on the TV up front, which I figured Baxter had flipped on, and with a big smile he thanked me and headed to the back where I knew he'd resume his sport obsession. Oddly, even though Baxter was certainly no athlete, he was always glued to the TV games, and particularly in the fall and winter when I'd noticed he absorbed every NFL game he possibly could find, although it seemed he could have cared less about the FHHS Rams or even Ohio State, which was certainly an ass-backward approach in Fort Harrison. It would still be a few years yet before we all came to understand the dynamic implications of that.

Krissy sat on a bar stool, her legs crossed, purposely flashing a glimpse of pink crotch the size of a small piece of pizza which she knew drove me crazy. Baxter was into Krissy, but very different from Brent. Even in front of me, Brent would have been unable to keep his eyes off darting to Krissy's crotch. He just couldn't have. Baxter, on the other hand, just adored Krissy but never once had seemed to stare or lust after her at all. Krissy'd once asked me if I though Baxter was gay and all I could say was 'I don't know,' cause I didn't.

All these years later we still don't know and have never heard whether he ever got married or not, at least he hadn't the last time I'd talked to Brent, but that had been over a year ago. I really didn't think he was gay though, I just didn't, and not because I didn't know a few of the *festives* because I did—and that included Dennis Shindeldecker who had even been a big shot lineman for Sam Giovanazzo a decade earlier. I mean you gotta be careful because you can get way too stereotypical with people sometimes and especially the festives, and when it really comes right down to it, what's the difference anyhow? There are much better things to tax your brain cells over and I'd long since believed that the greatest problem facing mankind was overpopulation . . . *and, well* . . . the festives certainly were leading the charge relative to that solution . . . or something such.

# Chapter Thirty-seven

"Billy, who was that *hot* guy again?" Krissy asked, dreamily. "You mean the priest? I just know him as Father Alex. He's new over at St. Johns."

"So he's like a minister, right, Billy? Preaches the gospel and all?" she asked, her wheels turning, I could tell.

"Well I never quite heard Catholics put it that way, but yes, I guess. He's a Catholic Priest, Krissy, just like Father Casey at St. Matthias. You know what a Catholic Priest is, don't you?"

"Well I don't know about all that religious stuff, Billy, but I know a little. He's awful hot; I know that much. Sure would be a shame if God got to keep that one all to himself," she said, giggling.

Krissy rotated on the bar stool toward me. Even with our familiarity, my autonomous eyes roamed every inch of her and my brain had to force itself to work in reverse if I were going to head off a painful erection for the next couple of hours . . . until she could take care of it for me much later. I loved her platinum hair and never understood why she went on her black kicks. Krissy never really had girlfriends like most girls. I don't know why I'd thought about that then, I just did. I always figured it was because she was not only drop dead gorgeous without even trying, but played the role of courtesan which all men (and boys—and more than likely even most priests) loved, unless they were lying or honestly *did* have a special pact with God. She had been very appropriate with Father Alex, but I think his neutrality had sort of thrown her.

I went behind the bar to start washing a tray of glasses Baxter had brought to the counter before heading to the back. I turned the submersible glass washer on, shooting a squirt of liquid soap in the already hot water Baxter had drawn and finished them off in about thirty seconds. Krissy had followed, reaching down to snag a hand full of the cumulus suds which she balanced on my nose, giggling, then just as suddenly turned to me, not ready yet to drop the Father Alex deal.

"I'm serious, Billy, that guy was hot. Isn't it supposed to be the deal or something that priests aren't allowed to fuck women so they're always messing with little boys? I mean how does that make sense? Mindy told me that once, but I don't get that at all, besides it makes me really sick. I mean I half understood Mom's perverts coming after me, but Priests and little boys, now that's really disgusting and especially a hot guy like that priest that was just here," Krissy pressed.

"Priests are *celibate,* Krissy. That means they take vows of *abstinence* and . . ."

"I *know,* Billy, I get it—*the guy's not supposed to fuck to honor God and all that*—but that's such a waste it seems, such a waste for a woman out there somewhere. Plus, I bet if you gave me ten minutes alone with him he'd forget about little boys and it just doesn't make sense that a good God would be pissed about it. And then we wouldn't have that *little boy problem*, would we? I mean how could a good God want that?" she asked seriously.

We had both gone into the kitchen off the left side of the bar, out of sight of even Winston. Jesus, Krissy could amaze me, but she probably had a damn good point. In a way she was dead serious, I could tell, and it troubled her, the part about the little boys. I knew it would always reside in a brain cell in that pretty head, yet she allowed the affliction but a momentary refuge before relighting the world with her playful humor and dancing wit, stuffing her hand into the front of my jeans and exclaiming, "Well here's *one thing* I ain't gotta worry about cause ain't no priest gonna bother you, Billy Bowling, cause you ain't no *little* boy . . . *you're a v- e- r- y big boy,"* she purred, before giving my balls that expected squeeze that delivered the masochistic pain I had learned to love. But I pulled away . . .

"Krissy, wait . . . it's not like *all* priests molest boys, just a few of them, and around here I've really only heard about the one in New Bremen a few years back."

"Oh, Billy, stuff a cork in it. My point was simple. Let priests fuck women and the little boy problem goes away . . . duh! I don't care whether it's here or in frigin' Rome. Is that so hard to understand? And as for Father Alex or whatever his name is, he got me *real* hot and bothered, so *you* better be able to take (she held her wristwatch up dramatically) care of that in exactly 3 hours 37 minutes and 8 seconds, Billy Bowling," she said, standing on her toes and whispering in my ear, "or I guess I'll just have to get in my car and go hunt him down now won't I? Cause I'm hot, Billy . . . *so so hot!*" she giggled, pushing a wad of saliva deep in my ear before heading off into the seats to pick up pop cans and candy bar wrappers, emitting a light laughter that trailed her like a long kite tail fashioned of larkspur.

Tic Forgett, Garth Schmutz and Joe Smith arrived, already smashed and arguing over some bet Tic and Garth had made about the 1978 FHHS football team. Their lives were pretty much football, beer, and probably jacking off thinking about Krissy or maybe even Busty. Garth had been married for like a year or so I once heard, but it didn't work out—surprise. Tic's only chance for a bride would have probably been through the Russian slave trade and Joe lived with his parents, unemployed, though surprisingly always with beer money. The open bowlers were leaving, returning their shoes, so I popped across to shelve them, taking a quick glance at my watch to see if I could break the record for holding my breath. Krissy ducked under the walkthrough, throwing open the cooler and pushed two Miller Lites and a Bud across the bar. The ogling of Krissy had commenced, and though the talk could be fairly crude, it was never directed *toward* her. Krissy and the Three Stooges had interacted for what now amounted to years and everyone well knew the acceptable script.

I had my own rounds to make, checking pins, spotters and ball returns, and making sure there hadn't been any alley or equipment damage so it could be assigned to the offenders if needed. As long as the bowlers knew you checked regularly, there were almost never any problems, which was the point. There were a few big scuffs on Lane 1 where the Fort Harrison junior high shit-heads had been bowling, but no serious damage. I might decide to scare Ronnie Seden, a cocky little seventh grader who thought he was a hot shit, by threatening to send a damage bill for $114 to his parents. I'd learned a long time ago that if you made it an odd number it would make the idiots nervous, but if you just said a hundred bucks, they'd think you were fucking with them right up front; the mysteries of the simple mind!

I had to laugh about Krissy and Father Alex. I knew Krissy pretty well and could tell that though she may have been attracted to him, more than anything she was trying to get a rise out of me. Krissy had not only made me comfortable with sex, but more than anything else she had helped me keep my head out of my ass—unlike Dad—and had helped me grow up to be much more responsible than I might been had she not been around. Yep, without Krissy Kurtz, I think I might have just cashed my chips in even *before* my entire world came crashing down. But above all else, Krissy had taught me to laugh, something I think I had 'dislearned' even before Mom and Libby were killed. And without that, I would have been doomed . . . *at each and every step along the way.*

I was chuckling about it all and smiling to myself as I made the rounds before the reunion group hit the door. With everything checked I went to the back of the alley, my apartment now of nearly three years. Baxter met me at the door on his way back up front since it was nearly time for the Barhorsts. I told him to get a bucket of cocktail ice and that I would be back up front shortly.

My space was really quite cool, but nevertheless it was time to get out and find a real life. I had gone to yard sales and thrift shops, trashed my original old couch years back for a nice hide-a-way, later adding a lounge chair and coffee table. I had a desk, 2 dressers and a wardrobe, all of which I had added over the years, along with a really nice 16x8 brand new thick shag carpet that Roger Edmunds, who owned a small carpet store up town had offered me for twenty bucks one night while bowling drunk. He said Mary Christman ordered it, then refused to buy it for whatever reason and he didn't figure it would sell too quick. Since he had little storage space he made a good deal for me and I loved it, especially after Krissy and I christened it in fashion the first night I set it in place.

I still had my original fridge and microwave, which was all I needed since I had a whole kitchen up front. I had CD and DVD players and a couple of months earlier had ditched my ole 19" Zenith for a 32" Sony that Baxter's parents sold me for $50 after they got a big screen deal. I'd had a few friends around off and on, but mostly it used to be Brent and now was Baxter who spent any time at my pad at all, except for Krissy, who for most of a year now had pretty much lived with me. It was actually all quite cool if you can picture living in an 'apartment' where a ball is striking bowling pins about five thousand times a night twenty feet away. And even after you lock everyone out—the sound still rings in your head.

Mops and brooms, tools and spare machine parts, I kept well organized in a large broom closet and at a workbench and storage cupboards in the far southeast corner, along with my weight bench, giving me quite a bit of space within the area which measured 70 x 9 across the whole back of the alley. It was definitely not your *normal* pad, but was a Manhattan penthouse compared to the despicable and depressing trailer where Dad and Busty lived.

There had always been a phone on the workbench, and as I pushed through the door to grab a mop, it rang. I had bought a large clock for a hoot at a garage sale at Sterile Cheryl Fox's commune. It was just like the kind in the school classrooms and I had been quite curious how she had come by it? It was a favorite part of my décor, however, and I honestly got quite a kick out of it. I glanced at it now as I reached for the phone, noting it was 6:55.

"Bowling's Bowling Center, can I help you?"

"Is this Billy? Billy Bowling?" a ladies voice asked.

"Sure is, what can I do for you?" I answered.

"This is Clare Putnam, Gwen's mother."

Immediately it seemed odd that she would call. I mean, Gwen might for some reason, but why Mrs. Putnam, I wondered, and an uneasy feeling crept upon me though for no particular reason.

"Hello Mrs. Putnam, how can I help you?" I asked, hearing and feeling a cracking in my voice.

"We've just arrived home, Billy, and we're trying to locate Gwen. Her brother, Mike, came over to meet her for milking they'd planned at five and he said she wasn't here. We circled her normal workout route, but didn't see her anywhere, although her car is here. I understood the two of you were going to the track meet this morning in Minister. Did you go then, and do you have any idea where she might be?" she asked pleasantly.

"Yes, Mrs. Putnam, we went to the meet. I drove and then we left early so Gwen could run and I could return to work. I dropped her off around one thirty or a little earlier and she went into the house through the back door to change for her workout. That was the last I saw her. And then I left to come back to the alley," I answered, nervously, I remember thinking even then.

"Well I'm sure there's *a simple explanation*. I just thought you might have a quick answer for us. Thank you, Billy," she said politely and hung up.

# Chapter Thirty-eight

*B*axter stayed till just after eight when Krissy and I figured we could handle the rest of the evening. There must have been forty people in the Barhorst Reunion and they were drinking like fish, particularly the men who stumbled every ten minutes or so to the bar for another beer, unable to take their eyes off Krissy, just as I had imagined. Winston Thermostat was taking a mysteriously rare trip on the bus to Dayton the next morning and had left early. Tic and his flunkies left just after Baxter, though a sprinkling of townies plus some guys from the outlying towns stopped by as usual on Saturday night—to have a beer or two, but mostly to see what Krissy was wearing that night. She was definitely good for business and many nights raked in a hundred bucks or so in tips.

I couldn't get the call from Mrs. Putnam out of my mind, but since I'd heard nothing further, felt pretty certain Gwen had turned up and everything was ok. The Barhorst group fazed out by 9:30, though four of the guys stayed another half hour to drink at the bar and ogle. Krissy told me later she got over a hundred in tips just from the Barhorsts and another seventy from the regulars, which was probably more than the whole damn alley cleared!

By 10:45 everybody had cleared and we locked the doors, deciding to do cleanup in the morning cause we were dead on our feet and Dad wasn't expected until late afternoon Monday. I didn't drink a lot, the occasional beer, and Krissy didn't that much either, but sometimes when she was planning to get really wild she would make some pretty interesting drinks and when buzzed could be like a wild animal.

"Billy, have a taste of this and tell me what you think," Krissy said, taking a spoon of something red from the blender and feeding it into my mouth.

It was kick ass strong, but good at the same time. "Wow, what you got in there? That's good," I said as she fed another large spoonful into my mouth and then frenching me, took most of it back out and swallowing it herself.

"You gotta guess, babe," she said, giggling.

"Ok, I know there's ice cream and tequila, right?"

"Keep going," she said, stuffing another spoonful into me and allowing me to swallow it this time.

"It's strawberry, that's for sure, but I taste coconut too. Must be some Malibu. Come on, just tell me."

"Oh, you're no fun, Bill Bowling! (the second time I'd heard that in a day so I was beginning to believe I just wasn't much fun). Ok, vanilla ice cream, strawberry daiquiri mix, Absolut, Malibu, tequila and crushed ice. So you like it?" she asked, having poured us each a full beer mug of the delightful red mix.

"I love it, Krissy. So what do you call it?" I asked jokingly.

"*Sex on the Bar*," she said, leering at me, but keeping a straight face.

"Great name, babe," I replied, somewhat clueless, before taking a big gulp straight out of the mug.

"I want *two* of them," she purred in my ear as she began to stroke my crotch.

"You sure about that? It's gonna hit us pretty hard *real quick*," I said dumbly.

"*Two I said*," she softly purred, now chewing on my ear and pushing her skirt to the floor before kicking it high into the air where it comically landed, and remained levitated atop, the Johnny Walker Red on the second level of the liquor shelf.

"Aren't we gonna go back and watch TV?" I asked, expecting to go back and get crazy in bed like we usually did.

"Billy, you're so dense sometimes. *Two*, don't you get it . . . *I want Two—Two Sex on the Bars*—one to drink, which I'm finishing right now and then I want the *real thing*, Billy. We always talk about it and still haven't done it. I want you to fuck me on the bar right here, right now, so that everyday I'm working and all those losers are sloshing down beers and dreaming about getting in my pants, I'll be able to see you drilling me hard—hard, hard, hard—right where their stupid beer bottles are sitting. Yeh, I want that to think about a lot. Maybe I'll even tell them that, Billy—tell them how you fucked me hard and how my legs and boots were pointed toward the sky as you pounded and pounded and pounded," she growled, pushing my pants to the floor and kneeling low to take me into her mouth.

I leaned back against the bar, feeling every muscle in my body loosen. I could feel my dick bouncing off her tonsils before she pulled back, dragging my penis in painful ecstacy across her perfectly fixed teeth. I took a big gulp of her *Sex on the Bar* and pulled off Jimmy's track sweatshirt that I had donned earlier that morning before leaving to pick Gwen Putnam up, throwing it across the bar. Together Krissy and I had learned each other and I knew tonight she didn't want me to just come in her mouth so I brushed her cheek when I was nearly ready to come and she stood up moving her mouth to mine where I returned the favor, sucking and inhaling her tongue the way she had been pleasuring me.

I kicked off my tennies and stood nude behind the bar as I continued to devour her tongue while caressing her moist womanhood with my left hand and working in three fingers as she squealed in delight. The instant I pulled away from her face I had her blouse and bra laying upon the bar, pulling first one then the other full breast into my mouth, letting them slowly escape before catching the nipple with my teeth, careful not to completely break the bond. Krissy's nipples were extremely sensitive and within seconds of my now rough game she was screaming for penetration.

Taking Krissy in my arms, I lifted her upon the bar where she too was now totally nude except for her pink ankle boots and white socks which capped the perfect dark brown legs pointing now toward the heavens. Krissy had quite a selection of sexy boots and these pink ones were the sexiest yet. I climbed upon the bar and pulled her wonderful female charms to my face, making her writhe and scream even more.

"*B i l l y* . . . don't make me wait any longer . . . *B i l l y* . . . I want it *now* . . . don't tease me . . . don't fucking tease me Billy—*N O W!*" she squealed.

I know it was passion and sex and all that and I know we weren't even supposed to be doing it from a moral posture, but it was at the pinnacle of passion that I fell in love more and more with Krissy Kurtz each time. You can preach and scold or shake your head in disgust at sinners purchasing a ticket to hell. I'm just telling you how it was and that I'm not all that sure it *was* a bad thing. Krissy was soft and thrilling and even funny in the apex of passion and it just felt right. More than anything in my life, it just felt right. I can't pretend that the bar was all that comfortable, but the passion was over the moon by the time I entered Krissy. She raked her turquoise nails across my back as she cried out in orgasm after orgasm until I finally joined her and we both collapsed in placid, if exhausted, satisfaction.

# Chapter Thirty-nine

*W*e lay in each other's arms on the bar and it was as comfortable at that moment as a hay wagon of down. Krissy draped her left leg over mine and dug at my balls with the sharp heal of her boot, an incredibly exciting, though painful game, that she often played as a *postlogue* to another wonderful chapter of love. The bar was lit by a string of pearl lights across and above the liquor shelves and by several beer signs, reflecting colors off the bottles like a favorite and cherished Christmas. Directly above us the circular Budweiser Hitch revolved with a dull hum, reflecting its age and bouncing strobe like colors off Krissy's perfect breasts. She looked up into my eyes with a gaze I knew I had never seen before.

"Billy, I love you." It was something that had *never* been said before—even after more than two years of teenage passion, which were now nearly history anyhow as within a few short weeks we would both turn twenty. It was like doing everything backwards and yet somehow for us it had seemed perfectly right.

"I know . . . and Krissy . . . I love you, too," I said, stroking her soft platinum hair.

"I've never said that to *anybody* before, Billy, not ever, not even to my Mom. I didn't even think I could say it at all, but it makes me feel good right now saying it to you cause I've felt it for a long time."

"I've never said it before either, Kris. I think my Mom said it to Jimmy and me when we were little, but I'm really not sure. I just *want* to believe it more than I really remember that she said it," I said, feeling good and sad at the same time.

"I've had guys say it to me, but it was bullshit just to try to get in my pants and I always knew that. I didn't want them to say it anyhow because they didn't have a right to. They didn't *know* me, but you do so I can trust you, can't I?" she said, laying her head upon my chest and softly crying.

"Yes, Krissy, you can trust me," I answered, sliding the back of my hand softly across her cheek.

"I've never loved another guy, not ever. I think I even hate men, but I learned to tease them even as a kid and I'm ashamed of that. There's a lot of stuff I wish I hadn't done, like I told you, but it was never really bad stuff, Billy. I was *never* like I used to hear the kids say—not even close," she gasped, and I could now *feel* her tears on my chest.

"I know, Krissy, and I always have," I said, stroking her hair.

"Billy, I never met my Dad. He left before I was even born and Mom won't talk about him and swears she doesn't know where he is. All I know is that his name was Sam Kurtz and that they were married about four years. Just long enough to make Tammy and me. I've hated Mom a lot, though it probably wasn't her fault a lot of the time and I know that. But when you're a little kid you learn to hate stuff like that— not having a Dad like other kids. And I've hated her because of those two asshole stepfathers, and especially Cal Johnson for messing with Tammy. But there were others, too. They'd stay awhile and maybe give her money to pay the rent for a month or so, stuff like that. I know she's been pretty much a whore, but Billy, she's not as bad as she used to be and in a way she's been a good Mom. I mean I see that more now. She tries—I really think she does—but she does what she has to do. *I just want something different someday, Billy, you know what I mean—something better—that's what I want,*" she said, burying her face in my chest and sobbing softly.

"I know, Kris, I know," I said, continuing to stroke her hair as she cried. "It's time for us to make a difference in how *we* live now. There's got to come a point where you say *no* to the people who are out there to steal your life, just like Dad stole Mom's, tried to steal Jimmy's, and like I finally realized, he has mine pretty much all along, just like Jimmy said he always would. But no more, Kris! We've learned to deal with stuff that would destroy most kids and now it's time to use that for us. God put you on the planet for me and you have helped me more than you will ever know. I don't know when or how, but one day all our bullshit's gonna help us get through stuff that would take anybody else down."

"Billy, I really respect you and a lot of people do; you just don't know it. Everybody knows you've had it bad, but you have always been cool, like you're thinking a step ahead of everyone else. People like you too, and they understand how hard you have to work. I've heard that before . . . a lot," she said, kissing me on the cheek.

"Thanks Kris, but life's tough for everybody at some point. It's just that even the little things make most people think the world shit on *only them* and then when something really big comes down it destroys them. You and me—well the way I see it—we've already learned how to play our hand during pretty tough times so how can it get much worse? It's our turn now for the good things, girl. Does that make sense to you?"

"Yep, Billy it does. But Billy . . ." she said, starting to sob again against my chest.

"What, Krissy?"

"Do you respect me? I mean I think you believed me when I told you I've never done anything crazy or sexy with anybody but you, but I know I've teased a lot and it's bad, isn't it? I could dress different too . . . or not joke around so much or . . ."

"Stop, Kris!" I said almost crossly, lifting her above my chest to look into my eyes. "We've been through this before. We don't live our lives for other people and that includes *you* for *me.* That's why I have known for a long time that I love you because I've never seen you do that. So let's don't start now! And Jesus, Kris, why would I *ever* want you to change—*anything!* I'm the luckiest guy in the world, but as much as I love your bod, babe, it's your spirit and humor and your energy that give me the biggest orgasms, Kris. So don't you *dare* change one single thing, Krissy Kurtz . . . not until you are ready to do it for *you!* And truthfully, babe, I hope that that day never comes. Do we get each other now, my beautiful girl?"

Her sobs started to subside and she hugged me tightly. "Yeah, Billy, we do. You're so smart . . . you really are."

"Well, I'm not so sure about that, but I do believe it's *our turn* now and that we are more prepared than most kids to move on, college or not, but we've got to stay us. I love how you dress and you do too. It's why you do it. I love your personality cause you are such a joy to be around and yes, to answer your question, *I respect you more than anyone I ever have met in my entire life.* I'm so proud of you, Kris, and have always wanted to SHOUT that you were my girl, but I didn't think that would be ok with you," I said as we both sat up on the bar and looked into each other's eyes.

Krissy kissed me, first softly, and then with again passion. "Billy, I love you and I love to hear myself say it. And Billy?" she queried, waiting.

"Yes, Kris?"

"You can scream at the top of your lungs that I'm your girl—*anytime and wherever you are when the moment moves you*—so how's that, big boy?" she bubbled.

"That's wonderful, Kris, just wonderful. God, I am so lucky. You are a wonder, dear girl—a wonder!" She kissed me again, licking my ear and reaching across to toy with my right nipple, first as a tickle, then suddenly pinching it—*hard!* "Kris, you'd better quit that," I said, reflexively jumping and knowing that I'd be ready for *business* again soon unless we changed the game—and fast.

"Did you like my drink, Billy? There's still part of mine left," she said, reaching down the bar and grabbing the partly filled red beer mug that had surprisingly survived the war. "Here finish this . . . while I attend to the *other one*," a line *at first l o s t . . .*

. . . The big gulp of Krissy's *Sex on the Bar* hijacked my tongue as it went past for Krissy had hopped off the bar and sitting now, on the stool directly in front of me, had taken my growing stiffness into her mouth where within minutes drained it again, spraying another surprising wave of white pearls across her blackberry nipples and laughing as she rubbed it into her perfect dark glistening skin. *( God, Krissy Kurtz, don't ever change, I thought to myself . . . p l e a s e girl, don't e v e r change! )*

*I was as peaceful as I'd ever been in my life at that moment . . . even as I was but hours removed from personal Armageddon.*

# Chapter Forty

Glancing across the room at the old school clock, I saw that it was 8:10 am and the phone was blasting in my ear. Just last week I'd run a line across the long wall and put a second phone on the small bedside table, for which I just then had sharp regrets. Having eventually reconnected with our clothing, Krissy and I had sat at the bar far into the morning, drinking another large pitcher of 'Sex on the Bar' and talking like we'd never done before—about life, about us, about families or the lack thereof, about Uncle Marco's phone call . . . and about dreams. *Our Dreams!* Now as the morning sun infiltrated the blinds, spilling bright plaid across the wild shag, I realized I had a genuine hangover for the first time in my life. Gently disengaging from a sleeping Krissy, whom the phone hadn't stirred, I sat on the edge of the hide-a-way and reached for the receiver.

"Yeah?" I answered with shortness.

"Billy, it's Baxter. Have you heard?" his voice queried.

"No, Baxter, I haven't *heard*, because *you* just woke me up. I was sleeping. It's Sunday morning, for Christ sake! Remember—nothing's on til this afternoon," I answered, pointedly.

"I'm sorry, I really am, but I thought I should call because we're friends. *Gwen Putnam's missing.* My Dad saw it on Lima TV."

A numbness invaded my being (not unlike that cold February night that was rocked by the explosion that killed Mom and Libby) as I tried to digest what Baxter had just said. But surely there was *a simple* explanation—I mean that's what Clare Putnam had said yesterday, hadn't she? Why was Baxter calling me anyhow and why would he call me about Gwen? And on TV? That was impossible. It was only yesterday morning that Gwen and I were at the track meet together in Minster. But it *was* Gwen Putnam, the thought flashed, . . . and that made *all* the difference in the world, didn't it?

. . . "Billy, are you there? Did you hear me? They say Gwen Putnam is missing and that no one has seen her since yesterday. I called you because Tim Otte and I went for pizza last night and he said you were with her at the track meet yesterday, sitting together at the top of the bleachers. I just thought you should know cause he said his parents were talking all funny, you know . . . about you being with her. I hope I didn't do the wrong thing to call. I don't mean anything other than I wanted you to know if you didn't," he'd said modestly.

I'd never heard Baxter say so many words at once, and though his voice had been louder than usual, it was strained. I just had to think. I stood up and walked across the long room, trying to grasp it all, trying to think, which wasn't working because suddenly I became scared . . . *scared for Gwen* . . . if still completely ignorant of the circumstances that would soon bring my own world crashing down.

"Billy, do you hear me? Are you there?" Baxter asked, quietly now.

"Yes, I'm here, but you can't be right. There's got to be a mix up, a mistake," I said, feeling like I should run out and jump in my Explorer and look for Gwen, certain that within minutes I could find her and she'd hop in joking with me, just like yesterday.

"So nobody has called you but me?" Baxter asked.

"Well, yesterday, just before you left the alley, Mrs. Putnam called. I was in the back and answered. She asked me about Gwen and I told her I had dropped her off at the back door and left. Around 1:30. She was real nice and said 'there'd probably be a simple explanation' and hung up. That was about seven and since I never heard anything more, I figured everything was fine."

"My Dad says on TV they're making it sound bad, like maybe somebody kidnapped her when she was out running."

I suddenly felt as if the alley was ablaze and all exits padlocked. Then there was the sound of the TV and glancing across the room I saw Krissy, now sitting up and framed by a bulkhead of cumulus pillows.

"Is there anything else? I need to think about this awhile, Ok? So is there anything else right now?"

"No."

"Ok then, Baxter, I gotta go. Call me if you hear anything else," I said shortly and hung up.

I walked slowly across the room toward Krissy whose big smile began to change as I drew nearer.

"Billy, what's wrong?"

"Remember last night when we were talking about everything and I told you about spending that time with Gwen Putnam, and about her college paper on the explosion that killed Mom and Libby? You do remember that, don't you?" I asked, thinking it could have easily passed her by—given the nature of our long evening.

"Yeh, so . . . I don't get it?"

I paused. Even though I'd told Krissy that part, I hadn't told her about going to the track meet, not that she and I answered to each other . . . at least not before last night. But I'd thought she still might have been hurt, or started doubting herself, so I hadn't brought it up. It just hadn't seemed that important.

"Baxter just called and they say Gwen Putnam is missing, and that it's been on TV," I said, trying to block out the TV in the background, perversely thinking that if I didn't hear it I'd wake up from a dream to find TV's had as yet to be invented.

"On TV? What do you mean on TV?" she asked.

"I don't know for sure, Kris, I haven't seen it. Baxter's dad was the one who saw it I guess, but you know how strange he is, so maybe he's wrong."

"Jeez, why are you getting so upset then?" she asked sincerely.

"Why am I so upset?" I shot back, feeling immediately bad I'd spoken crossly to her, before continuing, "I'm worried about Gwen. What if something *really has* happened to her?"

Then suddenly it hit me . . . and I froze in panic.

"What's wrong? Talk to me. You're scaring me, Billy," Krissy said, having learned to read me like a book.

"Ok, I'll tell you what's wrong," I answered, desperately trying to make sense of this insanity. "Because if nobody's seen Gwen Putnam since yesterday, then I may have been the last person to see her!"

"I don't understand?"

"Gwen Putnam and I went to the track meet together yesterday morning in Minster. She asked me to go and I figured that she had a few last questions for her paper so I went because there really wasn't anything to do at the alley. I drove since she'd bought me lunch two days in a row and I thought that would sorta pay her back. We left the meet a little after one o'clock and I dropped her at her house cause she had a long workout to do. That was the last I saw her. She disappeared inside the backdoor of her house and then I left to come back to the alley for work. I can't possibly see how anything could have happened to her. There's got to be some mistake," I said, wracking my brain over Gwen, still not seriously admitting to my own precarious situation.

"Billy, if people saw you leave the track meet and then you came back here to work and Baxter was here, then you have an alibi, don't you, and . . ."

"Alibi? What are you talking about—*an alibi*? Why do I need an alibi? I'm worried about what happened to her . . . *oh, my God* . . . you mean you think people might think *I* did something to her?" I gasped, slumping on the bed and grasping exactly what she'd just said.

"Well, you did say you might have been the last person to see her. But, Billy, I'm sure she's fine, don't worry about it," Krissy said, scooting closely and massaging my shoulders.

Suddenly a loud knocking resonated across the lanes from doors up front and glancing again at the clock I saw it was now 8:35. It was all falling into place—someone wanted to talk to me about Gwen Putnam and very possibly it was the cops, either Wade Borger or the sheriff—and I became frightened in a way I'd never before known.

The pounding grew louder. "Kris, you'd better get dressed. I'll go see who it is," I said, pulling on my jeans and throwing on the same sweatshirt I had donned to that very minute, 24 hours earlier—when all the world had been happy and wondrous.

Approaching the double doors I could see it *was* Sheriff Sam Oberly, and with a deputy I didn't recognize. He saw me approaching and the pounding ceased.

"Billy Bowling, right?" he asked as I opened the door.

"Yes, that's me," I'd answered, trying to be casual, which I'm almost certain I hadn't been.

"Glad to meet you, Billy. I sure remember your brother, Jimmy. Hell of a football player, that one. And I remember your family tragedy, Billy. Real sorry about that."

"Sheriff, it's about Gwen, isn't it?" As soon as I said it I knew that had been a big mistake. 'Jesus, Bowling, let them ask the fucking questions. Don't go volunteering shit like you've rehearsed a fucking script!' No wonder innocent people get nailed all the time. I mean criminals know how to act cause they probably take '*Who Me? 101*,' but when you're innocent—you're fucked—and hanging yourself without a rope is the easiest thing to do in the world.

"Yeah, Billy, it is. I guess you were with Gwen Putnam yesterday, right?"

"Yesterday morning, we . . ."

"Well look, could you take a ride with us down to Chief Borger's office in town? It shouldn't take much time. Or you can follow us down in your car if you'd like. We've just got a few questions for you, Billy, standard stuff you know. Besides there's probably *a perfectly simple explanation* for this little mess anyway, I'm sure. Nothing to worry about, I certainly wouldn't think," he said, though I could have sworn he had a half smirk on his face and his nameless stooge of a deputy seemed to be turned away as if stifling a laugh.

# Chapter Forty-one

*K*rissy ran up the catwalk, meeting me just inside the door, hugging me tightly and burying her face in my chest, softly crying. I had answered questions for maybe forty minutes for Sheriff Oberly, Deputy Marty Piquad, I later learned, and Wade Borger himself. I'd explained the simple course of the day events as they'd unfolded—Gwen and I heading to the meet at 9, then leaving a bit after 1:00 so she could do her twenty mile workout and I could return to the alley to work. Straight forward it had seemed, and everyone was really quite pleasant.

But even as I held Krissy, I began to fear for Gwen again, having now shed my own selfish fears. Where could she be? She and her parents must have gotten mixed up and she had returned to Notre Dame with a friend or had some other important appointment that they hadn't known about? It had to be something like that, surely, even if she hadn't used her car, which we had discussed during the questioning.

Krissy and I crossed over to and sat at the bar. Even with the time spent at Chief Borger's office, it was still only 9:45 and we weren't open until 2. I knew she wanted to ask me about the questioning, but there really wasn't much to say. Then, at eleven, Baxter called again: "Billy, the cops stopped at my house and my parents are really upset. It was the county sheriff and Wade Borger. They asked me questions while my parents stood there listening. I'm a little nervous about it all and my Mom says I can't come to work today."

"Why? I mean why wouldn't she want you to come to work? What did they ask you? I don't understand?" I protested, taking the phone and walking into the lobby.

"They asked me what time you got to the alley yesterday afternoon. I had to tell them three, Billy. Then they asked me if you seemed upset or different and I thought you were, so I told them that. I couldn't say anything else. I couldn't lie. My parents were standing right beside me," he said, rattled in a way that I would have never believed Baxter Sturdivant capable of.

Why would I have expected Baxter to do anything other than tell the truth? Then I remembered that I'd told Sheriff Oberly I'd gotten back to the alley a little after two I thought. Sure, I *had* fucked off for maybe forty-five minutes or so driving around and at the culvert on Indian Creek doing pretty much nothing, but no one knew it or where I was so I hadn't figured there wasn't any reason to even bring it up. But now there was an hour gap between what Baxter told them and what I had said—*then it struck me like a bolt of lightning*—it was nearly three when I had left that asshole, Clint Obringer, and I hadn't told them about that either. This was not good, I suddenly understood—and particularly if they talked to Clint by any chance.

. . . I remembered Baxter on the line, but he spoke up before I could. "Billy, the cops acted funny when I told them when you got to the alley. I mean they like looked at each other kind of funny and all. I had to tell them the truth, especially with my parents standing there glaring at me," he repeated for like the third time.

"It's ok, Baxter, nobody wants you to lie. Nobody needs to lie about anything, but I don't get you not coming to work? There are a couple of big groups due this afternoon and I need your help. Can I talk to your Mom?" I asked innocently, since I had known the Sturdivants for years.

"No, Billy, I don't think that'd be a good idea. I gotta go. I'm real sorry. My Mom just came . . ." . . . and then there was only a dial tone.

I hung up, feeling an alien panic set in. Insanity was everywhere. Taking a few steps, I sank backwards upon a barstool.

"Was that Baxter? What did he want?" Krissy asked sweetly, but knowing things were going all wrong fast.

"Yeh, it was Baxter. Says he can't come to work; that his Mom won't let him because the cops went to their house to ask him questions."

"About what?"

"About when I got to work yesterday, which was an hour later than I should have," I answered, not wanting to talk more or explain.

"Why?" she asked, softly.

"Krissy, can we let it go? You don't believe I did anything . . . *do you?*"

"Jesus, Billy, *of course not*," she cried.

"Then can we just let it go for now. It's just all so insane."

"You want something to drink or a burger or something? You're probably hungry," she replied, dropping the subject.

"Just get me a coke, Kris."

I had been so caught up and worried about the questioning, I had forgotten how truly hung over I was. Of all days to be hung over for the first time in my life, it had to be the day I get questioned by the cops for a potential kidnapping. I'd hoped no one had smelled the rare liquor breath I hosted, but I'd snarfed a pocketful of cinnamon mints and had no reason to believe they'd detected it—or I was fairly certain they would have asked a few different questions. At least that was what I was trying to convince myself to believe.

"Krissy, can you put a couple scoops of ice cream in a mug with the coke? Coke and ice cream sounds like the trick I need right now."

The coke float mellowed my stomach and I started really worrying about Gwen Putnam again even as I refused to admit to the gravity of my own situation. Krissy kneaded my shoulders and I began to relax. I had given her one of the dressers in the back and she had at least half her clothes at the alley now, having cleaned up and dressed for the day while I was gone. She'd begun to dress a bit 'traditional' at times, though not because I encouraged it, cause I loved the short skirts, heels and tight tops, which we'd beat to death again just last night, but it was a change she was ready to make a bit at a time in her own way. Today she had on a pair of tight jeans and a Courtney Love T-shirt, though with cork pumps and was still drop dead sexy, which at least for a few minutes helped take my mind off of everything else.

It was me who started it up again. "Krissy, where could Gwen Putnam be? I left her at the farm. She went straight in the back door and I left."

"The cops didn't doubt you when you answered their questions, did they? I mean they believed what you told them, right?" she asked, willing it to be so.

"I think so. I mean, they were nice and all. I'm just really worried about Gwen Putnam. You understand that, don't you, Krissy? I mean nothing can happen to me. I didn't do anything," I said, looking into her eyes.

"Yeah, I understand. I didn't know her or anything, just that she and Tammy were in the same class, but Gwen Putnam and Tammy Kurtz were not exactly the type to hang out," she said with a short chuckle. "Billy . . .?"

"What, Kris?" I responded to her waiting question.

"You're not in love with Gwen Putnam, are you?" she'd asked, cautiously.

"*Jesus, no, Krissy—I am not in love with Gwen Putnam.* Not in the way you're thinking. She was in my brother's class! We spent those days together because of her project. I told you that."

"But if you were maybe older and if you could, you might love her instead of me, wouldn't you? I mean I think I know that—and it's ok," she said, not sobbing, pouting, or seeming to be playing for sympathy.

"Everybody in Fort Harrison has a crush on Gwen Putnam, Kris. I mean, like married guys, junior high kids—hell I even think women do. It's kind of hard to explain, but that has *nothing* to do with us. One thing about you is that you're not like other girls, so don't be like them, Kris. You and I may have screwed up families, but we don't have to join hands with them. I want to know where Gwen is because I'm worried that something's gone terribly wrong and I'm afraid for her, but there's nothing more to it than that. When I told you I loved you last night, it didn't mean till the next better thing comes around cause it's not out there. I've spent the last two years so much in love with you, but I didn't know how to say it. Then when you did first last night . . . well—*that* was the greatest moment of my life! I would *never* trade you for Gwen Putnam or anyone on the planet—even if I could—because you and I are a fit, Krissy, and we were *meant* to be together. We're the missing pieces of the puzzle that got thrown out in the trash. Don't you get that?"

"Yeh, I do . . . I mean, I think I do . . . and I'm sorry," she said, hugging me.

"Don't do *sorry* either, Kris. It's not necessary and it doesn't fit you. I understand why you asked that, I really do, but just trust in me Kris. You are my girl—*period*!

"We're in a whole new world now, Kris. Just be honest and up front, and that's what I'll be for you. That's what you need and that's what I need, and that will separate us from the lives our parents led us to," I said, kissing her softly on the forehead.

"I know, Billy," she whispered as I inhaled her clean blonde hair and marveled at the charms of the girl from 'across the tracks'—the girl I had gone to school with for nearly ten years yet only recently had come to truly understand—a girl not another of our classmates even had a clue about . . . *or could hold a match to!*

Krissy ran to Schaff's IGA for a few things we needed before we opened at two and had been gone nearly forty minutes, which was strange. I went through the motions of cleaning, stocking the coolers and sweeping the alleys, but I was numb. I'd had enough numbness in life and didn't need more. What was going on? Where was Gwen Putnam? And now where was Krissy?

. . . "Billy, Fort Harrison's insane," Krissy called out across the alley after pushing through the front door. "Schaff's was packed with strange people buying groceries, and when I was leaving town I saw a TV truck with a satellite dish on top of it—and vans, cars and even a bus parked in the big lot down by the football field. And there's a news van in our parking lot right now. I think it's the Lima station. Someone yelled at me when I came in the door, but I didn't turn."

It had been just over 24 hours since I had dropped Gwen off at her house. Sheriff Oberly and Chief Borger had said they were trying to keep things quiet because they still expected it would easily be explained—and yet this! How? Why? How could these news people have known so quickly and why would they be here when everyone knew that soon Gwen Putnam would walk right in her door or at least call her parents on the phone? But Gwen Putnam was not your normal 22 year old, never had been . . . or ever would be. Gwen Putnam, as one of America's top hopes for an Olympic Gold Medal in just a few short months, was now owned by the world. And here I was, Billy Bowling, the last person to see her—and though I knew no more than anyone else—somehow I began to understand that my connection to Gwen Putnam was no longer to be envied.

I looked around the corner and could see people outside the door, though no one I recognized at a quick glance. It was twenty til two and bowlers wouldn't be standing there, not that early. Nobody waited in line at Bowling's Bowling Center. I went back to the bar. Krissy flipped the TV on and the blonde news chick from WHIO, Dayton, was on the screen interviewing Al Samsal, right in front of his store on Main Street. . . .

*"So Gwen Putnam was home on break from Notre Dame and you say she had been here at your soda shop the last couple of days. Can you tell us about that, Mr. Samsal," she said, sticking the mike in his face.*

*"Well . . . yeah. Gwen was in here a couple of times talking with this here Billy Bowling who runs the bowling alley outside of town for his ole' man," he said with a drift that struck me like a lightning bolt.*

*"So you thought that was kind of odd?" she asked, leading Al who wasn't all that bright anyhow.*

*"Sure did. I mean Gwen Putnam and Billy Bowling—that just didn't fit the way I saw it. I mean that didn't fit at all," he replied.*

*"Why would you say that, Mr. Samsal?"*

*"Well Gwen, you know, she was the town darling. Great athlete, beautiful, and I mean like real beautiful. But Billy? I never knew him all that well, but seemed kind of odd, I thought. He had an older brother, Jimmy, in the Marines now. I can remember him and Gwen coming in a few years back. Now Jimmy—he was a big star football player and him and Gwen made quite a pair, but I sure didn't get this Billy thing, didn't get it at all," he said, shaking his head.*

I reached up and turned the TV off. I could see where it was all going, but where was Gwen Putnam? That's all I really wanted to know so we could just get this all over with. And what was I going to do if it really was reporters outside? It was all just too insane.

"Krissy, let's just leave the TV off for now. I don't know what to do. What do I do about those news people outside if they want to talk to me? I'd just close the alley right now and keep the door locked, but what about the groups we have scheduled?"

"Billy, it'll be ok. I know it will," she said, hugging me and kissing my cheek. "Billy, I love you. It's you and me together— remember. And remember last night how we said we could handle anything together? We'll get through this. I know that in my heart."

"Krissy, I love you and I need you no matter what happens," I answered, kissing her lightly on the lips and heading to the door. It was five minutes til two and I had learned that there are times in life that you had to face things head on, whether you wanted to or not . . . and for sure, *this* was one of those times. . . .

*. . . That Sunday was a nightmare. It wasn't bowlers that greeted me at two for open bowling, just as I'd expected by then. It was insanity—yet an insanity still tame compared to what it would become the next morning.*

# Chapter Forty-two

Gwen Putnam was found dead early Monday morning in the big old barn at the edge of the maple woods behind the burnt out house Darrell Byers and his family had once lived in. She was stuffed into a crude cave fashioned from the dusty old mountain of loose hay that had sat rotting for decades. That she had been viciously raped and tortured was apparent long before an autopsy would be performed. One of God's brightest earthly lights he'd now reclaimed, but not before Satan had played his hand, and life in Fort Harrison, Ohio, *would never be the same.*

I was arrested later that day, but not before the massive onslaught of media had invaded Fort Harrison. Those who had surfaced upon Gwen's disappearance were mere pretenders compared to the national, even worldly press, which now descended upon the village. Most notably was Geraldo Rivera with an interview that aired on the noon news on Dayton TV—just before the police arrived at the alley.

Our two Sunday groups had cancelled amidst the chaos of the day before, so Krissy and I had managed to lock the doors by 2:45 against the incredibly rude media, although I had had to physically push to get the doors closed. Even then they'd stayed in the parking lot all night, beating on the doors, and we had felt like caged animals as we clung to each other and cried together, trying to make sense of it all, getting no sleep. To this day, that terrifying night is one reason Krissy and Billy Bowling will *never* take one thing on this earth for granted—and why we will *always* take the time to appreciate the small things.

We took the phone off the hook, for it never quit ringing, and there was certainly no one we wanted to talk to. It nagged at me, however, that the police themselves might be among those we were hiding from and I wasn't certain how to handle that at the time. Dad and Busty had decided to stay in Cleveland til Monday evening, for whatever reason, having left that notice on the answering machine Saturday morning, so it wasn't related to Gwen Putnam, and I was honestly thankful he wasn't around. Thin Jim Bowling was not a shoulder to lean on—*and I had learned that all life long.*

After we heard about Gwen the next morning, we put the phone back on the hook, although it had mysteriously quit ringing—something that to this day we have never really understood. I knew the police would be coming and I didn't need a swat team to bust down the front doors, so it was essential to answer the phone.

Krissy and I were sitting at the bar when the interviews came on. We had decided to watch TV, knowing this wasn't something we were going to be able to hide from nor would just go away. I had become desperately ill when I'd learned of Gwen's murder, invaded by a suffocating emptiness and nausea, and stumbled through the morning not only feeling caged, but in a personal vacuum. I watched the News as stunned as everyone, and even though I was certain I would be questioned again, never truly doubted that my innocence would be understood—until the bomb that was soon to explode on TV.

. . . Geraldo Rivera was inside Samsal's Drugs and Sodas, and beside him, Al Samsal stepped into the camera—now apparently the darling of the media. Geraldo turned toward him, pushing a mike under his chin . . .

*"Hello, ladies and gentleman. Geraldo Rivera here with a special live report from tiny Fort Harrison, Ohio, where the brutally murdered body of Gwen Putnam, one of the country's top hopes for a gold medal in the approaching Olympic games, was found this morning in an abandoned barn a mile from her parent's placid Western Ohio dairy farm. I'm here with Al Samsal, the proprietor of a small soda shop on Main Street, who we learned has an interesting theory regarding this tragic murder. Mr. Samsal, I understand that Gwen Putnam was recently in your shop and that you found the circumstances unusual. What can you tell us about that, Al?"*

*"Well G-e-r-aldo, ever since Gwen left high school and went to Notre Dame we ain't much seen her in these parts.*

*But a few years back when she was here in school, she'd come in like all the kids, and a lot of the time with Jimmy Bowling, who was a star football player from her class. But then the other day, in fact two days in a row, she comes in with Billy, Jimmy's little brother, and that just seemed real odd to me."*

*"And why did you think that was so odd, Al?"*

*"Well G-e-r-aldo, this here Billy, I never really seen him much until last year when he was a senior and started coming in here for lunch like most of the seniors. I kind of figured him to be a sort of loner. Everybody I talked to pretty much says that. So what's he doing coming in here with Gwen Putnam, I'm thinking to myself? That just didn't make no sense at all to me. And then all of a sudden she comes up murdered. Seems pretty suspicious to me."*

*"So you're saying Gwen Putnam dated Billy's older brother? Were they still dating? That might explain a lot, couldn't it, Al?"*

*"That's just it. Them two never had nothin' to do with each other senior year. That's what my kids said, anyhow. Jimmy, he was a hell of a football player and went to college, but didn't last. Flunked out they say and up and joined the army. Now he's in the Gulf somewhere."*

*"What else can you tell us about them being in the soda shop that you found strange?"*

*"Well, Billy, he just seemed real nervous I thought. I picked up on that right away and I'm around these kids all day long. You can tell when something ain't quite right."*

*"And what about Gwen Putnam, Al? How did she act?"*

*"Well you know, Gwen Putnam was something real special around these parts, always upbeat and all. The kind of person who would trust anybody and never suspect that anybody could be evil."*

*"Didn't you also say that your son saw them together the day of Gwen Putnam's disappearance? At a local track meet?"*

*"That's right, G-e-r-aldo. My son, Josh . . . well, see, he throws the shot-put for the Fort Harrison track team and he*

*said they was together Saturday morning at the track meet over in Minster. I guess for some reason they left real early and everyone thought that was real strange. Then Gwen turns up missing. I mean put it together—don't seem like much of a mystery to me."*

Krissy looked at me with tears in her eyes and I put my arm around her. We neither spoke, but in a few seconds I would become certain my life was over. Al Samsal had withdrawn from the TV screen and now Clint Obringer took his place beside Geraldo. . .

*"Joining us now is Clint Obringer, a former close friend of Jimmy Bowling, and a farmer just down the road from the barn where Gwen Putnam's body was found. Clint also had unusual contact with Billy Bowling the day of Gwen's disappearance and at approximately the time that the authorities believe the murder occurred. Thank you, Clint, for agreeing to talk with us. What light can you shed on this tragic situation?"*

*"I knowd Gwen since she was just little. Knowd the whole Putnam family real well. I don't know how nobody could uh' murdered Gwen, but I seen Billy coming right up the road from where Gwen was murdered. Even talked to him that day."*

*"Tell us more, Clint. I understand you were good friends with Billy's brother, Jimmy?"*

*"Oh yeah, me and Jimmy, we had some good times all right . . . this one time we . . ."*

*"I'm sure you did, Clint, but let's try to stick to the story. Now am I right that Jimmy Bowling and Gwen used to date, but that was over some time ago?"*

*"Yup, Jimmy had a thing for Gwen big time, but it never much worked out. He tried though, I'll say that. I figure maybe somehow little Billy there was trying to get back at Gwen for Jimmy. I mean that's what I sorta figured when I heard about this and remembered Billy coming down the road from the old Parker Farm where they found Gwen. I mean I ain't never seen Billy out this way in my life. It had to be him the way I figure."*

*"Well, Clint, of course we don't know that yet. Anyway, were Billy and Jimmy close would you say?*

*"Oh yeah them two was real close. Billy woulda done anything for Jimmy."*

*"So you say you actually talked to him, Clint? I mean, why would he slow down and talk if he'd just committed a murder. I'm not sure how that fits?"*

*"Don't know, Garaulldo, but I think he was drunk. Pulled his car up right beside my tractor and got out and started an argument with me and yelled for me to give him a beer cause I had a few in the tractor and I guess he was out. I tossed one over to him and he turns and flips me off and called me a bunch of bad names—you know what I mean—stuff like that. I mean something was wrong with that kid—real wrong. I could tell he done something, but I sure never figured he just murdered Gwen Putnam."*

*"What time did you say this was, Clint? And you say he was coming from the direction of the barn where the body was found?"*

*"It was about three Saturday afternoon. Remember it well cause I seen it on the John Deere clock . . . and he come straight from the old Parker Farm where Gwen's body was found."*

*"Well I want to thank . . ."*

"That's insane, Billy. How can they say stuff like that on TV? You didn't do those things Clint said, did you?" she asked, sobbing.

"No, Krissy, it was nothing like what Clint said—*nothing!* Everything he said was a lie."

I was glad I had leveled with Krissy and told her about going to the track meet with Gwen Putnam, but now, after all that, I had to wonder if the one person I believed I could count on was thinking the same thing I knew everyone else was . . . and I wondered just how long until my next visit from the cops?

"You don't believe that stuff, do you Kris? Just tell me the truth because this isn't gonna just go away and we both know that."

She pulled me close, kissing me and then looking deeply into my eyes. With flowing tears she held my face in her hands and whispered: "Billy, I *know* you'd *never* be mean in any way. You are the gentlest person I have ever known and it's why I love to be around you cause I've seen too many of the other kind. You didn't do this and so you will be ok. You've got to be! It can't happen any other way, but no matter what, when I decided to love you it was forever cause nobody I ever knew in my whole life has ever *stayed in love.*"

I held her tight—trying to keep from crying, trying to be strong—but nothing I had ever experienced in life had prepared me for this. Outside I heard the noise of the building crowd along with the shouting and banging reporters at every door and window. Everything in my world was falling apart and I knew it would only get worse, but for right now I had Krissy Kurtz in my arms, and even at that moment, I thanked God for that much. . . .

. . . Suddenly there was a pounding on the door that I somehow knew was different from the media—a pounding that I had expected and had even tried to prepare for. I knew it was the police. I gave Krissy a kiss and a broad smile and then did what I had to do, rounding the corner of the bar and sliding the dead bolt on the front doors. Wade Borger, Sam Oberly, Marty Piquad, and two Ohio State Troopers entered with purpose and behind them it seemed now there were hundreds of people and cameras flashing from every angle. There were even more state troopers outside who seemed to be holding back the crowd, many whom were yelling at the top of their voice, but with all the competition for volume it was so muddled that I never really understood what they were saying at the time.

*It was Monday, April 22, 1996, at 4:43 pm that I was arrested for the murder of Gwen Putnam . . . exactly five days following her fateful phone call to solicit my help with her masters thesis on kinetic explosions.*

"Billy Bowling, we have a warrant for your arrest in connection with the murder of Gwen Putnam. You have the right to remain silent (Miranda Rights)." Sheriff Oberly read them to me in the short hallway beside the cases that entombed Dad's bowling trophies and even a few of my own . . . while the troopers kept the ever pressing media at bay just outside. I turned toward Krissy, standing behind me, who was now frozen in terror. She rushed toward me, hugging me in fear.

"Billy, we have to cuff you now," Wade Borger said

"Kris, don't worry. It'll be ok," I said as Sheriff Oberly pulled me gently away from her. I put my hands behind my back as asked and Marty Piquad cuffed me. I looked away from Krissy cause I could no longer bear to see her pain. She was sobbing loudly as I was led out the doors and pushed forward with my head down and through the hords of people that I never made eye contact with, even as I could hear the reporters yelling for a comment and the never ending clicking of cameras. Then finally I understood the first of an almost infinite stream of obscenities being hurled at me that I would come to eventually find would be unending for months.

There were five police cars in the escort to Sidney and the Shelby County jail. I rode in the center one—Sheriff Oberly's cruiser—which had an iron grate between me and the Sheriff and Marty Piquad. As we pulled away I could see people running beside the cruiser though I didn't look directly at them. I was petrified of the world I had just abandoned Krissy to and more helpless than I could ever imagine a human being on the planet earth could ever possibly be. My world as I had known it—fucked up as it had generally been—had just come to a horrendous end.

*I had murdered Gwen Putnam—everybody knew that—and even the lamest justice would demand my death . . . and preferably, I would soon find, well before a trial could even take place!*

# Chapter Forty-three

*M*y father, Thin Jim, came to see me—*once*. He was even accompanied by his wonderful wife, Busty, who sat in the corner behind him like a toad hiding from a cat. It took about nine seconds to understand he believed I was the murderer that everyone said I was, so it didn't much matter what he said to me or that he never came back again. It was all bullshit small talk, for there was only *one thing* that was really worrying him . . . *how would he possibly run the BBC without Billy Bowling?*

Thin Jim did utter one profundity before he and Busty left: "Understand, Billy, we have no funds for an attorney, but I know that you will have one appointed by the court. We gotta go, got senior leagues at two and I've got a lot of fucking shit to do now, don't I?" he'd spat, trying to saddle me with a guilt trip even as I was but a fourth down away from death row, which was really almost comical under the circumstances if you really thought about it. Then he left without ever saying anything hopeful to me and certainly never saying that he loved me, which, of course, I had been used to my entire life. Even now, all these years later, it really didn't matter though. He was no different than a stranger living in the New Zealand countryside, I remember once thinking for some crazy reason, and I had long since ceased even thinking about the family I never really had anyhow.

I was incarcerated in the Shelby County jail in Sidney, Ohio, for nearly five months. The Fifth Amendment and Right to Speedy Trial Act of 1974 had little bearing when you have an attorney who petitions *stays* in order to *'prepare his case'* (which of course was supposed to be mine, but after awhile I understood it was really just *his own)*. The delays, which I hadn't understood at the time, were primarily to provide more time to construct his own *'larger than life image'* upon the world stage though it was a strategy that would ultimately serve to take him down.

Oh, yeah, I had an attorney all right, and before my father's footsteps were an hour removed from the jail—and *not* a Shelby Country court appointed one, mind you! My attorney was Demosthenes Stavros who had flown into Dayton from Miami, Florida, two days following my arrest, appearing at my cell at exactly 4:00 pm April 24, 1996. He was preceded by a hint of $200 an ounce Versace Vendetta cologne, which I hadn't remotely understood at the time. Even I had heard of Demosthenes Stavros, a frequent legal 'guru' on TV talk shows who had gained national notoriety for his critiques of the O.J. Simpson trial. His personal reputation had been gleaned defending, usually with success, a string of noted criminally indicted professional athletes, along with a dabbling of South Florida organized crime figures.

That he would show up to defend me, *Billy Bowling*, was incredible—only serving to depress me even more as I contemplated the evil that I had come to represent, not only to the local people, but also to those across the country and I supposed even around the world. I was not entirely stupid and understood that this guy came to get his own mug plastered across the papers and on TV as much as for wanting to really help me, but at the same time I still had imagined that it surely had to be a good thing . . . *didn't it?*

I was kept isolated the entire five months, and denied bail, which would have been millions anyway. I was never ass raped or anything; in fact I really never saw another prisoner the entire time, but around the clock somebody, somewhere, both inside and out of the jail, was screaming '*murderer . . . rapist . . . burn in hell . . . die you fucker,*' which was apparently acceptable to the Sheriff and guards, for no matter what I told my attorney, nothing ever changed. I learned early on that Stavros didn't really care about me and assumed I was guilty no matter what I said to him. There developed a nagging feeling that I should have exercised my right to fire him, but he pretty much bowled me over and I thought maybe he was really working for me behind the scenes somehow and that I just didn't understand it all and one day he would uncover the truth and I would be freed. And, of course, I had no money or contacts on the outside to help me acquire anyone different so I tried to convince myself that I should consider myself fortunate.

A year or so later I was to read the following account of Stavros in an article Krissy's mother had saved from *People Magazine*. I'm going to throw it in here to give you an idea of just who Demosthenes Stavros was, if you've never heard of him, and how the media even then was completely out of control and just what they would do to create an even superficial story for print. I am not going to include the entire article, just the description of my wonderful attorney who was decked out in togs and jewelry that would have exceeded the appraisal of half the houses in the town of Sidney, Ohio, (population 20,000) where I was being held in the county jail.

> . . . *Demosthenes Stavros flew in from Miami to represent Billy Bowling in his upcoming murder trial. People Magazine (May 3, 1996) has an exclusive account from our on-site correspondent, Lisa Strickland, regarding Demosthene's noted flamboyant apparel as he addressed the hords of reporters from the steps of the county courthouse in the small town of Sidney, Ohio. With some assistance from our research staff we estimate Mr. Stavros to have been wearing approximately $43,000 worth of clothing and jewelry upon his first visit with client, Billy Bowling, and during the subsequent news conference.*
>
> *These included: a $5035 Valentino dark blue pin striped suit - $2100 Berluti shoes - $800 Finamore dress shirt with a $475 Pancaldi silk tie and $355 Gianfranco Ferre leather belt. Mr. Savros was also wearing $465 Montblanc sunglasses - an $11,000 Naloni Canova 18K white gold and diamond wrist watch - a $6375 Versace Saffo 18K white gold and diamond bracelet - $1605 18K white gold Torrini cufflinks - a $580 Forzieri Difulko 18K white gold tie clip and a $7296 Torrini Wallstreet white gold and diamond ring upon his right ring finger. As always, there was a hint of $200 an ounce Versace Vendetta cologne and he carried a sleek rich brown leather $6410 Gucci valise. All in all as Mr. Stavros addressed the press, he was entombed by $42,606 in threads, leather, hardware and diamonds. Of course that doesn't include*

*his socks and underclothing, which our staff was unable to account for. The value of all items is given per current list as established by our People Magazine research department.*

At the time I was also ignorant that the suffocating media had invaded, not only Fort Harrison and Sidney, but greater Dayton, forty miles to the south—following in the footsteps of the Simpson case since they now possessed a truly organized militia. The only time I had contact with the outside, other than to hear the hordes of vigilantes, which in organized shifts screamed for my lynching, was when I was rushed off to my grand jury hearing. At that time perhaps twenty deputies and state troopers escorted me across the forty-yard distance between the county jail and the courthouse. I was completely engulfed by scores of reporters with microphones and even more photographers with cameras. Incredible venom filled the early summer air, and I witnessed a state trooper to my right pelted by a rock the size of a baseball, which bounced off his throat and fell at the base of my feet right as my head was being pushed down and I was shoved forward up the courthouse steps.

Uncle Marco came to see me at the end of the first week, but couldn't stay because he said Grammy Romano could die at any moment. She hadn't understood anything for months so never knew about me. Marco was genuine and knew I hadn't done this crime. He told me to *'hang in there'* because there was something that he was working on, whatever that was. He said he didn't have time to visit Krissy, but that when he could, he would be back to help me put this all straight. Then he was gone, seemingly like everyone else in my life.

Krissy, because of not being a blood relative (I was repeatedly told), was barred from seeing me throughout my entire incarceration while Stavros was my attorney, no matter how much I pleaded with him to establish my rights to allow me to see her. I was allowed to send (but not receive) two letters a week, which I always sent to Krissy and prayed that they had been delivered. I was, however, told there were hundreds, even thousands of letters that had come addressed to me from around the world—cornball freaks and prisoner *groupies*—along with triple that amount of *hate mail,* according to Sheriff Oberly who had managed to treat me civilly for the most part. I never heard once from Jimmy, nor the Sturdivants, or anyone in Fort Harrison, and like I said, my father had withdrawn completely from my life that first day he left the jail.

Stavros gave me the run around with no good answers other than that 'he was working hard on things and it would take time.' Throughout the entire period he only showed up to talk to me in person that first time, and then once about a month after that. His questions never made any sense to me and they always seemed to have little to do with establishing the facts as I knew them. Twice a week he'd call me on the phone for maybe ten minutes of bullshit and always said, 'Billy, I think we're turning the corner. I think things are beginning to look up.' Like an idiot I'd buy it since I had no supporters other than Krissy and Uncle Marco whom I couldn't even talk to anyhow, and who might have advised me to question his counsel if I could have. Mostly I was just empty and had pretty much given up, so I just vegetated. I no longer *observed and thought* like I had always prided myself for having been able to do all those years through school. I was just numb.

Grammy Romano hung on for another five weeks before she died. Marco had called me a few times, but after the funeral he called me at least once a week. Mostly it was just *up-beat* stuff and I was pretty certain there was nothing he could much do to change anything. He kept telling me to *'hang in there'* because he said he was working on something that he believed could make a difference, but Stavros had said the same thing, hadn't he? So after a while I never much thought about it and certainly never stuck my neck out at all to get excited.

*But on August 10th . . . after exactly 111 days in the Shelby County jail, a wonderful thing happened . . . God gave me family.*

# Chapter Forty-four

*F*or whatever reason (fatigue I supposed), most of the lynch mob evaporated by August and there were nights that I could almost sleep. I was still isolated from the other inmates, who were pretty much transients and in county lock-up for DUI, domestic violence or drug offenses. Sometimes it would get quiet for a day or two, before a new inmate would scream at me profanely all-night, as if he (or sometimes she) had gotten himself arrested for that express purpose.

The guards would occasionally quiet them, but only as it bothered them, for it had nothing to do with me since several of the guards themselves called me '*scum, murder boy, rat turd, piece of garbage etc,*' and some guard I'd only seen once said that if he could get away with it, he'd '*go get a big nigger to fuck me up the ass and murder me like I did that pretty white girl.*' It was a daily thing and the role of numbness that I had accepted for much of my life, particularly after Mom and Libby had been killed, in a way served to help me survive.

It's funny how your senses change as your environment does, so when I heard the footsteps coming down the corridor one early afternoon, I felt something unusual must be up. No one ever came to my cell early afternoon unless it was Stavros and that had only happened twice. Also I could easily tell by the footsteps that it was the big fat guard that everyone called Jelly Roll.

"Bowling, you have visitors. Come with me." It *was* the fat guard who had the personality of a ground mole. I had heard him called 'Jelly Roll' by the Sheriff, the other guards, and sometimes even the inmates themselves, which he had seemed to accept without resistance.

"Visitors?" I asked, but he just looked at me stupidly and began to open the cell door, before pausing to say, "Do I need to cuff you, sissy boy? I'm supposed to, but I really want an excuse to kick your fucking ass. I kind of think you're innocent though, sissy boy, cause I don't think you could fuck a girl if you tried." Wow, wasn't that a clever one—and I remember thinking to myself: 'Oh, that's right, you stupid fat fuck—as if you could, ever have—or ever will.' Then Sheriff Oberly yelled from somewhere down the corridor to get a move on it as he yanked me out of the cell.

"Want me to cuff him, boss?" Jelly Roll yelled back.

"Yeah, if you think you can't get him fifty feet to the conference room without him escaping or kicking your ass," Oberly yelled back as Jelly Roll shoved me forward down the hallway ahead of him, swearing under his breath and snorting like a rutting hog.

I had no idea what was happening. Except for the day my Dad and Busty had come, and twice with Uncle Marco, I had never been to the conference room. It was a room where you looked through thick Plexiglas at your visitor and spoke through a tiny speaker in the wall. There were four separate stations, but no one was in the room as I was brought in. I knew that visiting was usually between 6:30 and 7:30 in the evenings, though it was something I had always tried to block from my conscious thoughts. So after having been arbitrarily shut down for months out of sheer survival, I allowed it to open up now—and tried to imagine who was there—entertaining a flash that maybe my Dad had finally decided to at least sort of be a father.

Sheriff Oberly was waiting in the room and as Jelly pushed me in he stepped forward, glaring at fat-boy, and said, "That's good, Deputy Kline. You can return to your station." At first I'd imagined that the professional formality was for my benefit, although that seemed unlikely when I thought about it since I had heard the Sheriff berate both the inmates and guards over the months, calling them any number of derogatory names without care for what I heard. Then I realized that what was said would likely be heard by whoever was beyond the wall so the Sheriff was practicing political correctness.

"Billy, you haven't had many visitors have you?" Sheriff Oberly then said.

"No sir, I guess not. You won't let my girlfriend talk with me," I replied, looking him in the eye.

"Whatever, Billy. Oh, by the way, yer Daddy's over in the Piqua jail on a DUI. Too bad it couldn't have happened in my county and you two could have caught up on old times," he said with his back noticeably turned from the speaker wall, then laughing, but not really loud enough to be heard very far.

"You're funny, Sheriff," I shot back, knowing I had nothing to lose as the image that my father was beyond the wall evaporated.

"Ok, wiseass, you got company—two guys who claim they're your uncles. Checked them out and I guess they're right. Waited long enough to come, don't ya think? Well, I guess the one guy's been here before. Anyway, twenty minutes and that's it," he said, then winking at me in a strange way it had seemed, he left, closing and locking the door behind him.

For a moment I was stunned. Since Mom and Libby's funeral in 1991 I hadn't seen my Uncle Dante and truthfully I hardly knew him at all. Marco had been in contact with me regularly and had even come up a second time to see me and spend a day with Krissy just last week, but I still felt overall he was helpless, much as I knew he wanted to help me. So I wasn't really sure what this could all be about.

I saw movement beyond the far right window and heard someone call out my name, "Billy, is that you?"

"Yes, Marco, it's me," I answered. I could see Marco now peering back at me, and my Uncle Dante standing several yards behind him.

"I know it's been hard, but Dante and I think we can help you now," he'd said, buoyantly.

"How?" I asked, wishing I could catch his optimism. "Like I've always told you, I didn't do it! Gwen Putnam and I were friends and more than anything in the world I want to know who did."

"Billy, we know and believe you. Dante says you need a new lawyer because he knows the guy you have and claims he's all show. He called me last month to explain how he thinks we can help you and then flew up from Florida yesterday to meet me so we could come talk to you. Billy, you've got to understand that you're our nephew—*you're family*. Dante has plenty of money and he would like to have you consider a suggestion he has. Will you listen?"

"Of course, Marco. I know Stavros doesn't much care and that he's in it for the publicity, but I don't get to see or hear much and I thought I was lucky just to have anyone at all for free, since I couldn't hire anybody and Dad wouldn't help if he could."

"We know about your Dad, but listen to Dante, ok? We've only got fifteen more minutes."

"Sure."

Uncle Dante stepped up to the window and I realized I hardly knew him at all and would have easily taken him for a stranger had he not been with Marco. He was handsome, like Marco, but overweight, and with a tan as dark as an old football. Besides being heavier than Marco, his thick head of hair was as white as Marco's was black. I knew that he had been the oldest of the three children, with my Mom the youngest. He had a strong presence about him, but also a sad look in his eyes that I was pretty sure had to do with his own life and probably not for my situation, a nephew he hardly knew.

"Billy, I know we don't know each other very well, but there's one thing I'm sure of, and that is that you didn't do this crime you are accused of. Your mother was the sweetest person to walk the earth and there is no way a son of hers could be a killer. I know that as well as I know that there is a God who will somehow help us put this all straight, but I am worried about you at present because of your representation. I've lived in Palm Beach and Miami most of my life and I am very familiar with Demosthenes Stavros. In fact, I've even been involved in court with him, though never on the same side. He isn't representing your best interests I'm certain. Stavros is all about Stavros and always has been. Are you following me?"

"Yes, Uncle Dante, I am," I said, and fell quiet.

"He has no idea I am your uncle and will not be pleased if you follow my advice, but I hope you will trust me in this. I feel very guilty for not having stepped in earlier, but with Marco's encouragement and after your grandmother's death, I know I must, for you are *family* and you and Jimmy are the only family we have left, since we have never had children of our own. *Family is important* and something I too often forget in the midst of my own problems. Please allow me to send you an attorney, Billy. He is from Dallas and his name is Cliffton Tremont. I am certain he will serve you well, but it is your responsibility to dismiss Stavros, which must be done before Cliffton can contact you. Could you do this soon, Billy? I am certain time is very important."

"Of course I will, but Uncle Dante, I don't have money to pay you back and . . ."

"Billy, to hell with money. Money has been my curse and only recently have I started to use my money to do good things, and there is nothing better I can do with it than to help my family. I have plenty of money, Billy, don't you worry about that, but I expect my employees to earn it—and I'm quite confident that Cliffton will do that. Believe me, whatever *needs* to be done, or *can* be done, Cliffton Tremont will see that it is."

"Uncle Dante, do you want me to keep your name quiet? I mean when I talk to Stavros? Should I make certain to keep you out of it all?" I asked.

Dante's face brightened and a big smile loosened up his skin and sad eyes. "Not at all, Billy, not at all. When you talk to Stavros, you tell him your Uncle Dante Romano was up to see you and thinks you're getting fucked—then you tell *him* to get fucked. And it's perfectly fine if you tell him that's from me. Do it however you think is best. I'm just sorry I didn't come to help you sooner and I hope you'll forgive me for that."

I looked through the glass, ready to cry, but somehow held back. "Oh, Uncle Dante, this means the world to me. I'll never be able to . . . " I finally managed to say, looking from Dante to Marco and back when Dante cut me off.

"We only have a few minutes. Can you remember a number? It's very important because I know they won't let me give it to you on paper and you need to call me as soon as you've fired Stavros."

"I'll remember it, Uncle Dante, don't worry about that—I'll remember it—shoot."

"5 6 1 - 8 6 4 – 7 5 3 1. Now are you sure you can remember that?"

"That's an easy number, Dante. 561 is all I need to remember. Then start 8, then start 7 and go backwards by twos—561-864-7531. Now how easy is that?" I'd said, actually chuckling for the first time in months.

"Well I'll be damned. I never saw that before and I've had that number for thirty years. You should be my company accountant!"

A bell rang. I'd heard it 3 nights a week from my cell, ringing at 7:30 when the visitors were to leave and the inmates returned to their cells. It was a bell that never rang for me, but I'd kept my brain in neutral for I had enough problems without being reminded by a bell, that on top of them all, I had no family either.

Marco leaned up to the speaker as I heard the door open behind me. "Billy, you're going to get through this and then you're gonna have a big choice to make," Marco said with a big smile.

"What's that, Uncle Marco?" I asked.

"Whether you want to work for Dante in Florida or for me in the north when I sell *Romanos* and move to Michigan. I've got some pretty big plans up there, Billy. Well actually we've both got big plans—*and no sons to help us.* But we'll fight over you later. Hang in there, Billy. Someway I know this is going to work out. *It has to.*"

# Chapter Forty-five

*F*or *two days* I told Jelly Roll and the other guards that I needed to see Sheriff Oberly and that I needed to talk to my lawyer, which fell upon deaf ears. I had never before requested to, but now I could see that behind these walls I possessed no rights at all, which was exactly how society believed every murderer should be treated regardless that it was a right to which I was entitled.

I hadn't heard from Demosthenes Stavros for nearly two weeks, or so it seemed, though I hadn't exactly carved the days on the wall with a tooth I'd busted out of my mouth like a prisoner I'd once read about in a long ago novel I could no longer remember. Then on the third day after my Uncles left, Demosthenes Stavros called and they came to take me to the private cubicle that was for prisoners to talk on the phone to their attorney.

"How you doing up there, Billy?" he asked in his wise ass European accent. I had to give him credit for even remembering my name, for I wasn't too certain he'd ever known it in the first place. Of course he probably ran across it often enough while searching for his own press so that after awhile it had somehow just stuck.

"Mr. Stavros, *you're fired!*" I actually shouted into the phone immediately, not wanting to risk the chance we could be cut off.

"What was that, Billy? We're breaking up," he said, feigning deafness.

"I said *you're fired*," I said, calmly this time.

"I don't understand. Why would you fire me? I've been working very hard on your case and I think something big is going to break here real soon."

"Well let's see . . . I'm firing you because my Uncle Dante Romano thinks I should. He says he has a much better attorney for me and he thinks you're an incompetent asshole. That's pretty much why, and it seems like a good enough reason for me!"

There was a pause before a panicked voice squeaked across the phone and it was obvious that ole' Demosthenes was rattled. "Billy, are you telling me that Dante Romano from Palm Beach is your Uncle? I didn't know that."

"Why should you? I didn't tell you." Dante was obviously a big cheese in Florida, though I hadn't really known that and was pretending I had. Of course you'd think Stavros would wonder why he hadn't stepped forward with his bucks earlier, but truthfully he was too rattled to employ rational thinking at that point.

"But Billy, your uncle is wrong. We've had our differences over the years, but I have spent months on your case and your best chance is to see this through. For you to change attorneys now would be a disaster."

It would indeed be a disaster, but not for Billy Bowling. To be dismissed from the case before the trial, when his exposure would be of epic magnitude, would be an image wreck for Demosthenes. He would also be without the first nickel for his already accumulated expenses and efforts, which to be certain were minimal, yet still a slap in the face because a big book deal, personal appearances and things of that nature which he had intended to capitalize on would almost certainly be trashed.

"But, Billy . . ."

Sheriff Oberly had been hawking the phone call and I had a flash of using that to my advantage. If I fired Stavros and he claimed different, it could make things tricky for hiring Mr. Tremont, so I figured I would use Oberly as a witness. Stavros was blubbering on the other end of the line and I knew there was no danger of him hanging up. I figured it was just a matter of time before he hopped a plane to come begging in person, but I thought we could end it all right then. Covering the phone, I turned to the Sheriff.

"Sheriff Oberly, I want to fire my attorney and I want you to be a witness. He's on the line right now," I said, knowing this would bring mixed reactions. On one hand he hated Stavros, I was certain of that—I mean who wouldn't—particularly in a town like Sidney, Ohio. But I also knew that changing attorneys would seem to put off a trial even longer, and no one in Shelby County wanted that.

"I want a trial Sheriff, but this asshole wants to drag everything out forever. I want this over with. I am firing Mr. Stavros and then my Uncle has another attorney for me—one who won't mess around. Just listen to me fire him, then talk to him on the phone and back me up. This way we can all move on. Ok, Sheriff Oberly?"

Oberly stood there with his mouth open. He knew I had the right to fire an attorney and if I was determined to do so why not get it over and move on. Besides, I had twisted his simple brain with my logic, although I personally had no idea what Mr. Tremont would do, say, or how he would handle my case. I only knew my Uncles were in my corner and it was pretty damn great to know that at least someone finally was.

"I guess so . . . sure," he finally returned.

I raised the phone and asked, "Still there, Stavros?"

"I'm here, Billy, now let's talk this over . . ."

"DS, now listen to me. You're fired and Sheriff Oberly is standing right here beside me to verify it and repeat it to you, so you have a perfect understanding and we can all move on."

"But . . ."

"Sheriff, will you please repeat my instructions to Mr. Stavros?" I said kindly to Oberly and loud enough I knew Stavros had heard me before I handed the phone over to the Sheriff.

Oberly took the phone, first hesitating before saying, "I guess you're fired *Starbucks*. Can't say that we're gonna much miss you around here though," he said, laughing out loud before handing the phone back to me which I placed immediately on the receiver, cutting short Stavros's *Donald Duck* sounds that seemed to be coming from a planet far away in a distant universe.

I knew that if I was returned to my cell immediately without making my next important call it could be days and maybe even weeks before I would have that liberty, especially now with no attorney at all. I also knew I had Sam Oberly exactly where I needed him to bring it all full circle. As soon as I placed the receiver on the hook I picked it right back up.

"I have to make another phone call, Sheriff . . ."

"Nope, Billy, that's all for one day, now let's go," he said, lifting the receiver out of my hand and putting his hand behind my forearm to lead me down the hall.

"But Sheriff, if I don't call my uncle that means I'll be without an attorney and nothing moves forward—besides Fifth Amendment rights, remember?"

Sam Oberly looked at me with almost human eyes. It was a funny feeling that I had just then and there was a communication between us at that instant that I would have never imagined possible. In fact there was nothing about that August 1996 day that I would have expected, nor could believe, as I reflected on it that night in my cell—let alone what would happen several days following that.

"You didn't do this, did you, Billy?" he then *said* (not asked), looking directly into my eyes.

"No Sheriff, I didn't. Gwen Putnam had become a friend of mine and probably was the best person I've ever known," I answered.

"But the circumstances look real bad . . ."

"I know they do, Sheriff, but let me have a chance with a good attorney—an attorney that my *family* wants me to have. Then maybe everyone else can know the truth, but especially because I want you to catch the *real* person who killed Gwen Putnam."

I dialed the number—the easy number—561-864-7531.

"Dante Romano speaking."

"It's Billy."

"Billy, great to hear from you . . . fire that asshole, Stavros, yet?"

"Sure did, Uncle Dante . . . sure did."

# Chapter Forty-six

*C*liffton Tremont flew into Dayton the very next morning and drove to Sidney, Ohio, in a rented car, taking a room for $59.95 a night at the Hampton Inn just off Interstate 75. He kept (and stayed in) the room for the entire duration of his representation of me, although he made side trips 'investigating,' including a trip to Youngstown for four days. Cliffton Tremont was 66 years old and had lost his wife, Ana, of 41 years, just the year before. He had retired from his primary practice upon her death, agreeing to represent me only at the request of Dante, his fishing companion for years off the coast of Florida and throughout the Caribbean. Cliffton Tremont wore Brooks Brothers suits and Florsheim wingtip shoes and no tie. He also wore a Fossil watch his wife had once given him at Christmas, having spent an extravagant $65 for it at Elder Beerman.

Whereas Demosthenes Stavros was a graduate of Athens University in Greece and Yale Law School, Cliffton Tremont had graduated from Ashland College in Ashland, Ohio, and Ohio Northern University Law School in Ada, Ohio. Yet for three decades Cliffton Tremont was the most noted criminal defense attorney in all of Texas, occasionally taking a case in South Florida where he had a home so he could go fishing with Dante Romano during court recesses. Dante later told me that Cliffton always said, 'I have solved more cases on a fishing boat than I ever did in my office or in a law library.'

Demosthenes Stavros had rented a top floor suite for $700 a night at the downtown Dayton Marriot, thirty five miles south of Sidney when in Ohio, employed a chauffeur driven limo to be on call at all times, and traveled with two blonde secretaries who not mysteriously were the reason the suite was required. Demosthenes and his blonde entourage dined at *l'Auberge* (of course) or *David's*, Dayton's most upscale and expensive restaurants, while Cliffton Tremont preferred IHOP to start the morning, Arby's for lunch . . . and Bonanza Steak House for dinner. Demosthenes Stavros could be and often was a brilliant attorney, but he could have cared less about Billy Bowling. It was all about exposure and not a big secret within the circles of serious law. Cliffton Tremont was old school to be sure. If Cliffton Tremont took a case, it was given his undivided attention— and even at 66—possessed a legal mind with the capability of transcending the most brilliant resolutions a screenwriter had ever bequeathed Perry Mason.

It was 10:00 am, Wednesday morning, August 14, 1996, that Sheriff Oberly came down the hall and unlocked my cell door. I had been in the Shelby County jail for 115 days. "Your new attorney's waiting for you in the conference room, Billy. He sure ain't no Starbucks, that's for sure, but maybe he can help you. Maybe this was a 'meant to be,' like my wife, Jane, is always going on about. She thinks everything that happens on the planet was a '*meant to be.*' Come on, Billy."

As Sheriff Oberly unlocked the conference room door I could see Cliffton Tremont inside. He was sitting with his back to me as I entered, an empty chair directly in front of him. What I remember most is that he didn't even turn as the door opened noisily and the Sheriff and I entered. I would later learn that simple observation pretty much told the story of Cliffton Tremont as he wasted little unnecessary physical energy and yet you were certain the wheels in his head were turning at all times.

He didn't even stand as I walked around and turned to face him. I was a bit thrown and could have easily taken it as disrespect, or perhaps his disbelief in my potential innocence and me as a client, yet within a few minutes I began to get the drift of Cliffton Tremont, soon actually becoming quite comfortable.

"Mr. Tremont, this is Billy Bowling. There is a buzzer beside the door if you need anything. Deputy Kline will be just outside. I will leave you now to your business," Sam Oberly said and again flashed a quick, though now kind glance.

Cliffton Tremont reached out to shake my hand, still not rising, just bending forward a bit. Then he began a low key, though lengthy expose. "Have a seat there, Billy, and let's see if we can make any sense out of this mess you're in the middle of. If your Uncle says you're a good kid he thinks is innocent—well, that's pretty strong stuff for me—but there's a lot more I need to know than that. Dante's a great guy, but he's had a tough run lately. His problem is he has too damn much money and it draws bad women like a cow pie draws flies. Hey, Billy," he'd said, suddenly changing the drift, "buzz that gizmo over there and ask them to get me some ice tea. It needs to be cold and ask them for extra ice. Get yourself something while you're at it. Tell them to put it on my tab if they have a problem parting with their dime. Can't much work without ice tea, now can I? Not in August; it's a federal law you know," he'd said with a thin grin, reminding me of a large toad that was a bit intoxicated.

I walked to the door, pushing the buzzer which I could hear ring in the hall. Jelly Roll Kline opened the door all puffed up with one hand on his gun as if ready for Tremont and I to make a jail break. He was about 6'4" and well over 300 pounds and I'd heard him talking with another guard one day and figured out that he had played football for Marion Local High School, one of Fort Harrison's biggest rivals. Who knows if he was any good, but one thing I could tell was that no college could pull a string long enough to get that fat ass suited up for even the first game of the season. But then I was used to guys like him at the alley and he could have easily been Clint Obringer's double, one fuck-head I had tried without success to get out of my mind, knowing that his lies were a big reason I was in here in the first place.

"Yeah, whad duh yuh want?"

"Mr. Tremont would like some ice tea and some extra ice too," I said as he looked down his nose at me.

"Yeah . . . wool why dunn he come ass for it hisself?"

In a deep booming voice that scared the hell out of me, Cliffton Tremont, without even turning around melted ole' Jelly Roll . . . "If you want to keep your job, son, you'd better move on it fast or I'll file obstruction charges against you that you're boss ain't much gonna like. Billy what do you want?" Cliffton demanded, as I stood frozen.

"I guess like Lemonade or Pepsi or something."

"Which, Billy?" Cliffton Tremont berated, "one thing you better learn *right now* is to be forceful and emphatic. I'm beginning to see how you got yourself in this mess. Cops look for easy targets when they're under pressure and they don't much care if you're guilty or not. Bring lemonade for the boy," he yelled, yet with a mysteriously controlled voice. "Now Billy, come back over here. The rest is their job and they better get to it. We've got a rats nest in our fishing line we've gotta straighten out."

I returned to the chair expecting an agitated Cliffton Tremont and yet he sat placidly, looking like everyone's favorite grandfather. Even after having felt brow beaten by Mr. Tremont, I still became comfortable as soon as I sat down. Throughout the course of my client association, and even later on my Uncle's fishing boat, I could never quite figure out Cliffton Tremont. Eventually, however, I came to believe that probably no one could, and that it was within that magical realm of the unsolved where his greatest power hibernated, to be called upon only when absolutely necessary—and exactly when most unexpected.

"Ok Billy, tell me how you became involved in this mess," Mr. Tremont asked, turning to look into my eyes, no tape recorder nor notepad in sight. . . .

. . . For more than two hours I pretty much spilled out the story of my life as solicited by Cliffton Tremont, and particularly Jimmy's relatively benign relationship with Gwen Putnam and the unexpected circumstances by which she and I had connected that week before her murder. Mr. Tremont listened intently, but never once did he take any notes and rarely did he ask me to repeat anything. A big old clock on the wall showed the time to be exactly 12:10 pm when he arose from his chair for the first time.

"I'll be going now, Billy. Thank you for your time. I do my own detective work for cases like this and I have a lot of people to visit, it sounds like," he said, patting me lightly on the back as I rose and starting toward the door.

"Do you need any directions, sir?" I asked. "I mean like where people live and all?"

Mr. Tremont seemed to freeze in mid stride and turning to me said, "Billy, I'm an Ohio boy, but maybe you didn't know that. Grew up in Ravenna where my father ran a coffee shop right across the street from the courthouse. All the lawyers and judges took breakfast and lunch there every day, and that's when I decided I wanted to be just like them," he said, chuckling and shaking his head as if wondering whether he had been right to do so. "He was also the mayor for a long time so I was pretty much around the law stuff *and* the small town stuff always, let alone knowing my way around Ohio which is about as easy as riding a horse on a carrousel. Did my law gig in Ada, maybe forty miles from here, and my old college roomie, Donald Verhoff, the Probate Judge in Bellefontaine, was a Minster lad. I've been around these parts and in not a few good old Catholic bars—probably more than I should admit to. So Billy, I think I can figure it all out. In fact it'll probably be *too* easy cause I like a good challenge. Now you go back to your cell and lighten up a bit. I have a feeling we might just be able to figure this all out."

# Chapter Forty-seven

*I*t was three days before I heard from Cliffton again, when once more at exactly 10 am, Jelly Roll Kline came to my cell door. "Lawyer's here, let's go," he said, opening the cell and standing aside for me to walk out and down the hall to the conference room. For whatever reason he wasn't being a smart ass and walked behind me without pulling or pushing like he so loved to do. Sheriff Oberly wasn't around that I could see, which surprised me, given Jelly's virginal manners. As I entered the door, Cliffton was sitting with his back to me just like before. I walked over to my chair and sat down.

"What can you tell me about Clint Obringer?" he said abruptly.

"I don't know, I mean . . ."

"There you go again. I don't have time for what you *don't* know," he said with seeming anger. "This might sound silly to you, Billy, but I like to work with what people *do* know, so don't beat around the bush with me. Just give me straight, quick answers. I want the very first thing that pops into your head when I ask you a question. Haven't you ever heard that your first instinct is usually the best? Now do you we understand each other?"

"Yes sir, we do," I'd said directly, later realizing that somehow, whatever it was that Clifford Tremont wanted, was usually what he got, even if it meant expecting a character change.

"Go on then," he said, but softly now.

"Clint was a friend of my brother, Jimmy. They played football together all through school and even got an apartment up town the last half of their senior year . . ."

"Moved away from home, from families?"

"Well, we really didn't have much of a family at that point. My Dad drank a lot and Jimmy and him fought all the time . . ."

"What about Clint?"

"His family was pretty upset I know. They went to the school board and principal and even Wade Borger, the town cop, but Clint was eighteen and so I guess there wasn't much they could really do."

Did they both work—Jimmy and Clint? Where'd the rent money come from?"

"Jimmy worked a little at the bowling alley, but only when Dad was away at tournaments. I don't really know how he did the money part. Dad must have paid him something, but it couldn't have been much. Clint worked on his farm was all I ever heard, but when he moved I don't think he even did that. I never knew him to work anywhere else is all I can say."

"Didn't you find that a little strange—that they could afford an apartment? I checked with a Howard Shaw who owns the building and he told me that their rent was $350 a month and that it was always paid on time. Pretty steep for a couple of kids without a job, wouldn't you say? And you're telling me you don't have a clue how they were paying for it?" Cliffton asked, looking directly at me and waiting as if he knew the answer, but wanting me to say it.

"Well Jimmy did once tell me that the football coach, Sam Giovanazzo, had helped them with the money at first, but I think they maybe did some work for him I'd heard once," I answered.

"I was waiting for you to say that, Billy. I already knew it. Your brother's buddy, Clint, isn't too smart is he . . . and not very skilled with a lie. He says Giovanazzo pretty much paid it all. Says that he even screwed a few high school girls right there in the apartment while he, Jimmy, and some other kids were right outside the door. Ever hear anything like that?"

"Not really . . ."

"Dammit, Billy, you either heard it or you didn't. Now what is it?"

"I never heard anything about Sam Giovanazzo being in Jimmy's apartment cause everybody I know is afraid to talk about him or what he does. But my best friend once stumbled on him screwing a high school girl in his office," I said, feeling nervous about saying it until I remembered my own position and especially since Brent had never visited me, made a phone call, or even sent a letter, so I sure wasn't going to worry about breaching *his* confidence.

"You mean to tell me people around town know about this guy screwing high school girls and they don't do anything about it? Hell, sounds like Texas with their damn football and cheerleading secrets. Tell me more about this guy, Giovanazzo, and then I'll tell you a little more about what our friend Clint said," he said, waiting.

"Sam Giovanazzo's been in Fort Harrison forever, and won like ten state football championships and maybe five in wrestling, or something like that . . ."

"Just eight in football and four in wrestling, Billy, but go on," Cliffton corrected. Of course I'd known the exact number, I mean how could I not have, but was just trying to make a general point, so I could certainly see that Cliffton Tremont did his homework.

"Well he's an asshole, Mr. Tremont, and I think most people know that, but nobody bothers him, because along with the championships the track and cross country teams that Gwen Putnam ran on have won, Fort Harrison has more state championships than any school in the entire state. The last I heard it was 23, and honestly that's pretty much how the people of Fort Harrison define their lives. I mean that's what I've always thought. So people don't mess with Giovanazzo. That's just the way it's always been and from what I've seen, that includes the school administrators, school board, and probably even Wade Borger, the cop," I answered.

"I picked up on a little of that around town these past few days and now I know why, when I asked questions about this coach, people would only rave about him. And you're right, Billy, nobody would say anything bad about Sam Giovanazzo no matter what I threw at them . . . except for our buddy, Clint Obringer," Mr. Tremont said looking me in the eye.

"I'm not sure I understand?" I said.

"Ok, Billy, here's the deal. I'm not even a tough guy, but when I tracked down the Obringer farm I found Clint on a tractor out near the road probably about where he must have been when you talked to him that day. He was swiggin down Buds just like you said and it was only 10:30 in the morning. Clint's not very sly around strangers and especially if you act important. I didn't say I was FBI cause I can't. I just started out saying that the FBI was investigating the Putnam murder and that they were pretty sure he had lied during the

Geraldo Rivera interview and also the story he had given the county Sheriff and that he could be some pretty hot water if he didn't come clean. The FBI has been investigating, though I don't think very hard, cause everyone thinks that you're their man. Somebody talked to him a couple of months or so ago, but nothing much came of it. He apparently just repeated the lies he told on TV and to the Sheriff, which a guy like that has probably come to believe himself by now. Anyway within two minutes your man, Clint, snapped like a green bean in the fingers of a southern maid."

Cliffton took a long drink of his ice tea, which he had remembered to bring himself this time, and slowly looked at me without saying anything for a long time, as if waiting on me to say something though I remained silent. Finally he took a deep breath and went on. "He admitted he lied about you being drunk, lied about you demanding beer from him and even said he guessed that maybe you didn't seem nervous like he had said in the interview, at least not until the very end when you and he argued about him making fun of you. Is that correct? Just like you told me last week?"

"Yes, just like I told you, Mr. Tremont," I answered.

"But you *did* come from the direction of Boeke Road, like Clint said, and it doesn't help that you stopped to mess around in the creek which burnt nearly an hour you cannot account for. I understand it was a beautiful spring day, and that in your childhood it had been a favorite place and all. Yes, Billy, I can understand that easy enough cause I could see myself doing the very same thing. But it does put you on the road where Gwen Putnam was murdered and pretty much at exactly the same time the murder occurred. You had also been with her all morning and after leaving the track meet nobody can account for either of you until Clint Obringer saw you coming from Boeke Road. So if you didn't murder Gwen Putnam, Billy, there had to be three people on or very near Boeke Road when Gwen Putnam was murdered . . . you, Gwen Putnam—and the murderer. No one else lives on the road except the Millers whose farm borders 66 at the opposite end from the creek. The Putnams were all away at a livestock auction in Springfield and the Millers were gone for the day, too, and down in Greenville. Are you *absolutely* certain that you didn't see or hear any other vehicles while you were walking along the creek or sitting on the culvert?"

"No, Mr. Tremont, I didn't, and I have thought about that day every night I have been in here," I said, starting to lose the confident feeling I'd began to cultivate after talking to my Uncles and then meeting with Cliffton Tremont.

"It's a small town, Fort Harrison. Can you think of anybody who didn't like Gwen Putnam . . . or know of her having trouble with anyone that she might have told you about?" he asked.

Cliffton Tremont couldn't have asked an easier question. "*Everybody* liked Gwen Putnam! I mean she was perfect and the whole town looked up to her, pretty much from little kids right through the adults. She was like this incredible bright light, but it's hard to explain to someone not from around here," I answered.

"So you are Satan, Billy—you understand that, don't you?"

Jesus, he didn't need to hit me with the sledge right at that moment, but who was I trying to fool anyhow—except myself. "Yes, yes I do, Mr. Tremont. The crazy thing is I would probably be enraged more than anyone if someone else were in my shoes and I was on the outside. I mean there is no nightmare I could have invented like the one that has happened to me."

"I know, Billy, but don't give up, not yet," he said, suddenly optimistic. "Now I have what you may consider an odd question, but I want you to give me your opinion. You see, I'm an outsider and so I'm not all tied in knots about state championships and all that. Neither am I intimidated by anyone, and never have been, though believe me I've had my share of threats over the years. But let me ask you this: did Sam Giovanazzo and Gwen Putnam have any kind of relationship? You and everyone else seem to say they are the two biggest shows in town, so I was wondering how Giovanazzo felt about sharing the spotlight with a young girl after he'd had it to himself all those years? From what I'm starting to see, I bet he wasn't all that excited about her and the way the town had put her on a pedestal, with a parade, a town key, and all that. What do you think, Billy?"

Cliffton Tremont had just led me to saying the very thing I had been turning over in my mind for months as I tried to imagine if it could have possibly been anyone I had known who did this to Gwen. I had first assumed it had to be someone from outside Fort

Harrison who was sick and attracted to her aura, to her beauty. Still, there were times I would lay in bed and try to think of the people of Fort Harrison. I knew almost all of them through the alley, including most of the idiot drunks and lechers, yet I still could not imagine *anyone* who would have ever committed such a crime against Gwen Putnam. *Anyone, that is, except for maybe Sam Giovanazzo!* I particularly remembered that day almost six years earlier when he had talked about her with disgust, and even as an eighth grader remembered him almost seeming to encourage my own brother Jimmy to rape her: *"she's getting pretty big for her britches . . . if she don't put out easy, just take it . . . that's what they all want anyway . . . women are to use . . . women are to fuck."* I may have been in the eighth grade, but I had understood exactly what he meant and had heard the venom in his voice.

"Mr. Tremont, I remember something very clearly about Sam Giovanazzo and how he felt about Gwen Putnam, but it was nearly six years ago now, although it made me hate that man more than you could ever know. Then when Brent told me years later what he had seen, I wanted so much to see him burn, but I stepped back in line with all the other chicken shits in Fort Harrison and tried to put it all out of my mind, though I never have."

"What is it you remember?"

"Like I said it was six years ago. Do you really want me to tell you about something that long ago?"

"Certainly."

*"I was going into eighth grade, Mr. Tremont, and it was late August. I was riding my bike past the practice football field when I decided . . ."*

I remembered absolutely every word that I heard that day and never forgot them throughout high school—when I had Sam Giovanazzo for class, or I would pass him in the hallway—when I watched him on the sidelines coaching during Jimmy's playing days—and particularly after Brent Sturdivant told me about seeing him fuck Mindy Dalinghaus. I had hated Sam Giovanazzo ever since that day six years ago. Could it really be possible that now at 20 years old I might soon be facing the death penalty, for not only a crime I didn't commit, but for *another one* that *Sam Giovanazzo had,* only this time having passed beyond rape and actually committing murder? No, of course that didn't happen! It was just something I wanted to believe, and yet here was Cliffton Tremont, a noted attorney from Texas, who seemed to have been thinking the exact same thing.

After my story, Mr.Tremont paused momentarily, then asked, "Billy, what do you know about Sam Giovanazzo before he came to Fort Harrison?" Again he seemed to have that look which said he knew the answer, but wanted to challenge me to come up with the same one. He had done that several times now.

This time, though, I was honestly pretty much in the dark except for one thing I had actually heard from Krissy. After I'd finally shared with her what Brent had seen our senior year, she told me about what Giovanazzo had once done to her. The very first week of our freshman year he had pinched her ass while she was at the water cooler in gym class and then given her a pass to get out of study hall to see him in his office the next period. Krissy saw things most girls just didn't get because of her background and could have cared less about popularity, so Giovanazzo was barking up the wrong tree when he'd targeted Kris. She told me she had torn the pass up right in front of him and thrown it in the wastebasket and that Giovanazzo had gotten furious, saying: *"Miss Kurtz, you have just made a very big mistake and you will pay for it, I assure you—you will pay for it!"*

Krissy wasn't scared of anybody and ultimately nothing happened except that he flunked her two years in a row and that was the main reason she had joined the Dedheds instead of going through school in the regular program which she'd wanted to do. She also told me most girls knew Giovanazzo screwed girls, but that everyone was afraid of him so they would never say anything. Then she told me something she had heard from one of her Mom's boyfriends once. He'd said that Sam Giovanazzo had been in the mob in Youngstown years earlier or something like that, and that his brother was a big shot mob boss. But should I say this to Cliffton Tremont? I mean what could that have to do with anything, even if it was true?

"Billy—you still with me, son?" Cliffton said, breaking my trance.

. . . "Well, he's been here like 25 years, Mr. Tremont. Nobody knows much before that, I don't think. I heard a few things here and there, but not much, and believe me I pretty much hear *everything* at the bowling alley. I did hear something from my girlfriend just a few months ago though, but she overheard it from one of her mother's lowlife boyfriends so I'm not sure you could much believe it."

"And what was that, Billy?" he said with the knowing look that I was getting used to, yet was still unnerving.

"Krissy said that Sam Giovanazzo was connected somehow to the mob or mafia or whatever in Youngstown, across the state. But . . ."

"*Bingo, Billy, damn straight he is*, and I suspected that the first time I heard his name, but I couldn't imagine why a Giovanazzo from Youngstown would be a football coach clear the hell over here and in a town the size of Fort Harrison. Billy, bear with me a little longer. I have a story about Sam Giovanazzo I think you ought to hear. In fact I think everybody in the town of Fort Harrison should, regardless of whether he has anything to do with our murder case or that he has won umpteen state championships. I'm gonna tell you an *Eastern Ohio Story*, Billy, cause they probably don't much make it over here and then I'm going to be gone for a few days because I have a few people in Youngstown, Ohio, that I'm pretty sure I need to have a talk with.

# Chapter Forty-eight

"*I* grew up in Ravenna, Ohio, which I've always called *a peaceful village in the midst of urban chaos*. It was five miles to Kent State University, fifteen to Akron, twenty-five to Cleveland, twenty-five to Canton and thirty to Youngstown. Wouldn't you pretty much call that the middle of chaos? Yet if you'd parachuted in at night you might have imagined you were in Vermont. It was the peaceful county seat of Portage County with the courthouse smack in the middle of town on Main Street and my father's coffee shop, *Tremont's*, catty corner across Main on North Chestnut . . .

. . . Growing up it was the Golden Flashes, the Indians, the Browns and the Ravenna Ravens. One thing *was* a requirement though, Billy, and that was that you had to hate the Pirates and the Steelers since it was also less than a hundred miles to Pittsburgh and we couldn't let them upstage our Cleveland boys. Oh, we had our few rebels, like my old friend, Ray Victory, who bucked everyone and rooted for the Steelers, but there sure was no shortage of teams to follow and big games to get excited about. But you know what else there was no shortage of in Ravenna, Billy?" Cliffton paused, looking at me.

"No, I don't, sir," I replied.

"Mobster stories! When most people think of mobsters or the mafia they think of New York or Chicago or maybe Miami and Las Vegas, but Youngstown, Ohio, from the thirties right up until now has always been a big mob town, and with no shortage of corruption, bombings and murders. Youngstown tied it all together: New York to Chicago, and they ran Cleveland, Akron, Canton *and* Pittsburgh. And all right there out of Mahoning County, right next door to little old Ravenna. Mahoning County was probably the most corrupt county in the whole damn country back then and maybe still is. Even as we speak, Jim Traficant, United States congressman from

Youngstown is in the mob's pocket and everyone knows it. (note: in 2002 Traficant would go to prison for corruption and mob ties). So it shouldn't be a surprise that even if every person in Fort Harrison knew about Sam Giovanazzo, he would still be immune because of the fear factor. I suspect you're right, though—that most people in your little town have no idea. But don't tell me the cops don't know cause I wouldn't believe that for a second."

"All the major crime families—Bonanno, Lucchese, Genovese, and Gotti—have had their hands in Youngstown at one time or another, although their activities have slowed down because of the loss of population and general depression of the area. The Cardones' and Giovanazzos' have juggled the leadership the last twenty years and there are still hits, still bombings. A hit on Lenny Strollo, big-shot mobster from New York, who had come to Youngstown to stir up trouble between the Cardones' and Giovanazzos' took place less than five years ago and made headlines in both the Dallas and Miami papers. And your buddy, Sam's grandparents, on one side are Giovanazzos and on the other side Cardones. Billy, mobsters often believe nothing can ever happen to them, which seems exactly what Sam Giovanazzo seems to believe, and yet there is something here that bothers me," he said, pausing for a long time and staring at me until I finally spoke up.

"What, Mr. Tremont?"

"First, I don't think Sam is *connected* these days, but more than that, I know of very few mobsters who were pedophiles or even rapists. In fact I'm not sure if I've *ever* heard of one, and particularly where minors are involved. It's an unwritten code of honor and just not done. It is common, however, for the mob to inflict their own justice on those who do and that usually involves cutting off the genitals and stuffing them in the their mouth, gagging them so they can't spit them out and then either strangling them or a single bullet to the head. So if Sam Giovanazzo is like you say he is, it's a good thing he's not around the mob boys cause I don't think that would fly at all, even if his brother *is* the boss, which I believe he still is, though I haven't had much contact with northeastern Ohio for a few years."

"That seems pretty strange to me, Mr. Tremont. You figure mobsters are criminals and pretty much bad all over," I said, thinking about what he just said.

"Kind of crazy, I guess, but honestly most mobsters are pretty big on family. You can find them on school boards and coaching soccer and little league teams all over the place, and believe me we have our share in Dallas, Palm Beach and Miami. Your buddy Stavros knows that well enough. Hey one last story about Youngstown and I gotta go. Can't wait to go ask a few questions about Sam Giovanazzo over in Mahoning County, and believe me, the *horse's mouth* is the only place to find the truth—once you can clear it of the bull's shit," he'd said, laughing at his own joke. Then he suddenly quipped, a bit absently, "Yep, Billy, always thought if I owned a pub I'd name it the *Horse's Mouth,*" he joked, reaching beneath his chair for his cherished ice tea, which had to be room temperature by then.

"You mean you'd actually talk to the mobsters?" I then asked, assuming that's what he meant.

"Of course. They only shoot you if you're messing with them over the big stuff, and only then after giving you a little time to understand it might be an option. Hell, they don't care about an old codger like me asking a few stupid questions. Let me tell you a story. It's true, at least that's the word on the street—and it's pretty funny. Prohibition gave birth to the mobsters. I'm sure you know that if you've got any kind of history teacher at all up there in Fort Harrison . . ." Cliffton began.

That was probably an even bigger joke than Cliffton's story would be, since my history teacher was Dick Hamilton, Giovanazzo's fucking sidekick, but I answered on cue, "Yeah, I pretty much knew that."

"Well in 1931 a two bit mob boss in Pittsburgh named Joseph "Yeast Baron" Siragusa was gunned down in his apartment somewhere downtown. So when the cops get the tip about the hit and go to the apartment, he's got this parrot named Polly, of course, and it's yakking away like crazy right above Siragusa's body: *'Youngstown boys shot Joe; Youngstown boys shot Joe.' 'Booze all comes from Youngstown; booze all comes from Youngstown.'* This parrot never shuts up with these two lines for days, so the Pennsylvania and Ohio staties, along with the Feds, launch big raids all over Youngstown because of a goddamn parrot and they find stills and warehouses loaded down with booze from all over that's being sent throughout the Midwest and into the south, and all being distributed from Youngstown, Ohio. And a parrot named Polly broke the case! Put a big hurt on the Youngstown mob, but within a decade they grew back stronger than ever, and the rest has pretty much been history. It's a tough town and it's a hub. Most people just have no idea, no idea at all," he said, finishing the last of his tea.

"But in the end it doesn't much mean anything for me, does it Mr. Tremont? I mean Giovanazzo could be a mobster, a jerk, and even a rapist, which I already know, but in the end it doesn't really mean all that much for me, do you think?"

It was true that I 'd gotten caught up in the Sam Giovanazzo mob stuff and it kind of blew me away, and the Polly parrot story was a hoot, but then reality hit and for me I realized it probably didn't mean all that much. If you want to know the truth, I couldn't even see Sam Giovanazzo doing something that vile. I mean it had to be a monster even much bigger than him, didn't it?

"I don't know, Billy, I don't know, but with what I've found out myself and with what you've told me, I think it's time to go to Youngtown and see what I can turn up. I've always been my own detective when I've had the chance, although I'm not saying I haven't used others. But I've done enough to know I'm never really surprised about anything and enough to know that *gut feelings and hunches* are more often right than not, and if I'm not wrong we've both kind of got one of those right now, don't we?" he said, standing and slapping me on the back, a good natured move that I really had needed right then.

Cliffton Tremont had an incredible manner about him. He could rip on you over something simple, though in a controlled way; he could challenge you, determined to not let you off the hook until you answered; or he could be nice and relax you if he decided to, but which I had found he rationed in small doses. He seemed to be a man with an infinite well of stabbing questions and yet with a definite sense of humor, even though it did seem to me largely cultivated to amuse himself. I could only imagine what he was like in court, but there *was* one thing I knew for by then—*I was glad he was on my side!* As he walked in front of me I decided to ask an aching question that I had not yet presented him, Demosthenes Stavros having told me there was nothing he could do.

"Mr. Tremont, I have a question before you go, please," I said, timidly.

"Well *speak up* then, son," he said, as if irritated by the unplanned.

"My father only came to see me once and won't anymore I'm certain. You know something about that, and other than my uncles I haven't seen anyone the whole time I have been here except for Mr. Stavros and you. Why can't I see my girlfriend during visiting hours, Mr. Tremont?" I asked, looking up at him and expecting him to dismiss me as Stavros had. "She's stood by me, Mr. Tremont, and she knows that I am innocent."

"Who told you that you couldn't?" he asked.

"Mr. Stavros said he'd asked and they said I couldn't. That was four months ago now," I replied.

"You have the same rights other inmates have regarding visitors, but they may require a different time since you're in isolation. If a trial's in progress, they can deny you visitors—or at least certain visitors. Give me her name and I'll clear it with Sheriff Oberly or he better have a damn good reason for denying it. What's her name?"

"Krissy Kurtz, sir."

"K's or C's . . . or a mix?" he asked.

"Both K's, Mr. Tremont."

"Ok, Billy, now listen. I've got eight days to file for a stay or arrange the date for a pre-trial hearing. I may be gone four or five, but you hang in there and I'll see what I can turn up."

"Thank you Mr. Tremont," I called after him, but by then he had rounded the door without looking back.

*Was there really a chance that I could see Krissy? It was all that I could think about as I was led back to my cell by Jelly Roll. Something inside of me felt that a corner had been turned, but when the cell door slammed shut, it was time to shed any optimism if you truly didn't want to have a panic attack. But tomorrow would be another day—and since Clifford Tremont had shown up—I had begun to look forward to each new sunrise.*

# Chapter Forty-nine

*E*arly the next morning, Sheriff Oberly, himself, came to my cell, keys in hand. "Billy, I'm going to make an exception for you, but this is my jail so I'll do as I damn well please and nobody needs to know any different. I don't know why I began to have doubts that you murdered Gwen Putnam, but somehow I don't think you did and I'm gonna tell you something I probably shouldn't, and don't tell your man Tremont I told you, cause he's gonna wanna tell you himself pretty soon. There's a chemical test for rape that's never been used in Shelby County, but Doc Snyder's involved with the Federal boys and they're working on using it in your case. So if you didn't rape Gwen Putnam, we're all gonna know it real soon, Billy. Your man Stavros is who really fucked you. He didn't push one button that he should have cause he knew about it, but now you got a good un' in this fellow Tremont, that I can tell you—a real good un,'—cause he set those wheels rolling the very first day he blew into town. Now I'm gonna trust you not to tell anyone I said this to you, Billy, including that girl of yours when you call her," he said, winking at me. I sat up on the hard bed and looked at him confused, first trying to understand his drift and then . . . *had he said something about talking to 'my girl'* . . . or was I still half asleep?

"Get some clothes on, Billy. I'm gonna let you make a phone call to that girl of yours," he said, turning his back to me.

"Yes sir, Mr. Oberly, thank you; thank you very much," I said, jumping up and pulling on the drab orange jail frock that lay across the sterile metal table beside the bed. My heart was wedged so tightly in my throat that I could hardly swallow. Sliding on hospital issue prison slippers, I walked with the Sheriff through the door and down the depressing hallway that somehow today seemed like a walk through a pristine forest beside a fairy tale brook.

Once inside the phone room, the Sheriff closed the door and said, "Billy, if you can get her in here at six today, I'll let you two have twenty minutes before regular visiting hours. I'm giving you ten minutes now and I want you to make your call before Jelly Roll shows up for duty, understood?"

"Yes sir, Sheriff, thank you." He then left, closing the door behind him. I picked up the receiver, hearing a dial tone for the first time in months, which gave me an incredible rush that anyone never incarcerated could possibly understand. Having had no time to think it through, I frantically tried to imagine where I could reach Krissy this early in the morning? I knew her home number, but somehow I couldn't imagine that she had moved back there. She had been staying with me at the alley for most of a year before I was arrested, but had she stayed there with me gone? For an instant I thought of calling Dad, but at this time of the morning he would almost certainly be passed out and the sheriff said I only had ten minutes so I couldn't afford to waste time even if he answered—and why would I think he'd help me find Krissy anyhow?

The only number I knew to try was the alley phone which I could picture now on the small oak table I'd bought at the Niemeyer sale and placed beside the hideaway. The same phone that had delivered the haunting phone calls of Clare Putnam and Baxter Sturdivant. The phone started ringing . . . one . . . two . . . three . . . four . . . fi . . . "Hello," came Krissy's sleepy voice.

My heart leaped. *"Krissy . . . it's Billy!"*

*"Billy—Oh my God—Is it really you?"* she screamed into the phone and I could picture her scrambling to sit up in bed.

"Yes Krissy, it's me, but you've got to listen cause we don't have much time," I said, trying to keep myself together when I just wanted to break out crying.

"Oh Billy, I didn't think I was *ever* going to hear your voice again. I . . ."

"Listen Krissy, can you come to the jail today at six o'clock? In fact can you be here even earlier so we don't miss any time? The Sheriff said we could talk for twenty minutes at six o'clock today. You'll be here, won't you? You know how to get here, don't you?"

"Oh, Billy, *YES!*" she cried into the phone, *"Of course I'll be there,* and of course I know where it's at. I've been there before to get my Mom out, remember? And Billy, I've driven by there a hundred times just to be close, thinking maybe somehow I could see you. I've been inside at least ten times asking to see you, but they wouldn't let me," she said, starting to sob.

"So you're still staying at the alley, Kris?"

"Yeah, cause I didn't know what else to do and your Dad let me stay because he knew I could keep the place going. Heck, Billy, I'm pretty much the only one who can. And I just wanted to sleep in *our* bed. I'm supposed to work tonight like always, but fuck it all, I hate it there . . ." she was saying when I heard the door start to open.

"Krissy, listen, I'm going to have to go. Just please be here tonight by 6 and we'll talk about it all . . . *and Krissy, I love you.* I have a new lawyer who says we might have a chance to get to the truth. We've gotta trust that."

Sheriff Oberly opened the door and stepped inside. "Billy, time's up. You've got to go back to your cell. You did get your girl, didn't you? I never told you that she's been here trying to see you, but I bet she just did. Quite the girl, Billy, quite the girl." he was saying in the background.

Trying to ignore him, I'd finished, saying: "Krissy . . . tonight . . . I love you . . . gotta go," and hung up as she was crying into the phone. "Yes, Sheriff, I got my girl. Thank you, thank you very much," I said as I walked with him down the hallway and back to my cell.

. . . A young guy, Deputy Voss, came to get me at exactly two minutes to six, Jelly Roll Kline having completed his shift at 5:30. I'd seen him before and knew he did the evening shift til 1 am, but I'd never talked to him. He was polite enough though so I thought pretty good of him. You would have too if you'd taken the abuse I did at first, especially from that fat ass Jelly Roll. I swear Voss looked like he should have been in junior high as he opened the cell door and led me down the hall to the conference room.

"The Sheriff said for me to allow you twenty minutes, Mr. Bowling. There is a clock on the wall, so understand that I will come for you at exactly six twenty. Your friend is here and in the lobby. She should be in shortly," he said as I went into the conference room where I was alone after he closed the door behind me. There are certain things about my story that I may be able to help you feel or understand, but that moment, waiting to see Krissy and almost frantically trying to catch her first movement from behind one of the four thick Plexiglass windows, is a moment you could *never* understand.

*Then suddenly there she was, meekly peeking into the first window, just inside the lobby door.*

I knew we shouldn't waste time crying, but honestly it ate up at least the first two minutes, neither of us able to loosen our tongues and twist our lips to form words. Finally I was able to speak first.

"Oh God, Krissy, you're so beautiful," I spit out through teary eyes, as if trying to focus through defective wipers in a heavy storm.

"Billy, when are you going to get out of here? It's not fair. You didn't do this. I just don't understand it all," she said, sobbing.

"Krissy we don't have a lot of time and I need to ask you some questions," I said pulling myself together.

"I miss you so, Billy. I hate it at the bowling alley. Everybody acts so funny around me and your Dad is a bigger jerk than ever. I should have quit, but I didn't know what else to do and I didn't want to move back with my mother and her new boyfriend. But mostly I just wanted to be around your things, so I could touch them and smell them—and I don't care if that sounds crazy," she sobbed.

"That's what I wanted to know most, Krissy. Right before you hung up you said you were staying at the alley. Have you been there the whole time?" I asked.

"Yes, I'm staying in the back because your Dad said he was ok with that, but the only reason is because he knows I can run the place. The only reason that asshole cares you're in jail is cause you're not there to work for him. He's drunk more than ever and he's right—without me, the place would go under. Candy hates me, but even she laid off when I threatened to leave cause she sure as hell doesn't want to work," she said between sobs.

"Is Dad paying you fair, Krissy?"

"He pays me $7 an hour, same as you did, Billy. I mean I guess that's what I pay myself, cause I do the payroll now, anyhow," she answered.

"How's it going with your Mom right now?" I asked

"It' better. She's been nice to me and she doesn't believe you did it, Billy, she really doesn't. If I could get a different job I'd move back in with her, at least for awhile. Her boyfriend seems ok, but I've thought that before so I'll never really trust them. But Billy, I just want you out. I want the life we talked about that night, a good life, a happy one," she sobbed.

"Krissy, listen. You tell Dad to pay you $10 or you'll leave. Even though you do the payroll you need to run it by him. Type out a paper that says you're getting paid that and make him sign it. He'll bitch, but he'll do it, believe me, I know. And if he gives you shit or treats you worse, just start packing some stuff and taking it toward your car when he's there and he'll come around. He knows you're his only hope right now, but if you want to leave anyhow, then just pack up and go. It's up to you. And one more thing, did Baxter come back to work?" I asked.

"For about two weeks after you were gone he didn't. He told me his parents wouldn't let him. Then one day he came in and asked if we still needed help and I told him of course, and he's been just great ever since, and he and I run *everything.* I don't think I could do it without Baxter. And Billy, the assholes are different now, too. They still come to the bar, but act really strange around me. Some of them get smart with me too, and think I'll be easy since you're not there I guess, and I don't think I handle things as well as I used to when you were always there for me. But you trust me, don't you Billy? I'd *die* if I thought you didn't. It's the most important thing in my entire life, Billy—*that you trust me,*" she sobbed, looking through the disgusting window deeply into my eyes.

"Yes, Krissy, of course I trust you. We've been there before, remember. No bullshit between us, now or ever. But Kris, if something happens and I don't get out, then you have a life to live and you've got to forget about me. *That you must understand—and it can't be any other way.*"

"*Billy don't talk like that,*" she screamed between gasps and I was sorry I had brought that up just then and tried to change direction . . . .

"Kris, calm down, please honey. I have a really good lawyer now and I think there's hope. You can't stay at the alley forever, but maybe it's the best thing for just a while longer. What do you think?" I asked.

Through flowing tears she looked up at me, "I don't know what else to do cause I don't know where I'd get a job if I lived with Mom. But Billy, *I just want you out of here!*"

"Ok listen, Kris. Uncle Marco and Uncle Dante came to visit me and hired my new lawyer. I know that I've got to be set free somehow, I've just got to, because I didn't do this. Marco's selling Romanos; I think he told you that, but when I get out we're going to move to Florida and I will work for Uncle Dante. He has a huge company and said I could pick my job. You've just got to focus on that, because one day it *will* happen. Look at me, Krissy, and tell me you believe it."

She looked into my eyes through the smudged and scratched Plexiglass. I imagined that the janitors left it that way on purpose and that everyone got a good laugh over it. Maybe we should have tried one of the other stations, but we hadn't the time now. I looked into her eyes so deeply that I could see her entire soul and it was good, it was pure—and it was honest. I glanced at the clock and there were about two minutes left.

"Kris, tell me about you and Marco having dinner. He told me a little and it made me so happy. We only have a few minutes so please tell me. I want to think about it tonight," I said, smiling softly.

"Billy, all I could think of was you not being there . . ."

"Tell me the fun part, honey, please."

"We went back to *l'Auberge* and had the same table. I never knew your Grammy Billy, but I could tell your uncle was sad cause she'd just died a few weeks earlier. Then he told me why he was selling *Romanos* and that he wanted to move to Michigan and be a writer. We had a wonderful meal, but I just wanted you there so bad, so bad, Billy," she sobbed.

"That makes me happy, Krissy. I'm so glad you had a chance to do something fun and relax. Marco's a great guy, and if I ever do get out, it's my Uncles who I will have to thank. Listen, before they come for me I want you to know two things. You know I love you, but as much as that I am *so* proud of you. You are the most incredible girl to ever walk those stupid halls at Harrison High. You're like another species compared to the others—and I want you to know that. And of course you know I love you—so, so much."

"Billy, you *will* get out soon, won't you? Please tell me the truth," she said softly, as someone opened the door behind her and she turned away to look.

"Yes, Krissy, I'm going to get out of here and you've got to trust that," I said as she turned back to me.

"They say I have to go, Billy. I love you so! Goodbye for now," she said, crying and beginning to turn away, but not before we each put our fingers up to the dirty Plexiglas, matching them together. For people who manage to manufacture so much of their own sorrow and fail to take advantage of the freedom and happiness right in the palm of their hands each day, they should just once feel the pain that a half inch of plastic separation can mean—then maybe, just maybe—they'd truly understand what is *really* important in life.

*Eric Voss came in from my side and took me lightly by the forearm, leading me out into the hallway, back to my cell. It was exactly 6:21 pm on Saturday, August 17, 1996, and activities flourished across the free world under the warm summer sun . . . life rushing across a flat planet . . . life taken for granted . . . for you to hold each night another small funeral . . . a funeral for another day you didn't even realize you had attended.*

# Chapter Fifty

$\mathcal{M}$y evening meal was on the small metal table when I returned. There were no surprises . . . chewy gristly swiss steak, playdough mashed potatoes that I actually liked and always had (even in the free world), sterile overcooked green beans, a small plastic cup of fruit jello and small wedge of chocolate brownie with two paper cartons of chocolate milk, which I had chosen for each evening meal. Seconds weren't a choice, but you weren't going to starve and the upside of not being able to invade a fridge at will was that you weren't going to gain much weight, even if you didn't get any exercise, which I didn't since I was in isolation.

My *apartment* was 8' x 7½' or 60 square feet, which I somewhere heard was the minimum required by the state of Ohio for a single person cell. The bed was a solid piece of metal with a very hard mattress, if it could even be called that, affixed to the metal with long bolts and covered with vinyl so tough that it would have taken a grizzly bear a week of serious rage to puncture. Several thick blankets and a very hard vinyl pillow were provided, but no sheets so that you could try to hang yourself by somehow tying them to the high bars. But the biggest hardship was not having a feather pillow, which I'd always had ever since Grammy Louisa had given me one as a small child, followed by a new one every two years or so.

An open toilet sat against the back wall about five feet from the bed and between them a small sink. Every couple of days someone did clean them for regular prisoners when they were in the exercise yard, but in isolation it could get pretty grim if I didn't take care of them myself, which was a trick without any cleaning supplies. Go to jail for months and see what things you'll no longer take for granted. Maybe three times total a guard watched me in the hall while a janitor carelessly attacked the stool and sink, leaving a thick chemical residue pretty much everywhere for me to gag on and that I could have easily bent down and slurped up had I really wanted to commit suicide.

The metal table was bolted to the wall and you used it for anything and everything, which wasn't much . . . I mean like your meal tray, your jumpsuit at night if you chose to take it off, and a book if you had one. After two weeks I had been allowed books and had probably read thirty or so. It would have been a hundred, but they didn't have that many in the jail. They'd bring around a list and you'd mark what you wanted and eventually, though probably not that day, one of the guards would bring it to you. Most were pretty stupid, and often, ironically, predictable murder novels and the type written for people who didn't have a very large brain to nourish. I could read one in a day if I chose, but usually didn't because you could only get two a week anyhow, which I suspected was written into the guard's job description by their union so they wouldn't be overworked.

Mostly though I just lay in bed, sparring with my brain and fighting to keep it in neutral, a battle I usually lost as it ran through all nine gears of a highway freightliner. Today though it was in 9th, bombarded with the images of my beautiful Krissy, but also sliding into a *Bowling family flashback*, which it often did, the resultant depression usually making me wish for a slush fund of chemicals on the toilet bowl to ingest. . . .

. . . Mom had been an incredible pianist and yet Dad would never let her have a piano; I suppose because it would have taken up space reserved for bowling trophies. Anyhow at Grammy's when Dad wasn't there, Jimmy and I were in awe when she played the white grand piano that Grammy had beside the huge window overlooking *Fountain Square,* nineteen stories below. It was magical—and she could play anything.

Jimmy was an Eric Clapton, Derek and the Dominos freak, and he would have Mom play the piano part to *Layla* over and over and I just wanted to cry when she played because it was so beautiful. Jimmy told me, more than once, the story about Jim Gordon, the guy who wrote it with Eric Clapton. Even though he was the Domino's drummer, he'd played the piano for *Layla* and Jimmy said he did all these drugs and then one day went berserk and killed his mother with a hammer. I knew Jimmy would never do anything to Mom, but there was a fascination that he'd seemed to have with that story which I remember bothered me even as a little kid. Jimmy was very talented and could have done anything in the world that he wanted to, but there were times that he frightened me, for his anger ruled him much more than he ruled it—and the process by which he made decisions was terribly flawed.

. . . A ringing bell cut short my drifting thoughts, almost like the school bells had so often done over the years. But this bell was to signal the end of visitation—a bell that had for months been like a dagger to my heart.

*But today it rang for me. For today I had gotten to see my Krissy.*

# Chapter Fifty-one

*B*y Thursday, August 22, 1996, I had been in the Shelby Country jail for exactly four months, having been arrested April 22. I would not be released yet for two weeks, although that was the day I would first understand with certainty I would soon be free, and I am at a loss to even write what I felt, I'm afraid, so you will simply have to settle with the circumstances and chain of events as they unfolded.

That was the day Clifford Tremont returned from Youngstown and finally shared a secret he had selfishly harbored for nearly two weeks—the drift the Sheriff had tipped me on, yet served to only confuse me at that time. Mr. Tremont's later excuse for not telling me earlier was that 'he didn't want me to get my hopes too high for something that could still go wrong.'

His little secret was to shield me from the knowledge that a still rare DNA test was being conducted that would establish my innocence in the rape and murder of Gwen Putnam—that is, if I hadn't actually committed the act as I'd maintained all along. DNA, or *deoxyribonucleic acid* is that genetic human blueprint that we all now know so much about since it's tossed about on every TV crime show with as much necessity as a ball is needed for a baseball game (as I write my story nearly twelve years later) and possessing that magical chemical element with the power to liberate or convict.

What you may *not know*, however, is that in 1996, though its validity had been nearly perfected and the results accepted by courts of law a few years earlier, there was still no national databank of DNA in this country until 1998, thus making the connection with a random or unsuspected criminal almost impossible. It could, however, establish my innocence, though quite honestly in those virginal days was not a standard practice used and not something that would have likely even been employed in Shelby County at that time without being requested by an attorney or petitioned by the accused criminal, outrageous as that may seem (which Stavros didn't do, but Tremont did).

In fact, my case in 1996 was not only one of the very first cases to free a suspect because of DNA evidence, but one of the very first in the country to later convict the rapist with certainty based on DNA evidence. It's hard to believe, but check the dates on the internet (now) and you'll be surprised. Some sites even list my case. The results are not instantaneous, however, and it was then not unusual at all for several months to pass from the time the samples were submitted to the time the test results were known, though I have never really understood that. It is true that upon my arrival at the jail, I had been required to submit urine and blood samples, which I was told could be used for various testing and identification, though at the time I merely thought it was a health issue or that they were testing me for drugs. The samples, therefore, were available for later DNA testing as Tremont requested immediately upon taking my case and finding there had been semen in evidence at the Gwen Putnam crime scene.

Sam Giovanazzo had committed so many sexual crimes by then that he believed with confidence nothing could ever happen to him, not in Fort Harrison, Ohio (along, of course, with likely possessing the mobster immune mentality that Cliffton had told me about earlier). That this time he had moved on to murder wasn't all that surprising as he had threatened several nervous girls with just such consequences over the years—a few times coming within a fragilely enraged moment of carrying it out. He had reasoned that should it ever become necessary, he would figure out the cover up at the time. After all, growing up the way he did he wasn't stupid about such things, you did what you had to do, then you covered your tracks.

In one way, however, Sam Giovanazzo did *not* cover his tracks and it was because of his own nauseating arrogance. Sam Giovanazzo hadn't used a condom in the rape of Gwen Putnam, heinously deciding that the last thing he had to worry about was whether or not she became pregnant, thus DNA evidence was very simple to extract.

Sam had actually planned the murder of Gwen Putnam nearly four years earlier at that point, ever since that day she had been awarded the 'Key to Fort Harrison' in the spring of her senior year and he had witnessed the whole town worship her in a way he had never been accorded. And from the very beginning he knew that he would also have his way with her when he extracted his revenge, the prospects of which had excited him very much—even though she wasn't one of his 'little' girl's just out of the cradle.

But that first time Gwen had left for Notre Dame earlier than expected, throwing a wrench into things before he had been able to put his game plan together. Sam became furious, and with a most unusual person . . . *himself*! For you see, Sam Giovanazzo's entire life and every waking moment was consumed by game plans, football games to be sure, even wrestling moves for the domination of opponents . . . but there was *absolutely* nothing that drove Sam like his sexual conquests. They not only had to be fashioned with perfection, but executed with zero margin for failure and this was exactly why Sam Giovanazzo had never been challenged, at least in *his* mind—*because his game plans were always perfect.*

But Sam Giovanazzo's game plans had always been focused on *intimidating the living*, and since Gwen Putnam was going to be dead and Sam was ignorant of DNA at the time, very little time or care had been spent on *the game plan that finally brought him down.* For in his twisted mind, a dead person meant—*end of game, period*—and short of being caught in the act, absolutely nothing to worry about.

Over twenty-six years Sam Giovanazzo had 'raped' 22 (minor) Fort Harrison girls, and probably another 'football team' of eighteen year olds—and yet had remained unchallenged at any time along the way. Still, he had slipped up on the Gwen Putnam thing that summer of 1992, and before he knew it the 1992/93 school year was upon him. It had been six years since he had won *both* the football *and* wrestling state trophies in the same school year, but he fully expected to do it that year, so Sam's mind attacked the football season and the Gwen Putnam mission was dropped out of necessity. After all, she was now gone and if this proved to be the year he expected, Fort Harrison would soon forget all about Gwen Putnam and she would become yesterday's news . . . besides Sam wasn't completely stupid and even *he* knew murder could be a messy and risky business, so maybe he should just leave well enough alone. Sam's real comfort zone anyhow was *young girls*—girls imprisoned by the walls and requirements of the public school system where he was afforded the perfect stage on which to conduct his business.

Things were coming along very nicely that fall with the cute little Dalinghaus girl so he focused his full attention then on her. He had, that summer, engineered her *off* the cheerleading squad then immediately ambushed her with the promise of regaining a spot the following year, one of Sam's patented *game plans* that he had recently started thinking was becoming too easy. But he did need to concentrate on coaching that year, so the simpler game plan would be fine this time around. In the meantime, Mindy could become one of Sam's *stat girls* that winter for wrestling as he *worked* on her, and especially because he was getting particularly horny and needed to have some young action real soon. He had Mindy Dalinghaus in the palm of his hand, all right—and what a killer body! Ever since being turned down by that *Kurtz whore*, Sam had been infuriated, but Mindy seemed to be the next best fit. If, in fact, it was murder he was going to turn to, perhaps he should have started with Krissy Kurtz—*cause no one says NO to Sam Giovanazzo—NO ONE!*

# Chapter Fifty-two

*A* couple of weeks had passed since Cliffton Tremont shared his DNA information with me when I heard three people walking toward my cell, just after 2 pm. I never quite decided if jail time sharpened or dulled the senses, or that it even much mattered, but I understood the language of footsteps like I never had before and it had become second nature that I now realized three people were approaching. I was sitting on my bed, leaning back against the dirty block wall and reading John Irving's *The World According to Garp*, a surprisingly decent novel that Jelly Roll had brought me the day before. I had about two chapters remaining when the footsteps were spawned, first like crisp, though distant thunder, before being diluted by muffled conversation and drawing nearer. With natural anticipation I now saw Cliffton Tremont, Sheriff Sam Oberly and Jelly Roll Kline before me. Though I had a gut feeling that this was the moment I had so waited on, I nevertheless had a comical flash that God had indeed baked the planet cake using a strangely bizarre mix of human ingredients.

*"Billy Bowling, you are being released by court order. You are free to go,"* Sheriff Oberly had said with as much formality as he'd used when he arrested me in April. Of the three, he was the only one with a smile, but it just wasn't Cliffton Tremont's nature to exhibit much emotion of any sort I had earlier learned. Jelly Roll fumbled with the keys, but in general seemed pissed, as always, though perhaps more so today than usual since people like him survive by dining on the bone marrow of other's misfortunes, so someone else having a good day usually meant his was particularly doomed to suck.

The Sheriff stepped inside the cell and handed me a grocery paper bag that held the same clothes I had worn to the jail the night of my arrest. "Here Billy, leave that nasty orange thing on the bed. We'll get it later. Oh, your stuff's been washed, by the way."

As the three men took a few steps down the hall, I quickly changed my clothing and threw the jumpsuit on the bed. Sliding my Reeboks on I again noted the small things taken for granted, like shoes. For nearly five months I'd had only those hospital paper-thin slippers to wear and the feel of real shoes was a rare thrill—as if I had just rejoined the human race—which was exactly what was happening.

"You might want to bring your things, Billy," the Sheriff added.

"That's a good one, Sheriff—you're quite the comedian, aren't you," I said, jokingly, looking about the vacant cell and trying to force a chuckle before asking, "Sheriff, think I could maybe borrow my book here to finish? Promise to send it back."

"Sure, Billy, but just keep it. Our little going away present that I'm certain no one will miss," he'd laughed as I grabbed the paperback and walked through the cell door. Then everything hit me and I nearly drowned in an emotional flood that I'm not now, wasn't then, nor ever will be able to explain. Cliffton Tremont stepped forward enveloping me with the strongest one arm hug I had ever known, holding me above the hall floor with singular strength at a time when, had he not, I would have crumbled.

"Now I realize that you've probably consumed a stellar institutional meal a few hours ago, Billy, but I'm starving and would like to take you and the Mrs. out for mid afternoon *lupper* if you will join me. Oh, and the tab's on your Uncle Dante by the way," Cliffton then said, relaxing his grip as my legs gained strength, then laughing at his lame lupper joke, the normal accompaniment to some of the corniest jokes ever coined. Then I froze. *What else had he just said . . . the Mrs?*

"What did you say, Cliffton?" I asked.

"Lupper, Billy, *lupper.* It's 2 o'clock, surely you've heard that . . . lupper. Not all that hard to understand, Captain," he chuckled, shaking his head..

"I *get it,* Cliffton, I mean the *Mrs.* part. What do you mean?"

But as the door swung open, I needed nothing further from Cliffton Tremont, *for there across the room stood Krissy*, and as the room began to spin, before Cliffton could once again employ his latent one arm mana, it was Krissy who now held me up with a strength I didn't even try to understand.

"How's pizza sound to you kids?" Cliffton asked. I'd heard and didn't hear him at the same time. Then Krissy was pulling away from me, but just far enough to talk.

"Billy, Mr. Tremont wants to take us for pizza," she said as I dumbly nodded, just wanting to touch, smell, and inhale her.

"Ya got a pizza day here in the jail, Sheriff? Some places do these days," Cliffton queried.

"Nope, Mr. Tremont, we've never started that one. They're prisoners, you know," he said, chuckling.

"Well, where's the best pizza in town, Sheriff? I'm starved for something really good so don't steer us wrong. Someplace that I can get a nice cold one, too," he said, grinning.

"*Jelly Roll*," the Sheriff yelled –*loud*—startling both Krissy and myself.

The door swung open, Jelly Roll obviously having been just on the other side, which the Sheriff had likely known all along. He'd probably been racking his miniscule brain to think up a reason to come ask Sheriff Oberly a question so he could scope Krissy, whom he'd obviously seen before as she returned to lobby time and again over the months for our reunion. "Yeah, boss?" he said, his eyes darting from Krissy's breasts to her legs and back, his mouth gaping like the village idiot's retarded second cousin.

"Where's the best pizza in town, Jelly, and where Mr. Tremont can get a cold beer? I got an answer, but everyone in Shelby Country knows you're the horse's mouth when it comes to pizza and beer, so what's the word?" the Sheriff asked with a huge grin as Jelly Roll's eyes lit up, suddenly thinking about pizza and beer, his lust for Krissy having evaporated as quickly as the first piece of fantasy pizza his powerful mind had already devoured.

"Oh, *Cassanos,* boss, nothing better . . . get the *double cheeseburger* pizza! God, I mean that's . . ." Jelly Roll was in his element when the Sheriff cut him off.

"Thanks, Jelly, better get back inside. Time for a check around."

"I mean you want to get . . ." he tried to continue.

"Thanks, JELLY," the Sheriff said sternly now, taking a step backward to open the door as Jelly Roll reluctantly passed through and Oberly closed it behind him.

"Like I said gang, right from horse's mouth. Cassanos is the place though; would have told you that myself, but thought we'd have an ounce of fun. Just across the road over there on 29. You don't even need to move your car, Mr. Tremont. Billy, good luck and I mean that. Stay in touch, will you?" the Sheriff said.

The lightness of the pizza romp had allowed me to clear my head and gain strength. The Sheriff hadn't needed to go through all the dramatics anyhow cause Krissy and I had both eaten at Cassanos probably a hundred times between us over the years, but I guess he figured the little opera with Jelly Roll would give us, or at least Cliffton, a rise. I stood beside Krissy, towering over her petite frame, circling her shoulders with my right arm and holding her tight, then released her for a moment as the Sheriff stepped forward offering his hand. "We'll see, Sheriff. Don't think we plan on staying around too long," I answered.

"I know, Billy. Well you kids get on along, and Krissy, sorry this all happened, I really am. I know one thing though, as unfortunate as this has been, Billy's very lucky to have you in his corner and I'm pretty sure he knows it," Sheriff Oberly finished with a wink as we stepped into the courtyard between the jail and courthouse and I took my first deep breath of free air in five months. The last time I'd shared that space with hords of reporters, photographers and vigilantes screaming for my immediate execution, but obviously my release had been a perfectly kept secret because there was not a human in sight and I knew that I had Sheriff Oberly to thank for that—and was grateful because of it.

It was Friday, September 6, 1996, and as Fort Harrison High prepared to play the Delphos St. John Blue Jays that evening, hall decorations were being pilfered and the varsity players were AWOL about the streets of the village. And more than likely a player I hardly knew was finger fucking a cheerleader I hardly knew on the bench beside the flag pole beneath the window of Wickerdick's office, while he fondled the photo of himself and Arnold Palmer from 1975 and slashed off another calendar week . . . dreaming of infinite golf and his condo in Palm Coast, Florida.

. . . Sam Giovanazzo's free period that year was 7th (1:22-2:17)—and as I walked out into the sunshine of freedom at 2:06 pm with my Krissy and Cliffton Tremont—not fifteen miles distant Sam Giovanazzo was spraying his sperm across the fifteen year old chest and face of Stacy Burson, a requisite step for his serious duties but a few hours later at Robbins Field.

*And taped beneath the gymnasium podium that had been comically constructed years earlier by the shop boys, a Lane Phillips stink bomb awaited its 2:45 detonation.*

# Chapter Fifty-three

*I*t would still be three weeks before Sam Giovanazzo would be arrested for the murder of Gwen Putnam while pacing the sidelines at Robbins Field during pre-game warm-ups for the Parkway High School game. With my release, however, a barrage of renewed questioning by the FBI (as a result of an *anonymous* tip) would be anything but comfortable for Sam. FBI agent Mike Tarver and Sheriff Sam Oberly would ultimately manipulate a warrant to search Sam's secluded home to coincide with an away football game . . . and what they would find would not only be nauseating, but truly beyond understanding.

. . . Even for a fall football Friday, at 2:15 in the afternoon, we had Cassano's Pizzaria completely to ourselves, so obviously the Sidney High School administration had a handle on their jocks and they actually were confined within the building during school hours, I remember thinking to myself for a brief moment. Krissy started to slide into one side of a booth before I noticed that the bulky Cliffton would be much more comfortable in a chair, so I gave her a sly wink and nodded toward a table.

"Krissy, why don't we sit at a table. That booth reminds me too much of my cell," I said, lightly joking, but noticing Cliffton had seemed especially comfortable that the issue of his squeezing into a booth hadn't shared the light of day.

We ordered an XL pan pizza supreme, a pitcher of Amber Bock for Cliffton and two cokes for Krissy and myself. We'd eschewed Jelly Roll's double-cheeseburger suggestion, though it had been appealing I'd honestly thought, given what I'd had on menu for the past five months. Again I started to feel overwhelmed by it all, but as Krissy slid her hand back and forth across my leg, I began to relax—and Cliffton Tremont began to speak. . . .

. . . "Ok, what I'm about to tell you two you must not discuss with anyone . . . until, if, and when it becomes public. So I can trust you, right? It is important and could even involve your safety, though I think that would be stretching it quite a bit, given where our friend Sam Giovanazzo stands with his quite notorious relatives," Cliffton said, pouring his first glass of beer and chugging it as simply as one might swallow a stifled hiccup.

I wasn't sure where he was going, but I looked at Krissy, then back to Cliffton, and we both nodded. "Of course, Cliffton . . . I think you would know that by now."

"Yes, Billy, but just the same it needs said and you must be cautioned. I learned some very interesting things on my trip to Youngstown and it appears that everything points directly to Sam Giovanazzo, just as we had suspected could be the case, remember?" Cliffton asked, refilling his mug.

"Yes, Cliffton, but I never really believed it. How can you have such confidence now? I'm confused. They haven't run the chemical tests on Giovanazzo, have they?" I queried.

"No, they haven't, Billy, but that's just a matter of time—once we point the Feds in his direction. No, I'm talking about *horse's mouth* . . . just like I said—*the horse's mouth*!"

"You mean you really *did* talk to the gangsters?"

"Let's say mobsters, Billy. For some reason they prefer that, who knows why? I have some good friends in the area that pointed me right and I wasted little time asking questions. On the second day I received a phone call to meet with Vincent Giovanazzo himself—Sam's brother—who by the way *is el Capitan* of the Youngstown mob. I was nervous, I'll admit, because it was so quick and I assumed I was going to be told to stay clear and probably get lost. But like I said, at that point I wasn't afraid and arrived promptly for my meeting with Mr.Giovanazzo at Cedar Lounge in downtown Youngstown. Cedar Lounge has been around forever and I felt comfortable with the meeting there," Cliffton said, finally pausing.

"So you actually met with Sam Giovanazzo's brother who you say is the main mob boss?" I repeated as Krissy listened wide-eyed.

"You got it, Billy, and within seconds I realized Vincent Giovanazzo had written Sam off as a brother. He turned to me and said, 'Mr. Tremont, I don't know what you want around here, but if it is about Sam, and whether or not he could be connected to your rape and murder, the straight answer is *yes, he almost certainly is your man.* So take that with you and then please leave us alone. I don't want his scum rubbing off around here, do you understand? You need a suspect, you got one now, if you didn't suspect him seriously before. Now please, just go do what you do. I have business to attend to,' he said and abruptly left, without emotion or offering a handshake, a 'good day' or anything of the sort. From the window I saw a big black Lincoln pull to the curb and Vincent Giovanazzo disappeared within and was gone. I finished my Heniken, trying to fathom perhaps the most unusual and unlikely, though productive, meeting I had ever been party to in my entire life—and all in a total time of less than two minutes."

I sat confused, part of me still disbelieving that I was free and another part of me trying to digest what Cliffton Tremont had just said. Had he just said that Sam Giovanazzo's own brother said that Sam was the murderer?

"So what does it all mean, Cliffton? I'm honestly lost on all of this," I said, squeezing Krissy's hand beneath the table.

"It means, more than likely, that Sam Giovanazzo raped and murdered Gwen Putnam, and that a *little birdie* needs to make a call to the FBI to point them in the right direction," Cliffton answered, setting down his mug of beer and looking me seriously in the eye.

"So how can it be proven? By DNA?" I asked innocently.

"Yes, exactly the same way you were freed. There was DNA evidence at the scene. That was shared with me as soon as I took your case because it was the first question I asked—and a question that your man Stavros hadn't. Apparently it was quite obvious that the rapist hadn't used a condom, assuming it didn't matter anyway, and my guess is Sam Giovanazzo is not the type of person to *ever* use a condom. That would be too much like sacrificing a chunk of his manhood. I've heard of this sick profile before in rape cases in Texas and Florida. From the description of both the crime scene and of your friend who witnessed the encounter in his office I would imagine he uses the same method every time, and either has never impregnated one of the high school girls or very possibly arranged for an abortion had it ever become necessary. The semen found at the crime scene, excuse me Krissy, was found upon the chest of Miss Putnam, not inter-vaginal," Cliffton said, pausing and looking directly at me.

The statement made me cringe and was something I did not even want to think about, but I had noticed that Cliffton Tremont pretty much said exactly what was on his mind and that had been on it at the time. Under the circumstances I guess there was no reason to tip-toe around the facts that had first freed me . . . and now were posed to hopefully convict Sam Giovanazzo.

"So now what?" I asked as a pimply-faced redhead brought our pizza to the table.

"They analyze now, son, just like they did when checking on you," he replied, sliding two large pieces out of the pan and onto a small plate meant to hold one.

"So will they ask Giovanazzo for a sample or something?" I asked.

"I don't know for sure. Tarver and the FBI are handling it and those bastards love surprises, so it will probably be easy enough for them to snag a pop can or something from Giovanazzo. Is Sam Giovanazzo a smoker, by chance?" Cliffton asked, before devouring the first piece of pizza.

"Yep, he sure is, unless he quit since I was in school. In fact he's a heavy smoker and the alley between his office and the gym was always littered with thousands of cigarette butts. He even smoked during outdoor gym classes and during football practice," I answered.

"Bingo, Billy, a cigarette butt works most of the time and the FBI will look for that first. Just keep this quiet and sit back and wait. If I were you I wouldn't go to Florida just yet. You deserve to be here when it all comes down . . .at least that's they way I see it, but you and Krissy might want to do it differently. Anyway, I'm going back to Dallas tomorrow after I meet with Tarver and Oberly to share with them my little Youngstown 'fact finding mission,' which I think will compound the little phone tip and really fire them up to get on Giovanazzo's tail. I understand that you're both considering a move to Florida to work for Dante in Jupiter. Have you been there before?" Cliffton asked, sitting back on his chair and working on his second piece.

"No, neither Krissy or I have traveled all that much and I honestly don't know Dante very well, except for his visit a month ago. Mom talked about him, but he never much came back to Ohio as far as I know, though Grammy and Grampy Romano went down and stayed with him a lot in the winters," I answered.

"Well, you're in for quite a surprise, kids—that's all I can say," he said with a smile and a shake of the head.

"I'm not too sure what you mean, Cliffton," I asked.

"A surprise, Billy, just what I said. Dante is a great guy, as good as they come, but I'm gonna let you find out the rest for yourselves. Just be prepared for a surprise—and not an uncomfortable one—so don't go worrying about that. Oh, and by the way, he wanted you to have this when you were released," Cliffton said, pulling out a wad of cash and extending it to me across the table," accompanied by a sheepish grin.

"Geez, Cliffton, are you serious? I mean what's it for?" I'd asked numbly, looking at Krissy who was as floored as I was. "God, how much . . ." I started to say, but Cliffon cut me short.

"Just tuck it in your pocket real good and count it later. It's *'getting back on your feet'* expenses, according to Dante. Things like gas and maybe truck rental if you two really do decide to head south," he'd almost jokingly said for the first time I could remember since meeting him. So I slid it to Kris, who put it in her small purse and we dropped the subject for then, as Cliffton had seemingly wanted.

After some smaller talk—and when the last piece of pizza disappeared—Cliffton stood to go, tossing two twenties on the table. Krissy and I stood too, drawn magnetically. I wanted to hug Cliffton, but somehow suspected he was old school and that wasn't much done. I'd learned he'd never had any children of his own and so, of course, no grandchildren, and I figured his feelings were on reserve, even as you could clearly see the gold that formed his backbone and heart.

"Mr. Tremont, you saved my life and I will never forget it. Thank you very much," I said, hugging Krissy almost unconsciously and holding back the tears welling in my eyes.

Cliffton stepped forward and *did* hug me—with that same one arm hug he had used to support me outside the jail cell when my legs had failed. I no longer tried to hold back the tears and forward they burst.

"Billy, I understand. I'm just glad I could be of help, and remember, you have your Uncle Dante to thank more than me. Oh, and by the way, if you and Krissy do plan on moving to Florida I shall likely be seeing you again sooner than later for I am selling my Dallas home and moving full time to my place in North Palm, just ten miles down the road from Dante's little homestead. Bless you both," he said, releasing me and leaning forward to give Krissy a nip on the cheek. "You two make quite the couple, but you know that I'm sure. Now take care of each other," he said, and turning, disappeared out the door as we stood watching him go.

Krissy and I moved to a booth where we could sit side by side and ordered another coke. We just wanted to talk, to kiss . . . *and to believe.* More than anything I just inhaled her. There is no magic like just inhaling the woman you love . . . inhaling her hair until you get a funny nose tickle and suddenly your shoulders shake until the thrill comes out the tips of your fingers and you want to do it again. That's how you can tell what real love is—just inhale her neck and her hair—*and then you will know for sure.*

. . . "Krissy," I said as a thought struck me. "Is there any chance Dad is at a tournament this weekend?"

"Yeah, Billy, I think Columbus or Cleveland or something. I know it started with a C."

"So he left today?"

"Yeah, a little before noon—just before Cliffton called me and said you were getting out."

"So *he* didn't know I was getting out, right?"

"Of course not, Billy."

"What about Busty; did she go with him?"

"Yeah, they both went. Pretty much like always, and then Baxter and me have to run everything all weekend. Oh, and Billy, he did raise me to $10 an hour when I threatened to leave."

"Good honey, I knew he would, but listen, we got some serious plans to make. Is there anybody who can help Baxter for the weekend?"

"Maybe. His buddy Tim Otte helps us once in awhile, but he's on the football team and can only help Saturday afternoons and Sundays. I'm the only one on tonight, but hardly anyone comes anyhow, except for the drunks after the game. It's a joke."

"Perfect Krissy . . . it's all perfect! We rent a truck right now and get my shit out tonight. We can store it over in Minster. They always have units free and I'll call right now. Then we shut the alley down tonight and Baxter can decide whether he wants to run it over the weekend with his friend. Or he can just close it all weekend and have a break. Dad can't afford to fire him or he'd have *nobody* to run it. We'll try to catch thim after school and see how he wants to handle it."

"Billy, Baxter's parents won't let him run the bar if no adult is there. They'd shit if they even knew he set up Beams for Thermie."

"Whatever, Kris, we'll figure it all out . . . he'll figure it out. I'm not gonna much worry about what Baxter Sturdivant's parents care about, now am I? Besides, Baxter can take care of himself. He doesn't have to have the bar open. This is perfect, Kris. The whole town will be at the game and no one will even notice the truck. We'll get a motel room somewhere out on the Interstate tonight and call your Mom in the morning and see about staying there a few days while we decide what to do. She's ok with that you said once, right?"

"Yeah, Billy; she'd be fine with that. I think you'll like her better now—she's changed a lot."

"Great. Now we've got some plans to go over and some calls to make . . . oh, yeah, I almost forgot, just how much money was in that roll of cash Cliffton forked over?" I'd said lightly, assuming it was probably a few hundred or so, but enough for the truck and a motel . . .

*A twenty encased ten hundred dollar bills . . . AND . . . a cashier's check for $5000! "Oh, fuck, Billy . . . oh fuck, oh fuck . . . OHHHHHHH FUCKKKK, BILLY, LOOK! And as for fucking? OHHHHHHH . . . F ..............!*

# Part Three

## Family

## 1996-2009

*"There are only two ways to live your life. One is as though nothing is a miracle. The other is as if everything is a miracle."*

*(Albert Einstein)*

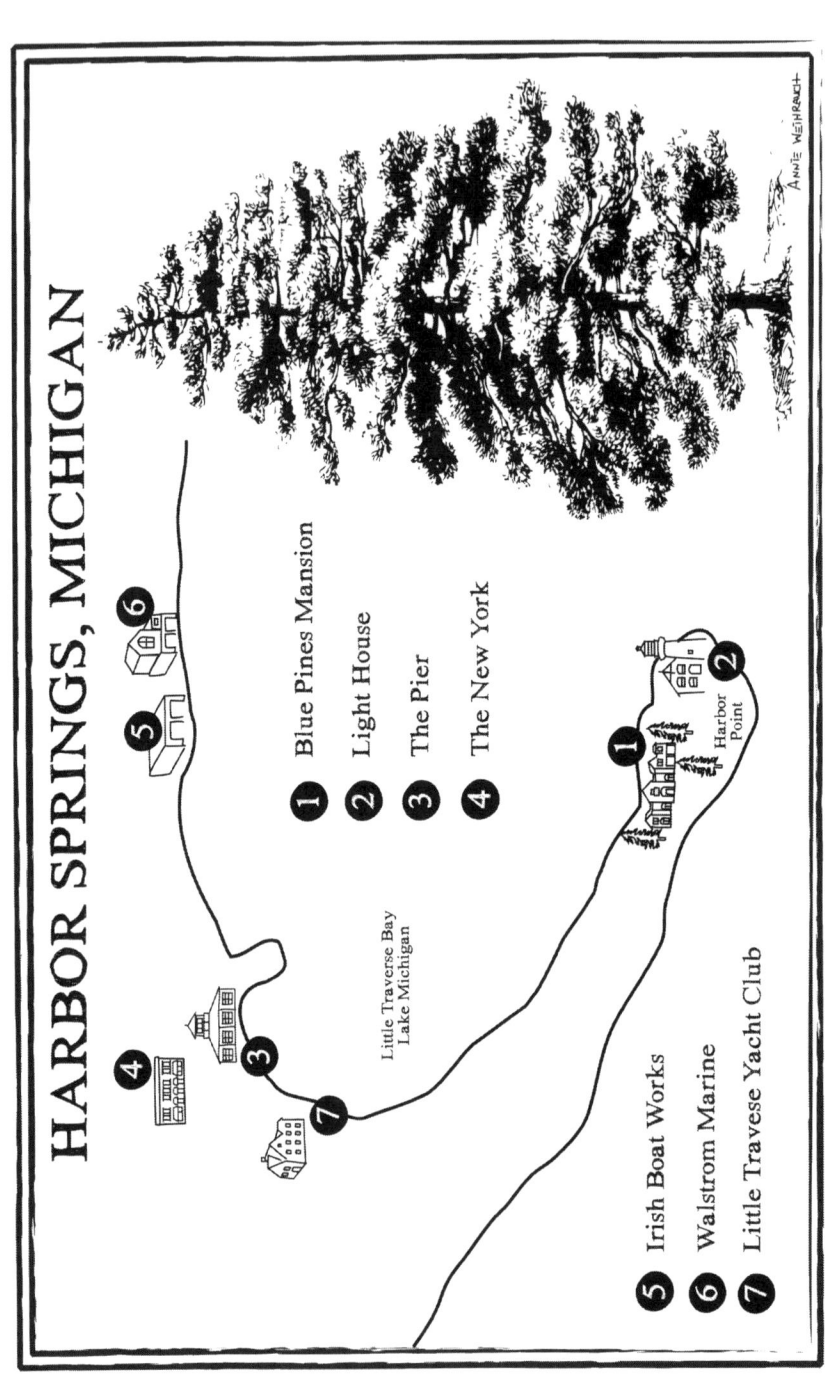

# HARBOR SPRINGS, MICHIGAN

1 Blue Pines Mansion

2 Light House

3 The Pier

4 The New York

5 Irish Boat Works

6 Walstrom Marine

7 Little Travese Yacht Club

Little Traverse Bay
Lake Michigan

Harbor Point

ANNIE WEIHRAUCH

# JUPITER ISLAND, FLORIDA

Atlantic Ocean

1 Blue Palms

2 Billy & Krissy's House

3 Romano Rinato

4 Jupiter Lighthouse

5 Crab House

6 Hobe Sound

7 U.S. RT. #1

8 Jupiter Inlet

ANNE WEIHRAUCH

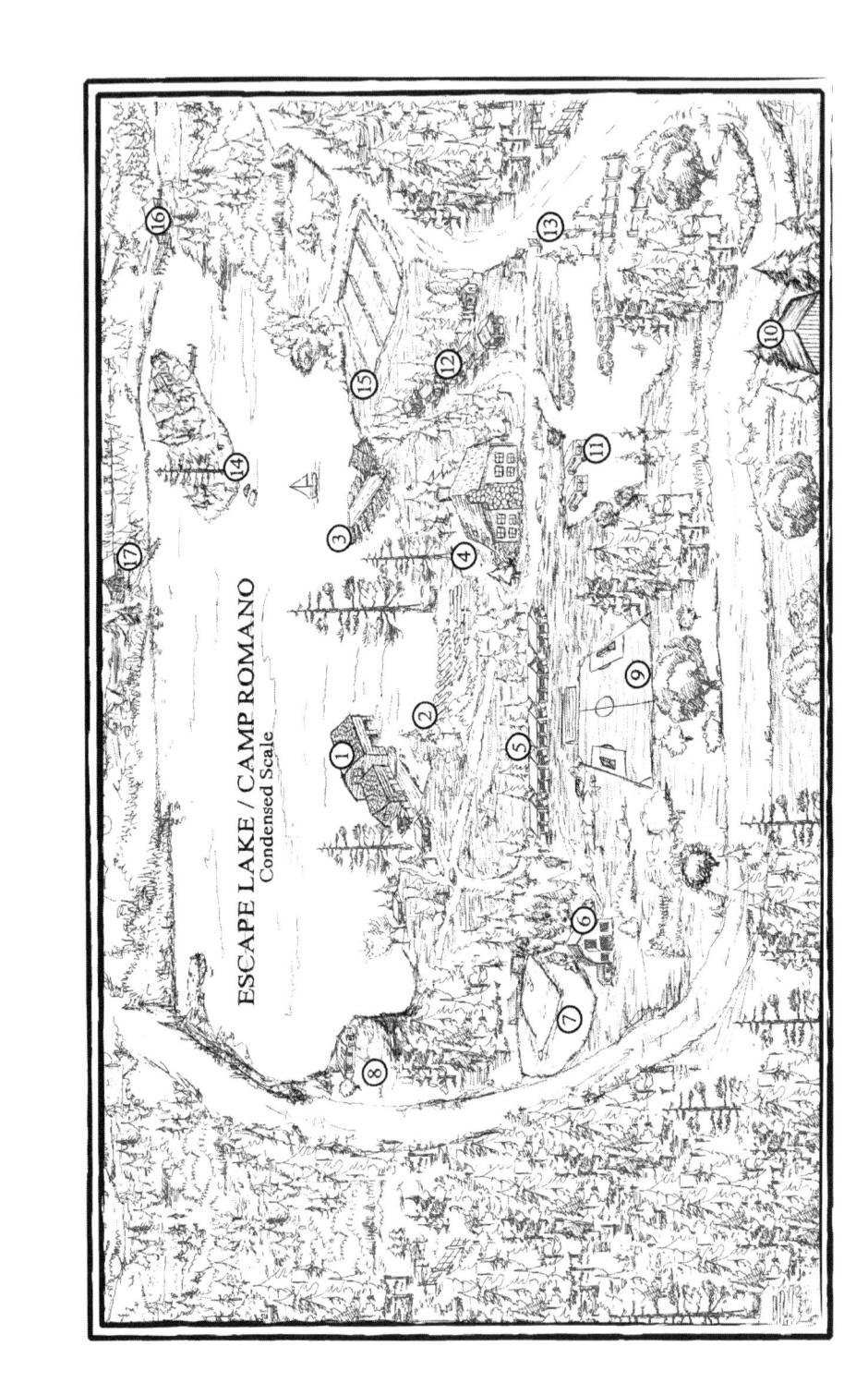

ESCAPE LAKE / CAMP ROMANO
Condensed Scale

# CAMP ROMANO, ESCAPE LAKE
## LEGEND

1. Camp Romano Classic Boat House
2. Camp Romano Amphitheatre / Fire Ring
3. Student Boat Dock
4. The Lodge
5. 'Rookie Cabins'
6. Sports Equipment Barn
7. Baseball / Softball Field
8. FORD CABIN / Marco & Mirella's Home
9. Soccer Field

10. Utility Barn / Boat Storage
11. Visitor Parking
12. 'Senior Cabins'
13. Escape Lake Road
14. Eagle's Nest Island
15. Clay Tennis Courts
16. Carston Cabin
17. CLIFFTON, Billy & Krissy's 'Home'

CAMP ROMANO
ESCAPE LAKE

# Chapter Fifty-four

*I*t's funny (well, not *really* funny*)* how when we've been totally victimized, our appetencies become so diluted by the injustice that even a scrap of good news or hope is cherished, although given what I had been through, I had come to understand that it can be a good thing. For even as I lived the nightmare of a potential death sentence/life in prison—and was the very picture of Satan himself—over the years I have come to truly understand just how lucky I had been in 1996 to have been vindicated through the use of DNA. Even now it is not uncommon to hear of someone innocent released after twenty-thirty years of prison time by contemporary DNA analysis, which is being improved even as I write. So I suppose it makes my nearly five months in a west-central Ohio jail cell pale in comparison—and I am thankful—though it was a nightmare that I can never quite extinguish from the recesses of my conscious mind.

However—short of plastic surgery or a beard and sunglasses—I would for many years be a marked person, never knowing when an innocent night on the town or a trip to the beach would create an awkward scene or even on occasion a spurious confrontation. My elevated profile during and after my arrest had rendered me forever guilty, and the assumption by some that society would line up to grieve with me over my horrendous injustices was a comical error that even I was eventually forced to laugh at . . . though 'funny' *it was not!*

After staying several weeks with Lacy Johnson, Krissy and I had decided to move to Florida where I would work for Uncle Dante as we had discussed. Marco had made definitive arrangements to sell *Romanos*, but was as yet uncertain what his future would ultimately be other than to move to Northern Michigan where he intended to write mystery novels. I'd made up my mind to see my father before we left, for in isolation I'd decided that should I ever be released, I would make *one last attempt* to fashion a relationship with him, and following that, make every effort to contact Jimmy. Otherwise, there *was* no Bowling family, period, which had haunted my entire life. So I would make the attempt—*I simply had to*—and should I be rebuffed, I could then move on with life knowing there was *absolutely* nothing else that I could have done.

. . . It was a Monday morning, the first week of October around eleven, that I pulled my Explorer into the lot at the alley and parked it near the back where I had thousands of times before. It had apparently sat there for months until the first time I talked with Krissy and told her to drive it and get rid of her rattletrap Escort. Dad had always left my things alone and never said a word to Krissy when she adopted it. He had a bizarre pinkish-beige '88 Lincoln Continental and Busty had always driven an old Taurus, but I didn't see the Taurus anywhere around. The Continental was parked behind the garage, not in it, because it was too long to fit anyway, so I suspected she was either gone or her car in the garage, although I couldn't picture Dad keeping the garage cleared out enough to get any kind of car inside. As I approached the skewered slab of steps at the side door to the trailer, I did find myself hoping that Busty was indeed gone, for if there was a chance for any sort of reunion, I would have preferred that it take place bereft the company of Dad's charming bride.

An old pickup and a newer Mustang sat parked in the lot, but it never surprised to see cars sit around for days before they were reclaimed and we'd never made a big deal about it—for we preferred that to being slapped with an 'accessory' charge in a fatal automobile collision. The dumpster behind the alley was bursting with trash—random paper and cardboard having blown off into Winston's field behind it. The trash barrel that usually sat behind the garage had been knocked over, spilling out everywhere. Much of it had found a home beneath Dad's gaudy Continental, though the lighter paper had blown into yard high weeds and tufted grass in what *used* to be our 'back yard.' Though only five years old, the trailer was the most God-awful and depressing piece of vinyl, pine and metal north of Mexico City. For whatever reason, the big convex end window that faced 66 was shattered and now hosted several long gray veins of duct tape, facing the cracks from both inside and out—the ends of the outside strips having baked to freedom in the summer sun and now, dancing like small paper skeletons in the light autumn breeze, were the only noticeable movement on the entire property. Where there had once been a storm door, now only rusty hinges greeted me, and as I began to knock I glanced down and could see five or six beer cans and an empty plastic two liter bottle of Popov wedged between the stoop and the trailer—along with ten or fifteen crushed and discarded empty packs of filter-less Camels, tossed into the weeds below with obvious purpose.

Part of me just wanted to turn and leave, but life is often like that I had come to find, and to face the unpleasant is sometimes the only way to preserve both dignity and sanity, and in the process liberating us enough to move on to something better, strange as it may sound. I knocked loud and waited.

The occasional car flashed by on 66, not 75 feet away, and even then it struck me how I'd known the drivers of the last two with hardly a glance—John Bertke, a truck mechanic at Northwest Towing out on I-75, and Joanne Niemeyer who lived just down the highway and was a secretary for Joe Amweg, the Farm Bureau agent. I wouldn't miss Fort Harrison, but it was ingrained within my being like a case of the herpes that could never be completely evicted.

Finally the door opened and there stood my endearing stepmother, Candy Busty Bailey Bowling, just four years my senior. Her expression dropped upon seeing me, like a teasing seven pin that finally bites the boards for an accidental strike. The stench of thick cheap perfume almost caused me to cough and her boobs sprung forth half naked from a tired old frilly blouse I remembered her wearing at the alley for years.

"Dad home, Candy?" I asked simply.

"He's not up yet, Billy. Are you back here to work?" she asked absently, with no secret that she planned on the answer being 'yes.' Of course there were no comments like, 'Billy it's great you're out' . . . or 'welcome home.'

"No, Candy, I'm here to see Dad. Would you please tell him I'm here," I said with a raised voice, but she stayed put almost as if blocking the door and with no seeming intention to do otherwise.

"There are a lot of things that need done in the alley, Billy. We've been waiting for you to come back. We heard you were being released. And what happened to Krissy? The storeroom's a real mess and why are all your things in the back gone?" she queried.

"Whoa, there a minute, Candy. Krissy and I got them, but we didn't take anything that wasn't ours. I'm not here to work if that's what you thought. In fact neither Krissy nor I are coming back to Fort Harrison, period. I just want to talk to Dad, that's all," I said as she looked at me, disbelieving.

"But, Billy . . ." she began as I made an impulsive decision and pushed past her into the living room where I immediately saw Dad passed out on the couch across the room. The TV was on and probably had been all night. Budweiser cans were strewn across the floor, giving even the bowling trophies a serious run for the money. A half empty two-liter bottle of Popov was precariously perched upon the edge of a cheap war-scarred coffee table that had been pushed to within inches of the vile golden velour couch. Without Billy Bowling holding things together, it appeared the *Absolut* days had bit the dust. A putrid smell of some sort invaded my senses from the direction of the kitchen—an odor that was probably the composite product of a myriad of both known and unknown disgusting ingredients—and the sum effect was to almost make my cell at the Shelby County jail seem suddenly less depressing.

"Billy, I didn't ask you to come in. This is *my* house now, you know. You should leave and if . . ." Candy was saying as I ignored her and approached my father where I now noticed his snoring and could smell his vodka breath from ten feet away.

"Candy, just shut the hell up, will you? This doesn't involve you anyhow. You might be Dad's wife, but you're not my mother, so why don't you just go and leave us alone," I said as I reached down to shake Dad awake.

She stood motionless at the end of the couch and once again I remembered how much she resembled a giant Toucan. But screw her I thought, and I began to shake Dad harder. The clock on the wall showed it was 11:17 am and it was time he was up. His eyes finally opened, settling for a moment upon me and I was pretty certain he figured I was a dream, and maybe even a bad one.

"Dad will you get up? We need to talk," I said with force.

For a long time he just stared at me, then slowly sat up on the couch and stared at me some more. There was no emotion at all, just staring in marginal disbelief, like I might have done had Dick Hamilton decided to actually teach ten minutes in a history class once. Then when he finally spoke, it spilled out, and was pretty much the script as expected . . . .

. . . "It's about time you got back. I heard you got out of jail a couple of weeks ago. Well that's good. I knew you never done that, but where you been? Why'd you move your stuff out? And where's Krissy been? We've had a hell of a time keeping the place going. Anyway, winter leagues start up in less than a week and . . ."

"Dad, I'm not here to work. I'm not staying," I said bluntly.

"What do you mean? Of course you are and I . . ."

"Krissy and I are moving to Florida. I have a job down there," I said, waiting.

"What are you talking about? *Krissy and you?* That's impossible. Billy, someday the alley will be yours . . . yours and Candy's, of course. We just need to get it up and running smooth again and then I can probably give you a raise this winter and . . ."

*"Dad, you don't get it. I'm leaving, like in ten minutes . . . for good.* But you don't care do you? You only cared about what Jimmy could do for you . . . or what I can . . . or even what Krissy could—right? You never loved any of us, did you Dad? Not even Mom, did you? Not the way you should have," I said with a burst of anger I had promised myself not to host.

Thin Jim Bowling arose from the couch and now took a couple of steps toward me, though seemingly with no particular purpose. I noticed that Busty had evaporated, then again acting on impulse, I took two steps toward Dad and enveloped him in a hug. It was eerie how I now towered over him and probably outweighed him by forty pounds and he seemed so frail in my arms. At first he had felt human enough—flesh and bone—but almost immediately had seemed to turn to stone. His arms never left their duty station, hanging limply beside his thighs. I could feel his grizzled beard and again was nearly overcome by the fumes of the vodka he had likely nursed far into the night.

"Dad, I love you—at least I want to. Didn't you ever love Jimmy and me? Didn't you ever love Mom? Isn't that what life's supposed to be about—to love people and to put family above everything else. Don't you feel those things at all?" I puffed through tears I never expected, gripping him even tighter before truly understanding I was merely embracing a life size wooden soldier.

Finally I disconnected, taking a step or two backwards and looking to Dad who now resembled a likeness of himself, though as if posed somewhere in a wax museum. I waited for a long time and he said nothing—absolutely nothing—much less respond to my questions, to my emotions. Had he even said 'Billy I need you' for any reason other than to run the alley I'm not certain what I would have done at that point, but he said absolutely nothing, even as I waited well over a minute.

Fumbling in my pocket, perhaps out of nervousness, I fondled the Explorer keys for a few seconds before I understood the message I was being sent and abruptly turned. The fresh air outside was as welcome as the day Cliffton Tremont had taken Krissy and me for pizza upon my release from jail, and the nippy early October breeze quickly dried the last of my lingering tears. Walking across the parking lot I paused to look at the old oblong red brick building that was *Bowling's Bowling Center,* in which I had spent most of my entire life. Inside that building I had *learned* to work, to short order cook and tend bar, and of course to bowl. It was where my character had been molded and where I'd honed my cynical philosophy of life and society, if equally shared with the Fort Harrison Village School System. It was there that I was stunned by the massive explosion that killed my mother and little sister, and from where I had stumbled into that thick ugly night in a trance. It was there I had last seen Jimmy and where I had truly discovered the angry and sad person that my brother was, despite his high profile and historical athletic achievements. But it was also within those four walls that I had fallen in love and experienced tempestuous passion. And inside that building I had been arrested for the rape and murder of an angel. But it was time to move on, for perhaps in an obtuse sense, the BBC had prepared me for something much better yet to come. At least it was all I could hope for at the time.

. . . Heading South on 66, I could see the spire of St. Matthias clearly in my rear view mirror for many miles, yet I possessed absolutely no nostalgic pull to ever visit the village of Fort Harrison, Ohio, again. I would also never see my father again, I was certain, but there was nothing further that I could do—and for as sad, and in a sense, alone as I felt—I was strengthened by knowing I had given it every effort I could to put things right *and that it was now time to leave that life behind and began a new one.*

# Chapter Fifty-five

Sam Giovanazzo lived a mile West of Fort Harrison on Rockport Road in a sprawling brick ranch that had been built in 1962 for the John Crouse family. At that time, Crouse had been the primary new homebuilder in the Fort Harrison area. Sam had purchased the property for $59,000 in the summer of 1977 after Fort Harrison won its second state football championship and he had made up his mind to stay and make state championships his life's goal . . . *supplemented, however, by his thirst for young, underage, high school co-eds.*

On Friday, October 15, 1971, the day of a big football game, Sam Giovanazzo had been caught fucking Mandy Butler (a 16 year old FHHS JV cheerleader) by his wife, Bobbie, in their second floor apartment in a big Victorian owned by Joe Amweg on Lawn Avenue. The house was only two blocks from both the high school and the bank where Bobbie worked, and she had darted home that day at 10 am (Sam's free period) to retrieve her reading glasses that she had forgotten to place in her purse that morning.

It was one week later that Bobbie Giovanazzo evaporated. An anonymous tip, apparently claiming foul play, had been sent to a young Chief Borger and sparked an investigation that had even involved the FBI sending an unsolicited agent to Fort Harrison. He left within a few days, however, apparently satisfied that Bobbie had left of her own free-will and reportedly had resurfaced in California in the company of Reldon Fox. Curious why the FBI had involved itself in this seemingly simple domestic conflict, Wade Borger had been provided at the time with Sam's connection to the Youngstown mob, something he had personally never shared with another person in town—*ever*—including his wife, Felicia.

At that time Sam Giovanazzo resolved that he would never again marry, for that would enable him to satisfy his lust for teenage girls as he wanted—when he wanted. The property at 7186 Rockport Road included four wooded acres and the house sat at the end of a secluded winding drive, all likely a part of Sam's master plan when he had decided to purchase it. Yet nice as it seemed to be, no one had *ever* been invited to Sam Giovanazzo's house—well, no one that is—*except teenage, usually minor girls,* whose clandestine movements would have stumped a Cold War spy.

That first Christmas in 1977, Phil Parsons, the FHHS vocal music teacher, had brought a group of carolers to sing outside Sam's house on a Wednesday night just before holiday break. Sam was furious and refused to open the door, fuming with almost murderous anger. The following day at school he stopped but a hair short of threatening Parson's life for having violated his space, which Parsons certainly never revealed to anyone—and least of all, to the notoriously chicken-shit principal at the time—Howard Bachman. Even Sam's assistant coaches, such as the trusted Dick Hamilton who joined his staff in 1983, had never been to his house. It was just not done and after awhile, like everything else odd and private about Sam Giovanazzo, had been diluted without questioning by the influx of additional state championships.

As the championships multiplied, the legend grew—and as the legend grew—Sam's immunity reached a status of inordinate magnitude. From almost the beginning, rumors had tip toed about the community of Fort Harrison concerning his impropriety around young girls. Eventually there were unnamed parents who pushed behind closed doors for answers, but since no girl had ever come forward to file formal charges, even the challenges seemed to fade with time—and particularly as the football championships mounted . . . one ('72) . . . two ('75) . . . three ('76) . . . four ('82) . . . five ('83) . . . six ('90) . . . seven ('91) . . . eight ('95). And then they started with wrestling . . . one ('87) . . . two (88) . . . three ('90) . . . four ('94). *Twelve total Ohio State Championships in 26 years and 22 of 26 Western Ohio Athletic Conference football titles.* Nobody messed with Sam Giovanazzo—and nobody was more certain that it would *always* be that way than Sam Giovanazzo himself.

Despite the size of Sam's home, it was sparsely furnished. An exception, however, was the kitchen and adjoining dining room, both of which had been set up for entertaining, and odd as that at first might seem, was something that would one day make perfect sense. Sam was a skilled Chef, having been taught the finer points of Italian cooking while living with his grandmother, Nana Ariello Cardone, in the mansion in Youngstown Heights. The Cardone's employed a large service staff, but Nana Cardone often took young Sam to the huge basement kitchen so he could learn the art of preparing Italian food and understand the appropriate role for the finer Italian aperitifs and dinner wines. Years later his apprenticeship would prove to serve him well, for perhaps more than anything else, it was the presentation of an exquisite Italian dinner with wine and candles that sealed and somehow successfully silenced the procession of young girls who had graced his home on Rockport Road over the decades.

Of the three bedrooms on the main floor, the one just off the dining room was beautifully furnished with expensive Henredon furniture, featuring a massive King bed with canopy. Of the other two, one was locked and never opened except for tossing in junk, and the largest, actually the master, was a complex and very complete workout room with a wide range of exercise equipment and free weights and the bath for showering after workouts. For even well into his fifties, Sam did keep himself in nearly perfect shape, anyone could note that.

The large living room had a modest TV and an old couch, but mostly plenty of just plain space and appeared to have hardly been used. It was simply not an important room for Sam and a very minor part of his life, for it was in the basement that his life was primarily lived when at 7186 Rockport Road. But how does someone explain the sickening and disgusting content of Sam Giovanazzo's basement—for that involves describing the basest debauchery to which a human could stoop. For you see, Sam Giovanazzo's basement was not only a sex dungeon and pornographic theatre, but also a sick shrine to document and commemorate every one of Sam Giovanazzo's sexual conquests over the years—starting the very first spring he was in town in 1971 with Jenni Strasbaugh, whom he had enticed into sex two months before even Lea Butler. In all, Sam Giovanzzo had violated 22 young Fort Harrison girls—the last being

Stacey Burson, a sophomore cheerleader at Fort Harrison whom he was having sex with even as I sat in my cell at the Shelby County lockup—arrested for a rape and murder that he had committed.

I was never there to witness all of what I have described to you, but the week after Sam Giovanazzo had been arrested, FBI agent in charge, Mike Tarver, called me to meet with him at Sheriff Oberly's office, saying that there was *debriefing* I should go through before Krissy and I could leave the area. . . .

. . ."Billy, you've been through a lot and when these things happen we can only say we're sorry it unfolded the way it did and wish you the best. We will provide you with therapy should you choose to utilize it, and at our expense. But you do understand that the circumstantial evidence was most incriminating and had it been only a few short years ago that could have very possibly brought a conviction. DNA is very new at this stage and still not frequently used. So without that national database and the information your attorney, Mr. Tremont, uncovered, it is likely Sam Giovanazzo would have escaped detection. I know that you have no plans to stay in the area for the trial, which won't be until next spring at the earliest, but I was wondering if you would like to see the incriminating evidence we found at Mr. Giovanazzo's home? Everybody's different, but for some people in your position, viewing our photographs might actually help you arrive at some kind of closure," he'd said straightforward and kindly.

"I would, I think, sir. Are they upsetting?" I asked.

"It all depends on what you want to view. The jury will view the photos of Gwen Putnam as she was found, but I wouldn't suggest that for you. I was thinking more of the photos taken at Giovanazzo's home—photos you will undoubtedly hear about during the trial—even after you have moved to Florida where I understand from Sheriff Oberly you are planning to go," he answered. "Oh, and one more thing, Billy. This is evidence that is not to be talked about publicly at this time, thus a confidence Sheriff Oberly and I are sharing with you. You do understand that, don't you, and will respect our responsibilities, correct?" he said quite seriously.

"I understand, agent Tarver. I do not want to see Gwen, but yes, I will take a look at the Giovanazzo pictures. I've heard something of them from Mr. Tremont, so I am curious."

Sam Oberly was sitting behind his desk and before I took the envelope containing the photos from Mike Tarver I looked at him and he gave me a brief nod, which I took to mean he thought I would be Ok with them. I withdrew them from the envelope as Tarver sat down and opened a bottle of Perrier.

I'm not sure how to even describe Sam Giovanazzo's sordid basement and have debated about even including this chapter, but finally decided it has value for truly understanding the twisted character of a man who irreversibly damaged the lives of so many young people in a small rural community.

The walls and ceilings were all painted with bright blues and golds—Fort Harrison High School's colors—and the entire floor of the largest room was a duplicate blue wrestling mat just like at the school, complete with a large gold Rams head in a circle right in the middle of the mat. Suspended from the ceiling in several places were leather and nylon contraptions of some sort which agent Tarver said were 'sex swings' that I guess were used for weird sex. There were several other despicable devices that I simply must refuse to describe.

In another area of the large L-shaped room a plush gold hide-a-bed was centrally placed. In one picture it was closed and in another open, complete with a blue coverlet with a gold Ram's head in the middle. At the far end of the room was a full wall screen; while in another picture you could see a projector mounted to the ceiling, which created a professionally designed home theatre. Another photo showed the open doors of a full wall built in cupboard in which you could clearly see hundreds of commercial pornographic films on one side, while the other housed a large grouping of obviously homemade marked tapes, some of which had been blotted out in the photo, for as I later found, they were of Sam's Fort Harrison conquests and included the names of students that you could sometimes decipher had they not been distorted.

In another photo, a series of multiple height tripods and two video recording machines had been placed on a table and shot for identification. As I started to pull that photo aside to view the next,

Mike Tarver spoke up. "Billy, I need to say a few words about the next few photos. They are photos of girls, some of whom you would undoubtedly know and that we assume had a relationship of some nature with Sam Giovanazzo. The faces have been covered, but you can get the impact of *the room*," he said, and I was curious by what he'd meant when he said '*the room*' in a disgusting sort of way. I was soon to understand.

The first picture I then looked at was of another smaller basement room off to one side. It was of a bright gold door flooded with light and the next picture showed the floodlights mounted on the ceiling and fixed directly upon the door. A large number of randomly spaced blue stars were affixed to the door, maybe two inches in diameter. I later found that they represented the Fort Harrison girls Sam had screwed over the years, but it was the inside of that room that nearly made me gag.

Inside the room were two trophy cases—exact miniature replicas of the trophy cases on each side of the high school wrestling pit. Inside the cases were small-scale replica state championship trophies, each one with a girl's picture affixed to the center, though as Tarver had pointed out, they had been blocked out in the photos. It's so incredibly weird because the floor was again a blue wrestling mat with a gold Ram in a circle, though this time on a scale to fit the smaller room. To top off the sick enclave was a series of miniature banners hanging from the ceiling just like in the pit, each one apparently with the name of a girl, although those few names that would have been visible in the photo had been blocked out too. I took a deep breath . . .

"Jesus, you've got to be kidding me. *These are pictures of Sam Giovanazzo's basement?"* I queried, knowing the answer, though somehow struggling to believe it.

This time it was Sheriff Oberly who answered. "Pretty sick, huh Billy? You *do* know where your buddy is right now?" he had said with an odd smile on his face.

At the time my mind was pretty exhausted and I didn't get his drift. At another time I might have found some bizarre humor, though I doubt it, so I turned to him, "You arrested him last week before the Parkway game. I heard that."

"Sure did, Billy—and he's right around the corner *in your old cell*. What do you think of that? Don't suppose you want to stop in and say hello, do you?" he said with a half laugh.

It seemed an odd thing for Sheriff Oberly to say to me, but I guess he meant well in some strange way. Agent Tarver stood and tossed his empty Perrier into a trashcan beside the Sheriff's desk, taking the envelope that I now handed across to him. I glanced briefly around the room for no particular reason, finding it a depressing place with pictures of wanted criminals on a large bulletin board behind the desk, some having now turned a putrid yellow/brown and with curling edges. I dropped my gaze to the dirty floor where I noticed a number of small tri-angular pieces missing from the corners of the neglected foot square floor tiles, as if a purposely-disgusting jigsaw puzzle awaiting completion.

"Thanks, Sheriff, and you too, Mr. Tarver. Will there be anything else?" I asked, standing, since they apparently had nothing further to say.

"Thank *you,* Billy, and again let me say it was most unfortunate this happened to you, but maybe somehow it will make you stronger. I have found that it often does," Mike Tarver said sincerely it seemed, reaching out to shake my hand, then opening the door and leaving before me.

"Billy," the Sheriff said, waiting.

"Yes, Sheriff?"

"You're a good kid . . . a goddamn good kid. Somehow I just started seeing that and it's when I knew you hadn't committed that murder," he said, looking up at me slowly. "You got some good people behind you, like your uncles and that kick-ass girl of yours, and I'm sure you realize that. She's quite the firecracker, that Krissy, but she never once doubted you. She was probably the person who convinced me about you the most. We talked to her quite a bit—maybe more than she'll ever tell you. You're a lucky guy," he said, reaching out to shake my hand.

"I am, Sheriff, and I know it, but I can't say it's been all that much fun finding out for sure," I said as I engaged his grasp.

"Can I say one more thing, Billy . . . and I hope it's not out of place cause I sure don't mean for it to be," he said, looking intently into my eyes.

"I think I can handle anything these days, Sheriff, so shoot—just not your gun please," I said, trying to be mildly funny, though I hadn't much humor at hand after having just witnessed the sick and disgusting world of Sam Giovanazzo that had thrived unchallenged in Fort Harrison, Ohio, for decades.

"My father was a bad drunk, Billy. My mother left because of it, but not soon enough the way I saw it. I spent too many years of my life trying to help him and making excuses for him. In fact I'd like a lot of those years back cause he didn't deserve the effort. We had to investigate you a lot Billy, so there's not much I don't know, you understand, and that's why I told you what I just did. I hear you're thinking of going to Florida with that cutie of yours and are probably torn about your Dad, and that's your business I know. I just wanted to tell you how I look at things now. Hope it wasn't taken the wrong way," he said as I withdrew my hand and stepped back before pausing at the door.

"Thank you Sheriff. I appreciate it and am fine with what you said. My father had a lifetime of chances to be an adult and never was, the way I've seen it for a long time. I saw him the second day I was in here and then he never came back. After I was released I tried to see if there was a chance for a relationship and found there wasn't, so I'm not torn Sheriff . . . I'm not torn at all. I only hope some day I have a son and that I have a chance to do things differently. That's what I most want out of life. I want the family I never had," I said with a soft smile, closing the door behind me and walking the five blocks down Black Street, East of the Shelby County jail . . . and back to Lacy Johnson's modest pink house in Sidney, Ohio.

# Chapter Fifty-six

*I* never wanted to write about Gwen Putnam's rape and murder, and truthfully possess few of the ugly details because I have never wanted to know them. Marco and Krissy, however, both felt I needed to include at least minimal details since it is a central reason for the book. In Fort Harrison there are a thousand bizarre stories that have circulated since Sam Giovanazzo's arrest—most in which I am still somehow considered a guilty party—and almost all of which have no distant clue of the basic facts or the tragic seeds of evil Sam Giovanazzo had sewn into the innocent spirits of Fort Harrison youth for decades.

. . . Almost to the minute, as I can remember—and told the cops a hundred times—it was 1:20 pm that Saturday when Gwen jogged to her back door and disappeared into the Putnam farm house to change for her workout. I had sat daydreaming in the drive, but for certain had headed down the lane by 1:25, turning right onto Boeke Road and driving very slowly. I had paused briefly in front of the old Porter Farm, where Darrell Byers and his family had lived, reminiscing about our carefree days in the tumble down old barn, and one thing I remember distinctly noting was how it was now nearly obscured from the road by a thick stand of young maples. At around 1:35 I turned off Boeke Road, north on Fletcher Road, which was the opposite direction I would have taken to return to the alley. I drove around some country roads just enjoying the spring and driving past the beautiful farms in the area before returning to Fletcher and pulling over to sit at the culvert that forded a drainage ditch directly as it passed into Indian Creek. It was likely just before 2 at that point and I messed around there for probably forty five to fifty minutes before driving on down Fletcher toward 66, but stopping first to talk to that asshole, Clint Obringer, a little before

3. After six minutes tops, Clint and I argued, and I took off for the bowling alley right at 3, plus or minus maybe two minutes, arriving there five minutes later via a short half mile jog south on Cole Road which nearly dead ended on 66 right at the alley—the entire distance to the alley from the Obringer farm being maybe four miles.

The total time elapsed between Gwen's jog to her back door until I returned to the alley was right at 95 to 100 minutes—and my unaccounted-for time between Gwen and Clint would have been about 85—which the cops had reasoned was plenty of time to commit a rape and murder at the Porter barn. They had at first questioned whether or not we had even returned to the Putnam farm, but since Gwen was found in her running togs, and her jeans and sweatshirt were found in her room, they had been forced to buy that much of my story.

That Billy Bowling's implication was a part of an ingenious master plan engineered by Sam Giovanazzo is completely false. In fact, as opposed to Sam's meticulous care in seducing minors, he had actually been quite sloppy with his attack on Gwen, and the timing of it all on the day of the murder an incredible accident. Sam Giovanazzo had no idea Gwen Putnam and myself were connected at all and had no knowledge of the three days we had just spent together—or of having been at the track meet in Minster only hours earlier. In fact it was really only by accident that he'd even known Gwen was home that spring weekend. . . .

*. . . Friday, April 19, 1996 - 9:20 am . . .*

*Gwen Putnam had darted into Fort Harrison Savings and Loan for a quick withdrawal before coming to meet me at Samsal's ten minutes later. She was standing at the teller window talking with Tilly Fisher, her best friend Kris's mother, when Sam Giovanazzo walked up behind her in line, not knowing for the moment even who she was.*

*"Coach Giovanazzo, so nice to see you," Gwen said upon turning and casting a bright sincere smile. "My congratulations on another championship last fall. That's is so awesome.."*

*Sam Giovanazzo was never social around Fort Harrison and seldom went up town except when absolutely necessary, such as that day at the bank. The irony was that he was so concerned about his legacy and yet had virtually no use for any of the people in town. He was simply an egomaniacal person with no regard for others, which in many ways made no sense . . . or that he should care at all how they viewed him. And now he was tongue-tied before his considered nemesis.*

*"Are you on a break, Miss Putnam?" Sam finally returned, awkwardly.*

*"Yes, home for a few days to work on a project. I'll be going back Tuesday. I still have a lot of training to do, but I love to run my Shelby County roads when I'm home," Gwen had responded innocently.*

*"Of course," Sam replied, his wheels turning.*

*"Well, I have an appointment, Mr. Giovanazzo. Very nice talking to you," Gwen said with a smile and pushed through the door into the spring sun where she turned right and headed for Samsal's to meet me on the second day of our interviews.*

Even with Sam's state championship that past year, it was now old news and all the headlines were about Gwen Putnam and the Olympics. *So she was home and would be running the roads where he had seen her before.* Gwen Putnam would *never* go away, and the plan he'd screwed up once before he determined at that moment to revive, and this time execute without error. As he stepped to the window and presented his bank book to a smiling Tilly Fisher, he had decided exactly what he would do this time before Gwen Putnam ever had a chance to return to Notre Dame—and certainly before she would ever have the chance to run in the Atlanta Olympics. The days of worshipping Gwen Putnam would soon to be over—*and Sam Giovanazzo would once again be the unrivaled King.*

. . . Sam started circling the country roads around the Putnam farm that Saturday morning, arrogant as always and with little concern that his car would be seen. In his sick mind—and especially given another championship that year—he was totally immune to anything and everything, he was certain, and that had been proven time and again as he deflowered the youth of Fort Harrison without consequence. That both the Putnam and Miller farms were deserted that day was also an accident, yet one that again played into Sam's hands because essentially the only traffic on Boeke Road was that traveling to and from the two farms.

At about a quarter til 2 that afternoon, Sam started across Boeke Road from the East, having turned off 66. While slowly passing the Putnam lane he noticed Gwen near the house on the wide-open lawn doing her pre-workout stretches that he well understood were the prelude to her workout. Sam probably knew the approximate route and that Gwen would take, heading west on quiet roads rather than towards 66, so he proceeded on down Boeke.

As with almost every case without a direct witness, no one can absolutely know the facts at this point, but it is assumed that he likely hid his car behind the 'Byers' barn and somehow distracted Gwen from her run—or simply showed up on the road where she would have stopped with innocence and then was forced to the barn. Sam Giovanazzo was 49 at the time, but physically imposing. As independent and athletic as Gwen was, she was still no match for a demented Sam Giovanazzo, once he had managed to get his hands on her.

The FBI assumed the rape, murder, and clumsily attempted cover-up probably all took place within less than twenty-five minutes, Gwen having been thrown beneath a mound of ancient moldy hay and further camouflaged by a rusty archaic combine which loomed in the foreground. The true method and manner of the rape/murder is abominable as imagined by the forensic people. Gwen was strangled with rusty baling wire which was laying everywhere about the old barn and it is suspected that she was raped *as* she was being strangled.

It almost certainly took place at exactly the same time I was loitering about Indian Creek—sitting on the culvert less than one mile distant. Tests for lactic acid had been conducted to determine whether Gwen was finishing or beginning her 20 miler and it had been concluded that she had just started her exercise, hence the pinpointed time frame. When Sam Giovanazzo left, he either went directly back Boeke Road to 66, which was more than likely, or west on Boeke then north on Fletcher, just a hundred yards away and over a small ridge from where I sat. I had never heard a vehicle and had wracked my mind relentlessly trying to be certain of that. Had Sam Giovanazzo turned south on Fletcher toward 66, he would have passed both myself on the culvert and Clint in the fields—or perhaps the two of as we talked beside Clint's tractor.

It had all been far too disgustingly simple for the twisted Sam Giovanazzo, and incredibly incriminating for nature-lover, Billy Bowling. Just as Mike Tarver and Sheriff Oberly had said—a few years earlier the case would have been open and closed and Billy Bowling would almost certainly be sitting on Ohio's death row. In fact, without Cliffton Tremont, it is very likely I would have found my way there anyhow.

. . . The stadium clock at Robbins Field had wound down to under eight minutes to kickoff when the procession of five police vehicles, including two Shelby County Sheriff Department cruisers, two Ohio State Highway patrol cars and one unmarked FBI sedan pulled alongside the Robbins Field home bleachers, blocking the road outside the main gate. Sheriff Sam Oberly, Deputy Marty Piquad, four State Troopers and FBI Agent Mike Tarver breezed past the ticket window where Constance Badderly sat gaping open mouthed. Under the concrete stadium they were not seen until they emerged from beneath a smaller grouping of bleachers reserved for the Ram marching band. There, single file, they passed through the band gate on the thirty yard line which led to the home side lines, not twenty feet from where Sam Giovanazzo stood, oblivious to them at first because of headphones and a conversation he was having with Charlie Herold, one of the assistant coaches in the press box.

To this day the Sheriff has fielded a lot of criticism for how the arrest was made because of the kids, the Parkway and Fort Harrison fans, the two teams and all that. Yet to me it was the most appropriate and proper act on the face of the planet that day, perhaps that week—or even the whole damn year.

Generations of kids at Fort Harrison High School knew *exactly* what Sam Giovanazzo was about, but since 'our' parents and school officials turned a blind eye, 'we' were at first anesthetized, followed by unwittingly allowing the abomination that was Sam Giovanazzo to—in some small way—become a part of 'our' own moral constitution. In their own way (and to their credit), the cops had finally come to that same conclusion and believed that there was a statement to be made—and what better forum than a home Ram football game! Shielding the youth of Fort Harrison from the realities of not only the law, but also basic right and wrong, had been practiced far too long and the public arrest of Sam Giovanazzo minutes before the Parkway football game was definitely appropriate.

While Marty Piquad cuffed Giovanazzo right in front of the home bleachers, Sheriff Oberly read Miranda rights before they even marched him away. Both Sheriff Oberly and Mike Tarver described it to me and, except for the fact that Billy Bowling didn't dare step out in public, I would have given the world to have witnessed it. Of course, had I been there I would have more than likely been lynched and hung from a goal post by the deaf, dumb and blind *because* of what had just happened to their *poor* coach.

Giovanazzo was then whisked away as 2000 people, coaches, players and students stared in disbelief. From what I later heard, the game was held up a half hour before Dick Hamilton took charge and the opening kickoff executed. The Fort Harrison Rams did win that night, 17-14, pushing their record to 5-0. As the players and fans left the stadium in muted celebration, Sam Giovanazzo was settling into my old cell in the Shelby County jail in Sidney, Ohio.

The Rams would finish the season that year 9-1, loosing only to Marion Local who went on to win the state championship for 1996. In the state playoffs, FHHS lost the second game to Covington High School, 31-6, ending the year with a 10-2 record. The entire town of Fort Harrison was not only in shock, but essentially in ruins. Their world had crumbled like perhaps no other village of similar size in the history of the country, short of being wiped off the map by a tornado or flood, which the more rabid citizens would have much preferred. But then again Fort Harrison prided itself for gleaning headlines, didn't it? And the world headlines throughout the year 1996 would make the legitimate headlines of Gwen Putnam's quest for an Olympic gold *and* Sam Giovanazzo's State Championships pale by comparison.

*Gwen Putnam need not have died though. It is truly that simple and enraging!* Every sign pointed toward Sam Giovanazzo's despicable and criminal behavior from year one in Fort Harrison. To say it was not known is total horseshit—people knew—and especially the school board members and school administrators because there had been plenty of parents over the years who had pushed to bring his depravity to light—only to be ignored because, all in all, they held virtually no clout compared to that of Sam Giovanazzo and his string of state record State Championships.

There *were* girls, especially after they had gotten older, who had considered pressing charges, but they were always scared off—and sadly often even by a family member who knew the scorn they would face and the nearly impossible battle they would have on their hands. We can also now assume that the (sometimes whispered) mob connection may have served to scare off at least some of the potential lawsuits, too. But, regardless of the reasons, no one had seriously challenged Sam Giovanazzo, no matter what they knew—and that group included Brent Sturdivant and myself, I say with great guilt. Nope . . . Sam Giovanazzo was the King of Fort Harrison, Ohio . . . just as he'd always planned—even as he should have been in prison many years before he could have ever gotten his hands on the wonderful light that was once Gwen Putnam.

As Krissy and I prepared to leave for a new life and an adventure we were now finally looking forward to, I was certain that when the true facts emerged in court, the village would finally learn a sad lesson that had been long overdue, and never again would another Sam Giovanazzo be allowed to not only survive, but thrive—in Fort Harrison, Ohio—or anywhere else. *But, sadly, Krissy and I would one day come to find out just how wrong we were to imagine that!*

# Chapter Fifty-seven

*N*early six weeks passed after my release before Krissy and I finally headed south. The Sheriff and FBI Agent Tarver had requested several additional meetings and we'd spent a couple of weeks following that to really decide if Florida was the right thing to do, neither of us ever having even been there before. But perhaps more than that, Krissy and I wanted to be *certain* that *together* was the direction we truly wanted to travel, since only one day after finally expressing our love, I had been taken away to jail. Did we really know each other well enough to embark upon this adventure together? We didn't want to make the same mistakes our parents had made years earlier.

We took day trips, hoping we wouldn't be found or noticed. One day we rented a powerboat on Indian Lake and spent the day tubing—illegally—since we had no lookout as required by law. Another time we drove to Indianapolis for two days, staying downtown at the Hyatt Regency and enjoying two memorable evenings, including an exquisite dinner at *St. Elmo Steakhouse.* Krissy was a saver and between us we had tucked away considerable savings for a couple of kids, I guess you could say, and we still hadn't decided what do with Uncle Dante's money—which we had spent very little of up to that point. We were originally going to go to Cincinnati, but thought we needed a neutral field and Indianapolis had seemed reasonable, for as much as we loved being with Marco, we'd decided we needed to be completely alone . . . and we fell *deeply* in love . . . and more certain than ever that we wanted to challenge the future together.

I learned early on that the press, prospective authors, movie types, and the slime that lives off of the sensationalism and the misfortune of others were going to hound me. We had found that holing ourselves up with Lacy threw most of the idiots off track and gave us time to think. Even in Indianapolis it soon became obvious it would be a long time before I could ever hope to regain much sovereignty, for on several occasions people studied me closely as if trying to decide who I was.

The time with Lacy had been good for Krissy, but overall Lacy would always be Lacy (we then thought), and though she and Kris had mended some fences, we were soon more than ready to move on. We'd decided not to rent a truck to take our stuff along until we decided whether Florida was really going to work for us—which turned out to be a wise decision, as we would soon forget about *anything* that Billy Bowling and Krissy Kurtz owned and had in a storage unit in Minster, Ohio!

So early on Saturday, October 19, 1996, we loaded up our '91 Explorer Sport (101,334 miles) with pretty much next to nothing and started south, preparing to stop first for several days with Uncle Marco, who was himself about to head in the opposite direction—north—where he had just bought an abandoned youth camp in Michigan's Upper Peninsula. For years as a child he had been invited by a friend to attend that very same Ford Motor Company Camp, and when he'd found it was for sale, he had, 'on a whim,' purchased the entire camp for 'peanuts,' according to Marco . . . even though he had no idea what he was really gonna do with the extensive grounds and buildings. Marco said his dream had always been to live in the land of blue lakes and pines—and that he'd *always* wanted to write mystery novels. So he was off to pursue his unique dreams, and apparently with the impending sale of *Romano's,* would soon be quite well set to do whatever he wanted.

Following Grandpa Romano's death three years earlier, Grammy had become ill soon thereafter, so Marco had forfeited the lease on his own apartment and moved to the 19th floor suite overlooking Fountain Square to take care of her. He had lived there now for nearly two years and was in the process of packing when Krissy and I stopped for our visit.

Krissy had been through Cincinnati on the interstate, but never downtown and as we circled the fountains and entered the parking garage she was gaping at the skyscrapers just as I had done as a child.

"Billy, I've never seen buildings this tall," she gasped.

"I know, Krissy; when I was a kid I loved this place, and still do."

"You mean Marco lives in one of these tall buildings?"

"Yep, Krissy," I replied as we wound our way up to the twelfth floor of the garage.

Marco met us at the door. It was a beautiful bright morning and the sun swept in through the window overlooking the Square so far below—draping a bright plaid veil across the sofa and around the room. In the background, *Pachelbel's Canon* played softly through speakers that seemed to come from everywhere. I didn't know that much about classical music, but Mom had taught me a little and that was always her favorite piece.

I had talked to Marco a couple of times on the phone, but hadn't seen him since my release and he practically lifted me off the floor with a bear hug before giving Krissy a gentle hug and kiss on the cheek. To this day Krissy is taken with Marco and I am still convinced that in her mind Marco and Michael Douglas are one in the same.

Spending three exciting days and nights in Cincinnati, we dined at Romano's twice, which was exquisite as always, and did a bit of fun shopping together, dipping into a bit of the money that Uncle Dante had sent. Krissy was in heaven and an eye magnet to have upon my arm as always, but more than anything was just such a joy to be with and to share in her child-like innocence.

Marco had sold the restaurant to second cousins, several of which were coming directly from Italy, and he was very pleased because he had confidence it would continue to maintain high standards along with bearing the name of his Grandfather, Julian. Julian had opened it in 1944 in the midst of WWII when most other restaurants were closing down, thus carving out a niche not only for food without rival, but a landmark destination for everything downtown.

It was early Monday afternoon, when after lounging around the wonderful apartment all morning, Marco said he had a place for late lunch that he wanted to share with us—and how could one go wrong with Marco Romano in Cincinnati? Taking the elevator to the street, I saw that Krissy'd be popping eyeballs, but I had been used to that forever and she was actually 'dressed down' from the old days. Still—her jeans were glued on an ass Rodin would have killed to sculpt—her cork pumps couldn't help but give notice—and though she wore a simple white blouse with a short light leather jacket that would have gone unnoticed on most girls (or women), her stunning face and platinum hair commanded 'impossible not to notice' attention.

Our destination: *Arnold's Bar and Grill* was Cincinnati's oldest tavern, actually dating pre-Civil War. Located on 8th Street, a few blocks north of Fountain Square, it had a delightful outdoor courtyard for dining and Marco commanded almost immediate attention by the staff as soon as we entered the bar.

"Marco, this is such a great town. We sure wish you weren't leaving cause we would have loved making a life together here," Krissy bubbled as we settled into our chairs in the quaint outdoor dining area, the mid October weather a bit nippy, though still pleasant.

"Cincinnati's a great town, Krissy, I'll give you that, and it hurts to leave," Marco answered. "It's just that I want a change before I die—and the lakes and pines in Northern Michigan have beckoned to me since childhood. You guys might not even know that Uncle Dante has a home in Harbor Springs, Michigan, do you? Well, it's a bit *more* than a home, but someday you'll just have to see for yourself. It's not far at all from the old youth camp I bought, which is about a hundred miles north and across the splendid Mackinac Bridge."

"No, I didn't know that, Marco, but there's a lot I don't know since I've been trapped in a bowling alley all my life," I answered. I'd been to Detroit once, I remembered (for one of Jimmy's bowling tournaments when I was a little kid), but knew no more about Michigan than I did Florida, though I *had* heard of and seen pictures of the Mackinac Bridge.

"Well kids, there's a lot about Dante maybe we should talk about before you head South in the morning," he said as a young waiter came to take our drink orders. Krissy and I decided on virgin Daiquiris while Marco ordered a pint of Newcastle Brown Ale.

"Marco, you know that Kris and I would have loved working with you at Romanos, but I understand following your dreams.

Uncle Dante seems nice, but you're right, I hardly know him and Krissy has never even met him. Cliffton really seems to like Uncle Dante, though for some reason once he mentioned he had lived a sad life. We just had to get out of Fort Harrison and anywhere would have worked, I guess. I tried to make peace with Dad and that will never happen, Marco . . . *never!* But even if it had, I wouldn't have wanted to stay at the bowling alley."

"I know, Billy. Cliffton's right, your Uncle Dante has had some rough personal setbacks, but there are certain things you should both know before you get there."

"Which we want to know. Are we making a bad decision?" I asked, leaning forward.

Marco took a large quaff of ale and laughed. "Oh no, Billy, you two aren't making a bad decision. Dante is the best man you will ever meet in your life. His problems have all been with the women in his life, most of whom unfortunately were after his money . . . for you see, Dante is one of the wealthiest men in South Florida and you really need to know this or you will be overwhelmed by it all when you get there."

"Go on, Marco," I said, as he had paused, looking from me to Krissy and back.

"Dante started his construction company in 1971 after working several years in the area as a mason for a man named Sal Greavu. It was Sal who put up most of the money when together they founded *Gold Coast Construction.* By the mid 1980's it had become the largest construction company in Florida north of Miami and they were building high-rise ocean front condominiums as quickly as they could ink the permits. At one time there were nearly 5,000 workers directly employed by Gold Coast, let alone the sub-contracts they farmed out. It was incredible. Dante once told me it took him till 1980 to make his first million, but by 1985 he was worth well over 20. Then Greavu wanted to go to Las Vegas where he thought the building boom would be even bigger, but Dante didn't want to be part of that, so he bought out Greavu for God knows how much—I sure as hell never knew," Marco said, shaking his head and then pausing to enjoy a few deliberate swallows of ale.

Krissy and I just sat listening. I didn't know what she was thinking, but slowly I was beginning to digest what Marco was saying and began to wonder just what we *were* going to find in Florida.

"Anyhow, Gold Coast started building in West Palm Beach, then moved to North Palm Beach to Juno Beach, Jupiter, Tequesta and is now building North in Stuart. In 1990 Dante purchased his estate on Jupiter Island for nine million bucks, Billy, and Jupiter Island is *not* a place you get into without major pull or big time celebrity status, no matter how much money you have. So you see kids, Dante is larger than life in Southern Florida, and when you get there I want you to be prepared. Recently he's started talking about selling Gold Coast—and his price tag is *half a billion bucks,*" Marco said.

"So how can he be unhappy? I guess I don't much get that part," I said, questioning.

"Because Dante always wanted a family, and particularly children. He was married four times and even I didn't know one of his wives. His first wife, Camilla, was a sweetheart and the love of his life, but like my Holly, died young with cancer. I guess us Romano boys weren't much lucky that way, were we, Billy?"

I didn't know much about my uncles at all I now realized, although Mom had talked about them when Dad wasn't around and I knew they were all close. I did remember, however, that she once told me they both had wives die young, but I never understood it all and it meant little to me since I was so far removed from it all. Still, I knew much more about Marco than Dante, hardly ever having seen him. I'd heard he had a lot of money once, but I had no idea it was anything like Marco was now telling us.

"Dante's last wife, Christina, left him six months ago and sued him for divorce. He was tied up with all that bullshit when your Grammy died and when you were arrested. He didn't get to see Mom before she died and he won't forgive himself. It's another reason he didn't help you sooner too, Billy. And his two wives before Christina have done their best to suck as much money from him as possible. Dante married Christina on a whim about three years ago. I met her once and she is stunning, I'll say that—a dark haired beauty from Rio de Janeiro that Dante had met in a Miami club where she was a dancer—a weakness of his, unfortunately. That's what Cliffton meant, and it's too bad, because Dante was a good husband and would have even been a better father, but now it doesn't look like that can ever come to pass. So soon he will have three ex-wives to drain his bank account although it certainly won't render him destitute. I just felt you should know this before you get there and I know he would probably prefer I gave you the background than for you to hear the distorted details from those you cross paths with in Florida. I don't mean to say Dante's perfect, or that I am either—not at all—but Dante is a good honorable man and it's too bad his personal life has taken such a beating because, despite the money, no woman could have had a more loyal companion."

Marco then fell quiet, seeming to be waiting for a response from me. There were a few things I was curious about so I figured it was a good time to go ahead and ask.

"Marco, is Dante a lot older than you and Mom? I just wondered because when you and he came to the jail he looked much older than you."

"Well, he's actually thirteen years older than me and I'm three years older than your Mother. Dante's 61 now cause I'm going on 48 and your Mother would have been 45 this birthday. But that's not old, Billy, it just sounds old when you're twenty."

"I know, Marco, but honestly Dante looks old and you look young, even given those years," I said.

"I know, and that's something else that I think you and Krissy need to understand. I don't think Dante is well, though he won't say a thing to me. Just keep your eyes open and please keep me posted. Once I get to Michigan and get a phone I'll get you that number, but in the meantime you've got my mobile. Anyhow, I think you kids will be a great lift for Dante and I know he is *so* looking forward to your arrival," Marco said.

"So, Marco, tell us about Dante's home in Michigan . . . where you're going to go to write," I asked because I had become quite curious with his enthusiasm to move north and I was intrigued by his ambition to be a writer. I had never known anyone who wanted to be a writer or had even thought about it.

"Well, like I said, first I'm going to settle into *Blue Pines*, Dante's home in Harbor Springs. It's a delightful old place on Harbor Point, a peninsula that sticks out into Lake Michigan just outside this small waterfront village. The Armstrong family—the hardwood floor people who actually started their company before the Civil War— once owned it. Herbert Armstrong was a close friend of Dante's in Florida and when he'd found that they were planning to sell their old vacation compound in Michigan, he bought it sight unseen, and especially since he knew I had such an attachment to the area. It's been about four years ago now. I've been there a couple of times and it is a treasure, but Dante's actually only been there once. He wants me to settle in and oversee a lot of work that needs done to restore it to its former majesty. I bought the camp in the U.P. cause I got it for a song. I'm just not all that sure what I want to do with it yet, but I figure it will be fun to work with and I've got enough money now to have it spruced up while I think on it. I'll just have to keep you both posted. Meanwhile, Harbor Springs is a delightful village and I think I can settle in there quite nicely and it will be the perfect place to write."

Chef Charles personally served us up a trio of incredible open faced prime rib sandwiches, smothered in a cranberry horseradish sauce that is impossible to describe, and surrounded by a necklace of honeydew melon wedges. Hanging with Marco might someday catch up with Krissy and me, and I saw that early on . . . but just then we were as far removed from worrying about anything like that as a human could possibly get.

# Chapter Fifty-eight

*I* will probably never write another book, but if I did it would be about the five years Krissy and I spent living in Florida . . . first working for Gold Coast Construction while attending classes at *Florida Culinary Institute* (and later in Italy) . . . and finally caring for Dante before he died. It was a magical life and one that could easily spoil a person, let alone a young couple—but our grounding before our Florida days and my months spent in an Ohio jail cell facing the end of life at nineteen allowed us both to grow amidst incredible wealth in a manor I think few could have done.

*. . . Dante paid nine million dollars in 1990 for 'Blue Palms' on Jupiter Island, just as Marco had told us . . . and in 2001, when Krissy and I sold it, it brought $19,800,000. Dante's yacht 'Inferno' sold for another three and a half million although we had decided to keep his 46' classic fishing boat, 'Matador.' But that was 'peanuts' (though please understand I don't write that boastfully), for a year earlier Dante had sold Gold Coast Construction for $440,000,000 and so after nearly three hundred million in charitable gifts, taxes, attorney fees, commissions and other expenses were settled (including generous payoffs to three ex-wives), Krissy and I inherited the remainder of Uncle Dante's estate, which at the time was nearly $135,000,000. Krissy and I were both 25. Marco had declined any inheritance other than Blue Pines in Harbor Springs, appraised at six million, and Dante's 1959 Frost Blue and White Chevy Corvette.*

. . . Two days after leaving Cincinnati, Krissy and I had been admitted at the gate to Jupiter Island by previous arrangement. It is not a place one just drives about on a whim. Given directions by the gate man, we wound through canopied streets of banyans and palms, and past mansions the likes of which I wouldn't have believed had I seen them in photographs. And of course the largest ones weren't even visible from the road. On South Beach Road we took a left in my old Explorer as people stared at us. *Ten South Beach Road . . . Blue Palms*, was mounted above a massive granite entry to Uncle Dante's estate. Mammoth iron gates stood open and we wound up a long brick drive, pulling to a stop beneath a canopy that could have shielded an entire army division from the elements. Lush palms, massive banyans and unrecognizable fauna and flora sprung everywhere, and fountains tumbled both near and distantly. When we got out, the first view of ocean hit us straight ahead, and soon the sound of the washing surf would eclipse the normal sounds of life as known before.

"Well I see you kids made it," came a hearty shout as Dante Romano approached from the direction of the beach. "Damn how wonderful to see some family down here. Come, come, let me see the two of you. Oh my God, Billy, where did you pick this lovely flower?"

Dante, with white flowing hair and tan as a discarded English saddle, came striding toward us. Barefoot with khaki shorts and a brightly flowered shirt, he was a huge barrel of a man and at first impulse, except for the weight, seemed the picture of perfect, almost radiant health. First he took my hand and shook it vigorously and then turned to us both; "Please, please come. Beulah has some snacks prepared. We must get to know each other for I know we hardly do. And so this is Krissy? I've heard about you from Marco. He was quite taken, you know, and now I see why. You are a very beautiful young lady indeed," Dante said, actually taking a curt bow and then kissing her hand lightly, as Krissy blushed, and I knew once again one of my Uncles had landed her in heaven. That type of stuff could seem kinda fake, and almost did, but a few weeks down the road I would come to learn it was just plain Dante. He lived in a very different world from most, at least while on the Island, but Dante Romano was far from a phony—very far from it—once you just plain got to know him.

Ahead of us a brief sweep of perfectly manicured lawn met a series of small dunes and grasses, spilling then beyond into the almost fluorescent blue ocean, maybe fifty yards distant. On the left side of the property as I faced the ocean, was an in-ground pool bearing little resemblance to any I had ever seen before—all boulders, lush greenery and waterfalls, and I'd only realized it was a swimming pool because of the diving board on one end. Just beyond was a massive house by Fort Harrison, Ohio, standards—which we were to later find was the *pool house—and soon to become our home.* To the right a series of intricate patios were laid out, some with gazebo covers, but the one with the table setting and snacks was open to the sun as the day was quite mild for Southern Florida. It was then I turned to view *The Mansion,* looming behind me.

Built in 1902, the main house of *Blue Palms* included seven bedrooms and nine baths and was just shy of 10,000 square feet. Besides the 3,000 square foot pool house, there were two smaller guesthouses, a six-car garage and a maintenance building the size of a tennis court tucked discreetly away in the lush landscaping. The property was nearly seven total acres and spanned Jupiter Island from the Inland waterway on the west to 500' of ocean frontage on the east.

At his own deep water docks on the inter-coastal side, Dante had *Inferno,* a *115' Christensen* fiberglass mega-yacht capable of easily traversing the planet, and *Matador,* a pristine, yet vintage, wooden *46' Merritt Sportfisherman* that *Ernest Hemingway* had once owned. That was the boat he and Cliffton Tremont plied the Atlantic in. The entire atmosphere was surreal and left Krissy and me almost without breath, which is about as close as I can put you to our real truth that day—and even during the subsequent years that were to follow.

"Kids, what can Beulah get you to drink? I will have my Dewar's as usual, Beulah. You name it kids—Beulah will get it. Come, come—don't be shy."

"Ice tea with lemon," Krissy said, speaking up and I gave that a second.

"You sure now, kids? Got no cops around here going to be checking your ID's. I've got every brand of beer you could possibly want and there's not a drink Beulah can't make. Or we can invade the wine cellar and see what ole' bro Marco sent me in his last shipment, if you'd like," he said, breaking into a roaring laughter.

Beulah was a black scullery maid and she 'came with the house' was how Uncle Dante once put it several weeks later. She lived in a small wing off the main house and did all the cooking and shopping—ordering by telephone for delivery—while she herself very seldom left the property. We would further find that another black couple, Leroy and Hallie Lincoln, lived in one of the small houses on the property. Leroy did most of the general maintenance and part of the gardening and Hallie was the housekeeper. Leroy used to work for Gold Coast and Dante had hired them for the position upon purchasing the property. I never did know or ask what Beulah's last name was and I guess it didn't matter; she was just Beulah, and that was good enough for us. Krissy and I would eventually come to find this was pretty much the norm on Jupiter Island and there were times it didn't seem that far removed from the plantation days of the ole' South.

From that very first day, we were comfortable with Uncle Dante. For two years we worked for Gold Coast Construction, Krissy being trained as an assistant secretary to Dante, while I began by driving a company delivery truck. We could have chosen any position we wanted, but those fit and we both enjoyed them. Dante paid us a wage that was more than fair and he refused to accept rent. At first I believed Dante wanted me to learn more about the business with the idea of playing a larger role down the road, but I wasn't really sure that was for me and he was a straight up guy with no games. One day the first year, and just before Krissy and I were married, he'd snared me at work and took me to lunch at *The Crab House*, a favorite of ours just down Highway 1. Settling into a booth overlooking the waterway and Jupiter Light House, I could tell there was business about him. . . .

. . . "Billy, what is it you'd *really* like to do in life? We've never talked much about it and you know you don't have to work for Gold Coast. We only get this one tiny life to live, so it's important to do what's in your soul. I was hoping to help you and Krissy, but don't ever feel obligated to Gold Coast or me. Do you understand me, son?" he said, looking me directly in the eye.

"I do, Uncle Dante, and you have been wonderful to Krissy and me and we are very happy," I answered.

"But what really hits you, Billy? What would you *really* love to do . . . other than make love to Venus, I mean," he said with his roaring laugh again, if somewhat subdued for the surroundings.

"I don't know why Dante, but since I was a little kid and I'd go with Mom to visit Grampy and Grammy, and we'd eat at Romano's, I've often thought I'd like to be a Chef, like Grampy and Uncle Marco. It's always really interested me, but maybe that's silly. I taught myself bartending at the alley and like that end of it too, except for serving drunks all the time," I said spontaneously— because Dante just put you at ease that way.

"That's fantastic, Billy. Then of course you shall be . . . *of course you shall be!*"

"But Dante, I like what I'm doing, I really do, and I think the construction business is pretty interesting too. I might like to do that, I'm just not certain," I replied, still afraid of hurting his feelings, which had I really known Dante, was ridiculous. For Dante Romano didn't get his feelings hurt—*except perhaps at love.* He just wasn't that sort.

"And what about that cutie of yours? What does she think she would like to do after you two are married? Raise little Billy's?" he asked, followed with laughter.

"Well, we've actually talked about running a restaurant together some day, but we know that's a long shot, of course," I replied.

"Nonsense . . . a long shot? No talk like that around Uncle Dante. Nope, you're on my playing field now and what we decide to do, *we do!* It's that simple, Billy. Ok, now listen to me . . . "

# Chapter Fifty-nine

*K*risten Cheyenne Kurtz and me, *William James Bowling V,* were married at St. Jude Catholic Church in Tequesta, Florida, on Saturday, October 4, 1997. We had both just turned 21 and know that some might question our decision to marry at that age. But *we were ready,* and eleven years later, would tell you we'd have probably gotten married at eighteen right out of high school—if you want to know whether we have had any *reservations.* For nearly eight months we took Catholic education classes as we had both agreed upon, and just the month before had been accepted into the church, although we were well aware the church was not without its own unique problems.

We sent Lacy a plane ticket and she flew down alone, her last relationship having just collapsed. Tammy could not come because she was involved in some mess of a marriage and living somewhere in Georgia, though we knew no more about her than I did about Jimmy—only that he was still in the service, God knew where, as he had contacted no one for years. Marco had flown down a week earlier and the four of us had spent some glorious times together around Jupiter and Palm Beach, even taking *Inferno* to Miami for a couple of days since Dante had a four man crew on call who also worked at Gold Coast. Marco in particular was in heaven driving Dante's Frost Blue and White '59 Corvette and a few days after the wedding even blew off to Key West in it for an entire week.

We were a funny family in a way, I know. Marco was really the only one with strong family ties with his parents over the years, while Dante, Krissy and myself had all been pretty discombobulated, I guess you could say. But it made what we'd evolved into stronger and more meaningful than most people could ever imagine.

Lacy arrived the day before the wedding and Dante immediately insisted she go shopping on him to buy whatever she wanted. As with Marco a few years earlier, Dante was quite taken by her stunning good looks and when she resisted, he whisked her away in his Bentley to West Palm anyway, and God knows when they returned in the wee hours of the morning. So now Krissy wondered about her Mom and *'both of my Uncles,'*—as honestly so did I. But again, we never found out anything, nor pushed very hard.

The wedding was in a tiny alcove of St. Judes, with only Father Pacininni, Lacy, Marco, Dante, Krissy and myself present. It was exactly the wedding we would have wanted and if we could have each had a wish, it would have been for Tammy and Jimmy to have their lives straightened out and have been with us. Yet we understood it just wasn't the way life was moving and we thanked God for the family that we finally *did* have.

Marco's gift was a case of the finest Italian wines that could be imported into the country, I'm sure. It is impossible to know exactly the expense, only that with his own *special* discount in all honesty, they were probably free, while on the open market would cost only God could know how much. His note read: *To Billy and Krissy—For the finest fifteen days of your life yet to come. Much love, as you know—Marco.* I figured out later that there were bottles that would have brought a thousand on the market—if that is, you could even sequester them at all. I suspect it was a lot like the box of Cuban cigars Uncle Dante had wrapped and presented along with the wine. Yep, Mr. and Mrs. Billy Bowling definitely had a couple of high roller Uncles, but as far as we could see, the best guys on the planet.

Dante and Marco didn't stop there! . . . "Oh wait, what's this," Marco had teased, dumbly reaching under the lounge chair where he sat, as we were all gathered on a deck built in the dunes just feet from the roaring waves. "Here's something else, and it says *Billy and Krissy* so it must be another gift or something," Marco quipped dumbly, handing a small wrapped box to Krissy. Actually an old check box, it contained round trip tickets from Miami to Rome for a two week paid up Italian honeymoon—

and was accompanied by *ten thousand dollars*—equally split between American and Italian traveler's checks . . .

> *Billy and Krissy:*
> *We are so happy you are family. It is very important to us Italians as we think you will understand, particularly after your trip. You are a wonderful young couple who has conquered great odds and the best of life is yet to come. Have fun.*
> *Marco and Dante Romano.*
> *P.S. Your mother was our beautiful little Sis and we miss her terribly, but she would be very proud of you both and we hope you think of Her and your own little Sis, Libby, often.*

. . . The first week in Rome was with reservations at the *Ateneo Garden Palace Hotel,* the finest hotel in all of Rome, and just blocks from the Colosseum, while the second week was a private flight to *Firenze* in Tuscany—and then a bus ride to the Chianti region and the hamlet of *Fabbrica.* There we had stayed in a centuries-old farmhouse in the heart of rolling vineyards and were carted about the countryside by any number of Romano cousins that Marco had set us up with. It was a magic even the movies could never have captured, but more than that, the deciding factor in establishing the dreams we intended to pursue with a vigor upon our return home. . . .

# Chapter Sixty

*T* hat winter Krissy and I became full time students at the Florida Culinary Institute in West Palm Beach, one of the best in the country. We worked for GCC part time for a while, but then Dante made the decision to market Gold Coast, proclaiming that the three of us would establish the *finest Italian Restaurant in all of South Florida*. He still held multiple land holdings, and one in particular, just South of the Crab House on Ocean Blvd. that a commercial developer would have murdered for. It was three vacant acres zoned commercial and the only such remaining spot with ocean frontage within maybe a hundred miles in either direction. It was just the sort of little toys Dante Romano kept in his back pocket to someday play around with, and as he saw it, that day had arrived!

By the spring of 2000, Krissy and I had both completed the three-year program for a B.S. in Culinary Management. It was the most extensive program offered by the school, and while Krissy's concentration was in food prep, I had majored in general staffing and bar management. We twice returned to Italy, once for a four-month Italian food and wine school in Tuscany at the *Villa Bordoni Chianti Luxury Hotel* in *Greve*, in the heart of the Chianti region that we loved so much. Krissy worked with Chef Bartolemi at the hotel while I traveled the countryside learning the wines and making future connections for Dante's proposed *Romano Rinato*. Marco even flew over and spent three weeks traveling with me and introducing me to his already established contacts. The three of us spent some wonderful time together, including perhaps the most memorable day of Marco's life (since he had lost his young wife) when he met Mirella Caracissi, whom he would marry exactly one year later.

About the time Dante sold Gold Coast, his attorneys had secured the necessary permits to begin construction on our restaurant,

*Romano Rinato* (Italian for born again), and on July 1, 2000, we held a groundbreaking ceremony as Dante had wanted. Krissy, Dante and myself wore hardhats and it was the kind of gig that I still found a bit goofy I must admit, although I had been making a concerted effort to temper my cynicism in recent years and since leaving Fort Harrison, Ohio, was actually finding it quite manageable. Dante had this gold plated spade for us each to turn over some sand, along with the mayor of Jupiter and some other big shots we didn't even know—except for Cliffton Tremont—who was right there beside us, hardhat and all. It was pretty exciting though, I've got to say in all honesty.

Then only two months later—and just after construction had begun seriously—Dante fell desperately ill and was diagnosed with severe kidney failure that had advanced even beyond a potential transplant. A full time nurse, Helen Spalding, was employed and took up residence in the mansion. With Dante's funds a dialysis machine was delivered to the property since he required twice daily treatments although even then, his decline was rapid.

In the early stages Dante was able to get out and around and I often chauffeured him to the construction site, which we monitored together with great pride, but he would soon tire, forcing us to return to Blue Palms and often within the hour. Even with nurse Spalding, either Krissy or myself tried to stay with him at all times. A week before Christmas, Marco flew down and moved into one of the guest cottages. He was working on his second novel at that point: *'The Murder of Chef Carmichael,'* having published his first, *'Murder Most Vintage,'* just the month before—which had been received, at least regionally, with rave reviews. Dante had done his best to put up a strong face through Christmas, but it was on January 5 that Marco approached Krissy and me one evening with seeming purpose as we sat watching night invade across the Atlantic, having long since drawn the curtain on Western Europe.

Crossing the lawn, he had a bottle of *Chianti Borgoconda* and three crystals in his hand. Such beauty and such pain, I can remember thinking at the time. But pain and death stalk us all, so the beauty must be gleaned whenever possible and at whatever cost. For *'it is the blending of a destined death with one's worldly responsibilities—while appreciating the beauty of God's grand play upon earth each day—that makes a life lived virtuous,'* Dante had once said to Krissy and me soon after his initial diagnosis.

As Marco set up the table, Krissy and I abandoned our chaises and joined him. There were still a few leftover snacks of cheese and crackers that Beulah had brought to us before retiring for the evening. Pouring us each an ample glass, Marco swirled his about in the manner of the professional *sommelier* he was—I, his budding disciple.

"Ah, *Saint Andrea via de Fabricca*! No better vineyard and winery in all the world and you are probably understanding that I'm betting, aren't you, Billy," Marco said, taking a soft sip to the palate, allowing it to linger.

"I would agree, Marco, from what I have learned so far. Of course, I am prejudiced. But I reserve the freedom for a change of heart as my education continues," I responded, grinning.

"Well put, Billy. Avoid prejudice at all cost, though . . . and most certainly not on my behalf. Tis only for you to discover—for as with snowflakes—no two palates are identical so we can only *suggest,* but never *decide* for another."

"Yes, Marco, I understand, but I must say I have uncovered none better yet," I replied honestly, though thinking very seriously about what he had just said.

"And Krissy, my lovely Mrs. Bowling; how are you feeling about this restaurant business these days? It is much harder work than people imagine, isn't it, and the management of cook staffs can be quite maddening as nearly every day you must work with a new face towing another set of personal problems. Yet our patrons don't understand this, which is exactly as it should be. We are servants to provide a dining experience as perfect as mortals can fashion, for that's what sets the truly superior restaurants apart from the pretenders," Marco said, sitting back in his chair, waiting for a reply.

"I think I have learned that, Marco, though even a year ago I would have agreed yet not understood, but I am different now. Working with Chef Bartolemi showed me that more than anything I learned at school or at *Marcellos*." (a fine West Palm Beach restaurant with whom Krissy apprenticed for a year).

"Wonderful answer, sweetheart. Still, Billy, burying your lovely wife in the kitchen is a sin against God's creative talents, wouldn't you say? Such beauty was meant to greet and host, the perfect prelude to an exquisite dining experience," Marco said with a gentle laugh, unlike the roaring laughter of Dante.

"You're right, Marco, I know, and exactly what my management sense tells me," I said, squeezing Krissy's hand softly and leaning across to kiss her on the cheek as she blushed.

"But kids, Dante wants to talk to us all tomorrow over dinner, for we have some big decisions to make and cannot pretend he will always be with us. Six, here on the deck, weather permitting. Is that agreeable?" he asked with a changed tone.

"Of course, Marco, but is there . . ."

"Billy, tomorrow. This is Dante's ball game. Excuse me, but I am beat. Tough life down here driving a vintage Vette around all day in this hot sun," he joked, and with that was gone.

Krissy and I nursed the wine. I had still never learned to really appreciate beer, and most liquor pretty much made me want to puke just thinking about it, but the wines—oh, the wines—how they had grown on me! Of course drinking wine that would cost a patron $300 or more a bottle may have spoiled me, but then it didn't appear the stock was about to run out anytime soon.

We filled our Riedels, kicked off our sandals, and crossing the dunes begin to walk along the edge of the gently washing surf. Jupiter Island was indeed a private paradise only the biggest money could buy, and even then usually not, just as Marco had once told us. We both laughed about our awkwardness and how Fort Harrison High's Billy Bowling and Krissy Kurtz were probably the most unlikely couple to ever make it past the Island gateman, who now waved us through as if we were royalty. The huge estates like Dante's were often vacant except for the caretakers—the owners away stirring another pot in some far-flung corner of the globe—so at times we could walk a mile along the beach without even seeing another person. We both well understood that the wealth was obscene and certainly that Dante's had not delivered him much true happiness, but above it all that mortality was an equal opportunity employer, and though often a courier for justice, for Dante Romano somehow now seemed exceedingly sad.

His wives had come and gone, each leaving their mark upon Jupiter Island society *and* a large dent in Dante Romano's heart, not to mention his bank account. There had been parties on *Inferno* to Miami or the Bahamas and back with over a hundred people, along with gala social events upon the grounds of *Blue Palms*, all usually at the whim of now long absent wives, while Dante himself seemed to take joy in the small things—Krissy and me these past five years or his fishing trips off shore or into the Caribbean on *Matador* with Cliffton Tremont. Dante Romano deserved his wealth, if anyone did, and yet it had sadly seemed to fit him with the comfort of a fiberglass tuxedo. Now Dante was terribly ill and things would soon change, yet just how much and when I didn't think anyone could predict—anyone except Dante Romano—*though Krissy and I would come to find it all out the very next day.*

# Chapter Sixty-one

*T*he large wooden deck nearest the ocean was submerged in the dunes so that it was invisible from both the back yard *and* the shore, yet was maybe within fifteen feet of high tide and the most wonderful spot one could imagine to relax and enjoy a drink, game of cards, or on occasion even a full course dinner. It measured fifty feet square and could easily seat forty people at ten imported Greek iron tables with chairs that Dante's second wife, Vienna, had ordered (Leroy Lincoln had told Krissy and I one day while he was gardening). They were beautiful, however, never left out and only set up when and as needed. Leroy saw to that with his bright orange Kubota and large wagon.

As Krissy and I emerged from the pool house the following evening at six, we could see Dante and Marco as we broached a steep rise to the south of the pool. They were both settled upon the discreet deck and we noticed further that both Beulah and Hallie Lincoln were setting up for what appeared would be evening dinner. Dante was in a wheel chair by then (which had actually been conveyed to the dinner deck by Leroy via his Kubota and wagon) and we could see Helen Spalding retreating in the distance, having seen that he was settled in and comfortable.

"Wonderful, wonderful, here are the kids now," Dante greeted us graciously as we approached, then adding with weakened laughter, "And my dear Krissy, I do beg your pardon for not standing."

"Oh, Uncle Dante . . ."

"But come, come, anyhow my dear and allow an old man a peck on the cheek and a whiff of that glorious bouquet," Dante joked as Krissy leaned over for his quick nip and gentle hug. Marco then approached and gave both Krissy and I a brief hug. There had always been an abundance of good natured joking and appropriate attraction all the way around, which was so very different from anything either Krissy or myself had known our entire lives . . . before Marco and Dante.

"We better be careful, Marco, and fall out of love with this man's wife cause I think Billy could probably kick both of our asses these days," Dante said with the roaring laugh, which was sadly becoming weaker as the days passed, then added, "Come, kids, have a seat and let's toast to your wonderful lives which are really just beginning."

One region of Italy neither Krissy or I had yet visited was *Trentino Alsto Adidge* in the Italian Alps on the Swiss-Austrian border. On the Adidge River, the region was bordered by the Phaetian Alps on one side and the Dolomites on the other and was famous for the Pinot Grigio grape dating back to Roman times—at least this was my education through Marco who traveled the region often to procure his favorite white table wines. Marco said the scenery was spectacular and promised that on our next trip we would visit the region since the connections for the whites were critical. A *Kossler 1978* Pinot Grigio we then raised in toast.. . .

. . . "Billy and Krissy, you have brought so much joy to my life, and into Marco's also, as he and I have just been talking about. Oh, but that I could live forever to enjoy your company and watch you both grow. But my time is thin and I know that, so let's toast to family, for you three are my family and this is as happy as I have been for many years, and for that I thank you all," Dante said strongly as our four Riedels softly kissed.

Though there was visible emotion, Dante possessed an unusual strength of spirit without a hint of self-pity. Marco then stood and though I hadn't thought about it often, I couldn't help feeling we were in the midst of a movie set and Michael Douglas was now taking center stage.

"First, I toast my brother, Dante. How I wish we had seen each other more often over the years, but no mind now, for today we are together and I cherish these moments. To Billy and Krissy. You've had some tough times, but you are an exceptional young couple and Dante and I are *very* proud of you both. Without you we might all still be drifting as lost pieces of a puzzle. *To us all*," Marco said, raising his glass for the second toast.

At that point I understood that a toast all the way around was called for, so I stood, collecting my thoughts. I now towered over Marco, having stretched by then to 6'3," a somewhat aberrant genetic characteristic for either a Bowling *or* a Romano and one which everyone joked about. Raising my Riedel and nodding in turn to the three, I began: "Even when life was tough I taught myself not to cry about my bad fortune, but that doesn't mean I ever expected much *good* fortune and now I know *I am the luckiest man on the planet*. I think I loved Krissy in about fourth grade and now she is my wife, so how could it get much better than that? But more than anything I wanted to be a part of a family, and Marco and Dante, you are the best, and are both a part of Mom which I feel every day I am around you. I only wish that Jimmy were here and I haven't given up hope that he will be part of us too, one day. But for now, no one could have a better life and I thank God each day that he has allowed me to be a part of all of your lives," I finished with tears in my eyes as I reached toward Dante for the third family toast.

Across the lawn I could see Leroy driving the Kubota toward us, pulling this elaborate stainless steel gizmo that Dante (or more likely a past wife) had procured to deliver hot meals to any one of a number of exotic and secluded locations around the grounds. But first, Dante spoke.

"Your turn young lady," he said, smiling warmly at Krissy.

Krissy looked to me at first, though briefly. I had seen her grow like no one could have possibly imagined over the past half decade in Florida. She was a beautiful, self-confident woman and yet that never surprised me because she always had been, and long before other girls her age. It was what I had always seen in her, yet that mysterious integrant that I had, for years, been unable to define. Krissy stood and raised her glass.

"I've always wanted just what Billy most wants . . . *a family*. Billy and I never talked for years, but I think I always understood him somehow, just like he understood me, and somebody beyond us planned that all out. I think *I* actually loved Billy in *third grade*, though, ha ha," she said with a light giggle and a wink from sparkling eyes. "Uncle Marco and Uncle Dante, you have both been so good to me and I thank you for that, more than you will ever know. I love the three of you so very much," Krissy said eloquently, extending her glass . . . *and I had never been more proud.*

The meal was grilled Yellowtail Snapper with a white bean salsa, linguine with collard greens and conch fritters smothered in a watercress dressing, finished off with apple rum cake. I realized then it was Beulah who should be head chef at the pending *Romano Rinato*. After everything had been cleared away and Leroy had lit a number of torches just off the deck, Dante turned serious.

. . . "Kids, as you know 'the best laid plans and all that' . . . well, you understand. The fact being that I am not likely to be around to oversee and enjoy the restaurant as I had hoped, which is often the case with so-called retirements, but it has been great fun just planning it and seeing the sparkle in your eyes. What I want you to know, however, is that you are not bound to our project at all and I certainly don't want you to feel that, particularly after I am gone," he said, pausing.

"Uncle Dante you will be around for a long time yet, I'm sure," I spoke up.

"That's kind of you, Billy, and I know what you're trying to do, but the fact is I won't. So we need some projection here and I do not speak of this lightly. Marco and I have had much conversation these past few days and I want you both to hear me out." Dante raised his Reidel and took a deliberate sip of Pinot as we all sat quietly.

"You see, Marco loves the North and he has a very exciting project in mind—a dream that he shared with me just yesterday and that I would like him to tell the two of you about," Dante said, nodding to Marco and suddenly looking very tired. We both looked to Marco as he began to speak.

"It is my plan to turn the camp I bought into a summer culinary school for low income kids that might have an interest in pursuing careers in the field. The setting on *Escape Lake* is perfect, particularly the Lodge and lodge kitchen, even though they need completely overhauled before we could begin. The thing is, I don't want to manage it full time for I want to continue writing, though I would like to be very involved and teach a bit of what I know about foods and wines. If the two of you might have an interest in the project,

I think we could create something that has never been done before anywhere. It would be a summer venture, of course, and exactly at a time when you might want to escape the ghastly humidity of South Florida. And it *would* be a family enterprise," Marco said, as Dante nodded with a smile.

He then stopped and there was a brief silence. It was true that Krissy and I had loved it the two times we had stayed at *Blue Pines* in Harbor Springs and it had thrilled us to cross the majestic Mackinac Bridge to see the camp and the wonderful Upper Peninsula cabin that had recently become his base for writing. The camp was run down, but it did have incredible potential and we could understand Marco's attraction and excitement.

"What do you think, Billy?" Dante finally said.

"But Dante, the restaurant . . . *Romano Rinato?*"

"Of course, of course, kids. It's all yours as you wish, but understand I will not be here nor will Marco be near, at least most of the time. We just want you to know your options and then Marco and I want you and Krissy to do exactly as you desire, even if it means you change your minds completely and decide to become comedians in Las Vegas. We know how you lived your life at that bowling alley and you must *never* again feel obligated to anyone. Marco can find able partners to help him pursue his dream if it's not for you; right, Marco?"

"Yes, of course, we just want to throw it all out there. It's the way families should be—kicking around options without horseshit and obligations," Marco said, looking from me to Krissy and back.

"Well, you're right on about that," I answered, looking to Krissy who softly smiled.

"Then enough said for tonight I would think," Dante said, raising his glass again for a toast then pulling it back. "Oh, and kids, what I have is going to be yours and I suppose you should know that, so I guess you wouldn't have to work at all, would you? But I know you both better than that and if two young kids could handle a *small* fortune with poise, I am certain it is you two. A big chunk's gonna go to charity—and to clean up that mess with my women, and Cliffton will handle all that—but *Blue Palms* will be yours and a sizable sum beyond that. You would certainly be free to stay here, but I'm betting you probably aren't much into that. I'd have never been here myself except for the occasional wife, you know," he said, chuckling, then pausing to gain his breath.

I looked at Krissy and she at me. We had never even considered such a possibility and yet, except for Jimmy, only Marco remained as family. My senses were numb, but I spat out, "But Uncle Dante, Marco is your brother . . . and besides . . . you are going to be around for a long time . . ."

"Nonsense, Billy, I wish, but I won't—and adults must face reality. Marco and I discussed this at length. I waived my inheritance rights and Marco did quite well for himself with the sale of *Romanos* and your grandparent's estate. I am leaving *Blue Pines* in Harbor Springs to Marco and that little toy car he so loves to scoot about in. Kids—*we have no shortages here*—it is now about living honorable and productive lives. And Billy, I trust that when Jimmy resurfaces you will consider his options on my behalf, but for now this is the way it needs to be done. I think we have covered all the bases. What say you, Marco?" Dante asked beginning now to raise his glass for the final evening toast.

"I have nothing further, Dante. It is just as we spoke."

"To family," Dante said, raising his Reidel, echoed by Marco and then trailed by Krissy and myself.

A gentle, yet very cool January breeze blew in off the Atlantic. The torches fluttered in the wind and the faces around the table flickered like an ever-changing slide show. In the distance I saw Helen Spalding approaching as if signaled somehow, which I was certain hadn't happened, yet it had somehow seemed a bit eerie. Both Dante and Marco looked at peace, even as a million brain cells bounced around my skull as if scrambling for shelter from an earthquake rumbling somewhere in the unknown distance. I just didn't know what to make of it all—it was so overwhelming. But the peace of Dante Romano counted for more than anything just then and as I looked at him being attended to by Nurse Spalding, he looked happy—and I was glad.

# Chapter Sixty-two

*D*ante *Augustus Romano* died in his bed at *Blue Palms* on April 8, 2001. He was just shy of 66 years old. Marco, Krissy and myself were with him, and Helen Spalding was nearby. Though very weak, Dante had remained alert and lucid to the very end. At exactly 9 am he had looked upon the three of us with a soft smile before closing his eyes. By 9:10 he was gone, leaving only the smile behind.

During the immediate months preceding his death, we had all made many plans, and it was with a grace and comfort that Dante passed on. *Romano Rinato* would proceed as planned and Krissy and I would retain ownership and general management, but two friends we had made while staying at Villa Bordoni, Alejandro and Taylor Del Sannio, would come from Italy and assume active management. Alejandro's family had for generations run a famous restaurant in Fabbrica, Tuscany, although Taylor had grown up in Vermont where her family owned and operated *Sarconni's*, a popular Italian restaurant in Montpelier right across the street from the state capitol. Taylor had gone to the same school Krissy had in Greve where she met and married Alejandro who was a part time instructor. We were all very comfortable with the arrangement.

Marco had shown us the detailed plans for his camp on *Escape Lake* and it was exciting—and something Krissy and I very much wanted to be a part of. Following renovation of the buildings, which he hoped could be completed that fall, the following summer he planned to extend the first invitations, along with the promotion of future scholarships. Although Dante, Marco and Mom had attended a private Catholic high school, Marco had always wanted to do something for the inner-city kids of Cincinnati because they were the ones he'd often employed over the years to work in the kitchen and bus tables and he had developed a fondness for them.

He understood that they often lacked discipline and, as a result, denied adequate training thus subsequent opportunities. The program he hoped to construct would be open to needy kids in the greater Cincinnati school system and a committee he was currently working with would set the guidelines for acceptance.

The initial class of 15 would be invited to return for a second year unless there had been a motivational or disciplinary issue that had not been resolved. Then each year an additional 15 first year students would join those returning for a maximum of thirty each summer. After completing a second year at *Camp Romano*, students would be awarded scholarships to culinary schools as needed. First year students would follow the completion of junior year in high school and second year students would follow graduation. If a kid could exercise reasonable discipline and stick with the program two summers, Marco would see to it that he or she would then be provided wonderful opportunities in the culinary field.

*Camp Romano* was also going to be designed for *fun*, just like in the 60's when Marco himself came north with his friend, Tommy Shuster, and it was called *Camp Dearborn*. Tommy's dad had worked at the Ford plant in Sharondale, north of Cincinnati. Camp Dearborn was for the children of Ford employees for nearly half a century . . . right up until the mid 90's when the American auto industry began to decompose. Marco purchased the entire camp of 14 cabins, a chapel, the massive Lodge, a large, though dilapidated boathouse and a newer metal 30'x 60' maintenance building full of canoes, day sailers and lawn equipment, situated on 20 acres and with 400' of lake frontage . . . all for $240,000.

He then negotiated separately, and bought what the Ford camp kids used to call the *big shot cabin,* which in the early days Henry Ford himself often stayed in, as did subsequent Ford big shots like Lee Iacoca, Robert MacNamera and, of course, a succession of following Fords. It had been the base for card games and strategy sessions for the big boys when they were up for the fall deer hunt, long after the summer camp was closed. Built of massive logs in the 1930's and sitting on a high bluff just east of the camp, the vintage log structure of about 3500 square feet with a massive stone fireplace included four bedrooms, two full, now modern baths, a large loft that overlooked the glorious lake (where Marco wrote), kitchen and galley . . . and a massive great room spanned by a full front porch to the very edge of the bluff which dropped sharply to the lake fifty feet below. Another 300' of lake frontage went with the cabin and met the camp frontage so Marco's holdings commandeered 700'on the pristine lake. *The Ford Cabin* had been maintained very well over the years, unlike the camp, and Marco had to shell out another $295,000 for the *executive cabin.*

Though Marco was no Dante, I found out later he had walked away from Romano's in very good shape and after the half million plus for the property purchases, and another half million to complete the camp renovation (the vast majority of which went into the lodge and a complete overhaul of the kitchen), he was still sound financially. He was even bringing in a contractor friend of his from New York state to oversee the complete restoration of the classic boathouse, a rare architectural design for that part of the central U.P. and seldom found outside the Les Cheneaux Islands, seventy miles to the east. By the time it was completed two years later, the magical building, extending far out into Escape Lake, and including an apartment for a caretaker above, he'd shelled out another 300 grand. By then, however, Marco's book, *Murder Most Vintage* had nearly brought in enough to pay for the entire boathouse project, let alone that *The Murder of Chef Carmichael* promised to do the same.

Krissy and I sold *Blue Palms* as I wrote. It was purchased by a famous NFL quarterback turned TV commentator whose identity I agreed not to disclose at the time of the sale so I have decided to respect that, even as I now write, some six years later. The buyer retained Beulah and the Lincolns, for which we were grateful, knowing that would have been very important to Dante. *Inferno* was sold to *Fantaseas Yacht Charters* in Miami for a relatively low price, but one Dante had approved before his death since he had a good buddy who operated the company and always had wanted the 115' Christensen.

Krissy and I still own *Matador*, but ever since the sale of Blue Palms, Cliffton Tremont has kept 'her' docked on the canal at his North Palm Beach home to use as he pleases. At least once a year we take an extended fishing trip with Captain Tremont, usually in the Carribean. Our trip last year had been the biggest event in *Eli's* young life (I'll get to that), and seemingly one of the bigger ones in Cliffton's and we are hoping Eli has many more such adventures to experience with '*Pa Pa' Tremont*.

Dante was cremated and Krissy, Marco, Cliffton and myself, from the bow of *Matador,* had dispersed his ashes into the sea as near as Cliffton could pinpoint to the spot where in 1989 Dante joined the elite 200 lb. Tarpon Club, having landed a tarpon that weighted 216 pounds. At the time less than forty—two hundred pounders—had been recorded around the world, with the world record just over 250. It had been his final request to merge with the sea where he said he had spent the most exciting day of his life, which was somewhat sad when you really stopped to think about it.

It was further distressing irony that the three most important men in our lives were men whom would have been wonderful fathers yet had gone through life childless. Now, as surrogate children, it was Krissy and I who had reaped the benefits of their earthly achievements and we often felt quite undeserving. Yet Dante had been '*in heaven*' his last few years, even in the midst of his illness, so we took considerable solace in that. Krissy and I so wished he could have lived to see Eli born just a year later, but it wasn't to be. Still, for as long as Cliffton Tremont was around, Eli was not going to be without a 'Pa Pa' and it was a wonderful thing to behold.

Krissy and I were now *Florida people*, having lived there for nearly six years (which in Florida easily qualifies one as a 'native'). True, we had lived on Jupiter Island those years, the most exclusive community not only in Florida, but probably the entire country, but we had worked in the *real world* and it was there that we were most comfortable. We could have *grand-fathered* ourselves in, despite the '*tsk tsk talk*' of the locals, and stayed on 'The Island' forever, never needing to work had we wanted that, but it was never an option in our minds and hearts—just as Uncle Dante had known all along.

The exorbitance of Jupiter Island was for those struggling with their own mortality. Krissy Kurtz Bowling and Billy Bowling weren't. In 1996, we had come to understand it about as well as any two nineteen year old kids had anywhere at anytime on the planet, and we weren't about to forfeit that lesson—not only 'not anytime soon' . . . *but ever!*

# Chapter Sixty-three

*T*he first years in Florida I was often recognized from my mug shots on TV that had bombarded the American public for months in 1996, and nowhere was I more recognized than right there on Jupiter Island which taught me that the obscenely wealthy—who could do anything they wanted on the planet—nevertheless thrived on the same gossip and TV trash that absorbed the residents of Sunrise Mobile Home Park in Fort Harrison, Ohio. Eventually the public recognition began to erode, but *never* on the Island, which was one good reason Kris and I were more than happy to leave.

On the other hand, outside of Sam Spade, one would have had a difficult time finding us those five years, for Jupiter Island is a great place to live if you want to be left alone—at least by the outside world. Lacy knew where we were, of course, and the phone number where we could be reached, but Krissy had sworn her to secrecy. If someone crossed paths with her soliciting us, it was to *never* be disclosed where we were and we didn't even want to know about the inquiry, nor could think of any reason for an exception.

Dad may have assumed we were with Dante, but according to Dante he doubted that he knew much more than that he lived in Florida and—given his lifestyle—it is unlikely he would have even stumbled across our situation. It was only Jimmy that I wanted desperately to contact over the years and with Cliffton's help we secured his location and an address that we knew would find him. By 2000 he had become a *Major* and was still stationed in Riyadh, Saudi Arabia, where he had been for an extended period of time, having decided on a military career. I wrote two letters without response, although Cliffton assured me he was certain they had reached him. After a time I just more or less gave up, but then a fortuitously strange thing happened just a month after Dante's death. . . .

. . . Lacy called and said that two fellows who were twins had been trying to contact me. She further said it had something to do with Jimmy and thought maybe I would want to know that. She had forgotten their names, but had taken their phone number if I wanted it. I passed the phone to Krissy for a chat and stared at the number, trying to make sense of it. It was a Fort Harrison number, but rang no bell. Then duh! It had to be Turk and Thad Otte, the only boy twins I knew and both in Jimmy's class. I remembered hearing that one of them went to play football at Union College, somewhere in Kentucky, and the other had gone off to study dentistry at Ohio State. I couldn't remember which was which and that was the last I'd even given them a thought. Nearly nine years had passed now, so who knew what their story was? . . .

. . . It was Thad who answered the phone and I was glad cause I always liked him a lot more than Turk who had been one of Giovanazzo's committed thugs.

"Billy?"

"Thad? Were you and Turk trying to reach me?"

"Yeah, we were. Have you heard anything from Jimmy lately?" he asked, waiting.

Part of me didn't want to even admit that I'd had no contact with him for years, as it seemed to throw me back to the old days and made me remember all too painfully what a fucked up family we were. But on the other hand, I knew I'd never connect with Jimmy if I didn't stick my neck out whenever I had a chance, like now . . . and I was to find I wasn't wrong.

"No, Thad, I haven't heard from him for years. I only know he's still in the marines and that he was in Saudi Arabia last I'd heard."

"We know, Billy. Turk talked to him just last month, but it's kind of a long story and we think you should hear it. We heard you were in Florida and weren't sure where, but Turk and I are coming down next week to visit our grandmother who is ill. She lives in *Fort Pierce.* Are you anywhere near there?"

"Yeah, real close, Thad, maybe thirty miles south," I answered.

"We're going to be there on Monday. How can we get a-hold of you?"

I gave Thad both our cell numbers and we agreed that when they were able, we'd make arrangements to meet sometime the following week. It was Wednesday morning that Thad called and we made arrangements to meet at *The Queen Mary British Pub* out Jupiter Farms Road. Krissy and I had been there a couple of times and liked it cause it was in a quiet spot and though, from the outside, didn't much resemble a British Pub, it served wonderful fare and great imported beer which I had slowly been cultivating a taste for. It was well off the coast and tucked away in what we had come to know as *old Florida*, but was nevertheless owned by some very British people from Yorkshire whom we had grown to quite like.

Kris and I were enjoying a beer on the long front porch when the Otte boys pulled up in a big old beige Buick—the make and color of car that every senior citizen over 65 must be required to drive by law. As they approached I could see that their eyes nearly popped out as they spied Krissy, who was dressed Florida-style in shorts, a halter top and casual, yet heeled pumps. We both stood and I reached out to shake, first Thad's hand, then Turk's. "Been a long time guys," I said as we all settled in and the Otte's ordered their beers.

"Jesus, Billy, we don't know much I guess—are you guys married?" Turk asked, having noticed Krissy's left hand and the huge diamond that Uncle Dante had given me to give Krissy just before our wedding.

"Yep, almost four years now," I answered.

"God, how life goes on," Thad exclaimed.

The Otte boys didn't look all that different except for the tattoos that crept up both of Turk's arms. We made small talk and just took awhile to get comfortable, as it wasn't like we were particularly good friends. I was far from the same person they'd remembered, it was obvious, and Turk, in particular, couldn't keep his eyes off Krissy. After twenty minutes or so we got to the subject of Jimmy. Thad broached it, but it was really Turk's story.

"Billy, Turk should tell you about Jimmy," he said, and then withdrew giving Turk the stage.

. . . "Well, I was in the Navy seven years and just got my discharge papers last month. I served on the *Yorktown* most of my gig and was often in the Saudi port of Damman to unload supplies for the Marine base in Riyadh. Jimmy was usually there to receive the supplies and the last time we got pretty fucked up drinking whisky all night. Jesus, Billy, what's happened to him? Do you really mean you haven't talked to him?" he asked, although I had told Thad on the phone that I hadn't.

"No, just like I told Thad . . . nothing."

"Well, I'm going to tell you this and I hope it won't upset you too much. In all my years in the service I've never seen a more angry person. I'm sure he spilled things to me that he doesn't let his superiors or his soldiers see, but he's downright scary. I mean Jimmy always had a temper, and a lot of anger, but he worries me. I'm surprised he can even keep his stripes. He must be a pretty good actor is all I can say," Turk said, falling quiet.

"I'm not sure what you mean, Turk?"

"Ok, I'll try to explain. He never found out about Gwen's murder until the first time I saw him maybe four years ago. I was actually the one to tell him, so of course he'd never heard that you'd been in jail for it, Billy. How could he not know that?" Turk said, pausing as if waiting for an answer.

"It's the way our family was, you should know that. We're fucked up. You know how Jimmy and Dad were. You were there. Jimmy wanted out of it all and I guess has made a point not to think about us or contact anyone."

"Yeah, well, I kinda know. Anyhow, when he heard Sam Giovanazzo had murdered Gwen, I was scared Billy . . . *real scared.* He hardly looked human and was overtaken by a rage I can't even describe," Turk said.

"Jimmy was always an angry person, Turk. Most of it was Dad I always thought," I replied.

"I know, but he's worse now. Billy, there's something else I want to say . . . and I think Thad does too. It's one reason we wanted to see you," Turk said, looking up at me in a way that didn't seem to fit the Turk I had once known.

"Go on, Turk," I said simply, more than a little puzzled.

"Billy, Sam Giovanazzo fucked a lot of us up. I'll say that now, but it took me a long time to admit it. *Jimmy loved football, but he hated Giovanazzo.* I probably did too, but without really understanding it. All of us *became* a little bit of Sam Giovanazzo I think. You couldn't help it; it just crept in the back door after years and years of his shit. You learned to look down on women; you learned to feel superior—hell, I even think a lot of football players fought with their parents because Sam Giovanazzo looked down on them too. But I think Jimmy was affected more than most—and especially because of how Giovanazzo always put Gwen down in front of everybody," Turk said, pausing.

I only knew of that one time, that day on my bike and Turk had been the other guy in the bleachers though he probably didn't remember that now and there was no need to bring it up. But had there been more times? Sure, why wouldn't there have been? So I decided to push the point, saying, "What do you mean Turk? What did Giovanazzo say?"

"Well, you know how Jimmy felt about Gwen. It didn't go anywhere, but he still loved her and everybody knew it. But Giovanazzo trash talked Gwen Putnam all the time. Honestly, when I heard Gwen had been murdered, the first person that came to mind was Giovanazzo, and I know a lot of guys probably thought that, maybe even adults too, but nobody would dare suggest it. It's the way it was, Billy, and you know that. It's a fucked up town and a fucked up school. Two State Championships I played on, and now I'm almost ashamed of it—ashamed to have played for Sam Giovanazzo. He left a lot of scars and I'm just talking about the guys. We all knew that he fucked the girls, and especially the young ones. Those are scars that haven't a chance of ever going away and then you got blamed for so much of it. Mostly Thad and I just wanted to tell you how sorry we are—how sorry a lot more people than you think are—but especially the kids who went through that school. It's the adults who are fucked, Billy. I just wish it would change now that that asshole is finally where he belongs, but Thad doesn't think it has. Dick Hamilton won a State Championship last year and honestly, Billy, he wasn't much different from Giovanazzo except that he fucks other guy's wives instead of students."

Turk Otte, one of Sam Giovanazzo's inner circle, was now saying exactly what I had seen all those years. He was on target all the way down the line; the kids; the adults—and the total abuse of Sam Giovanazzo—but it was a conversation just to vent and a conversation far too late to make a difference now. Yet it was something that needed to be known and heard by all the adults who thought they were so much smarter than the kids in a small village in West Central Ohio. Thad had remained quiet, but now, after we all ordered another round, spoke.

"Billy, I remember a day when I was a senior and was on a pass to gym class with Giovanazzo. We were killing kids with balls like Giovanazzo always thought was so funny and some girl got her face wiped out and some other girl got into it with Giovanazzo about it. I don't remember her name, but I remember Giovanazzo ripping on her dad because he was a nurse. I also remember you were standing under the basket and watching it all while Obringer, Jason Bertke and me were supposed to laugh with Giovanazzo about it all. You were there, Billy. Do you remember?" he asked, waiting.

"Yes, Thad, I do."

"I didn't want to be part of that, Billy, but I didn't know how *not* to be because that's what you had to do if you played for Sam Giovanazzo. You *always* had to make him know that you understood he was the *King*. Turk didn't really see it like I did, not back then. I saw the bullshit every day, but I never did a thing about it and I am ashamed. It has always haunted me a lot, but particularly since Gwen Putnam was murdered. Giovanazzo never should have gotten away with what he did. Maybe if some of us would have spoken up or tried to do something, Gwen would still be here, and a lot of kids feel the same way I do, but there's nothing we can do . . . not now," Thad said, fighting back tears.

There was silence all the way around for a minute before I spoke. "I appreciate you fellows more than you can know. You can imagine how it haunts me, let alone the struggle I had with five months in jail for something Sam Giovanazzo had done, but Krissy and I are learning to move on and to take from the past what can benefit us both now and in the future, then leave the rest behind. It's all we can do, Thad . . . Turk. So let's just order some good British fare and enjoy ourselves. It's on me."

"Billy, that's not necessary," Thad began . . .

"Thad, on me I said. How long are you guys here for?" I then asked.

"We don't know—a few more days or a week. We wanted to see grandmother, though she was doing much better this morning."

"Ever go deep sea fishing?" I asked, as Turk's eyes lit up.

"No, Billy, but I'd love to. Do you know someone with a charter around here?" Turk asked.

"Krissy and I have a boat. If you guys want to drive back down tomorrow, we'll take you out. How's that sound?"

"It can get pretty rough out there, can't it? How big is your boat?" Thad asked, concerned.

"Big enough, Thad. Here let me write down directions to our place. There's a gateman, but we'll give him your names," I said, turning over a place mat and pulling a pen out of my pocket.

To say the least, the next day was quite an experience for the Otte twins. Matador was still docked at Blue Palms, as we had not sold at that point. Maybe we shouldn't have let them in on our little secret, but what the hell we figured. Perhaps it was a bit pretentious to set it up that way, but it really was the only way to go out on the boat that made sense. We went into no particulars, but yes, we told them—we owned the place—having inherited it from my uncle. We spent a great day fishing, but without any particular luck since I was no Cliffton Tremont, and whatever they wanted to relay to Fort Harrison was fine by me and Krissy we had decided. After all, what else could be said about *Billy Bowling* that hadn't already been said . . . one way or another? So have at it . . .

# Chapter Sixty-four

*I* had this odd feeling that the appearance of the Otte twins was a meant to be, sort of like Sheriff Sam Oberly had said his wife, Julie, told him was the reason for everything that happened in life. Nothing had been resolved of course, but there was reasonable comfort in knowing I had a kindred connection to not only the Otte's, but apparently a number of FHHS graduates over the years. I had hoped that was true, but had never had it revealed like both Turk and Thad had those two days we spent together. Yet from everything I heard, there had never much been a change in the attitude of the adults in Fort Harrison as I had hoped would happen when the disgusting nature of Sam Giovanazzo was laid before them at the trial. (A trial, which by the way, would never take place).

Administrators like Wickerdick had moved on, trading his 'row of ducks' for the golf condo in utopia and chasing a little white ball into the weeds each morning, or fishing them out of a lagoon with whatever newfangled retriever *Golfsmith* had come up with that winter. The old *State Championships* survived for most I was certain, and still became the reason for living as guys like Tic Forgett and Garth Schmutz were laid off from Ford and went on unemployment. Al Samsal and Clint Obringer probably still watched the videos of their interview with Geraldo Rivera, and I had heard that the Fort Harrison Savings and Loan had recently been turned over to Carl Robbins IV, which meant pretty soon they would eclipse the Bowlings as *Fort Harrison's first family of royalty*—and especially since it was unlikely that the Bowlings would be producing any more William's and James's; at least by me they wouldn't!

There was an unintended strength that Krissy and I had both absorbed from the Otte's and it served to pave the way for the major change that we were now about to make in our lives. It was exactly a week after Turk and Thad had met us at The Queen Mary—on

Wednesday, May 23, 2001—that we found out for certain that Krissy was pregnant. We had just put *Blue Palms* under contract and were planning to move to *Blue Pines* in Harbor Springs, Michigan, by the first of July, where we would stay until late fall, getting 'used' to the north and visiting with Marco as his camp restoration neared completion.

Before we left, however, we bought a wonderful home on Ocean Drive in Jupiter Colony where we planned to winter—or stay if we ever needed to come down to help at *Romano Rinato*. Though right on the Atlantic, we'd snared it for just over a million, and within less than four years it would be worth double that. It was private and comfy and, though still obscene by standards we would understand, was certainly no Blue Palms! If you have money or access to it you can make more, that's for certain—*the American Way*, that is—which of course most Americans have absolutely no access to.

July and August in Harbor Springs, Michigan, was a treat and yet something we would be just as happy to do without in the future, having found that it was the *off-season* months that were the real treasure, for it was then the beautiful village truly blossomed— and in the company of *real* people. Having spent five years living on Jupiter Island, nothing surprised us anymore relative to the extravagance and arrogance of wealth, yet we found that summer the obscenity had actually followed us—which had quite surprised us—having had no real education as to the background of the small harbor parish.

Harbor Springs *harbors* a legacy of Gatsby type old-money estates that are quite charming, even though now often peopled by obtuse and arrogant heirs. Normally *old money* arrogance means that your grandfather, or more often great-grandfather, did something very clever legally (or especially sly illegally) and amassed a fortune . . . which is then sucked on by a succession of heirs who, within time, will most certainly deplete the coffers— just as certainly as a favorite lolly-pop eventually becomes a bitter paper stick. In and of themselves, the heirs of old money people deserve little intrinsic respect—unless they have actively managed, maintained or improved the family legacy—which to be fair, a *rare few* actually have.

I must admit Krissy and I did find the turn of the century summer estates and Victorian traditions charming and certainly not something we would wish to see come to an end. In general we were snubbed on *The Point* even more than on Jupiter Island, but we had been educated honestly and so it certainly caused us no distress. There was, of course, no shortage of lechers, either on The Point or in the village—when Krissy was out and about.

When we awoke September 4th, however, we did so in a very different world. The Labor Day Weekend had passed and in a blink the summer people of Harbor Springs had vanished, many to return to their downstate or Chicago lives, while others had evaporated to re-establish winter residence in Florida, Arizona or Southern California. The true charm of the village for us then unfolded—*until exactly one week later, when on September 11, 2001, the numbness of tragedy struck again, only this time to be shared by all Americans.*

Wanting to just be around others, we had stumbled numbly downtown to visit our favorite spots, *The Pier* and *The New York*—both now peopled by a handful of stunned locals. Dale, the bartender, had held court at *The Pier* for generations and I could only imagine the stories buried deep within his brain, though secrets that would never see the light of day because that's what money expected—and thus how those who served money survived.

There were maybe ten locals in the bar and the tension was obvious. Both TV's spewed venom none of us as yet understood, only knowing that the world as Americans had always known it was about to change radically. We slid onto two bar seats as Dale approached.

"What can I get you kids?" he said cheerfully, though shouldering the worried look we all wore.

"Two Bass," I answered, "and what's the bar special today, Dale?"

"Two steak or chicken fajitas for five bucks," he answered, setting the two frosty drafts before us. Krissy actually quite enjoyed a beer now and then and I was engaged in an apprenticeship with the fermented beverages at the time and could say that I was slowly coming around.

"Sounds good to me. What say you, Kris?"

"You want them both, don't you?" she asked:

"I don't know, probably."

"Good, cause I want the broiled whitefish and salad bar. That ok?"

I had to laugh to myself. We were multi-millionaires and could have called Stafford Smith, the owner, to tell him we wanted to buy the place and it would have probably washed. And yet my beautiful Krissy was looking into my eyes to make sure that $15.95 for her broiled whitefish and salad bar was ok . . . *since I was only spending five bucks on the bar special.*

"As long as you smuggle me a cup of cole slaw, it is," I returned, trying to smile.

We stayed in Harbor Springs that fall until the last week of October since Krissy was due right around Christmas and we planned on being in Florida for the birth. We purchased a used Jeep Wrangler to travel about the bucolic countryside—south through the beautiful harbor town of Charlevoix and on to 'cosmopolitan' Traverse City—but especially north to Wilderness State Park where we spent many hours on the miles and miles of beautiful and abandoned sand beaches that were the exact antithesis of our Florida haunts.

We traveled often across the dramatic Mackinac Bridge to stay with Marco in his breath-taking northern retreat and observe Camp Romano as it neared completion. Michigan's beautiful Upper Peninsula was a world unlike Krissy and I had ever experienced or could have even imagined . . . in fact it was like a foreign country I would eventually come to feel just a few years later when it would, in essence, become our home. *Escape Lake* was sparsely populated, especially since the Carston family still owned about a third of the lake frontage directly across from the camp. Because of health issues, however, John and Florence Carston lived most of the year in Arizona, maintaining a modest cabin on the lake even though they could have pretty much built whatever they wanted—since the Carston family owned numerous dolomite quarries around the U.P. and throughout Northern Wisconsin. But they were just wonderful regular people whom Krissy and I had hit it off with on one of our visits to see Marco a year earlier. When they understood what we were planning with the old camp, they had offered us an incredible piece of property without us even having solicited it. *And so Krissy and I began to plan our own first real home!*

*Escape Lake* is most unusual and beautiful. Only a hundred eighty acres, yet nearly a hundred fifty feet deep in spots, it almost gave the appearance of a crater lake as probably eighty per cent of it was bordered by a very high ridge. Camp Romano commandeered the only level ground leading to the lake; the terrain then sharply rose to where Marco's cabin sat and then gently rose even higher around the south and western sides of the lake before dropping again just shy of the camp. The four acres and three hundred feet of frontage that John Carston sold us was literally to die for. Almost directly across from Camp Romano, it sat high upon a dolomite cliff in an area of massive old hemlocks—and with spectacular views of the lake.

In mid October, Krissy and I bought some camping equipment and spent nearly ten days camping on *our land*, planning our home and making careful love in the tent late in the evenings. To that point it was the most wonderful ten days of our lives, even transcending Italy. I'd had a friend in Florida try to teach me to play the guitar for well over a year and had gotten decent. I would play the guitar around the campfire, but I would always remain a lousy singer so Krissy had to learn to sing and had gotten pretty good. Our favorite duo was *'Friends In Low Places.'* I laugh now because later on we would hold 'talent nights' at the camp around the big old fire-pit and the second year Krissy and I finally agreed to do our thing, and everyone said we were good. But they were at that age (not much older than I was when I'd told Jimmy that he and Clint Obringer's 'Shack Up Shack' above Gibson's bakery in Fort Harrison was 'tits') when I had learned it's better to lie about stuff like that than to tell the truth . . . just to be pleasant. So I guess we'll never really know the truth, will we?

*Blue Pines* was a wonderful place, and to this day we often stay there, loving the small village of Harbor Springs during the off-season months of October and May—just before and after Florida. Marco had overseen many remodeling projects at Blue Pines before Dante had died, so it was a great place to be while our home was being built in the U.P., which ended up taking over a year. Eventually we bought a 34 foot Erickson sailboat from *Irish Boat Works* in Harbor which we named *Missy* (for Mirella and Krissy), and both Marco and myself learned to sail, often sailing from Harbor Springs to Beaver Island for a night—then on to Manistique, which was only a twenty-five mile drive from *Escape Lake*. We kept an old Land Rover there in a garage we rented from Turner Grable, who also ran a charter fishing boat out of Manistique and owned the slip we docked *Missy* at while at the lake.

*Those were idyllic months we spent sailing out of Harbor Springs and the 'near' off-season was a paradise and so unlike the rat race in Florida. But, then again, in Florida it didn't snow, did it?*

# Chapter Sixty-five

*. . . Eli Dante Bowling was born December 23, 2001, at St. Lucie Medical Center in Port St. Lucie, Florida. He was 8 lbs 4 ounces and very healthy, but would be bummed for years that his birthday was that near Christmas, making him somehow always feel a little cheated. Guess Kris and I hadn't thought about that one whatever night it was he happened along. For us, however, it was the best Christmas ever!*

*L*acy came down and spent most of December with us and it was nice. Our money was a very tricky thing and at first we had hoped to keep it as quiet as possible, but somehow that never seemed to work. Lacy was never expecting or ever had been, though we had helped her and she certainly no longer needed to strip or work at Three Blind Dice. Her relationships were still usually a mess and we didn't go there very often, but somehow, on her own, she had learned not to become involved with men who understood our money. She knew how to handle things appropriately and always did, so we made sure she was comfortable, often staying for months at our home in Florida and especially that first winter helping Krissy with Eli and later staying the summer when we were up north. For several years, however, she continued to maintain her small pink house in Sidney, Ohio, and spent more than half the year there.

Then eventually a funny thing happened . . . she and Cliffton Tremont became good friends and, well, I guess you could say companions. There was a twenty-year age gap and the physical diversities were almost comical, but they seemed to be quite compatible and for all the right reasons it seemed to Krissy and me. Lacy's intelligence no longer surprised me and she was still a striking woman, so it was without difficulty that I understood

Cliffton's attraction to her as he had been lonely for a number of years. We purchased a condo in a high rise on Juno Beach 'for an investment' and Lacy moved there full time in '03. It was exactly half way between our home on Ocean Drive in Jupiter Colony and where Cliffton lived in North Palm Beach. Though she wouldn't have had to, she took a hostess job at *Romano Rinato* on her own *without* using our connection at all, having interviewed with Taylor and landing the job while we were still in Harbor Springs. We were at first stunned and Krissy was obviously quite proud. It was several months before Alejandro and Taylor made the association since Krissy and I were north and Lacey simply had never brought it up. When it eventually was revealed, the Del Sannios told us she was a tremendous asset.

Tammy has been another story and one our biggest challenges. On her third marriage and with four children by age 30, we began to get phone calls and letters almost weekly from her flat out begging for money—after she had somehow put the whole story together and managed to track us down. Lacy said she had never told her anything of substance, which we believed, and she had done her best to deal with her. We would certainly have tried to do something positive for her, but she became especially obnoxious and we finally decided on NO, period, for it seemed we had no other choice. We continue to try to come up with a way to help her and her children because we want that very much. It's just that right now the circumstances of Tammy's contact border on blackmail tactics and we simply won't be a part of that. Whether that will ever change we just don't know. It has been very difficult to know what to do. We did set up an education fund for the children should their lives evolve so that they could someday make use of it. So far we have not told Tammy that, however, as we are not sure that would be a good thing to do. It is all very sad.

. . . Throughout the summer of 2002 our home on Escape Lake was being built. Marco also brought the first class of culinary campers to Camp Romano that June, although it would take several years for the camp to become what it is today. There were 13 kids that first summer, and except for a few minor disciplinary problems, things went quite well. That summer was just cooking classes and lots of fun on the lake. As much as anything, the students helped Cornelius Whiskins, a true *Yooper* (as the natives of the U.P. were often called as opposed to the *Trolls* who lived south of the bridge) whom Marco had hired as the full time caretaker. They spruced up the canoes and day sailers, cleaned up after the construction crews and completely landscaped the grounds under *Whisky's* direction—and quite professionally—given that he'd owned a cabin maintenance and landscaping service before Marco hired him.

By the first week of October amazing changes had taken place at Escape Lake and Camp Romano would be ready for full operation the following summer. Our home, which we had named *Cliffton*, was also nearly finished. I know we didn't need to, but we had been extravagant, although unless you visited our home you wouldn't know it from the lake—which is exactly as we had planned, having found that money allowed you to move large trees around like chess pieces.

Our home on the lake was not particularly large, just a bit bigger than Marco's if you included the basement. It was unique, though, I have to say. It had 3 bedrooms, 3 baths and a very large loft. The logs were brought in from Ontario although the labor force was local and overseen by the designer Hans Van der Treft from Blind River, Ontario. Our plan, similar to Marco's, was a huge great room/dining room with vaulted ceiling and a massive stone fireplace. The porch ran the entire front and had its own exterior fireplace in addition to a large sunken hot tub tucked away under hemlock branches on one end. The kitchen was actually modest and the appliances uniquely disguised—and it was nearly surrounded by a circular bar of rare finished hardwoods. A large pantry with second frig and freezer opened off the kitchen. The loft had a corner fireplace and Krissy and I used it for our own bedroom since the elevated view through the pines and across the lake was breathtaking. Rare *Northern* antiques that Krissy had purchased at *Moving Mates*—a business north of Harbor Springs that liquidated the old estates and cabins in the area—outfitted the entire place.

The basement was where we departed from Marco, who had none. It was designed for kids, for we didn't plan to stop with Eli.

It included another fireplace, walls of cupboards and a very clever glass front that looked to the lake yet was camouflaged by the landscaping and nearly invisible from the lake itself. We could turn it into whatever we later wanted, but for now was a place to ride plastic trikes and other plastic crap that a one year old monkeys around with. It was a hope of mine that one day Eli would want to play pool and we would certainly have room for that.

We had a five car garage built into a steep ridge behind the cabin and *outfitted* with toys like snowmobiles and wave runners in two bays, an F250 pickup to haul firewood or supplies for the camp, Krissy's new *Escape*—and my *1991 Ford Explorer Sport* (147,345 miles)—which I'd had completely overhauled. I'd long ago told Krissy that no matter what, it would *never* go because it represented who she and I really were, and we didn't ever want to forget that. Regardless, we definitely were *Ford People*, which somehow seemed completely appropriate—given our circumstances.

Oh, and we also had a pristine 1955, 16' classic wooden *Chris Craft* inboard runabout that we kept stored in the camp utility building, but would dock at the cabin (once we had a dock built, that is). The road around the lake was crude and rough. We could have paved it, but I didn't want to, much to the chagrin of the few other residents who struggled with it, particularly in early spring when it turned to mud. But the way I looked at things was that you didn't get any 'rubber-neckers' snooping about, which was exactly the way we wanted to keep it, and it never much bothered me to drive a dirty car when Up North—just as long as it kept moving!

We understood how fortunate we were and were thankful. We were fortunate in where we could go and what we could do, but with it all, *Cliffton* became our *real home* and the only true place where the worries of the world just seemed to completely evaporate.

# Chapter Sixty-six

*I*t was Christmas Eve, 2003, that Sam Giovanazzo was strangled to death at the Southern Ohio Correctional Institution in Lucasville, Ohio, where he was beginning the sixth year of his *plea bargain life sentence*. He was 56 years old. Rumor had it that it was an inside 'mob arrangement' just because his brother, Vincent, had decided that he no longer deserved to breathe—for as long as he did it somehow would continue to blacken the Giovanazzo name—which was, in a manner of speaking, quite the oxymoron.

Krissy and I didn't think much one-way or another about it since his crimes against the students of Fort Harrison High School had been buried the second his plea deal was consummated and a jury trial dismissed. In fact, for several years we had evolved to a point where most of that life had been left well behind—and Sam Giovanazzo was certainly one person whom we no longer allowed to enter our thoughts—*period. . . .*

*. . . Until March of 2006, when Jimmy Bowling wrote headlines that would pale even the darkest days I had suffered through ten years earlier . . . and I knew that Sam Giovanazzo was as much to blame for the tragedy as was my estranged father, Thin Jim Bowling. Not, of course, that James William Bowling VI was blameless, if the charges were true . . .*

. . . I had given up on contacting Jimmy, assuming he had opted out of my life for good. I had once considered getting a visa and flying to Saudi Arabia, but with the onset of the Iraq War in 2002 that became impossible. Never having received a response from Jimmy over the years, I could only assume he was involved in the war, but never knew his location when the incredible news came to us one day in early June, 2006 . . . even as the horrific event had taken place several months earlier. Marco had asked us to stop by for drinks at his place when Krissy and I were finished that afternoon at the camp. His request seemed quite solemn, but we were busy at the time so I hadn't much thought about it.

Marco and Mirella had been married at the time for nearly four years—having had an idyllic Italian ceremony in Fabbrica, Tuscany, that Krissy and I had attended. They now spent seven months in Michigan and five months in a wonderful chalet they purchased in *Cortina d'Ampezzo,* in the heart of the Italian Alps, where Mirella could visit with her family who would come to spend ski holidays. We had further started a tradition a few years back that together we would all spend two weeks in May—and all of October—at *Blue Pines* before and after the summer crowds, sailing Lake Michigan by day and visiting our favorite haunts, *The Pier* and *The New York,* evenings.

Of the inheritance we received from Dante, Krissy and I donated nearly ninety per cent of the total amount to charities, including five million set aside in a fund for the operation of *Camp Romano* and for the scholarships. All charity gifts had been placed in *Dante Romano's* name. That left *more* than enough for her and I to do whatever we wanted in life and we had no intention of just handing chunks of money over to Eli or any future children. Early on they would be schooled in where our good fortune had come from and that life was meant for challenges not gifts.

Through Cliffton Tremont we had set up a substantial OHSAA (Ohio High School Athletic Association) scholarship fund to honor Gwen Putnam, which would be in accordance with guidelines as determined OHSAA and by the Putnams. Anonymity was impossible, though technically how we set it up, but the Putnams knew where the money had come from. I once had an extended phone conversation with both Clare and Don Putnam, which I believe was strengthening for all of us, although that was as far as it had ever gone.

Aside from the charitable donations, we paid for our homes, established an education fund for Eli and future children (and Tammy's), set aside a sizable amount for Jimmy, made investments and tucked some away that we could get to as needed or to travel. And even as absentee owners, *Romano Rinato* was bringing us a very nice income by the second full year of operation. So life moved on and we had hoped for no more great surprises, *and certainly no more family tragedies.*

Mirella had done wonders with Marco's cabin and it was incredibly homey. It was 5:30 before Krissy and I could get away from camp and turn it over to the three college-age counselors Marco decided to hire each summer. We had begun to accept reservations from small groups for lunch most days and dinner three nights a week, which had become quite popular (and especially from the 'elite' summering families south of the bridge), but on Thursday's nothing was ever scheduled except classes until 1—and then the *complete Lodge scrub-down* until 4:30. After that, Thursdays were for the students to do their own 'outside thing,' which usually included a cookout on their own, loading up their food and taking the canoes to Eagles Nest Island for a bonfire on the shore.

As Mirella opened the back door, we were greated by the whiff of exquisite Tuscan cuisine and discovered it was a dinner invitation although Marco hadn't said that. Though of the four of us, Mirella was the only one without professional training, she could sadly put us all to shame.

Mirella was a classically beautiful Italian woman, exactly one day Marco's senior. Her husband of twenty years had been a famed violinist who had been killed in a plane crash several years before she and Marco met in *Torri*, a village in Tuscany where Marco and I had traveled together to review a small vineyard that her parents owned. She had moved back there after the accident to stay with her family . . . and the rest is history.

Every family makes spaghetti and meatballs with a spinach salad right? *Wrong!* I won't even try to describe Mirellas' *S&M,* but it's a different animal, believe me, just as are her salads. Marco, as always, had the perfect wine, which I cannot now recall, but the meal was superb as always. Krissy and I had, of necessity, learned to temper our intake of food or we would have both been blimps by the time we were thirty, given our circumstances. We also worked out religiously, especially sculling early mornings on the lake and so even at thirty were fit—*and Krissy has never been anything other than a knockout her entire life.*

Marco acted odd throughout the meal I'd thought, and as Krissy helped Mirella clean up, he and I went out onto the porch and settled into a couple of Adirondacks, still sipping the superb wine. . . .

. . . "Billy, I've got something very disturbing to tell you," he said, looking directly at me with an unsettling presence..

It couldn't be about Eli or we certainly wouldn't have eaten dinner first, and something happening to Eli was what would have scared me most. He was staying at the Carstons with Florence as he often did during the day since she said she so loved having him around. We were to call when ready to leave to pick him up. But something was very wrong here.

"Billy, its Jimmy."

Before Marco could say more I felt my heart leap and was certain Jimmy must have been killed, yet somehow that didn't fit either cause Marco would have told me that immediately.

"Was he killed?"

"No, Billy, he wasn't, but I was watching the news this morning and it seems he was involved somehow with what the military is claiming was a criminal execution of civilians in Iraq. Apparently there are several men involved and I honestly don't know the particulars. His photo was on the newscast I was watching and the actions are being condemned by the United States. They suggested a military trial would be held and that five soldiers would be charged with the pre-meditated rape of a young girl and the murder of her family of six. Jimmy was singled out as the platoon commander."

"Rape? What do you mean rape? Jimmy would never do anything like that!" I nearly shouted.

"I don't know, Billy—it's just what I heard—but we both know not to trust TV," he returned, quietly.

I sat numb and suddenly sick to my stomach—a feeling that I'd had far too many times in my life. Trying to calm down and put it all together, I turned to Marco and asked, "Marco, what can we do? There must be something that we can do to help set this straight," I said to him, willing that to be true.

"I don't know. First we need to get the facts. We all know we can't trust the TV to give them to us. If I were you, I think I'd call

Cliffton and ask him to find out what he can. If anyone can get it straight, he will."

Mirella and Krissy joined us on the porch and I suspected Marco hadn't told the story to Mirella as she had been her wonderfully humorous self throughout the meal and emerged laughing along with Krissy. Her Italian accent was intriguing and Krissy and I had joked with each-other about her attraction to *Michael Douglas* and mine to *Sophia Loren,* whom we had stumbled upon once our senior year in high school when we had gone to Sidney to see *Grumpier Old Men* in which she had played a role. I found out later who she was and that she was 60 at the time and still, I had thought, the most beautiful woman I had ever seen (except for Krissy Bowling, of course). In all honesty, however, Mirella bore an eerie resemblance to Sophia, if considerably thinner.

"Mirella, an exquisite meal as always. Thank you so much for your trouble," I said, standing.

"Oh, Billy, every meal you eat is 'exquisite' and you know it, but thank you, dear," she laughed with an accent that could melt anyone.

"Well, I can't say you're wrong there," I answered, chuckling, but catching Krissy's eyes I knew she had detected something was wrong. Krissy Kurtz knew Billy Bowling forward and backwards and would have been impossible to play charades with, though it was something we had never yet tried.

"We really need to get Eli. Thank you both very much for everything. We'll talk tomorrow," I said, winking at Krissy as we took our leave.

Kris never asked me a question until we had Eli settled in bed and both went out onto the porch just following. We had long since acquired an eerie communication and she knew exactly when to (and when not to) ask questions or volunteer an opinion.

"Something's wrong, isn't it Billy?" she finally said.

"Yes, Kris, it's Jimmy. Marco says he's been involved in a war crime in Iraq and that his picture was on TV this morning."

"I don't understand . . . a war crime?"

"I don't know, Krissy," I said softly. "We both know not to trust TV. Marco suggested I call Cliffton and I think that's a good idea."

Krissy came and sat on my lap, holding my head against her chest and stroking my hair. For a long time neither of us said a word because we didn't need to. Tomorrow we would face what we needed to and do whatever we could. It was a life with which we were both familiar and another chapter that needed written, like it or not.

# Chapter Sixty-seven

*L ieutenant Colonel James William Bowling VI* was the highest commissioned officer ever convicted of a capital crime in the history of the United States military. He was tried and convicted by a military court for the rape and murder of a fourteen-year-old girl and the murder of her parents and three younger brothers and sisters in the Iraq village of Mahmoudiya in March of 2006. He now sits on death row at Fort Leavenworth Military Prison in Leavenworth, Kansas—along with eight other military personnel. Four other soldiers in his command were involved, two of which had trials and were sentenced to life in prison . . . two more with trials pending.

The evidence against Jimmy seemed substantiated—two of his subordinate soldiers having testified against him for consideration in their own trials yet to occur, along with the testimony of both soldiers who received the life sentence. Of course, how can we ever know the real truth? As for me, no matter his anger or how Jimmy's life unfolded, it is impossible for me to believe he could have ever committed such atrocities.

With the suggestion of Cliffton, I had hired Thomas Blackford from Arlington, Virginia, who specialized in military defense to represent Jimmy at his trial at Fort Bragg, North Carolina. Upon trying to meet with Jimmy, however, Mr. Blackford was repeatedly rebuffed and Jimmy chose to be represented by a TDS (Trial Defense Service) attorney as provided by the marines. I'd spent four days in Fayetteville trying to see him, and though I was told I could if he would agree, he never would. No matter how many questions I asked at the base, I was never afforded much helpful information. That was in November of 2006 and so I was eventually forced to fly back to Florida, later to read in the press, see on TV, or find on the internet what everyone else did right up until his conviction in January of '07.

I could only remember too well the echoes of Turk Otte five years earlier and I too wondered how Jimmy had maintained his commission without being seriously challenged. Then this horrendous event might not have ever taken place. I could only suppose he was another casualty of another insane war that was completely out of control and, with not only little purpose—but particularly without organization as well. And yet within Jimmy I knew there was more than just the military circumstances . . . *so very much more!*

The most frustrating thing ever in my life—even more than being imprisoned myself—is that Jimmy would not talk to me then . . . and will not talk to me now . . . and I can only assume it is the result of a deeply disturbed psychiatric state, *even as it was not allowed (or used) as a condition for his defense.* I spent a week in Kansas City in late February after Jimmy was sent to Leavenworth, petitioning to talk to him, only to be told twice that I was refused because he would not agree to it. I was forced again to return to Florida. . . .

. . . Throughout my school years, and particularly after Mom and Libby were killed, I used to wonder about our father and the *Vietnam War,* having heard and read about soldiers who had suffered from flashbacks and thinking somehow that perhaps that could possibly be a reason for his maladjustments. It had never been discussed in our family at all nor had my mother ever once mentioned it to me and I doubted ever to Jimmy, if indeed she even had knowledge of my father's role in the war. As noted, when she used to talk to us she would say things like: 'your father is not happy because he didn't want to run the alley and you need to try to understand him,' but she'd never mentioned the war, which one might have thought would have been part of such a request had he been struggling with related demons. She would always add, however: '*There's something else, but I can't tell you now, boys— maybe when you're older'* . . . but then '*she never got older'* so we never got to hear that secret, did we?

In no way could I picture Jimmy *ever* raping a young girl or *murdering an infant*, and still have not allowed myself to believe it nor likely ever will. Yet I didn't understand war, and for that—in and of itself—I felt very guilty. I had done research and found that the *My Lai Massacre* in 1968 in Vietnam was a well-documented U.S. atrocity where 504 innocent children, women and old men were murdered—and many of the women raped. Lieutenant William Calley, the commanding officer, was court marshaled and sentenced to life in prison, only to be pardoned by President Richard Nixon two days following his conviction, after having served a sum total of 4½ months in a military prison . . . ironically the exact time I had spent in jail for a crime that I hadn't committed. A pardon now for Jimmy's conviction would be highly unlikely, given the current political and world atmosphere; not that I think it should happen, no matter my brother or not.

The seeds of Jimmy's anger had been sewn long before his enlistment with the United States Military machine. To be certain, Jimmy Bowling was head strong and full of anger from a very young age, which was likely destined to be a part of his personality for life without serious professional intervention—which he had never received and most likely wouldn't have agreed to in the first place. However, with a positive and strong adult male role model, Jimmy Bowling could have been a much different person, I am convinced. I can't know exactly where Dad's problems originated, or even Sam Giovanazzo's, since his brother seemed to have had at least positive family values, but I do know that they were the two men who influenced Jimmy the most, and both clearly troubled souls although I *certainly* do not render any serious comparison between Dad's issues and the perversions of Sam Giovanazzo, please understand. In almost every way, the men in Jimmy Bowling's life failed him— and on his own he was unable to rise above the damage.

. . . Krissy was waiting for me at West Palm Beach International upon my return from Kansas City. She had stayed in Florida for both trips, and even though I could have used her moral support, it was better that she stayed home with Eli I thought at the time and still did after my second trip. It was something I needed to confront on my own, just like I had when I made my last attempt at a relationship with my father. She was standing and holding Eli's hand behind the ropes as I cleared customs . . . *and it was the most beautiful sight in the world!* I must say that at times I've felt almost ashamed of having so much personal good fortune now, but it is where our life has evolved—a life which my story, I'm sure, has shown hasn't always been easy for us, either. I do know for certain that there is one thing that stands above all else—*that we have a moral obligation and responsibility to each other, and particularly to Eli, to get it right this time around and to build a family that can never be torn apart no matter what is thrown our way!*

Krissy and I embraced and kissed, and at five Eli looked up at us with a big sheepish grin. I had long been committed that it would always be that way. I picked Eli up, hugged him and said 'I love you,' even as he began to jabber a mile a minute about some kind of monster crab that had washed up on the beach and we had to rush home so he could show it to me. Krissy had a squirrelly manner about her and said she had some interesting news too (after she understood I really didn't want to talk about Jimmy and Leavenworth.)

"Billy, Thad Otte called last night. He's at their place in Fort Pierce and would like to get together," she said, still oddly hiding some sort of joke I was almost certain. *(I, too, knew Krissy Kurtz Bowling . . . if though nowhere close to the way she knew me!)*

After their grandmother died, the Otte's had kept her modest home in Fort Pierce which was just a few blocks off the water and very charming. It had been in the Otte family for years by then and Thad once joked his grandfather had bought it in 1981 for $35,000 and everybody said he was crazy at the time, though now it would bring probably ten times that amount. The Otte family was huge and I guess it was Thad's turn that week, as the house was usually occupied by an Otte off and on all winter and most of the summer.

"Oh really," I said. We had seen Thad a couple of times, though never Turk again, after that first time nearly six years earlier, but it had been awhile and I certainly could use some friendly company so I thought it would be nice to visit with him. We started to walk down the corridor, but Krissy stopped me with a naughty sparkle in her eyes, as if trying to stifle a laugh that she wasn't certain would be appropriate, given the journey I had just returned from. Neither of us, however, was worth a damn at fooling the other so I smiled widely and said, "Come on girl, spit it out . . . something else is up. It's ok, shoot."

"Well, Billy, Thad's married . . . and he has his family with him," she answered, though I knew there was much more to it by the way she was looking—and especially when she deliberately waited for my response.

"Really . . . and he has a *family already?* Jeez, he wasn't married last year, was he? Must be a pretty fast worker. Is it anybody I know?" I asked innocently enough as Krissy burst out in almost hysterical laughter.

Eli was pulling on my arm because he wanted to get home to show me his treasure from the sea, but I could tell that whatever Krissy had up her sleeve wouldn't wait until even the parking lot, so I picked him up and started the bouncing game that he liked, knowing it would quiet him for a while.

"Billy, you're not gonna believe this," she stuttered, almost unable to talk.

"Jesus, Krissy, you're worse than Brent Sturdivant used to be. Spit it out, girl," I said, confused.

"Thad married Marcia Schweiterman, Billy—Turk's first wife. Isn't that the most hysterical thing you've ever heard in your life? And what's more, Turk's two boys now live with Thad and Marcia. I'm afraid I won't be able to entertain them with a straight face, Billy, and I mean that," she gasped.

That *was* hysterical—a twin brother marrying his twin's ex-wife. I mean I had to wonder how many times that had been pulled off before? Only in Fort Harrison, Ohio, I thought, and burst out laughing along with her as we started for the car.

"So have you already set this rendezvous up, Mrs. Bowling?" I asked, clicking open the hatch of Krissy's Escape and pushing my suitcase in. She goosed me with a giggle as I closed the hatch and I jumped (something she had so deviously perfected behind the bar at the BBC all those years ago), but turned to kiss her again as Eli looked at us with a grin, yet an impatient one.

"Tomorrow at six. We're grilling at home instead of going to Romanos cause Marcia said her boys would love to play with Eli on the beach. But honestly, Billy, I don't know if I can pull it all off with a straight face . . . *and I mean that*," she said laughing, yet worried at the same time I could tell. I looked lovingly upon my beautiful wife who had such a wonderful free spirit—*a spirit she had never allowed anyone to steal from her*—and a spirit that would bless our children with a peace Krissy and I had never known . . . *and I was happy.*

"Sweetheart, we'll be fine. There's *nothing* you can't handle, for you always have, and I have faith that will never change," I said, climbing in to drive, even as I fought a momentary flashback—the type that would never completely allow my soul to be free. . . .

*. . . For as I drove away from Palm Beach International Airport with a grin on my face, the fuzzy warmth of my beautiful wife beside me and my young son in the back seat, I could see with frightening clarity Turk Otte finger-fucking Marcia Schweiterman on the bench below Wickerdick's office my freshman year as I looked down from the window in Room 211. . . where Dick Hamilton had failed to put in a showing for history class . . . and while behind me Mindy Dalinghaus squirmed and stewed with her own still wondrous spirit that would an hour later allow her to cry appropriate tears—after the freshman space cadets fucked up their shot at the big-time!*

# Postlogue

*K*rissy loved working at *Romano Rinata* in the winter with her mother and especially since she could come and go as she chose. It was a charming and professional restaurant and we were very proud of it, just as Dante would have most certainly been. Alejandro and Taylor had done an incredible job with it and it truly had become a landmark pilgrimage in Southern Florida, which had been Dante Romano's goal from the very beginning. I spent most of my time with Eli on the beach or the two of us fishing with Cliffton off shore; much more at home working with the summer camp kids than sticking my mug in at Romano's where I had early on seen that, even with my 'professional expertise,' I was simply not needed—although I must say I had certainly never felt unwelcome. My notoriety had largely evaporated, but if I were going to be recognized it would be in Florida, thus I preferred a lower profile while there. By chance, however, I *was* there one evening a few weeks after returning from Kansas City—when I noticed Taylor approaching me with purpose.

"Billy, there's an older couple dining who would like to talk with you if you are free. The gentleman says he knew your father." After momentary pause, I followed her into an alcove. The architectural design which we'd chosen rendered two large common dining areas and two long alcoves that resembled catacombs and provided very private dining for couples. Taylor steered me into the catacombs where a pleasant elderly couple sat smiling.

"Mr. and Mrs. Trout, this is Billy Bowling. Billy, the Trouts," Taylor said graciously before retiring.

The gentleman stood to shake my hand. "Billy, I'm Arnie and this is my wife, Carol. Do you have a moment?" he asked.

"Of course, sir. How may I help you?" I said politely, but with natural reticence given the brief bio Taylor had given me. There was ample room for a chair at the end of each private booth, so turning, I pulled one up and took a seat.

"Billy, your father and I were in the service together. Carol and I live in Stuart now and we started coming here to dine last year. Such a delightful place you have and we look quite forward to our nights here. We noticed the picture of you and your wife with the Del Sannios in the lobby one evening and, I beg your pardon if I'm out of place, but I recognized you. All along I knew you were Jim's son, for I grew up in Eaton, just down the road from you. Jim and I were drafted together, went through boot camp together, and served side by side in the 25th Infantry in Nam."

Mr. Trout paused and I felt uncomfortable, although I knew it wasn't his intention. Yet I had wanted answers, right? Well, as Cliffton Tremont would say, the best place to get them is the *horse's mouth.* I decided to speak next.

"Were you in combat, Mr. Trout?" I asked simply.

"Yes, Billy, we were, and your father was very brave, but I'm afraid the war took a terrible toll on him. May I go on or would you prefer me to stop," he posed, seriously.

"Yes, please continue, Mr. Trout," I answered.

"Thank you, Billy. Your father was our platoon commander and he was assigned a mission one night to go up river with seven men and exterminate a Viet Cong machine gun battery. I wasn't chosen which has always haunted me very much. He was the only one to return, Billy—and he was never the same—in fact not even close. I thought you should know that because I know the incredible tragedies your family has been through. Everyone in Western Ohio knows. I hope I haven't been out of place. Carol advised me against seeing you, but I'd want to know. *I'd want to know*," Mr. Trout said, his eyes tearing.

I sat numb for a while and didn't know how to feel, or what to say. Then suddenly I knew Mr. Trout was right—*I did want to know*—and I needed to make certain he knew that he had been right to tell me.

"Mr. Trout, thank you very much. I *did* want to know, sir. *I did*. It can't change much now, I'm afraid, but I am indebted to you, please understand that. Mrs. Trout, it *was* the right thing to do," I said graciously, standing. "And dinner is on *Romano*'s. Now not a word, please, I insist," I smiled as they started to protest.

I then excused myself, but made a point to stay long enough to catch them as they took their leave, making pleasantries and thanking them for their patronage. Somehow I could feel that Arnie Trout knew nothing else need be said—no other questions asked, nor answers required. And for those few brief moments we had connected in a way that had been necessary for us both.

*Skeletons?* That was actually one of the titles I had kicked around for this book, but Marco boycotted it, so I listened to him and allowed him to actually pick the title—which of course makes me feel rather funny (you know . . . one of those 'funnys' that really isn't funny). Anyhow, Billy and Krissy Bowling have enough *skeletons* to build a high-rise condo on Jupiter Beach with the bones, we sometimes joke. We don't talk about it a lot, but I know Krissy would like to meet her father one day. I wish I could talk to Jimmy, but I honestly have little hope for that. Krissy still racks her brain almost daily about what she needs to do in order to have an honest relationship with Tammy. And as for my father—I honestly don't know what to do—but given Mr. Trout's recent revelation, I have begun to think about trying to re-connect with him, for I have heard he isn't well. So that's where Krissy Kurtz Bowling, Eli Bowling and Billy Bowling are right now. . . .

. . .*One thing Krissy and I DO believe with certainty is that every single day is a miracle! And that when you stop believing that, it doesn't matter how old you are, or how healthy, how wealthy—or who you are—for if you don't see the miracle each morning right upon your doorstep, you're not really living anyhow. Some days are better miracles than others, though—*

*we'll give you that! Like yesterday at the Doctor's office, for example, (well, we cheated this time)—for Elizabeth Maria Bowling (our Libby) is due right about Christmas—and the complications of explaining the timing to Eli pose a challenge that we may need a very special miracle to solve.*

*God Bless,*
*Billy, Krissy, Eli and (Libby) Bowling*

*Admmix*
*Jupiter, Florida*
*Harbor Springs, Michigan*
*Escape Lake, Michigan (Upper Peninsula)*

8527126R0